we
have
shadows
too

nicole t. smith

we have shadows too

Published by Lightpen Publishing.

For additional information on this book, its author, or to schedule a live event, please email: nicole@shadows.group.

ISBN: 978-1-936753-09-3 (paperback)
ISBN: 978-1-936753-10-9 (ebook)

Cover design and art by Nicole T. Smith and Ryan Vaillancourt.

This book is a work of fiction. The subject matter, however, is sadly real. As you read these pages, please be mindful of the family, friends, acquaintances, and strangers whose pasts you do not know. And an earnest word of caution: There may be triggering situations and themes present in this book for certain audiences.

For TG

we
have
shadows
too

To guard

a secret

remember...

there isn't one.

Eastport, Colorado—July 1993

Behind the glass, her eyes remained level, hands steady at ten and two.

". . . a big responsibility. Rella, are you hearing me?"

She blinked. Her grip relaxed to nine and three. "I'm sorry, Mrs. Delain. You were saying?"

"You've been absent this entire conversation."

"I'm a little—off, is all," Rella responded.

"Well, it's no wonder. Lack of sleep under these circumstances, I'm sure."

They passed a sign: HOSPITAL NEXT EXIT.

"There," Janet Delain pointed.

Continuing up the road, they turned right, following the circuitous asphalt drive to a secluded area behind a chain of buildings, pulling into a small parking lot.

Rella stepped out into the sun. Closing her eyes, she tilted her head skyward, asking its rays to transmit enough warmth to take with her inside.

"How did it feel to be in the driver's seat?" Janet asked, exiting the passenger side.

"Unusual," Rella replied.

Windows gaped from the institutional brick edifice. Trees stood guard. Letters in gray stone spelled BROWER over the weighty door's crest.

Upon entering, a sense of confinement enclosed Rella.

"Name, please," the front desk person asked without looking up.

"We're here to see Leah Cooper. Janet Delain, and this is her daughter, Rella Cooper."

A loud buzz sounded, followed by a click.

"You must be excited to tell her," Janet said cheerfully as they proceeded down the hall.

In the large common room, odors of coffee, green peas, and gravy, the powdered kind made of corn syrup solids and yeast extract, lingered suspended in the stale air. Most patients were in their pajamas, at three in the afternoon, which made Rella uncomfortable.

"Leah, darling." Janet glided to her. "Rella and I are here."

Sitting alone in one corner, fully dressed in a cotton shirt, light brown pants, white ankle socks, and canvas shoes, Leah made an effort to raise her head.

Rella saw the prison in her eyes and resisted turning away. She glazed on a smile, hoping it wouldn't crack.

"Rella has something to show you," Janet announced proudly, smoothing her tautly pinned graying hair.

Rella opened her palm and extended her arm. "I got my license today, Mom."

The mother she knew would have brightened with joy. Instead, she sat, dulled, her expression melted like heated wax.

Rella slowly lowered her hand, eyes cast downward to her sneakers.

"Rella handled the test beautifully," Janet reported, seating herself next to Leah. "Our star pupil, as always."

Rella saw her smile somewhat, the real mom still inside, trying to get out.

"You'll be leaving here soon." Janet straightened her knee-length skirt. "They said you will be just fine. Though, you've lost ten pounds, with scant to spare."

Leah didn't reply.

Rella stepped back from this shell of her mother. She walked over to the puzzle table. Others in the room didn't acknowledge her.

Invisible, she moved her hands over the broken landscape.

Electroshock therapy, the doctor had called it. The way to fix her.

Rella hadn't known she was broken.

Her mother was missing pieces. It wasn't until many years later that Rella would become conscious of the forgotten. And that's when her own puzzle fell apart.

Part One

Maybe, I think, when you've waited a long time to see something, you need to find your way to it in glimpses.
—Laura Kasischke, *White Bird in a Blizzard*

One

Colorado—September 2016

Trevor Cooper walked into his elder sister's apartment. Gray sweatshirt thrown over the back of a chair. Mismatched gloves on the floor. Yesterday's pizza box on the couch.

"Just get here?" Morgan asked, shuffling into the room.

"Yeah."

She pulled on the sweatshirt. "Sorry for the mess."

"My place doesn't look much better."

"Third shift, fourth night in a row. Drive-through breakfast. Then on to her hospital. Visiting hours start early."

"How is she?"

Morgan sighed. "Mostly sedated. She knows I'm there, sort of. I wonder if she really meant to, or if it was an accident."

Trevor sat on the armrest of the couch. "I thought she had been doing pretty well. Morgan, how old were you, when Mom told you about how she grew up?"

Morgan rubbed her forehead and eyes. "I was in college. Twenty-something."

Trevor shook his head. "Why didn't you tell me sooner?"

"I don't think she had even meant to tell me. I'd stopped in to surprise her, take her to lunch. She was at the kitchen table, staring off. I sat down in front of her. She didn't say anything at first. And when she started talking, it was more like she just needed to say it out loud, into the air."

"A lot for you to carry."

"I didn't want to burden you. And she made me promise not to say anything to Rella. But I think now I need to."

"Why?"

"Mom's been holding this in, all her life, but there were signs she wasn't right. Someone as traumatized as she was, there are moments when they just need to escape, and maybe this attempt was one way." Morgan sighed. "It makes me worry for Rella."

"What do you mean?"

"What if she tries the same thing?"

Trevor looked at her in disbelief. "What? No way. Rella is the most put-together person I know. She'd never even think about doing that. There's no reason."

"I know Mom doesn't want to die. But she struggles living with the thoughts. I've been doing a lot of thinking, reading. I wonder if something might have happened to Rella. Like what happened to Mom."

Trevor's heart stalled. "That's not possible. Rella's never said anything."

"Mom didn't either, all that time. Something's always been off about Rella. I could never put my finger on it." She pointed, as if she knew what she was aiming at.

Laguna Beach, California—September 2016

Rella leisurely strolled along the street, her long, brunette hair glistening in the sun, past colorful art galleries, surfboard rentals, and boutiques with aquamarine and turquoise jewelry.

One shop caught her eye, a mahogany barrister bookcase, rolltop desk, and antique library catalog outfitting the display window.

She climbed the stairs and pushed open the door.

"Greetings!" the shopkeeper sang.

"Good morning!" Rella returned. "Beautiful day out there."

"Always the right temperature." She approached Rella. "Exquisite piece, isn't it?"

Rella lightly ran her fingertips over the bookcase, imagining what used to be held inside. "Quite."

"Early 1900s. We offer delivery! Are you local?"

"I am now," Rella said, smiling.

"Well, welcome to Laguna Beach. 'A resort for all seasons,' as they say. Where are you from?"

The room edged in. "Recent graduate," she answered, dodging the question. "Architectural and building sciences."

"Ah, wonderful. Diverse inventory here for all design tastes!"

"Yes, so I see. Once I'm settled, I'll be sure to come back." Rella exited the shop.

She followed a curving path up along the bluffs. It had taken her eight years to finish the five-year architecture program, concurrently holding a full-time job to cover expenses. Despite the ceaseless work with little rest, the days had passed like a vacation.

Her mind embraced the challenging activity, her thin, athletic frame thrived in the sporty outdoor lifestyle, and the strange physical pains she'd suffered from for as long as she could remember had diminished a bit.

She rested her hands on the metal railing, the sparkling water reflecting in her emerald eyes. A rising breeze skirted around her crisp capri pants and bare ankles. The coastline stretched, California vast and protective at the same time. An open world charged with energy and possibilities.

She had escaped. From what, she didn't know. But memory echoes lay sunk far offshore, where they couldn't touch her.

Trevor splashed cold water on his face. Ran his hands several times through his hair. Pushed up the sleeves of his crewneck shirt.

He called his younger sister.

"Hey, Trev! What's going on?"

Trevor willed an upbeat voice. "Rella! How's sunny California? In the new house yet?"

"Got the keys a few hours ago. I still can't believe it!"

"All your hard work—you deserve it." Trevor paused. "I was thinking of coming and seeing your new place, check out that view. I could leave tomorrow, if that works. It's been a long time. I miss you!"

If only he could put Rella in a parallel universe where horrible things didn't exist.

"Yes, of course—I'd love to see you. Sorry I haven't been back in a while."

"It's cool. I understand."

Eleven years ago, he'd stood in the Denver Airport terminal as her plane flew away, heavyhearted to see her go, even though the buoyant change in her voice upon arriving in California clearly evidenced that she'd made the right decision.

"The only problem is, I still need to furnish the house."

"No worries. I'll find a motel close by."

Trevor blasted the radio, flipping to any station not disbanded into static, unsuccessful at drowning out the noise in his mind.

He chugged cold coffee as he passed through Primm, Nevada, hints of motor oil and dust scenting the white paper cup. Two hours later, he reached Barstow. He strode into the gas station. Hot coffee to the right, refrigerator cases of cold beer to the left. He stayed to the right.

As dusk fell, he arrived at the address Rella had texted him.

"I've come to hire the best architect in the business," Trevor announced upon entering.

"Trev! You made it!" Rella put aside the papers in her hand and rose from the couch in the first-floor foyer.

"I've missed you, Rella." He gently hugged her. "Working on a Saturday?"

"Just organizing. I officially start in two weeks."

"It worked out nicely, then, especially with the new house and all."

"Sure did!"

Her childlike countenance lit up. Although thirty-eight, most people took Rella for ten years younger, her face locked in time.

"Except for the fact the guest room isn't ready yet," she continued. "Otherwise, perfect timing for you to visit!"

He was sick at the thought of contaminating her happiness.

"You look good. Been working out more?" Rella asked.

"Increasing my weights at the gym."

"Nice. You must be tired and hungry from the drive."

Wired from the coffee, food far from his mind, Trevor said, "Sure am."

"I've explored a little and have a place in mind. Want to take one car?"

"I'll follow you there. That way I can head to the motel afterwards."

Trevor pulled up in his gray 1994 pickup, behind Rella's new, sporty, powder blue convertible, a recent present to herself after she'd retired the secondhand car she'd used while in school.

"You're all set," the valet told him. "Car in front of you paid."

The restaurant's exterior terraces twinkled with rows of stringed lights.

Inside, a young hostess with chopped bleached-blonde hair in a thigh-high, sleeveless dress handed Rella a disc, as black and polished as what clung to her body. "Have a drink while you're waiting," she cooed with a curl of the shoulder, throwing an unabashed smile at Trevor.

"Still turning heads, I see," Rella commented as they headed toward the bar.

"It's the blue eyes," Trevor said.

Once the disc buzzed, they were seated in the quieter upper patio area.

"Pretty nice place," Trevor remarked.

"They have organic and vegan options," Rella said, removing her navy-blue bolero blazer and folding it neatly, placing it next to her on the bench.

"Nice." Trevor picked up the menu. "Sheesh, nine dollars for asparagus?"

"Since when do you consider ordering vegetables?" Rella said with a laugh.

"What are you getting?"

"The vegetable curry."

"Works for me." He folded the menu. "I'll be right back. Going to scrub up."

The waitress soon returned, balancing large white plates. Enticing aromas of cinnamon, cayenne, turmeric, and coriander drifted up, awakening Trevor's deadened appetite.

"Wow, this is delicious!" he declared on the third forkful.

"See, vegan food is yummy."

"I'm impressed."

The server returned. "Here are the mazavaroo fries."

Trevor picked one up from the basket in front of him. "So, what's a mazavaroo fry anyway?"

"They are made with a type of African green chili."

He popped one in his mouth. "These are terrific! You're not going to have any?"

"Too spicy for me. I ordered them for you."

Trevor's attention hopped between the curry and the fries.

"How's the area? Meeting new people?"

To Rella, people were mystery side dishes, sometimes compatible, but, like mazavaroo fries, often seasoned with ingredients that burned.

"I haven't had much time to make friends."

"Seeing anyone?" Trevor asked, aware of the improbability. His sister was attractive, friendly, and likable, but dating and nightlife were relegated to the bottom of her list.

"No. How about you? Anyone special in your life?"

Trevor's fork paused in midair.

"Oh, Trevor, I'm sorry. Completely insensitive to assume."

Although several years had passed, wounds have no calendar or clock. Trevor's heart had been broken by a girl he had intended to marry, and he hadn't pursued a relationship since. Boyish looks and an easygoing disposition belied the fact that he was about to turn forty, and he'd regressed into an adolescent lifestyle, as worn-in and without risk as his high school team jacket.

He shook his head. "It's fine, really."

Unwilling to spoil the evening, he put off revealing the real reason why he'd paused—what was behind his visit.

Twenty minutes later, he put down his fork, plate clean.

"That was one of the best meals I've ever had."

"I'm so glad. You had a long day on the road." She flipped her utensil in the curry. "How are things back there?"

She'd felt obliged to ask the question.

"You know Eastport. Nothing changes."

Trevor saw her flinch at the mention of the city's name, as though she'd been punctured by a tack.

Rella pushed her plate away. "I'll have to take the rest to go."

Outside, waiting at the valet station, Trevor looked up at the sky. The stars sparkled happier and brighter in California than they did in Eastport, where their light was somber, tearful.

He wanted to give her one more night of peace.

Two

During his drive into Orange County the day before, Trevor had noted countless communities of clean rows of neat, tightly packed houses photocopied in variations of beige. He liked this area much better. Upcycled beach shacks and cottages painted in bright mint and purple shared the hillside among extravagant residences of varying elevations.

Trevor leveled onto the drive. Unprepared for the grandness of Rella's house, he faced the towering facade. His eyes traveled from copper-colored natural stone up soaring redwood plank walls. The black metal roof took a blunt angle toward the sky. A massive oak front door rose double overhead, waist-high ceramic blue urns overflowing with fragrant white sweet alyssum on each side. He touched his finger to the bell.

Rella opened the door wearing a big smile and shorts, hair in braids, and unclad feet. "Welcome!"

"You're bright and chipper," Trevor said.

"Up at five, went to the gym, ran a few errands, and started in on the house." Rella wrinkled her nose. "I made sure to instruct them *not* to clean after closing. They'd use a bunch of chemicals."

Trevor had rolled out of bed a half-hour ago. "Rella, this place is incredible."

"Wait 'til you see the inside!" She bounced with excitement.

"It's huge!" Trevor exclaimed, his voice echoing. He passed a wide wrought-iron staircase, drawn to the floor-to-ceiling windows in the kitchen and great room. "This view is outstanding." Beyond the abundant eucalyptus, palm, and cypress trees growing along the slope, the ocean waters glinted like crystals in the sun. "I guess this is what making the big bucks looks like!"

"I love what I do. It was never about the money."

Trevor ruffled her hair. "I know. I'm sure you still shop in secondhand stores."

She smiled. "It's like a treasure hunt, and I feel good giving items a new home."

"Quite contemporary a place, for you."

"I considered that. But the floor plan and location are perfect. There's lots of privacy, and inside it's pretty much a blank slate. Let me show you upstairs!" She practically ran, taking two steps at a time. "Here is my room," she said, pushing back the double doors. "And this attached area will be workspace," Rella explained, gesturing to the side room. "Plenty large for a drafting table. I still prefer sketching the old-fashioned way."

"A workplace next to your bedroom will keep you up."

"Better not to let the mind rest."

Trevor thought he saw a flicker behind her eyes. "And where's the bathroom?" he asked.

"Down the hall."

"Huh? A house like this without an attached bathroom?"

"I didn't want one." Rella left the room.

"Why not?"

Ignoring the question, Rella led the way down the hall.

"This wing was designed to be one extended suite. Here's the walk-in closet. All this space!" Rella squealed, pirouetting. "I can't wait to arrange it when all my things arrive."

"My stuff would fit here." Trevor traced a four-by-four square with his hands in a nook of the closet.

Rella continued on. "Lastly, the bathroom." She opened the door and stepped to the side, but not inside.

"Whoa. Is this a crime scene?" Trevor bent to excavate from the rubble.

"I'd been hoping they would have finished more by today. I'm having the tub removed and the tile replaced."

"It's all brand-new."

Rella swiped the piece from his hands and flung it back into the pile, the black square cracking from the force as it landed.

Rella concluded the second-floor tour with the guest wing.

"I have a little surprise in the kitchen. Follow me!"

She practically hopped down the stairs. With a flourish, she opened the door to the refrigerator. "I love a new fridge, glistening clean, nearly empty."

"Mine's empty, too, but can't say it's clean."

Rella withdrew the one item inside, presenting a bottle of champagne.

"Haven't heard of this one, and I won't attempt to pronounce it," Trevor said.

Rella brandished two crystal flutes.

"Champagne glasses! All I ever have are plastic cups."

"Absurd." Nose lifted, she placed them on the countertop

with a lyrical cling. "Such a delightful, crisp sound upon the stone."

Trevor smiled.

"What?" Rella said, pouring the liquid.

"Remember how you used to dress in those big old hats and wear lace gloves and serve tea?"

"I did?"

"Yeah. You'd pretend sometimes that we were in the 1800s. You got frustrated once when we didn't dress for dinner."

"Huh. I don't remember."

"You spoke in the same voice you just used."

"I long for that time period," Rella said, her eyes traveling, "as though I were from back then. I remember on weekends I'd ask Mom to take me to historic open houses."

"They did a great job with this poured concrete," Trevor remarked, running his hand over the island's smooth blue-gray surface.

Rella handed him a glass.

"Thank you," Trevor accepted.

"Thank *you*, for driving all the way here. It means a lot to me."

Trevor wished he could just enjoy this time with his sister. His phone buzzed. Morgan, surely.

"Do you need to answer?" Rella asked.

Trevor shook his head, setting his phone to silent mode and putting it facedown on the counter. He then lifted his glass and drained it.

"I guess the champagne's a hit." Rella studied him. "Trevor, is something wrong?"

Trevor sighed. "Mom's in the hospital again."

The bottom of Rella's glass hit the counter. "Oh, no!"

"She—she tried to end her life. At least, it appears that way. You know how she's out of it sometimes."

Rella put her head in her hands.

Trevor rubbed his palms on his jeans, as if trying to muster the power to continue telling Rella about their mother's past, and what Morgan suspected. None came.

Three

"Rella—finally! I've been worried about you. Is Trevor there? He's been ignoring my calls."

"Yes, he was here earlier. I had some house stuff to do, so I'll be catching up with him in a couple of hours."

Morgan listened to her sister's breathing. Growing up, Rella could go hours without saying a word. "I'm sorry he had to give you bad news on this trip."

"How's Mom doing? I realize I can't call her when she's in there."

"No, and I think it's best anyway. She's—spacey. You know. I'm sorry if this brings up bad memories," Morgan said.

"Just from the day I got my license. It was nice of Janet to make sure I was still able to take the test."

"She's been a loyal friend to Mom all these years."

"She was very kind."

"You saved every penny to get your first car." Morgan laughed. "Remember the day you threatened to take off and never come back?"

"I did? Oh, yes, I remember now. I'd been upset about something. I just wanted to drive away, to a place where no one knew me."

"Yeah. There's been some rough road. Remember when you were—I think, nine—and you found Mom in the closet?

She'd drunk a jug of rosé. I felt terrible you were alone that day."

"Huh? You were there too. We both found her."

"No, you were the only one home. You called the paramedics, remember?"

"That's not how I recall it. I distinctly remember being told 'Rella, call now!' "

"That's not possible. Anyway, I was there the next time it happened, the day the police came to the house."

The harsh sound of a knock caused Rella to jump, jarring her hand and sending a mark through her drawing.

Morgan looked up from her schoolwork. Sighing, she went to answer the door.

"Is there a Leah Cooper here?" Rella heard a gruff voice ask.

"Why?" Morgan responded confrontationally.

"We need to come in, please."

Rella saw a man push his way past, with another one. Police. She rose off the carpet.

"A call came in," the officer said. "We need to check on her."

"A call? From whom?"

While Morgan spoke with the patrolmen, Rella ran up the stairs, two at a time.

"Mom?" Rella spoke softly into her mother's darkened bedroom, where the blinds were drawn. She heard a faint exhale.

She walked to the other side of the bed and found her mother on the floor, the phone receiver in her hand. "Who are you on the phone with? Did you call the police?"

"The police?" her mother mumbled.

"Maybe you should come downstairs."

Her mother didn't answer, made no attempt to get up.

Rella left the room, quietly shutting the door.

She descended, encountering the two cops on the landing.

"She's in her bedroom, resting," she said, obstructing their path.

"We need to see her," one said firmly.

"She's in her pajamas." Rella wondered if it was too early to say that.

"We just want to make sure she's all right," the second cop said, with kindness.

Rella followed them.

"Which bedroom is hers?" the first one asked.

Rella pointed straight ahead.

He rapped on the door. "Mrs. Cooper? Can you come out, please? It's Eastport Police Department."

No sound came from the other side.

"Mrs. Cooper, we have to come in."

"Mom, can you come out, please?" Rella said through the door.

The two officers marched in, around to the other side of the bed.

"Mrs. Cooper, we need you to stand up, please."

Her mother responded in incoherent mutters, same as she'd done that day in the closet, after the rosé.

Rella wondered if this was this like drunk driving. These officers didn't have record of the first offense; or did they? Would she go to jail? And where was Morgan? Didn't she care about what was going on up here?

"She's just tired," Rella said, crossing the room. "She goes to bed early."

They ignored her.

"Mrs. Cooper, stand up, please," the first one repeated.

Rella thought she heard her mother tell them to get away, her arms jutting out.

"Calm down, Mrs. Cooper."

"Please, leave her alone," Rella said.

The first policeman reached for his two-way radio. "This is Officer Hoff, requesting paramedics."

The sound of a siren grew closer. In minutes, the house swarmed with trespassers, and Rella had to fight to maintain position in her mother's bedroom doorway.

"What's the situation?" a medic asked, furnishing a blood pressure cuff, the sound of Velcro tearing apart abrasive to Rella.

"Empty wine bottle, two pill bottles—prescription. She's coherent but slurring, answered a few questions. Guess she called her therapist, who then called 911."

"Copy."

Her mother surrounded by medical personnel, Rella followed the first officer downstairs.

"So, you were both down here—you hadn't been upstairs?" the second officer asked Morgan.

"Correct."

Morgan's voice was laced with annoyance—at their mother rather than at the officer, Rella surmised.

"And where is your father?"

"He doesn't live with us."

Two medics descended, carrying Rella's mother strapped to a gurney.

"Mom!" Rella cried, running over. Her mother didn't respond.

"We're taking her to Brower."

Brower. Rella had heard of that place. It was where crazy people went. Her mother wasn't crazy. She didn't need to go there.

"Mom! Mom, can you hear me?" Rella said.

"Please step back," the medic on the right instructed.

No more regarded than a lawn ornament, Rella watched her mother being loaded into the ambulance. The rest of the medical team filed out, and Rella saw the two officers hand Morgan a piece of paper before they left too.

Rella went inside.

Morgan had already gone back to her schoolwork.

Rella stood, wondering what her mother would do. She went through the house, picking up scraps of medical debris, wanting to make sure the house was tidy when her mother returned.

"Rella," Morgan said gently, bringing her back to the present.

"I'm still here," Rella replied quietly. "Why did they take her to Brower back then? And why did she have to keep going?"

Morgan was silent for a minute.

"Rella, there's something I've known for some time now. Mom wanted it kept from you." She paused. "Trevor didn't tell you everything yesterday. This isn't easy to talk about, but it's going to be even more difficult for you to hear. It's about Mom—how she grew up."

I found an empty chair

and sat on it

to find myself even emptier.

I found a broken glass

and looked at it

to see my dissolved face

a little prettier.

I found a steep doorway

and entered

in order to close my exit.

—Munia Khan, "Blue Stanzas"

Four

Eastport, Colorado—1963

Leah woke with strange pain in her abdomen.

She carefully climbed down the small ladder from the loft bed, stubbing her toe on the desk chair underneath as she walked by.

Using the bathroom, she noticed red spots in her underwear. She'd turned twelve several months ago. Her best friend Janet had gotten hers last year.

Leah opened the door under the sink, rummaging through a wasteland of items before finding some gauze and a thin, elastic belt-like contraption with clips as a probable solution, but with no idea how to use the apparatus. She wadded up toilet paper instead. She'd ask Janet about it later.

She returned to bed. Unable to sleep, the affliction made her nauseous and sore inside, but she was hopeful. Maybe now it would stop. She wanted to have a baby one day, but not that way.

She stared at the sloped ceiling, inches away from her face. It was the only place she could breathe in the house, and she imagined the roof lifting and a cloud descending to carry her away.

Later that afternoon, at lunch recess, Leah bypassed the cafeteria and went out the side door. She found a spot on the grass, glad it was warm enough to sit outside. Opening her tin lunchbox, she removed the thermos and pulled back the sandwich wrapping, nibbling the white bread. Turkey and mayo. Yuck.

"Where's Janet today?" Leah's classmate Angela dumped her books on the grass and dropped down next to her.

"Not feeling well, I guess."

"I love her hair. I wish I had hair like that. Yours, too. So thick. Hair quality says a lot about a woman."

"It does not. And we aren't women."

"Your brother is so cute. Get me a date with him."

"Get one yourself." Leah bit into a crisp McIntosh apple.

"But he's *older*. You have to help me," Angela whined. "Oh, Cal . . ." she crooned.

Leah pushed her food away.

"You don't want it?" Angela grabbed Leah's discarded sandwich. "Yeah, your mom makes the best lunches," she said between chomps. "You must be *so* happy to have a mother like that."

Every day after school, for a couple of hours, Leah worked at a law office, filing. So far, she'd been able to keep the job a secret from her family. She'd asked the senior clerk about working Saturdays too, but the office closed over the weekend.

After spending Saturday morning walking, she peered around the hedges at her house, a white two-story with a peaked roof and small windows. The driveway was empty. She walked up the steps to the front door, putting her ear against it. Hearing nothing, she quietly stepped inside.

She exhaled at seeing the empty living room. She went into the kitchen to get a soda pop from the fridge.

"Leah, where've you been?" Her brother came up behind her and grabbed her arms.

The refrigerator rattled as Leah stumbled against the door. "Cal, let me go."

"Sorry. Hope I didn't hurt you."

They both heard yelling coming from the yard. Cal released her. "Stay inside," he said.

The door flung open. Wiping blood from his nose, their father's friend, Lester, scuffed in. "He's at it again," he sneered.

"You like it," Cal returned.

Lester smirked. "Grab me a beer, will ya?"

"Make it two."

Leah jumped at the sound of her father's voice as he entered. She edged behind Cal.

"You threw some good punches today, Silas," Lester said.

"Don't I know it. Still went easy on you."

Leah's insides crawled.

Silas kicked the back door shut. "Cal, the beer."

Cal ushered Leah to the other side of him. Lester's red eyes bored into her.

"Here." Cal handed one to Lester and tossed the other to his father.

Silas bent back the flat tab and chugged. "Come on, Les. Take a look at this mower with me. You too, Cal. You might learn something. Get your hands dirty at least."

Leah kept her eyes averted as they went through the living room and out the front door, and then she fled to her room.

A few hours later, Leah sat on the floor, reading. She thought she heard footsteps on the worn, carpeted stairs. She waited. The third stair to the top always groaned under the weight of a foot.

Eek.

Her breath caught in her throat. She wondered if her mother had gotten home yet, if Cal was out, or if her father was still with Les.

The strip of light under the door disappeared. She pulled her legs up to her chest, crushing them in her arms.

24

Cal entered. His eyes told her what he wanted.

She followed him into his room. He shut the door. Spun his favorite record. Turned up the volume. She'd grown to detest the song. It filled her ears. Then she felt full all over. She wished she could eject it. She turned her head away.

Afterward, he stood, looking guilty, as he always did. But it never stopped him. He made a point to remind her every few times, "Keep quiet, Leah, okay?" He wouldn't look at her. She'd been very confused, the first time. It hurt. It still hurt.

Leah ran the shower water close to scalding.

The one bathroom in the house had pink tiles near the sink and around the tub. The boxy shower stall was tiled in black. Steam filled the air, the walls shaping a coffin. It happened in here, too. Not with Cal.

Leah clenched. It was worse with her father. She'd rather it be Cal.

She put her palm on the slippery tile. Blood trickled down her legs. She pushed back the curtain, relieved to see no one standing there.

Desperate for fresh air, Leah went for a walk. She sat under a tree and twirled a twig in the ground, drawing shapes that didn't mean anything.

Once, she had stood up for herself. And Cal had stopped. He'd left the room with his head down, disappearing for three days afterwards.

Her mother had confronted her, angry. "What did you do, Leah?" she had demanded. "He left because of you." To her, Cal could do no wrong.

She looked up at the tree supporting her back. Studied the leaves. Birds congregated in the heights. Several butterflies fluttered by. She imagined wrapping her hands around each branch, pulling herself higher and higher, away from harm and monsters.

Five

Laguna Beach—September 2016

"Rella. Hey. How are you doing?"

"I'm sorry I didn't call you back sooner, Trevor."

"Don't worry about it. Are you okay?"

"Keeping busy." She exhaled a broken sigh. "Morgan called."

Trevor swallowed.

"She told me, about Mom—her childhood."

Trevor let out a breath. "I didn't know any of this, Rella."

"How could anyone . . ." Rella sniffled.

Trevor wanted to cry, but the tears remained elusive. "Do you want me to come over?"

"No. Thank you. You came all this way but, I'm . . . I . . ."

"I'm here for you, Rella. No pressure."

They hung up.

Trevor left the motel and walked to a nearby liquor store, buying a six-pack of beer.

Back in his room, he cracked one open and downed it. He went for a second. Before reaching his lips, his strength gave out.

He placed the can on the end table and dropped onto the bed, pounding his fists into the motel pillows as the waves broke into surf below.

Tasks of the day helped distract Rella. Her bed and dining set arrived. She directed the delivery men where to place the heavy, solid wood acacia table and watched as they removed the protective plastic from eight tufted chairs, upholstered in cream fabric. She transferred new sheets from the washer to the dryer as they set up her king-size bed between two end tables she'd found antiquing.

After the movers left, she made the bed, smoothing the sheets, tucking in the corners and arranging the pillows.

It would be her first night in the house.

A strange awareness encroached. She spun, sure she would see a face on the other side of the glass.

No one.

She slowly approached the windows and gazed down the hillside. The angle of her house on the steep slope made it impossible for anyone to look in.

"What am I afraid of?" she said aloud to the empty house.

She resumed making the bed.

The sun descended expeditiously. Rella grabbed the remote for the blinds and quickly pressed it, unable to bear the thought of darkness outside, obscurity. Her heart palpitated uneasily in her chest. She was glad she hadn't eaten much all day. There wasn't enough room in her stomach for both food and fear.

In the hall, she hesitated at the top of the stairs. They curved, the end sneaking out of sight. She eased onto a step. She pictured someone waiting at the bottom. Living alone for years, Rella couldn't recall ever being scared like this.

Turning the corner into the kitchen, she spotted the

remote for the downstairs blinds on the counter, gauging it would take five long strides to reach it. She averted her eyes until the entire length of window was covered.

She surveyed the great room, stark other than her new dining set. Nothing for anyone to hide behind. But she didn't feel alone.

Brring!

Rella let out a cry at the abrupt sound of her phone. Shaking, she laughed at her own baseless jitters.

"Hi, Morgan," she said, forcing stability into her voice.

"Rella, did you call Trevor? Tell him to come over?"

"I'm fine."

"I'm serious. Call him. He can sleep on the floor. He won't care."

Rella didn't listen.

Two hours passed.

Night spread, diffusing like poisonous steam. A feeling slithered over Rella. Her hands rigorously abraded her arms and thighs as she fought the urge to gouge her nails into her flesh.

She ran into the kitchen, opening cupboards. A can. Any heavy object. She needed a weapon. She banged each door shut, incensed at finding mostly empty space.

Then the sensation broke, like a fever, as quickly as it had come.

Rella stood, shaking. She gently opened the refrigerator door, the lone bottle of champagne there, most of its contents remaining. She poured a glass. The bubbles soothed her nerves and stomach.

Rella washed the glass, then filled a new one with water to take upstairs. Approaching the landing and hallway, slivers of half-open doors penetrated like eyes.

She quickly ran into her room and shut the door.

She put on pajamas and folded herself in the covers on the bed, the glass of water untouched, afraid of needing to leave the room for the bathroom. She brought her knees to her chest.

Four white walls. A concealed window. A closed door.

As a child, at bedtime, she'd make up fanciful, adventurous stories to prepare herself for sleep. Now, she couldn't access that part of her imagination.

Her mind off-gassed, like a new house, with suffocating toxic thoughts.

A recurring dream she'd had between the ages of nine and thirteen wafted in.

Someone at the front door. Somehow, she could see through it, to the other side. A man stood there, tall, in a long, gray trench coat, a low hat hiding his face.

He knew she could see him.

Malice oozed through the cracks around the hinges.

The figure remained motionless, mocking, waiting for her to open the door and let him in. Her muscles congealed, knowing no escape, until she woke, and its presence vaporized with the dream.

Rella picked up the phone.

"Trevor?"

"Rella, what's wrong?"

"I don't know." The calming effect of the champagne had completely worn off.

"I'm coming over."

Rella didn't want to tell him she was afraid to leave the room. "Never mind. I'll be all right."

"Rella, I'm coming."

She heard him reach for his keys, then the sound of a door shutting as he left the motel room.

"Do you want to stay on the phone with me until I get there?"

"Yes, I think that's a good idea."

The line remained mostly quiet during the eight minutes it took for Trevor to get to Rella's house.

"Rella, I'm pulling up. Is the front door locked?"

"Yes."

"Can you come down and let me in?"

She pictured the man in the trench coat on the other side of her bedroom door.

"I'll keep talking to you, Rella. It's going to be okay."

She slowly pushed back the bedding, uncovering her knees and feet. She extended her legs off the bed, then quickly retracted them, envisioning a hand reaching out to grab her from underneath.

Get a grip, Rella, she told herself. It's not possible anyone is in this house. They would have snared you already.

Unconvinced, she thought of another way off the bed. Prepping herself, she made a jump for it, landing far enough away so no one underneath could reach her.

Mentally shutting out thoughts of eyes ogling from under

the bed, she made her way to the door. The handle felt cool in the heat of her palm. Once open, she would have nowhere to go, no place to run. If someone was on the other side, they would get her. She was letting them in.

She couldn't do it slowly. A partially closed door was a hundred times more chilling than one open all the way. She flung it back.

No one there.

"Are you out of the bedroom?" Trevor asked.

"Yes." Rella advanced down the hallway. "Sorry. I'm a little spooked."

"Take your time."

Rella approached the stairs. Her sense of dread returned, not as strongly, subsiding.

She descended quickly and paused at the front door.

"Trevor?"

"Yes, it's me, Rella."

Rella heard his voice through the door and the phone simultaneously. She turned the locks.

"I've got you," Trevor said, as she buckled into his arms.

Six

Rella woke to a dark room and no memory of going to sleep. She felt around the bed. Soft covers. Lots of pillows. A remote.

She hit the button. The blinds hummed as they slowly lifted.

Rella squinted as sunlight poured through the glass. The intense foreboding from the night before had gone. She couldn't explain why it had taken over, or how it had left.

She stood and went to the window, soaking in the warmth on her skin. Her stomach slowly settled, and her shoulders relaxed. She then remembered her brother's arrival last night.

"Trevor?" Rella called as she descended the stairs. At the bottom she saw him asleep in one of the dining room chairs, forehead resting on his arms, folded on top of the table.

"Trevor?" She lightly touched his back.

"Yeah?" His head snapped up.

"Sorry. Didn't mean to startle you."

"No, I'm fine. How are you doing? You okay?"

Rella pulled out a chair across from him. "I think so. Last night is a little foggy."

"Rella, Morgan wants you to call her. She has more to say."

Rella gazed out over the ocean, having chosen a quiet spot on the beach to phone Morgan.

"Rella, do you know what PTSD is?"

"Yes. Post-traumatic stress disorder. People get it from going to war."

"Not only war. It can come from any type of trauma. And, if the person was young at the time, the brain can make them forget the incident, but it's still there, under the surface. And it will come out in different ways."

Rella wasn't sure why Morgan was telling her any of this.

"I got to thinking about you, Rella. Growing up, there were certain ways you behaved that didn't quite seem normal, especially now, after the research I've done. And then there's your patchy memory. You've forgotten even some of the good times. The health problems you've had since you were little—sleep trouble, the pain in your body that no one has been able to figure out. What seven-year-old gets migraines all the time? You still get them."

Rella couldn't recall a time when she hadn't felt ill, or when she wasn't experiencing some sort of pain. Batteries of tests had proved inconclusive. She refused to bow to drug-pushing doctors. She'd learned to live with it, making healthy choices, not allowing her physical ailments to slow her down, limit her potential, or decrease her enjoyment of life.

"Maybe there's a hidden reason for your symptoms," Morgan continued. "These days, doctors pick from a menu of diagnoses. Depression. OCD. Bipolar. GAD."

"GAD? *Egad.*"

"Egad? What, were you born in 1892? It stands for

generalized anxiety disorder. Rella, I'm making a statement here. I've worked in the medical field for over twenty years now. Doctors don't usually see what's really there, the cause underneath. They don't even look for it. They just slap a name on the symptoms, followed by medication. But from what I've read and studied, you have all the signs of PTSD."

"How silly. I do not."

"Rella, you now know how Mom grew up. And you were in that house, alone, more so than Trevor or I ever were."

The words moved through space and time and distance slowly, as if detained by an invisible force. Rella suddenly realized what Morgan had insinuated. "Nothing happened to me!"

"Rella, your memory has never been good. Maybe you completely blocked something out. I just think it would be prudent to see someone who specializes in child sexual abuse and PTSD."

Rella wished she could put her hands over her ears and never hear anything damaging again.

"It can't hurt," Morgan said. "And maybe you won't have to suffer with these physical symptoms anymore. Promise me you'll consider it."

Rella buried her feet in the warm, coarse sand. Millions of tiny grains, sizable collectively, but when solitary, nearly invisible. She cupped a handful. Memory measured in elemental specks, recognizable when complete, but, as single particles, easily swept away.

Seven

Laguna Beach—October 2016

The first floor of the design firm was outfitted with sleek forest green couches and accent tables made of various shapes of repurposed driftwood, which sold for thousands.

The Escheresque staircase angled three times. Rella held the floating banister until she reached the second level, the workspace. Completely open, with no interior dividers, natural light flooded from windows that ascended on all four sides.

Rella arrived by eight a.m. for her first official day. By noon, the others had yet to show. She left to take a walk in the sun, returning an hour later.

"Hey there!" a voice called from the kitchen area, causing Rella to startle.

A young girl came billowing toward Rella, tall and thin, like a cattail, with skin unblemished by the California sun. She wore a silver and purple angular sleeveless top, a tiered ankle-length cotton skirt layered with vintage-inspired aprons, and laced, brown combat boots. The ensemble suggested a meager budget for clothes, but Rella had seen the skirt in an ad and knew that it cost nearly as much as one of the upmarket end tables downstairs.

"You must be Rella." She extended her hand, standing soundly on her frame. "Virginia Derry, but everyone calls me

Ginnie." There was a light smattering of freckles across her upturned nose, and a shock of wild orange-red hair tumbled abundantly around her.

"Yes, that's me," Rella said, her whole body moving as a result of the woman's lively handshake.

Rella glanced at the white mug in Ginnie's hand, her eyes straying to a nearby desk that held three more coffee cups.

"You caught me," Ginnie said, chuckling. "Terrible habit. Not the coffee—that's an elixir of prime perfection. I couldn't possibly live without it. My dilemma is the potpourri of choices! White chocolate macadamia, salted caramel mocha." She nestled the mug in her hands and inhaled deeply. "Ah. Southern butter pecan." She savored a sip, then gave Rella a closer look. "Aren't you a little slice of sweetness. Adorable outfit."

Rella had donned a jumper with a collared undershirt and saddle shoes.

Ginnie moved behind her desk, settling narrow wire-framed glasses on her slender face. She looked regal in her high-backed chair.

"I can tell you're not from around here," said Ginnie, glancing up, expecting a response. "Madison, Wisconsin," she volunteered on her part. "Well, Cedarburg, to be exact." Ginnie shivered. "Don't miss those Lake Michigan winters."

"The home state of Frank Lloyd Wright," Rella said. "Have you visited Taliesin?"

"Oh, yes." Ginnie surveyed her desk. "I suppose it's time to send these mugs to the graveyard." She swooped them up, humming merrily as she sauntered toward the kitchen.

"I see you've met our future coffeehouse designer." Lifetime Laguna Beach resident and owner of the firm Garrett Pageant entered the room, wearing a floral print, buttoned shirt, khaki shorts, and open-toed sandals. "Virginia would be in eternal bliss."

"Ginnie!" she corrected amid the clanging of dishes.

Garrett shook his head. "Virginia is a much more suitable name for such a talent," he said to Rella. "Solid." He delivered a closed-hand motion toward the floor, as if putting a stamp of approval on his name choice. "VID Designs," he voiced, loud enough for Ginnie to hear.

"Already plotting to get rid of me." Ginnie reentered the room, a new mug in her hand, the southern butter pecan on her desk already a bygone.

"Never!" Garrett said.

"VID?" Rella asked.

"Virginia Irene Derry," Ginnie clarified, resuming her position behind the desk.

"Or Visions in Design," Rella thought quickly.

"Hmm. I dig it. And for you," she mulled it over while inhaling the new flavor, "Relevant Designs. Get it? *Rella*-vent." Ginnie smiled widely at her genius.

Rella liked her.

Two weeks had passed since Trevor's visit. Morgan's call pushed to the back of her mind, Rella focused on work. She still wrestled with sleep, however. If anything, it had gotten worse.

"You don't look so good," Ginnie said one day, folding her arms and leaning on Rella's desk. "Are you sick?"

Rella shook her head.

"Pregnant?" asked Ginnie.

Rella's face contorted to a look of repulsion.

"Right? Why any woman would go through *that* is beyond me."

"I couldn't agree more," said Rella.

"And the *delivery*? What a use of the word. As if you were sending a package or giving a speech. Hmph. Atrocious. I used to deliberate whether I'd rather come down with leprosy or pregnancy," Ginnie said, looking up at the ceiling in a philosophical way.

"Hi, girls!" Garrett greeted them. "What's the talk of the day?"

"The monstrosity of childbirth!" Ginnie announced.

"Impeccably timed entrance," Garrett said with a laugh. Rella had learned Garrett had married the first and last girl he ever dated and had four daughters.

He unloaded several rolls of plans on his desk, saying, "Rella, I have a question for you."

"Talk later," Ginnie said, tossing Rella a wink.

Garrett laid a business card on Rella's desk, facing her direction. "They called me this morning. Want us to design their new headquarters."

Rella glanced at the card. *TripWire Alarms and Security.* "They're the leading surveillance company in the nation."

"Yup." Garrett smiled proudly. "Their corporate offices are located in Atlanta. When can you go?"

Rella looked up at him. "This project is for me?"

"Of course!"

From across the room, Ginnie grinned with an excited thumbs-up.

Atlanta—November 2016

The week in Atlanta sped by, nearly every moment occupied.

One early evening, after finishing her last meeting for the day, Rella descended the hotel staircase, finding the lobby milling with well-dressed people. She'd noticed signs posted throughout the hotel advertising a conference. Normally the words would have melded into the background, become part of the wallpaper, but not this time.

TDT—Uncover the Wounds of the Past that Affect the Present.

Rella mingled purposefully through the crowd, picking up snippets of conversation.

"Excuse me," she said, interrupting two women. "I was wondering if TDT is a type of therapy?"

"Yes! I have been using it with patients now for several months, and what a considerable difference in their progress."

"It's striking how fast it works!" the second woman agreed. "What used to take me weeks, sometimes years, with a patient, I can do in days."

"Has anyone ever come to you with no specific memory of trauma?"

Both women turned thoughtful. "No," the first one answered. "But I believe this therapy would pull it out of them."

Rella thanked them for their time and returned upstairs

to her room, where she did a search with the term "TDT."

She learned that it stood for Trauma Desensitization Therapy—a form of treatment for PTSD.

A traumatic event or events can sit like a block in the brain, causing disturbances and preventing healing. TDT helps remove these blocks. During the session, the client is in control of his or her mind the entire time.

Rella wrote the word *block* on a blank sheet of paper and then free-associated all the related words and concepts that came to her.

Barrier

Building

Brick

Foundation

Construction

Constructive

Smart

Strong

Protect

Back off

Conceal

Entomb

Long-standing

She'd learned this technique in a creative writing class, resulting in a few dark and enigmatic poems, but had also found it helpful when designing client spaces. Now, she attempted to ask her subconscious mind its opinion.

She studied the list, her eyes lingering on *protect, back off*, and *entomb*.

Maybe her blocks were there for a reason.

That night, she awoke to shooting pain in her abdomen. Curled into the fetal position, she took short, shallow breaths. Sitting up, she turned on the lamp and rocked, pushing her fists into her thighs, tears in her eyes.

She remembered in detail the first day the red curse had arrived.

Although she loved learning, summer was her most anticipated time of year, filled with sunshine, warm nights, pool parties, and sleepovers.

That day Rella woke with an alien feeling in her stomach. Skinny, but a ravenous eater, she had an extra slice of peanut butter toast at breakfast.

By noon, all the girls were over to swim in their pool—three friends of Morgan's, and five of Rella's. Despite their age differences, in summertime everyone got along.

Four large boxes of pizza arrived. Still suffering the strange cramping pain, with even more of an appetite than usual, Rella dove in, devouring three slices.

"I gotta pee!" she announced, bounding up from the table, skipping happily to the bathroom.

She wiped. There was red on the toilet paper.

Confused, Rella wondered how pizza sauce could have gotten there.

She wiped again. Red.

Then it occurred to her. She'd overheard Morgan and her friends talking about this around a year ago. It all sounded awful. And stupid. She'd done some reading, about where the blood came from, and it appalled her. A girl either had to have a baby inside of her, or bleed? Why was there no other choice? She had daydreamed that maybe she'd been born free of all the parts that would trap her in this malediction.

She squeezed the toilet paper with one hand. Normally she would've had to take a spill to see that much blood, like the time she'd grabbed her sled and barreled down a hill covered in fresh snow, before hitting a concealed rock and being thrown, proudly getting the first stitches in her life.

That wasn't the case now. She'd done nothing courageous. And there were no stitches for this.

She wiped away the rest of the blood, pulled up her shorts, and went back to her friends.

Rella never wore a bathing suit without both a T-shirt and shorts over it, self-conscious even with her thin body. It took a few minutes for the blood to show up on her shorts.

"Hey, Rella, you got sauce all over you," Chelsea said, pointing. Seven-year-old Chelsea was the youngest in the group, the sister of one of Rella's friends.

Rella grabbed a stack of napkins. "I'm such a slob." Her eyes met Morgan's, and then Morgan's best friend Nina caught on.

"Who wants ice cream?" Nina cried out, and all the younger girls squealed.

Morgan lead Rella to the bathroom.

"Why do I keep bleeding?" Rella asked plaintively.

Morgan opened the cabinet under the sink. "When did it start?"

"When I went to the bathroom."

"Okay. It's okay. Is it painful?"

"Like someone kicked me in the stomach and I can't catch my breath."

Morgan acknowledged this with a nod, opening a box with the quick precision of an EMT readying bandages to treat a victim. "Here, you'll have to learn how to use these."

"I'm not wearing a diaper!"

"You don't have a choice."

"I'll just be more careful next time I pee."

"Rella, you don't just bleed when you go to the bathroom. It's not like urine. Your body doesn't hold it or wait till you're on the toilet."

"You mean it just keeps coming out of me?"

"Yes."

"For how long?"

Morgan shrugged. "A week."

"A *week*?" Rella shrieked.

"Rella, calm down. It happens to every girl."

Rella broiled on the inside. It was the first time she'd felt a loss of control over her own body. Her only offense: She was a girl.

"No! I don't want this!" She stomped her foot on the ground.

"Rella, why are you talking like that? You're thirteen, not seven. Here, take this, and I'll go get you some underwear."

"I'm staying in my suit."

Morgan's shoulders dropped. "Rella, you can't," she said softly.

Rella's eyes filled with tears.

Morgan put her arms around her. "I'll tell the girls you aren't feeling well after eating the pizza, and you can't swim the rest of the day." Morgan gave her a squeeze. "Be right back."

Morgan shut the door.

Rella looked down at the pink, artificially scented wad in her hand with contempt. Boys didn't have to bleed and wear a diaper and miss out on swimming. Punished and betrayed, her body was programmed to do something she'd never consented to, and she couldn't escape it.

Eight

Rella sipped tea in the hotel lobby just after one p.m. She'd had the final meeting for her project that morning, completing a few days ahead of schedule.

Fragments of her conversation with Morgan menaced like wasps, three words delivering repeated stings. *Child sexual abuse.* She often had to pretend certain things didn't exist in order to be able to live. She never read the newspaper or watched the news.

Nothing had happened to her. Of that, she was certain. But that still left no explanation for her ailments.

She sat for an hour, her mind a pool she barely dipped a toe in. Her tea grew cold.

Then, it came to her. Genetic memory. She'd learned about it in psychology class. The professor had cited several examples of studies showing how fears, aversions, and sensitivities could be passed down. Her laptop with her, she searched online, finding one article that discussed how DNA could carry memories of traumatic stress. Rella sat back. That was it. That must be the answer. If she had somehow inherited her mother's memories in her DNA, perhaps that's why she suffered so.

She thought about what Morgan had said—how maybe she could rid herself of the pain. Maybe that could mean period pain, too. She wondered if the TDT could fix it.

Rella searched an online TDT directory and clicked on a few names. She could easily change her flight. If she took care of it now, she could leave it all behind when she flew back to California. She wondered if anyone would be able to see her on such short notice.

She absently twirled her cup in the saucer. Maybe it wasn't a good idea. She would have to talk about a lot of unpleasant things. Why put herself through it? She tapped her fingers on the table. If she could lessen even some of the pain, maybe it would be worth it. She did suffer more than she should, especially as someone who took such meticulous care of her body and health.

Even though she knew DNA was a complicated thing, not to be pulled apart easily, like thin strands of delicate necklaces entwined together, she still envisioned the genetic mark plucked out as simply as removing an eyebrow hair. She could handle that.

She sent out five e-mails to people in the listing and then went for a walk.

Two hours later, she'd received four replies. Three of the people were not available, but one was. Seth Jabez. He was a bit of a distance away, but she didn't mind long drives.

I don't normally work weekends, but I can see you Saturday and Sunday. Two hours in the morning, two hours in the afternoon. Three hours on Monday. Eleven hours total. Confirm as soon as possible.

Rella found this reply cold. A warning bell pinged softly in her mind, but the pain from last night rang louder. And the treatment certainly couldn't do any harm.

On Friday morning, Rella picked up the rental car and set out. Fiddling with the radio, she found an oldies station.

The familiar opening lines to "Suspicious Minds" by the Mississippi-born legend immediately returned her to the past, to thoughts of her mother, and a road trip she had surprised her with right before she'd moved to California.

Her mother had told Rella that she'd once taken three days off to see Elvis live at a Vegas concert, one of his last, and mentioned how she'd always wanted to visit Graceland.

Rella had mapped out the route, and off they went. Her mother enjoyed the tour with fascination, and after the enjoyable day, put her arms around her daughter and said, "Thank you, Rella. Thank you for making this dream come true for me."

"Of course, Mom. And I have one more surprise, if you don't mind a detour."

"More time with you? Are you kidding! I'll go anywhere!"

They had extended their trip, and two days later, upon entering a town, Rella slowed down and pointed to a road sign.

"Las Cruces," her mother read aloud. It took her a moment to make the connection, then, "Maybe it *was* Las Cruces!" she exclaimed, mimicking the grating nasal tones of a character from the sitcom *Wings* who'd coined the phrase.

Although Rella had never seen the appeal, the show had been a favorite of her mother and sister, who would often repeat the line amid peals of laughter.

Rella drove to a nearby store, ran in, and came out with a black marker and a large piece of neon orange poster board on which she wrote: *Maybe it* was *Las Cruces!*

They found a spot in town, on a small hill at a busy

intersection, and took turns holding up the sign, taking pictures of one another, howling, "Maybe it *was* Las Cruces!" as passing drivers beeped and waved.

Rella's current road trip was miles away from that happy expedition. How difficult it must have been for her mother, keeping so much inside. Perhaps it felt like living a dual life.

She spotted a restaurant off the highway and pulled in, bringing her briefcase inside.

After ordering the only vegan offerings on the menu, a side salad and plain baked potato, she removed an item from her case.

By age three, Rella had already begun carrying books around the house, spending hours drawing at the table in her playroom, creating houses with secret doors and numerous rooms.

Always encouraging Rella, her mother had presented her with a book called *Need a House? Call Ms. Mouse!*, a story about a female mouse architect named Henrietta, owner of Ms. Mouse & Co., who designed clever abodes for all kinds of animals, insects, reptiles, and fish.

Rella cherished the book to this day.

She opened the cover and removed a card she'd saved, one of many her mother had given her over the years, in her efforts to encourage Rella to communicate, conscious of the fact that her daughter often locked her feelings inside a vault. A white bear in green overalls, its paws covering its eyes, sat on the front, positioned above the words: *It's okay to show how you feel.* Inside, her mother had written:

Sometimes it's extremely difficult to be a parent, and it's almost impossible to be the kind that can smooth over life's troubles, taking away the pressure, pain, and heartbreak we all endure each day.

You are always in my thoughts. I don't have all the answers, but I can be a good listener. I know it's difficult for you to talk. Please write, if that would be easier for you.

Remember, goals can be reached, and dreams can be realized. You can do anything you want to do. Life may be hard at times, but you are strong, capable, and independent.

Remember this too: It has to rain sometimes, or we'd never see the rainbow.

I'm here. I love you.

Mom

Nine

Rella consulted the GPS in confusion. She glanced at the address she had jotted down. There didn't appear to be a mistake. But she saw no offices, only boxy, cinderblock, residential apartments.

Reaching number 610, she parked on the opposite side of the street. The area was run-down, bland, like chewed-up and spit-out gum.

She gathered items from the passenger seat. Small notebook. Pen. Bottle of water. Sweater.

She encountered a keypad at the entrance door. The e-mail had given no information other than the building number. She studied the names on the panel, and found *Jabe*, the *z* smudged off. She pressed it. Waited. Pressed again. The buzzer sounded.

"Third floor," a female voice scratched through the intercom.

Rella climbed the empty, dusty stairs. The hallway's sallow green paint flaked to the floor like dandruff, and the thin baseboard bore scraping lesions of tenants moving in or out.

A lone door waited at the end of the hall, ajar.

She knocked.

"Come in."

Outside light, grayed by thin curtains, filtered in from the far side of the room. A woman approached, her face as aged and lusterless as the apartment.

"Wait here," she instructed. Passing Rella, she rapped on a door.

"Your appointment is here. Cleaning's done. I'll be back next week."

She gave Rella a depleted smile before exiting.

Rella wanted to run out and never come back.

The door opened, and a tall, thin, balding man in his mid-fifties, wearing a brown polo shirt, tan slacks, and slip-on loafers, stood in the doorway.

"Hello," he said. "Seth Jabez."

"Hi, I'm Rella."

"Come in."

She followed him into a small office where a desk faced the window. Rella didn't like the room, and she didn't have a positive impression of him.

Sitting, he swiveled, facing her, gesturing to the only other chair, straight out of a seventies dental lobby, backed up against the wall.

She sat. The synthetic material crunched. At least there was no brown paneling on the walls.

He handed her a clipboard with paper, and a pen.

"It's important to establish your background. Please write down as many of your family members as you know, go back as far as you can, their names, ages or birth order, if they are alive or dead, their relationship to you, and marital status. Start with yourself."

Rella began.

Rella May Cooper. Age 38. Single.

Trevor Brayden Cooper. Age 42. Brother. Single.

Morgan Jean Reisert. Age 46. Sister. Widowed.

Leah Beth Cooper. Age 63. Mother. Separated.

Jack Thomas Cooper. Age 65. Father. Separated.

Her hand shook.

Edith Stein. Grandmother. Dead.

Silas Stein. Grandfather. Dead.

Cal Stein. Uncle. Dead.

"I don't have anything to write for my father's side. He was an only child and I never met his parents. I don't know their names."

"You can leave it blank, then."

"I'm finished." Rella held out the paper, the assignment already taking a toll.

"I see your parents are separated. When was that?"

"I was very young."

"Neither remarried?"

"No."

"How is your relationship with your father?"

"Pretty good. We talk here and there. He travels for work, and I'm so busy all the time."

"I see your sister is a widow."

"It happened a long time ago, more than ten years back, now. It was horrible. Quite a shock. A work accident. They'd only been married about a year and a half."

"This Cal—do you know how old he was when he died?"

"No. Young. Before I was born."

"How did he die?"

"Shot himself."

"I see." He put the clipboard down. "Tell me why you are here."

"Well, as I stated in my e-mail, I've had health problems my whole life. Pain, migraines, sore throats. Doctors have never been able to find an explanation. I exercise every day and eat a nearly perfect diet, no animal products, nothing processed."

"Do your siblings have health problems?"

"No."

"Do you have a history of nightmares, depression, troubles with intimacy?"

"Some nightmares. No depression. As for intimacy, I'm not with anyone at the moment. Haven't been for a long time."

"Why is that?"

"I have no desire; I see no value in it. I abhor the idea of getting pregnant and refuse to take hormonal birth control. I have pain in my abdomen, all the time, which increases after intercourse, for days afterwards." Rella hoped this would end the topic.

"Any self-harm—eating disorders?"

It was so long ago and no longer a problem, Rella hardly thought about it anymore. "Anorexia."

"How old were you?"

"Around seventeen."

"How long did it go on for?"

"Several years. And it doesn't make sense, because I was always skinny. But I later read that it's not about weight; it's about control."

"Do you recall a particular incident or a time when you felt out of control?"

"No."

He glanced at the clipboard. "You're thirty-eight. Why seek out help now?"

Rella's heart thumped in her chest. "I found out something, about my mother. She had a horrible childhood." Rella lowered her head, pulling at her hands. "Sick, disgusting things happened to her." She couldn't bring herself to say the words out loud.

"Sexual abuse?" Seth asked.

Rella nodded.

"Who did these things to her?"

Her stomach churned. "Her father. Her brother."

"And how does this relate to you?"

Rella's hands tightened.

"My sister Morgan. She researched PTSD. She thinks my health problems might be . . . She thinks something might have happened to me, too. But nothing did. It's not possible. I would remember." Rella brushed back her hair and drank water.

"Your sister thinks you might have been sexually abused? By whom?"

"I wasn't. Here's what I think. I must have *her* memories, my mother's memories—or rather, the repercussions of them— in the form of all this pain, these symptoms. They're stuck in my body, passed down to me. I've read about genetic memory. I mean, that has to be it, right?"

"Possibly." Seth angled his chair to face her more directly. "We are going to access your brain, to enable it to give us the information we need. It does this in images. Let them come and tell me what you see."

Rella took a deep breath.

Ten

"Since you don't have a memory of any major event, we can use something else." Seth consulted his notes. "You said you'd get upset when you were woken up, as a teenager. Who would wake you up?"

"My mother, usually. I've always been a light sleeper. A turn of the doorknob was the same as an alarm to me, as if my ears had been listening for it."

"And why would you be listening for it?"

"I wasn't; I mean, I didn't plan to. That's just how I'm describing it now."

"And why did it upset you?"

"My heart would race. It was hard to calm down."

"Any emotions?"

Rella thought. "Anger, maybe?"

Seth wheeled his chair in front of her. "Close your eyes. Focus on being woken up unexpectedly."

Rella closed her eyes.

"I'm going to be tapping your knees. Stay connected to anger, and notice what you see, as it comes."

She felt tapping on the left knee, the right knee, continuous.

At first, denseness. Then, like swimming in murky water, minimal light leaked through. She floated above a bedroom.

A girl was asleep on the bed. The doorknob turned. The girl didn't notice. She stayed asleep. The door opened, letting in a crack of light. A face jutted in front of Rella, distorted, inhuman, its mouth curving into an evil smile.

"Uh!" The sound leapt from her mouth. Pressure clamped her chest.

Seth stopped tapping. "What did you see?"

It took Rella a moment to realize where she was.

"A—a bedroom. Someone opening the door. A girl on the bed."

"Was it you?"

"I couldn't see who it was."

"How old was she?"

"I'm not sure."

"Who was going into the room?"

"I don't know," she said, tears coming to her eyes.

"A man or a woman?"

"A man, I think."

"But you can't see the face?"

"No. Just this awful . . . smile."

"Close your eyes again."

Rella didn't want to, not if she was going to see anything like that again. Hesitantly, she obliged.

The tapping recommenced, wrenching her from the room, dropping her back into the same scene.

No one in the doorway. Movement, on the bed, someone getting on.

She lurched.

"What happened?" Seth asked.

"The bed moved."

"Close your eyes."

The tears returned. "I don't know about this."

"Watch it play out, like a movie."

Rella's idea of a movie was *Pollyanna* or *Anne of Green Gables*. Those were safe. This was no film she wanted to see.

The phone on the desk rang, the unexpected shrill jarring her.

Seth rolled his chair over to answer it. He spoke for a few minutes before replacing the receiver and facing Rella again. He circled his right forefinger in the air. "Let it roll out."

Scared at what would come next, Rella closed her eyes again.

"What do you see?"

"Nothing. White." She was relieved.

"Think about the movement on the bed."

"It wasn't me on the bed."

The tapping on her knees continued. The white stillness didn't last long.

She floated above a bedroom again, but this one was bright, as if it were the middle of the day, or all the lights had been left on, a different room altogether from the previous one.

White walls. White sheets. The girl on the bed had blonde hair in pigtails.

"What do you see?" Seth repeated.

She told him.

"How old is the girl?"

Rella couldn't see her face, only her hair, and that she was wearing a white dress, but a number popped into mind. "She looks about four."

Seth kept tapping.

Rella twitched.

"What is it?"

"She's standing. There's blood. There's blood on the dress." Rella's voice quivered.

"Where did it come from?"

"I don't know."

Rella gasped and recoiled in the chair.

"What is it?"

"A face." She pressed her cheek into the chair, trying to get away from the face, its breath.

"Whose face?"

"It's . . . it's a mask. Hovering above my face. Black and red and white. With an evil smile."

"Can you take the mask off the person wearing it?"

Rella's head swung. "No, no—I don't want to."

Lightheadedness engulfed her as she separated, floated up.

"What's happening?"

"I'm an onlooker."

She exhaled in relief.

"But that little girl . . ." She wanted to reach down and snatch her out of there. "I see someone entering the room. It's—it's my dad. He's come to the rescue. He yells at the intruder, hits him, leaves him crumpled on the ground, and carries her away." Rella furrowed her brow. "No, that didn't happen. No one came. I only imagined it. It's up to me to save myself. I could die, or live, but no one is coming to save me. I will live. I beat him off, and the blood, it's gone, no more around, it's white and yellow, and I *stomp* out of there. No one is going to save me. I need to take care of myself and find my own way home."

"Rella, your voice changed." Seth had paused the tapping.

Her eyes fluttered open. She looked around the room, disoriented. "The little girl. She's still in the room. With the blood." She rocked back and forth in the chair.

"Rella, can you remember this happening in your life? What you saw?"

"That wasn't me," Rella said after a few moments.

"Who was it?"

"No idea. But I don't have blonde hair."

Rella didn't like Seth's proximity to her.

"But you were there, beating off the person."

"I see two people. Me, and the little girl with the blonde hair. Maybe I rescued someone? Or wanted to?"

She didn't understand these pictures. She shook her head, wishing it were a Sketch n' Shake she could reset to blank. "This little girl with the blonde hair. Who is she?"

"Did you have a friend who resembled her?"

"I can't remember what friends I had at that age."

"Can you remember any significant events at age four?"

"No. But my memory is terrible. It always has been. I have to rely on Morgan to remind me of things from my life."

"Maybe you can ask her, then. Or your mother."

Rella didn't want to tell her mother about any of this. It would just upset her.

"You said you were about three when your dad moved out?"

She nodded.

"Did other people watch you? Family members? Babysitters?"

"Yes. I had many babysitters, after my mom went back to work. My father watched me as often as he could, of course, but he was out of town a lot for work."

"Did you have male babysitters?"

Rella shrugged. "I don't remember."

"What about your grandparents?"

"Yes, I was there a lot."

"Did you like it over there?"

"No. It felt dirty to me, cluttered, and it smelled like cigarettes. I hated sleeping there. We actually lived there for a time, right after my dad moved out, because my mother had lost the apartment we'd been in." Rella shuddered. "I hated that bathroom."

"The bathroom?"

"The shower was narrow and black. Have you ever heard of tiling a shower in black? There was no light in there. The rest of the room had pink tiles, like the fifties or sixties style, around the tub. I didn't like it. And I hate bathtubs. I won't take a bath."

Seth made some notes. "How was your grandparents' relationship with each other?"

"Not great. His bedroom was in the basement."

"Why is that?"

"I don't know. I never saw them being affectionate with each other. Maybe my grandmother didn't want him near her."

"It's time to break now. I'll see you in an hour."

Rella gathered her belongings and stood. "Have a nice lunch."

"Yes," Seth said, picking up his phone.

She let herself out.

Stepping outside, the ground tipped off-axis and pressure in her head swelled, as though acclimating to an unfamiliar planet, one cold and harsh, a Neptune arctic giant, farthest from the sun. The air, heavy with condensation, weighed on her shoulders.

The image of the little girl, and the sheets saturated with blood, had come from a place light-years away.

Her phone rang, rocketing her from this alternate reality back to her own.

"Hi, Morgan."

"How's it going?" Morgan asked. "What have you learned?"

"I hate it. I shouldn't go back there."

"Why?"

She felt as though she were lowering herself into an abyss she might never climb out of. Rella didn't want to describe the images, relive them. She sighed. "Let's talk about something else."

Back in Seth's office, Rella said, "Listen, what happened this morning—I've never had anything like that come into my head before. I couldn't eat lunch. I can't get the images out of my mind."

"That's why we keep going. We search out the upsetting events so the brain can reprocess them."

"Maybe they don't want to be found."

Seth picked up his notes. "You mentioned widespread pain in your body. Describe how this makes you feel."

"Old. Deteriorating from within. In warm weather it abates. Somewhat."

"If you had to pick an area in your body where it's the worst, where would it be?"

"My inner legs; hamstrings. I stretch all the time, but I'm still tight."

"Do you clench your teeth?"

"Yes, and my fists too, at odd times. Even when I'm content, calm, I find myself doing it."

"What emotion would you associate with the pain?"

"Emotion?"

"First one that comes to mind."

"Anger."

"You mentioned this earlier. Are you often angry?"

"No."

"What kind of situation bothers you the most?"

"Feeling trapped."

"Close your eyes again," Seth instructed.

She did. He wheeled closer to her, started tapping. She feared what her mind would produce.

"Can you remember the first time you felt anger in your legs?"

"No."

"How about anywhere else in the body?"

Metallic rigor wrapped her neck. "I can't get up."

"Where are you, Rella?"

"Can't move my legs."

"Why can't you?"

Rella's body tensed, bracing against something she couldn't see, didn't want to see.

"Can you remember the first time you felt trapped?" he asked, tapping.

"No."

"Where do you experience it in your body, when you feel trapped?"

Rella couldn't respond.

Seth repeated the question.

"Nowhere," she said flatly.

"Nowhere? Any pain or tension in your legs right now? Tightness?"

"No."

"Are your legs confined in any way?"

"No."

"Has there ever been a time when you weren't in control of your legs?"

"No." She sat composed.

"That's all for today." Seth returned to his desk. "I think you should come an hour earlier tomorrow."

Her eyes stared ahead. "I will be here," she said.

Eleven

Shackled in a fitful sleep of soundless screams, strangling cords, and arm constraints, Rella woke with a stiff spine and racing heart. A sense of dread settled in, her stomach so queasy she felt carsick even before driving to her next appointment. Somehow, she made it to Seth's office.

"Today I thought we'd start with how you don't like bathtubs. I'm assuming you don't know why."

Rella shook her head.

"What words come up when you think of bathtubs?"

Rella thought. "Before yesterday, I would have had no answer. But now, 'dirty' and 'concealment' come to mind."

Seth wheeled closer. "Think of only those words."

Reluctantly, Rella shut her eyes.

Tap. Tap. Tap.

Losing any sense of the room around her, she descended.

"I'm being pushed underwater. Or, I've slid down. No, I'm being held down."

"Who's holding you down?"

Rella tried to see the arm, couldn't make out if it was male or female. "I'm swallowing water. Lots." It swirled. She coughed.

"How old are you here, Rella?"

Lost in the liquid, falling backwards, she reached up,

fighting against the perception of drowning.

"Where are you?"

Her mother appeared above her, nebulous through the water. She couldn't have been the one who pushed her down.

Her vision cleared. She was up out of the water.

"I see a bathroom. The tub is pink, and the tile is black. There's a little girl in the bathtub."

"Is it you?"

"She has the face of a plastic doll."

"Is she older or younger than four?"

"Younger. Maybe two."

"Who else is there?"

"My mother, sitting on the floor."

"What's going on?"

"She's smiling, playing with the little girl as she washes her."

Rella's brow furrowed. She felt the presence of someone else in the scene. Her mother's expression twisted to ire.

"Get out of here!" her mother yelled, pushing her hand at the air.

Rella's mother never yelled.

Lurking in the partially opened doorway was a man, his eyes leering.

Rella pushed herself forward in the chair, surfacing from the submersion of the image. "What is this?" she asked Seth. "What are you doing to me?"

"What happened there at the end, Rella?"

"There was a man, in the doorway."

"Could you see who it was?"

Rella shook her head. The image of the evil smile flashed in her mind, wider, taunting. "I don't want to do this anymore."

"We are seeing what is inside. Your brain is showing us what is already there."

"These are not my memories."

"Close your eyes. Connect back to it."

Tap. Tap. Tap.

Her head turned unnaturally to the right.

Tap. Tap. Tap.

"Rella, what do you see?"

Her hands fisted, pushing against her thighs. "Mm. Mm. Mm." She protested in short bursts.

"Rella, what's going on?"

Tap. Tap. Tap.

Her hands flew up and she kicked the air with her feet, her noises becoming louder.

Seth spoke evenly to her, bringing her back to the present moment.

Rella recovered a few minutes later, opening her eyes.

Seth turned from the desk. "Rella, have you ever felt separation anxiety?"

"Yes."

"At what age?"

"Five. When I was dropped off at school, I'd scream and cry. I never wanted my mother to leave. The teachers told her that once I settled in, I was fine. I loved learning."

Seth wheeled closer. "Recall the scene of being dropped off."

Tap. Tap. Tap.

"Have you always felt safe around your mother?"

"Yes."

"And your father?"

"Yes."

"Your sister?"

"Yes."

"Your brother?"

"Yes."

"What about other family members?"

"I've never felt unsafe with a family member."

"Center your thoughts on being alone, abandoned."

Tap. Tap. Tap.

"Anything, Rella?"

"Nothing."

"It's important to resolve this. Center your thoughts on being alone, abandoned," he repeated.

Her brain must be protecting her for a reason, she thought.

"Do you have a photo album from your childhood?"

She did, with photos from her birth until about the age of three or four. She hadn't looked at it in ages. "Yes."

"Mentally hold this photo album in your hands."

Tap. Tap. Tap.

Blues, yellows, and greens wheeled into focus, and she saw cartoon giraffes and bubbles on the front cover, the binding a little torn in the top left corner. "I have it."

"I want you to think back to the mask you described. The one with the evil smile."

Tap. Tap. Tap.

"Picture that mask, Rella."

She writhed, pushing away with fisted fingers and curled toes, strained noises captive behind closed lips.

"Mask, Rella. Mask, Rella," he repeated.

"No." She pushed back into the chair.

"Can you see it?"

She rolled her head.

"See *who*, Rella."

The mask sprang out, in front of her, on top, on all sides, like a demented clown in a box.

"No!" she screamed, but only in her mind, her eyes squeezed shut.

"Flip through the photo album, Rella. Turn the pages."

Tap. Tap. Tap.

It flashed in an instant, stung like radiation. The face. The eyes. A cry jammed in her throat, swallowed in the past, locked inside for decades.

Eyes flying open, she pushed up and back in the chair, as far away from Seth as possible.

"You recognize the face."

The page from the photo album scorched her mind.

"What did you see?"

Rella reeled from the revelation.

"Tell me."

Reality crumbled away, and Rella felt alone in the chair, the walls gone, only a few square feet left of the floor remaining beneath her.

"I'm in the photo, maybe two, three years old," Rella began, her voice hoarse. "My grandmother is holding me. I'm on her lap, facing the camera. Next to her is my grandfa—"

She couldn't say it. His face as Rella had never seen before, the eyes drilling into her, a look she had erased.

"It was your grandfather," Seth said.

Rella hadn't inherited repercussions from her mother's memories. They were her own.

Back at the hotel, nightmares plagued Rella's sleep—of being held down, unable to lift her head or move her legs, eyes and faces at windows, doorways, being submerged in water, drowning, and the evil mask.

The bathtub. Her loathing of pink and black tiles. That house had always felt unclean. She now saw where the real filth had come from.

She'd never open her childhood album again.

She woke with a start. Movement on the bed.

She quickly turned on the light, sure someone was there, but she was the only one in the room. She glanced at the clock. Two a.m.

She kept the light on as she carefully closed her eyes, not at all confident she wouldn't regret it.

Horrible pain in her abdomen awakened her at four a.m., as if she had her period, but didn't. She thought of the little girl, the blood on the sheets. She curled into the fetal position, knowing she would not sleep again.

Morgan called her later that morning.

"Hey, just calling to see how it's going."

"I never should have come here."

"Why?"

"I was fine before."

"No, you weren't, Rella—all the pain you experience."

"I'm worse now!"

"It will get easier," Morgan said calmly. "Hopefully after this treatment, you won't be as affected as you are now."

"That's like saying you can jump into water and not get wet."

"What time is it there? When is your next appointment?"

"I—I can't see the numbers on the clock. My vision . . . I can't see straight."

"Can't see straight?"

"I hate that house!" she burst out.

"What house?"

"That basement!"

"Rella, your voice sounds different. What are you talking about? Which house?"

"The grandparents' house!"

"The grandparents?"

"I can't believe her!" Rella screamed. "Why would she leave me there? Alone in that house, with him!"

Her skin squirmed at the sudden memory of passing his bed in the basement in the summer, with shorts on, the sheets brushing against her exposed legs. Her nose filled with musty dust particulates.

Her hands flittered in front of her face.

"Rella, what are you talking about? What have you found out? Are you saying that something *did* happen, in that house?"

Rella openly cried, for the first time since discovering, and then she hung up, unable to voice what she'd learned.

Morgan stared at the phone. She took a few deep breaths, reining herself in from immediately calling Rella back. She reviewed what Rella had spurted out, adding in what she already knew about her grandparents—her grandfather was an abuser, and her grandmother had turned the other way. Leah had paid the price. From Rella's outburst, Morgan surmised that Rella had too.

She called her back.

"What?" Rella snapped.

"Rella, I know talking is hard. I don't want to put any unnecessary pressure on you. I just want some clarification."

Rella sighed. "Fine."

"Rella, did our grandfather molest you—abuse you in any way?"

Rella sobbed. Took a breath. "Yes. I mean, I think so."

Morgan gripped the phone, fighting not to slam it on the counter. "Rella. I don't know what to say. When I told you to see someone, it's not because I wanted to be proven right."

"I know." Rella paused. "We *lived* there. We lived there, Morgan. What was she thinking?"

"I don't know. She's not right in the head. Maybe she thought there was no danger anymore. But now the repressed memories will come out, and you'll be better."

"I don't *remember* anything."

Her last session. Three hours long. Seth called it processing. At noon, she'd walk out of there, brain restored, torment over.

Seth wheeled his chair over.

Tap. Tap. Tap.

Methodical, like a hammer hits a nail.

Tap. Tap. Tap.

Like a knocker strikes a door.

She wasn't a person. Solely a mind he tap-tap-tapped to access.

An image came.

"I'm in the dining room, at my grandmother's house. He is at the head of the table. Coughing. Always coughing. Phlegmy, spitting into a handkerchief. He was a smoker. I'm there. Pretending to eat. My face is down. 'Rella,' my grandmother says sternly, "you make sure to clean your plate.' She always insisted on that. My mother never did. 'What's wrong, why aren't you eating?' she says, standing over me now. I look up at her, then over to him." Rella's body tensed. "His face—it's not what I remember." Rella shook her head forcefully. "I want this face out of my mind."

"What does the face say, Rella?"

Tap. Tap. Tap.

"*Don't say anything. You can't. Ha. I win.* My grandmother says, 'You eat every last bite.' I pick up my spoon, even though I don't want to, even though the food is making me sick. It's like swallowing a secret."

The tapping paused. The comprehension arrived.

"The eating disorder," Rella whispered.

Having no previous issues with food or weight, overnight

there'd been a reversal. Rather than nourishment, food had become poison, harmful. Starvation imparted power, discipline. She'd prided herself on her strength, her ability to resist food. On minimal calories she'd exercised incessantly, running, insensitive to the searing pain in her legs, relishing the lack of restraint. Light, unencumbered, asexual. Superhuman. Her period had mercifully ceased.

Deprivation had its risks. Anemia. Fractures. Chest pain. Frailty, on the brink of disintegrating, blowing away.

Tears formed in Rella's eyes. She couldn't remember a time in her life when she physically felt good.

She'd been warned not to tell. And she'd kept it hidden, even from herself.

The phone rang. Seth reached for it.

"Could you *not* answer the phone?" Rella said, indignation rising in her voice. She'd had enough and couldn't believe a professional would do such a thing, especially repeatedly.

Seth regarded her with slight annoyance but left the phone where it was.

He attempted another round of tapping, but Rella's mind had bled enough. It wouldn't offer a drop more.

"We are out of time. You need to continue with phone sessions, a minimum of once a week."

"Continue?" Her hands and lips trembled.

"E-mail me to set up a time." He turned his back to her, facing the desk.

Rella sat speechless—at his lack of empathy, at how the sessions had ended. It wasn't what she had expected at all.

Numb, she picked up her belongings and left.

I, D-503, Builder of the Integral, am only one of the mathematicians of the One State. My pen, accustomed to figures, does not know how to create the music of assonances and rhymes. I shall merely attempt to record what I see and think, or, to be more exact, what we think (precisely so—we, and let this We be the title of my record). But since this record will be a derivative of our life, of the mathematically perfect life of the One State, will it not be, of itself, and regardless of my will or skill, a poem? It will. I believe, I know it.

. . . It is I, and at the same time, not I. And for many long months it will be necessary to nourish it with my own life, my own blood, then tear it painfully from myself and lay it at the feet of the One State.

But I am ready, like every one, or almost every one, of us. I am ready.
—Yevgeny Zamyatin, *We*

Twelve

The bright light of the outside world flicked on.

Margaret's eyes opened. The couch she slept on faced a solid glass wall. She preferred a couch rather than a bed.

She rose, picked up the blanket, folded it neatly, and placed the two pillows on top. She lifted them so as to keep their form and went to the armoire in the corner. She opened the deep bottom drawer and placed the articles inside.

She retrieved her exercise clothes, and went into the

small, adjacent room that contained an elliptical machine, mat, and one bench. No mirrors.

An hour later, she indulged herself with an extra three minutes under the hot water in the doorless shower. Even though it was unlikely anyone would see her today, or any day, she still insisted on dressing in a trim, gray and white business suit set.

She closed her eyelids with deliberation, then opened them widely. Her onyx eyes shone like two marbles. She was glad they weren't an ambiguous color, like hazel. She rested simple, black-rimmed glasses on the bridge of her nose. Once her long, dark hair was dry, she pulled it into a bun.

There was no television in the office. She felt it a waste of time and neurons. She was far too busy for frivolity. She didn't allow useless print material either. She'd lined up her current three books on the end table next to the couch according to size, on the subjects of organizational skills, management, and data storage.

On the wall to the right was a brown and gray kitchenette with a single-basin stainless sink, under-counter refrigerator, and a cabinet above with neatly folded hand towels and minimal dishware. Margaret washed, dried, and returned items right after using them. A cabinet hid the trashcan. It was cleared daily.

Small bites of tomato, carrot, and sprout sandwiches curbed any pinch of hunger. She dabbed the corners of her mouth with a half-piece of paper towel, always frugal. Searching for crumbs, she inspected the floor for any stray particles, leaving nothing behind.

She would prefer no reliance on food, sleep, or drink. Invincible, free from necessities or dependencies. Shrewd, untouchable, impervious to cold or hot, drafts and exhales. No need for bathrooms or showers.

She went to the sink and placed a glass under the faucet, keeping the filtered water slightly warm. She watched the water rise, stopping it at a third of the way to the top. She took a sip, paused, then took another before dumping the rest.

She rinsed the glass, filled it, and carried it to the fern in the corner near the window. She emptied the water into the soil, taking a moment to press her forefinger into the potted earth.

Beyond the living quarters was a middle room, the walls a light blue. Rather than the wood floor of the living area, it had plush, royal blue carpet.

A round, heavy, cherry table sat in the center, a bouquet of flowers positioned at exactly the midpoint on top, each bloom without scent. She was sensitive to fragrances of any kind.

Margaret admired the discreet power of flowers, their ability to flourish, even after the harshest weather.

Two paintings covered the walls, with matching frames of gold—one of a massive ship at sea, the scene dating to the early 1900s, and one of a pastoral landscape, a farmhouse in the distance. The paint glistened under the curved brass lights that shone above each of them, the only artwork in the entire office.

The carpet continued into the front room, blotting out all sound. File cabinets, made of the same cherry as the center table, stood guard around the perimeter, against all four walls, diminishing the room. Margaret was used to confined spaces. Of impressive size, they could prove deadly if one were to be trapped under their crushing weight. Each was fitted with a lock. Margaret held the key. She shut files inside, but did not take them out, or read their contents. She didn't care to.

Nearly hidden, encased by the cabinets, was the only exit, protected by an access code, an additional precaution for the safety of the files. She stepped out of the office now and again, but only if necessary. The exertion made her quite dizzy, and she had plenty to do inside. There were no clocks, no timecards. She was always on duty.

Margaret assessed the two rooms. The carpet had no signs of wear or fading. No lint. She ran a paper towel, damp with only water, over the wood surfaces and paintings to check for dust. Immaculate.

Holding order, cleanliness, and routine in the highest regard, she'd been appalled at the state of these rooms upon her arrival. A chaotic, disorganized mess, as if someone had left in a hurry, or had been told to leave. She hadn't asked any questions; she'd learned early on not to. She nodded in accordance when given direction. Those first few months had been hard, working and existing under such conditions. There had been no living quarters. She surmised the former supervisor had not been sequestered there. It was now required to be confined. It suited her. She did her job best from a distance.

She stood at the wall of windows in the living quarters, looking through the spotless glass, eyes level. Located in a high-rise, not much impeded her view. She allowed herself a moment of pride at her years of successful service.

Below her were several floors, each one containing rooms that had been created, re-created, altered, substituted, replaced, or repaired. Never removed; that wasn't possible. But emptied, echoing a former identity. Off-limits. The elevator never landed there, the buttons dark on the panel, circuits aptly rewired.

Her office commanded the top floor. No matter how many Others were added, she would remain at the summit.

Holding up the foundation.

Part Two

In another moment down went Alice after it, never once considering how in the world she was to get out again.

The rabbit-hole went straight on like a tunnel for some way, and then dipped suddenly down, so suddenly that Alice had not a moment to think about stopping herself before she found herself falling down what seemed to be a very deep well.

. . . Down, down, down. Would the fall never come to an end?

—Lewis Carroll, *Alice's Adventures in Wonderland*

Thirteen

Laguna Beach—January 2017

"There's the rock star!" Ginnie declared, heralding Rella's arrival in the office. "Garrett reported that the Atlanta project is ahead of schedule, all due to you. How were your holidays? What did you do over the two weeks?"

"My family and I don't celebrate holidays. I just stayed around here." The time off had not been pleasant, days spotty like a muddy windshield and time distorted, and she was glad to be back to work and in a routine.

"What say we get a drink tonight?"

Rella had only interacted with Ginnie in the office thus far.

"That sounds really nice," Rella replied.

Ocean waves gently lapped the sand below, like a cat lazily offering affection to a hand or cheek. The Monday-night scene at the Beachcomber was equally mellow. Barely audible piano music lulled itself to sleep in the background. Outside on the deck, the girls chose a seat next to the fire pit, which dried out some of the moisture from the misty air.

Ginnie preferred her cocktails as Rella did, with no sugar

or chemical concoctions, and they elected to share a pitcher of margaritas. The server poured the mixture of organic tequila, agave, and fresh lime over ice into their glasses, placing the remaining amount on the table.

Ginnie took a sip, wrinkling her nose. "I love extra lime."

"It's rare to see it so stormy here," Rella noted, lifting the thick glass.

"I kind of like it. A chance to wear my scarf," she added, petting the puffy, pink trim around her neck.

Ginnie's ensemble of the day was a pair of jeans, riddled with rips as though she'd gone after them with a pair of scissors in a moment of madness, bright watermelon-colored ankle socks, and a black, short-sleeved sweatshirt with white writing splashed across the front:

architect [ar-ki-tekt] – noun
solves a problem you didn't know you had, in a way you
don't understand
[See also: genius, marvel, exceptional]

Her hair, loosely piled on top of her head, spouted into a cascading waterfall. She could have been taken for a struggling grad student if it weren't for the light gray designer low-top sneakers on her size nine feet.

"Doesn't rain so much here," she continued. "Can't use my Hello Kitty umbrella."

"You have a Hello Kitty umbrella?"

"Yup." She took a hefty gulp.

"I still have my Punky Brewster doll, and most of the Strawberry Shortcake collection."

Ginnie slammed her glass, rattling the table, causing

Rella, and a couple of nearby patrons, to jump. "No way."

Rella giggled. "Yeah. How do you even know about those things anyway? Are you even thirty yet?"

"Just a smidge under. I *love* eighties stuff," Ginnie drawled, collapsing into the pillows on the bench. "I just drink 'em up, like this margarita. Vibrant, highlighter colors. I have Rainbow Brite sheets on my bed."

"You do not."

"Totally do. I never got why those Dimple Dolls were all the rave, though. Such chubby, homely things with straggly yarn for hair. Like this mop," Ginnie indicated, dropping her hand atop her head.

Rella laughed. "About the dolls, I agree. But your hair— it's rambunctious! I love it. Mine's kind of thin. My sister Morgan has nice, thick hair."

"You have one sister?"

"Yes, and one brother, both older. How about you?"

"Only child. I would have liked siblings."

"Except when you're vying for TV time and the only one rooting for *Punky Brewster.*"

"What did Punky say all the time again?" Ginnie pondered, raising her chin thoughtfully into the air.

Rella didn't have to think twice. "Holy macanoli!"

"Right!" Ginnie walloped the table, causing a few more stares. "Every time she said that I had a hankering for pasta."

Rella laughed. "I loved that show. I have all the episodes. Such positive morals and lessons—not like TV nowadays."

"Isn't it the truth? I refuse to have cable."

"Me too. Zippo worth seeing."

"Hello, ladies."

Neither girl had noticed the approach of the Southern Californian beach guy replica: tanned, T-shirt, confident smile, drink in hand.

"I couldn't help but overhear laughing." He settled his left palm on the back of the chair closest to Rella.

"You mean my big mouth!" Ginnie corrected him.

He gave her a polite smile, then turned to Rella. "I don't mean to interrupt girl time, but I wondered if I could have your number."

"Umm, no," Rella replied.

Ginnie made a noise somewhere between a snort and a hiccup.

"So forward of me. Why don't I give you mine?"

She pursed her lips and sat up taller in the chair. "No, thank you."

"Ah, sorry, you must have a boyfriend."

She shook her head. "No, I do not."

"Well, then, there's no harm in taking my number, is there?"

"Not to me, but perhaps to you."

"How's that?"

"You'll be expecting me to call, but I won't."

"You won't."

"No. So, I'll save you the inconvenience." She turned away from him.

"Nicely done," Ginnie praised after he shrunk away.

Rella rubbed her eyes.

"You okay?"

"Yes, fine. Just a little off." She steadied her gaze, her vision soggy.

"You looked on your game to me. You handled that brilliantly."

Rella touched her hand to her forehead, a little dizzy. It had been happening a lot lately. She blinked a few times.

Ginnie cast her eyes down at her drink. "Guys never hit on me."

"What? I don't believe it."

"You're pretty and petite."

"You're very pretty," Rella said, with all honesty.

"I'm pale, with the face of a pixie, and the fashion sense of a cartoon character. I stand out like a beanstalk among the girls here."

"Why would you want to resemble them?" She couldn't believe the self-adhesive bandages passing for dresses. "Besides, he was *grossaroo!*"

Ginnie laughed. "Another one of Punky's sayings, right?"

"That's right. And like Punky—a girl who skipped merrily past all fashion expectations and colored the world with her signature style—stay authentic you. I wouldn't change a brushstroke."

"Those are the nicest words anyone's ever said to me." Ginnie wiped an eye and took a sip of her drink. "It rivals prom night, when my mom declared, 'Finally, a dress that makes you look less like a giraffe and more like a gazelle.' "

"She did not say that."

Ginnie nodded, swallowing. "Oh, she did."

"Well, both creatures are equally lovely," Rella asserted.

"You're sweet. And also an original. Never the same look two days in a row. I'd love to see your closet. Chic ensemble today."

Rella traced a fingertip over the border of her chiffon top, ruffled in front, paired with a black, collared vest, mid-calf cuffed pants, and ballerina shoes with magenta bows.

Ginnie straightened in her chair and smiled. "Wanna come over and watch *Girls Just Wanna Have Fun* this weekend? You can be Janey and I'll be Lynne. I was obsessed with Helen Hunt's hair in the last scene."

"Another girl who wasn't afraid to be herself," Rella emphasized.

Ginnie smiled appreciatively. "I'm so glad we're friends."

Friends. Rella hadn't had one of those in a long time.

Rella headed to Ginnie's on Saturday night. She rang the doorbell of her one-story cottage, nestled in a bed of goldfields, daisies, sunflowers, and sea lavender.

"Come in!" she heard Ginnie call.

Rella stepped inside, carrying a bag of goodies she'd brought for movie night.

A modular sofa sat to the right, with cushions of bright pink, purple, and lime-green accent pillows. A hammock chair hung in the opposite corner, tassels dangling. The wide-planked wood floor was painted a cream color; the white walls displayed colorful cubed photos of sea creatures. Moroccan-style lamps, knickknacks, and a tea set sat atop mismatched end tables with differing geometric prints, and a bulky rattan rocking chair on the opposite wall was buried in socks.

"They're all clean," Ginnie assured, swooping into the room. "I leave the drudgery of pairing for last."

"I could help, if you want," Rella offered.

"That's a fine welcome your first time here—come over and fold my socks!"

Rella laughed. "Such a fun, eclectic room."

"Just placed the last piece a week ago. I give the pieces time to come to me. Aren't you cute in your white jean jacket and headband!"

"An eighties original," Rella said, touching the denim, "from my teen years."

"Looks brand-new. You take marvelous care of your belongings."

"You look fabulous yourself! Positively like Lynne in the movie."

Ginnie sported an off-the-shoulder mustard-yellow-and-brown-striped top with metallic spandex pants.

"Told ya I love the eighties. Come on into the kitchen."

"Wherever did you get those hair clips?" Rella asked as she followed her into the next room.

Ginnie touched the light blue dinosaur barrettes on each side of her head, which closely resembled those worn by Lynne in the film.

"Stick with me, kid, for all the outlandish accessories."

"I've accumulated quite a hat collection myself," Rella said, putting her bag down on the counter. "Needed them, for the long winters."

"Oh, so you're from a cold climate too. Whereabouts?"

Rella regretted bringing it up. "Colorado," she muttered.

"Cool. I always thought it must be such a pretty state. Do you miss where you grew up?"

"Not at all. Mind if I put these in the fridge?" Rella asked, holding up the salad ingredients she'd brought.

"My house is your house. Your mom must miss you. Mothers always do. Even mine."

Rella paused in front of the refrigerator door, glad to be facing away. She swallowed.

"Yeah, mothers always do."

Rella remembered clearly the day she'd told her mother she'd been accepted to the university and was moving to California. She saw the momentary pang in her expression, at losing her youngest, but her mother quickly swapped it for one of elation. She had placed her hands on Rella's shoulders. "I am so proud of you. I always have been. Your every endeavor results in success—and you'll blossom like a desert flower under all that wonderful sun."

"So," Ginnie said, bringing her hands together in a loud clap, "what do we have here?"

Rella ordered her light tears to stop. Turning, she saw Ginnie checking out the wine she had brought. "White for the salad, and red for the popcorn."

"I like the way you think," Ginnie said with a tap of the temple. "I just need to start with a little coffee first. Had a headache earlier. It's gone now, but I'm still not quite myself."

"Headaches are like that."

They played the movie in Ginnie's large bedroom, dancing with the music between handfuls of popcorn. As the credits rolled, they agreed that one eighties film wasn't enough.

"*The Goonies, Pretty in Pink, Footloose,*" Rella read, flipping through DVDs, "and *Annie.* Leaping lizards!"

"Leaping lizards!" Ginnie repeated, Miss Hannigan style.

"*Back to the Future.* I've always been fascinated with time travel, going back to the past."

"Me too," said Ginnie. "Except I'd pick the future. I wonder what I'd see there. I wouldn't mind being married one day, if I found the right person. But I'm in no rush, just cruising."

"When it comes to career, I'm in the high-speed lane," Rella said, pointing her finger ahead. "But relationships? My car isn't even on the road."

"Ha!" Ginnie laughed. "*Rev*-olutionary. What do you usually do in your *spare* time?"

Rella giggled. "I like puzzles."

"I'm no good at them—and I always lose at least one piece!"

"That is the worst!"

"I like to color," Ginnie admitted.

Rella crossed her legs, facing her. "I love to color. Still have the coloring books I had as a kid. I always used the big box of crayons. Periwinkle was my favorite."

"Mine was Burnt Orange. I used to wonder why one would burn an orange. Most of my crayons ended up broken. I'd imagine all yours were intact."

Rella grinned.

They ended up choosing *Footloose* as their next film so they could dance. By the time it ended, it was close to one a.m.

"Did you bring your pj's to sleep over?"

Rella had brought them, as Ginnie had suggested, but she wasn't sure about staying. Strange thoughts of feet sticking out from around corners and fingertips curling around doors had enslaved her nightly since she'd returned from Atlanta. She kept her bedroom lamp on all night, unable to close her eyes without a fully lit room.

Being with Ginnie had so far banished these troubling thoughts; maybe spending the night would mean peaceful sleep for the first time in a long while.

She helped Ginnie clean up, then went to change in the bathroom. She peeked in before entering. White tiles. She went in, shut the door, and walked to the vanity. In the mirror, she saw it. A shower curtain. Clasping the end of the counter, she turned to face it. It had butterflies of different colors on a white background. Rella mobilized her courage and pulled back a corner. The tub was clear. She changed and exited.

"I have a guest room," Ginnie said, leading Rella down the hall. "It's small, but quiet." She switched on the light.

White walls were trimmed in bright cobalt. Short curtains made of gray burlap framed the one window, with red, white, and matching cobalt-colored flowers painted on. An armchair and ottoman were situated in one corner, a petite writing desk in the other. The bed took over the center of the room.

"Waterbed," Ginnie said, placing fresh, folded towels on the ottoman. "Didn't think they existed anymore, right? Me either. It was a gift. I'm not partial to them myself. I hope it will be okay for you?"

Rella hadn't seen a waterbed in years.

"Fine," she replied hollowly.

"We can go to breakfast together in the morning. Maybe champagne brunch!"

"Sure."

"Nighty-night!" Ginnie said, closing the door behind her.

Alone, in a strange room, with a waterbed.

Rella wasn't so sure this had been a sound idea.

She left the overhead light on and turned on the lamp next to the armchair. The curtains flanking the windows were only decorative, not made to be closed. There was no mirror in the room, at least.

She went over to the bed. Set on a platform, framed by white beadboard and covered by a puffy duvet with matching pillows, it didn't look like a waterbed. She put one hand lightly on the surface. It rippled. She leapt back.

She transferred her overnight bag to the floor and sat on the armchair. Eyeing the bed suspiciously, she filed through her memory. She'd disliked the unsteadiness and movement of her mother's waterbed as a child, and the feel of cold vinyl through the sheets. She tried to remember what time period her mother had had the bed but couldn't.

An image flashed in her mind, of a room darkened with reddish curtains. A waterbed. Movement.

Rella jumped up and walked around the room, staying far from the bed. She couldn't let her mind go to any disturbing images.

After a long night in the chair, she warily approached the bed, messing up the sheets and pillows to make it appear slept in.

Fourteen

A week after her sleepover at Ginnie's, Rella drove to the beach.

Pain suddenly struck over her left eye. Her fingertips lightly touched the slight indent above the eyebrow. Her migraines had increased, pounding from inside her head.

She sat in the sand. The typically placid water churned tumultuously, agitated from unseen undercurrents and riptides. Waves ran to shore and crashed against clusters of rocks, foamy water seeping between fissures, treacherous to anyone reckless enough to approach.

Whitecaps rose into sharp triangles, pointed fins, like circling sharks barring entry. Her brain had protected her. There was a reason she didn't remember. A reason for the sharks.

She stood, hoisting her legs through the sand. She'd lost all desire for food and drink but welcomed fresh air. Rounding the bend, she came to a crowded area of the beach, with colorful umbrellas providing patches of shade, smoke rising from cookout grills, and sprinkles of chatter and laughter.

Without provocation, Rella bolted. Like a spooked horse, she took off down the strand, putting distance between herself and an unseen threat, the sensation of being hunted quelling all reason.

Winded, she slowed momentarily. *Run*, a feeling inside urged. Her legs propelled her forward. Finally, unsteadiness incapacitated her, and she veered off the track toward the water as her joints gave way in the sand.

Her head spun as though she were strapped to the needle of an internal clock, simultaneously turning clockwise, counterclockwise, around past and present, a centrifugal force compromising her circuitry. The illusion of control she thought she'd had, gone.

She rubbed her forehead, sat up, and drew her knees to her chest.

"I'm okay. I'm okay," she whispered, her arms wrapped around her legs, as the world decelerated.

Drops of rain fell on the windshield as Rella pulled up to the house a few hours later. She exited the car, cold moisture lightly pelleting her skin. She gazed at the secluded yard. The driveway stretched like a slick, barren desert. The wind whispered. Leaves rustled a warning. She pictured stones hurling themselves at her. Nothing could be trusted. Everything had turned unsafe.

She would never have the same life back.

She pulled into the garage. The door descended.

Rella stood at the bathroom counter, washing her face, careful to keep one eye open. An image encroached, someone coming from behind with eyes of fiery rage, ready to bludgeon her.

She spun around. Empty space.

The sense of being watched. Torturous. Outside every window. In each crack of a doorway.

Midnight. Three a.m. The looming peril of falling asleep laid low in the corners, a leopard waiting to spring. Her mind growled like a rabid animal, frothing at the lips.

She left the lights on and worked at her desk. Vigilant. Four a.m. She fluttered her eyes, widened them, in an attempt to keep them open. Six a.m. How long would darkness last?

She succumbed to drowsiness as the sun began to lighten the sky.

Someone climbing on the bed. Sinister faces over hers. Then, in water, held down, by an unseen force. Her hands flailed to strike at the source of the pressure on her matted hair. She gulped the air before being pushed under again, her chest burning.

Next, on the top floor of a glass-domed building. A tsunami rose, the impact imminent. She wondered what would kill her first—the shards of glass or the crushing weight of the water.

She awoke, panicked that she'd fallen asleep.

Rella sat up and reached for the glass she'd left on her nightstand, taking a small sip. Since the TDT sessions, she'd had to be careful about how much water she drank or it would pool in her body, sloshing in her stomach. At times, she felt compelled to spit it out.

She sat, rocking, her mind hijacked, her body not her own. She wanted to scream at the thoughts battering around in her head but knew it wouldn't stop them.

She should have trusted her instincts and left that office.

The images played relentlessly in her mind like a film that had broken loose from its reel. No rewind. No pause. No stop.

———

She e-mailed Seth Jabez.

Please, please tell me you can reverse what you did to me. I have been destroyed.

She received a two-sentence reply: *We have to keep going with it. Call or e-mail for an appointment.*

She cried out in frustration.

Rella opened the fridge, nervous about eating, but nauseous because she hadn't touched much in days. The smallest amounts made her bloat, as if her body had unlearned how to digest, the bites she swallowed now routinely coming right back up.

She talked herself through each nibble. *You need nourishment. It's not bad for you.*

She just wanted to feel clean. Unused. Unaffected. An empty fridge couldn't harbor tainted food. A blank mind couldn't contain rancid memories. And dreamless sleep couldn't frighten the night.

She'd try a salad.

She put her cutting board on the counter and washed the lettuce. Dried it. Removed a knife from the drawer. Rella only kept small knives around. Big ones scared her.

As she chopped, bothersome thoughts infiltrated.

She'd cleaned the leaves individually, but were they *really* clean? Did the lettuce smell funny? She examined it. Bright green and crisp.

An image of tapeworms wriggled into her mind. She gagged, a sensation down her throat. She scraped the lettuce into a bowl, uncertain if she would be able to eat it.

Tears collected. Thoughts of pain and suffering occurring around the world at that moment. Anger replaced the sadness.

She squeezed the handle. Raised the knife and drove it into the board. Over and over. She then lifted the board above the counter, smashing it repeatedly against the edge. The wood finally gave way and splintered.

The savagery of her actions snapped her back to reality. She looked down at the poor cutting board, one of the first household purchases she'd made for her little apartment after moving to California.

"I'm sorry." A torrent of sadness poured through her. Tears landed on the wood.

She hurriedly rummaged in the drawers for Krazy Glue, but it was too late. No matter how carefully she handled the board, it was damaged beyond repair.

The small hours of the night serene, silent, she went downstairs. She removed the car keys from the kitchen drawer and went out to the garage. Got into the car. Shut the door.

She glided both hands over the smooth steering wheel.

Started the car.

She'd self-harmed in the past, the first time her mother had gone into the hospital. She never knew what had possessed her to think of it—to actually do it—cutting the underside of her upper forearms with a razor blade. The effect was satisfying, tranquilizing, standing in the shower inflicting stinging slits in her skin, red blood turning pink as it mixed with falling water and flowed down the drain.

She'd been scared to go near her wrists back then, craving the peace of death but fearing its finality. She found it funny that it took bravery to end torment.

With resolution, she calmly removed her hands from the wheel and sat back. She debated listening to music. Soon, there would be no sound. No need for food or drink or sleep or dreams.

Her peripheral vision caught sight of a ladybug, its tiny black appendages beautifully scaling the window. Crimeless. She loved all bugs, all creatures. Thoughts of their suffering pained her profoundly. While out walking, she made a deliberate effort to stay alert so as not to step on any fellow insect pedestrians, and she carefully rescued those she saw in the middle of any path. She was particularly attentive after rain, for snails.

She couldn't hurt the ladybug.

She turned off the car. Pushed the remote to raise the garage door, keeping the ladybug under observation. It seemed unharmed.

She waited thirty minutes. It meandered around before finally flying out and away. Seeing the ladybug had caused a change in her, shutting off the plan. Mentally exhausted, she sat for some time before exiting the car and returning inside.

The rest of Rella's night passed in disjointed pieces. She

locked the garage door. Upstairs, pajamas on, she got into bed. That night, for some reason, bad thoughts were wiped away and she remained in a state of disconnect. She closed her eyes. She slept. She dreamt.

Down a chute she fell, topsy-turvy, head-first, images cascading, lunging at her along the way. No sense of bottom, no way back to the top. Like Alice, she'd tumbled into a vortex to another world, and had no idea how to get out.

Fifteen

Colorado—January 2017

Morgan wiped the counter down. The smell of bacon and eggs saturated the air. She shook her head. She needed to eat better.

She went for a drive. Lost in thought, she looked up, realizing where she'd unintentionally ended up. It had been years since she'd been on this avenue.

A main thoroughfare since its founding in the early 1950s, the remains of its former commercial glory sat neglected and forgotten. Lots once occupied by thriving businesses were now ravaged by weeds. Discolored RETAIL SPACE FOR LEASE OR SALE posters hung in empty windows. Several had NO TRESPASSING signs. Most didn't need one.

A sullied white cloud-shaped sign caught her eye, the original exterior still intact, from the time when it had been called Dreamy Donuts, according to her mother. The "y" had been dropped at some point after the term became outdated.

Nearly every winter morning, Morgan had marched confidently into Dream Donuts, a big girl at six years old, with real money in hand. She'd turn around to wave energetically through the window to her mother, not minding the fact that she'd have to wait in the morning-rush line. No place on earth smelled as scrumptious as Dream Donuts.

Nearly four decades later, the familiar fragrances of doughy crullers and artificially flavored French vanilla coffee grounds still sweetened the air. Morgan inhaled deliberately.

"Can I get a chocolate frosted?" the little girl in front of her asked her mother.

Morgan smiled. Those had been her favorite too. They had been allowed three sweets a week growing up, and Morgan always chose a donut for at least one of them.

She approached the counter. "Small coffee, please, two creams on the side, no sugar." Exactly the way her mother had ordered it.

"Anything else?"

"A chocolate frosted, please." She hesitated. "Make it two." She paid for the items and found a seat.

Morgan lifted the Styrofoam cup between her hands, remembering how much larger and more awkward the container had seemed when she was young. She removed the plastic lid, placing it next to the creamers and donuts. Tomorrow I'll start my diet, she thought.

An elderly woman sat alone, on the opposite wall.

This reminded her of a time when Rella was around seven, and she, her mother, Trevor, and Rella had gone out for pizza.

"Rella, you're not eating your pizza," Leah noticed.

Rella kept her head down.

"I'll take it!" Trevor reached over to nab her slice.

"Trevor, sit down, please. Rella? Are you crying? What's wrong?" Leah asked gently, leaning forward.

"That old man is eating *alone*," Rella whispered in her ear.

"Oh," Leah said. "Well, there's a solution for that."

"There is?" Rella asked, wiping tears between irregular breaths.

"Of course. We'll see if he wants to join us."

Rella's face lit up.

"Would you like to go with me to ask him?" Leah stood, holding out her hand.

Rella nodded eagerly.

Morgan left Dream Donuts, warmed by her conversation with Elaine, the elderly woman she had joined for a second round.

The sky had become overcast. She continued down the avenue of faded familiarity. The ice-cream and sandwich shop they had been allowed to walk to as kids. The drugstore she and her friends had frequented in search of new makeup and hair accessories.

Morgan drove past one of the many hospitals her mother had been admitted to over the years. Her mother had confided in the doctors after her first breakdown, what had happened to her as a child, and they had silenced her rather than treated her, shocking her brain and then numbing it with pills.

She would pass the street soon. Morgan abruptly took the left turn. The house was the second one on the right.

It was beige now, instead of white. Morgan looked up to the dormer on the left, her mother's former room, and pictured a young Leah on the window seat, staring out from behind the glass, long, straight strands of dark hair framing her face.

How many times had she cried within those walls, screamed, dreamed, hoped? Plotted.

That's what Morgan would have done. Plotted and schemed and retaliated. She took after her father. She was loud. Boisterous. Outspoken. Leah was not. And Rella took after their mother.

Her primal urge was to drive her car right through the house. But different people lived there now, ones that had put up flower boxes. Would they stay if they knew what had gone on inside? That kind of information was never part of the real estate listing.

Its windows stared silently, as if horrified by its past, entreating absolution.

Sixteen

Eastport, Colorado—1964

"I can't believe you missed *Dobie Gillis* this week," Leah's best friend Janet said.

"He's dumb. Thinks girls are pats of butter."

Janet expelled a short laugh. "Whatever are you talking about?"

"Wants a 'gorgeous, soft, round, creamy girl.' Said so last episode."

Janet waved her mascara wand dismissively.

Leah picked up one of Janet's magazines, skimming the headlines.

Successful Marriages Start in the Kitchen!

The Harder a Wife Works, the Cuter She Looks!

"How can you read this junk?" Leah said. "As if a woman's happiness comes from a new washer and dryer." She tossed the magazine aside with contempt. "It's blighting your mind!"

"*Blighting* my mind? Such a big word."

"Girls are more than just wives and cooks and cleaners!" She wanted it to be fact. Why did evidence always point to the contrary?

Janet heavily applied the inky liquid to her eyelashes.

"You're going to use up the entire tube," Leah told her.

"Sometimes, you just have to make the world pretty."

"You're pretty without it."

"That's your opinion."

"Why don't you stay home rather than go on a date? I could sleep over."

"Wouldn't be right to cancel last minute."

Leah watched Janet. "Why do girls work so hard to be pretty for guys anyway? I wish I were fat and ugly and had pimples all over my face!"

"Oh, you do not." Janet brushed her hair in long, slow swoops, her arm machinelike in its rotations.

Leah didn't exactly wish that. She liked her thin body, and received many compliments on her long, velvety, straight hair. She knew she stood out because of the exotic shape of her almond eyes. She only wished she was undesirable to boys.

Janet put the brush down and rose, smoothing her dress. "Time for me to go," she said, fastening her sweater around her shoulders. "Now, don't pout. We'll see each other tomorrow."

Leah headed to a nearby park. It was deserted most of the time now, ever since a new playground was built a year ago, closer to the school.

Leah preferred the solitude. It was also where she had chosen her new secret hiding spot. She'd invested in a small waterproof box she could hide in the ground, bought outside of town where no one knew her or her family. Ten paces from a tree on a crest of a small hill, in the direction of thick bushes edging the playground, her treasure lay buried.

She sat with her back to the tree, as she always did before digging, keeping an eye out for anyone around. Confident she was alone, she went to fetch a small spade she'd hidden on the opposite side of the park.

She smiled as she removed the box from the ground, wiped off the loose dirt, and opened it. The smell of money and autonomy rose to her nose like a hello. She removed three stacks, comprised of ones, fives, tens. A bag of coins. Lastly, she extracted a single twenty. A whole twenty. She eagerly anticipated the day she'd add a fifty to her trove.

She knew the exact total already but counted anyway. Each snap of a crisp bill represented the hours spent in the stuffy file room, alphabetizing cases won and lost, subjected to Paul Anka's "Puppy Love" at least five times a day, playing from the local radio station. It was worth all the caked lipstick kisses from female family members reeking of department store perfume and glass cleaner as they slipped her the bills in generic greeting cards, each dollar enabling a decision in the future life she was building toward, rather than paying for.

The money was her friend.

After finishing, she held on to ninety-five cents. A sundae at Mitchell's Ice Cream Shop cost forty cents, a soda for ten cents, and, if she was feeling indulgent, a piece of pie for thirty-five cents, with ten cents left over. She always tipped the waitress.

She patted the box before returning it to its hiding place and covering it back up with dirt, kicking leaves over the top.

Not quite yet ready for her sweet treats, Leah trekked down the hill to the playground as the sky dimmed, heading for the swings. The seat was askew. Leah took the chains, one in each hand, stuck the tips of her shoes in the sand, and pushed back.

Squeak. Squeak.

She moved her legs back and forth, relieved to be in pants. Girls weren't allowed to wear pants in school. Only skirts or dresses. Boys tore through the schoolyard at recess. Girls couldn't run and play freely with dresses on.

She kicked her toes further into the earth and wondered why there were so many stupid and impractical rules. During the cold winters, on the thirty-five-minute walk to and from school, the cold air reached up her skirt like icy fingers, forcing her to take short, fast steps on rigid legs.

The seat a little too low for her, her white ankle socks accumulated dust as she swung. Her mother would chide her for it. She didn't care. Her brother never got reprimanded for getting his clothes dirty or torn.

Leah had once convinced herself that her mother didn't know, couldn't know.

But she did.

Leah went somewhere in her mind each time it happened. Her body wasn't hers. It stole her soul. Reduced her to one-dimensional and voiceless, like those girls in the magazine ads.

Leah gripped the steel links and leaned back in the swing, relishing the strength in her legs, enlisting the muscles in her arms. She was as good as any boy, no matter what the TV and magazines said.

Leah walked into the bathroom at the ice-cream shop to wash her hands, picking up the white bar on the side of the sink.

110

Sometimes there wasn't enough soap in the world.

She ordered a basic sundae, with three scoops of vanilla, chocolate sauce, whipped cream, and a cherry, even though the waitress proposed she try the new flavor, with chunks of bright red and green pineapple. Leah declined. Who'd ever heard of a red or green pineapple?

Leah dangled her feet from the seat of the booth, savoring every mouthful.

"You ate that right up," the waitress commented, clearing the dish. "Check?"

The clock on the wall read quarter to eight. "I'll sit for a while, thank you."

For lack of a more wholesome pastime, Leah picked up a newspaper that had been left on the table. An ad entitled *Your Future* spread across two pages, listing five careers: men depicted in the roles of physician, chemist, and geologist, women as nurses, and "machine operators"—a fancy label for typists.

About to push it away, the words *Love your future!* caught her eye, an illustrated smiling young girl's face drawing her further in.

She continued reading.

Choose any one of these exciting careers:

Fashion Coordinator

Interior Designer

Medical or Legal Secretary

Airline Hostess

Court Reporter

Call Broad Ridge Junior College of Business for Women today!

Leah wasn't much into clothing or interior design, but airline hostess sounded neat. She closed her eyes and pictured herself flying to exciting new places.

She looked at the related ad on an adjoining page:

Airline Hostess ~ Welcome Wing Airlines

You can fly with the finest airline in the world, with routes in both the United States and overseas.

In order to be eligible, you must meet the following qualifications:

- *High school graduate*
- *Age 21–27*
- *Height, 5 feet 2 inches to 5 feet 8 inches*
- *Weight, 100–135 pounds*
- *Attractive*
- *Unmarried*
- *Eyesight 20-50 or better*

Apply to: Welcome Wing Airlines Employment Office
110 State Street, Chicago, Illinois

"I saw you eyein' that pie over there, honey. Fancy a slice?" the waitress asked, patting her apron.

She was moderately overweight. Leah wondered if she had ever dreamed of being an airline hostess.

"Well, maybe I shouldn't have any more sweets."

"How 'bout some fries, then? I cut 'em up myself this mornin'."

"Sure," Leah agreed absently.

Trim, attractive, and unmarried. That's what the airlines wanted. But Leah aspired to have both a family and a career.

Why did she have to settle for one or the other? Who made those rules? She was a hard and smart worker. She'd also make a good mother. No, a better mother. Much better. If she had a boy, she'd teach him to be different. If she had a girl, she'd teach her to be strong, and instill confidence in her, that she could be whatever she wished to be.

"Here's your fries, honey. Ketchup?"

"Yes, please."

The woman nodded and went to get it. Leah turned the page, where a bright ad splashed across the entire right side. A woman held a bottle of ketchup, eyes wide in surprise, her lips, as red as the ketchup, rounded into a circle, her perfectly manicured red nails poised over the bottle. Underneath the picture it read: *You mean a woman can open it?* The response? *Easily—without a knife blade, a bottle opener, or even a husband!*

"Here you go, honey!" The waitress placed the bottle on the table and padded away.

Leah spun open the top quite easily on her own and dumped its contents all over the page.

Seventeen

"Why can't we stay at your house tonight?" Leah asked Janet as they walked down the street.

"Mom and Dad are on a date night," Janet said, rolling her eyes.

"Oh. Well, what time will you be over?"

"I'll just pack an overnight bag, so, like an hour or so? Angela mentioned coming too."

It was Leah's turn to roll her eyes.

"That okay?"

"I guess."

Janet arrived. The two sat on the floor of Leah's bedroom, playing Spill and Spell.

Angela burst in.

"Hello, gals!"

"Ange! What are you wearing? That skirt is so short!" Janet exclaimed.

"Don't be such a prude," Angela said, popping her gum. "I see I got here just in time," she added, eyeing the game. "Time for the fun to begin!" She whipped out a bottle of vodka.

"That stuff tastes terrible," Janet said.

"Not with soda. Got any grape-flavored, Leah?"

"You can check the fridge downstairs," Leah replied unenthusiastically.

Angela left the bottle and hopped away.

Leah shook her head. "She's a soap opera waiting to happen."

"She'll probably have kidney failure by the time she's forty."

"She doesn't need to be this way, thinking she's cool dressing like that, bringing alcohol around. They're just props for the person she thinks she ought to be, to get boys."

"The wrong kind of boys, that's for sure." Janet shook the cup and spilled the cubed letters onto the floor. "Let's see what we got here."

Leah's door flung open again, but this time Cal stood there.

Leah jumped, her face tight.

"Leah, hey, sorry, didn't know you had company. Hey, Janet."

"Hey, Cal." Janet looked back and forth between Cal and Leah.

"You sleeping over?"

"Yes, she is," Leah said. "Angela too."

Cal nodded. "Have fun." The door shut.

Leah picked up the cup and took her turn.

"Everything all right between you two?" Janet asked.

"Fine." Leah kept her eyes on the letters, rearranging them.

Angela entered with two cans of soda under her arm. "You only had one grape, so I got root beer too." She put them down on the table. "Ugh. I forgot glasses. Be right back."

"I don't want any," Leah said.

"Me either," Janet seconded.

"Two sticks in the mud. All the more for me, then." She spun on her heels and exited.

"Leah, you're shaking," Janet told her.

"There's my word." Leah counted up the score.

"Maybe you should have that drink," Janet said. "Have you ever had a drink?"

"I tried my mother's wine once. She doesn't drink so much. My dad does enough for both of them."

"And what about Cal?"

"Sometimes, I guess. I don't think he likes it, because he's seen what it does to my father."

Janet didn't like Leah's father. She glanced down at Leah's word. *Brutal.*

"One glass, just for me," Angela said, returning. She poured the soda first, followed by the vodka. "I saw Cal in the kitchen. Think he'd squeal if I offered him some too?"

"Let's just hang out, the three of us," Janet said.

A week later, sitting in the living room working on school assignments, Leah jolted when Cal walked in. She'd thought he'd be out all night.

He shoved his left hand into his jacket pocket, throwing his keys to the floor.

Leah's first inclination was to ask him what was wrong, but knew it was best to remain unnoticed. He passed by her on his way to the kitchen. She packed up her books, went up to her room, and quietly shut the door.

Thirty minutes later, he entered her room.

"Cal, I don't want to," Leah said.

"Leah, please, come out."

"I have to finish this. There's a math test Friday."

"It won't take long."

He turned up the volume on the record player. Tears coursed down her cheeks.

Cal noticed. He stopped.

"Leah, don't do that." He moved off of her. "Why do you have to cry?"

Leah pulled her dress down, mad that she hadn't changed after school.

"Leah, stop, okay?"

Leah sat up. "No, *you* stop. You stop, Cal. I hate this. And I hate you."

"You don't hate me, Leah. You can't hate me."

And she didn't. It's what tore her apart even more. She hated her father. But she didn't hate her brother.

"I don't want you to do this anymore," she said.

"Leah, I have to."

"No, you don't."

"I need to."

"You're a pathetic brute then, just like Dad."

Cal's face looked stricken. He pulled up his pants and left the room.

Leah lifted his favorite record off the player and slammed it down, splitting it in two.

Eighteen

Laguna Beach—February 2017

Rella sat working at the dining table as the persistent Santa Ana winds howled outside. When embarking on a new design, she meticulously calculated the numbers, knowing that even a sixteenth-of-an-inch mistake could compromise the entire structural integrity.

Hours later, the turbulent gusts spun shades of night. Rella stood to illuminate the room. Returning to the table, shadows hinted at a presence, reaching out.

She slowly raised her eyes from the carefully measured framework she had constructed with her pencil and ruler. Someone was there.

A tall creature, hunched over, head down, stood at the entrance of the room, the skeletal, angular body cadaverous. The wraithlike figure reminded Rella of when she'd been in the grips of anorexia, dying inside, her body swallowing itself.

Rella sat transfixed as the female form raised her head slowly, turning her face toward Rella. Her mouth opened, expanded, wider, soundless, as if screaming through water.

Then, as unexpectedly as she had come, she was gone.

Rella found herself at her laptop, tapping on the keyboard. *TDT practitioner near me.* She paused. What was she doing? Why would she ever subject herself to that again?

She placed her hands in her lap. Whatever Seth Jabez did had severely damaged her. And while the garage incident had withdrawn to the back of her mind, like a distant train car rumbling onward to another destination, she couldn't ignore the fact that it had happened. Something was very much wrong. If TDT had caused it, maybe it could reverse it.

Rella dreaded the thought of enduring more torment, but it might be the only way. This time, she would only go to a female.

Her eyes landed on a name. *CJ Laurino-Deter, LCSW.* In her photo, the smiling woman looked about ten years older than Rella. Rella looked up "LCSW" and learned it stood for "licensed clinical social worker." Rella didn't recall any initials after Seth Jabez's name. She continued reading the listing, which included *trauma* and *PTSD* under the "Specialties" heading, along with *TDT consultant.*

Although she got the best feeling from this listing compared to any others, she still worried. She shut her laptop.

The next day, a phone call was placed to CJ Laurino-Deter and an appointment made for the following week.

The social worker's office was located in Huntington Beach, several blocks from the water, in an older medical building.

Rella climbed the stairs to the second floor, taking a seat in the waiting area. Minutes later, a trim woman in her late forties came into the room. She had shoulder-length, black, wiry hair, and wore a fitted button-down shirt, short black skirt, and three-inch strappy heels.

"Hello, I'm CJ Laurino-Deter," she said, smiling. "You can call me CJ. I have some preliminary paperwork for you. Take whatever time you need. The door is around the corner." She handed Rella a clipboard.

"Thank you." Rella completed the forms in five minutes. She stood and walked to the doorway, giving an almost inaudible tap.

"Come in."

The office was pleasant and spacious, with hardwood floors, light-colored walls, and plenty of natural light from three large windows. There was a fireplace with several knickknacks on the mantel.

"Please, have a seat." CJ gestured to two oversized armchairs in front of the windows.

Rella chose one. It was wide and soft. There was a table with a box of tissues between the two chairs. Rella put her small purse on top.

"It's nice to meet you, Rella. I'm sorry for what you have been through. You mentioned seeing someone recently, a TDT practitioner?"

"I don't know *what* he was, exactly, but he used that method on me, yes."

"On the phone, you mentioned you've been suffering ever since, with symptoms you've never had before."

"I'm a mess. A complete mess. People often use the word 'great' to describe their life, even though they may not mean it at all, but my life really was. All of that's been taken away from me." Rella reached for a tissue. "I've had symptoms my whole life, but these are intolerable."

"What symptoms did you have prior to seeing—what was his name?"

"Seth Jabez," Rella answered, never wanting to say or hear the name again. "Migraines since the age of seven, body aches starting at age thirteen, that have worsened, sore throats, horrible menstrual cramps."

"Seven is young to get migraines."

"I guess."

"Where are the migraines located?"

Rella touched her forehead above each eye. "Here."

"How often do you have them?"

"Every day. To different degrees."

"Every day since you were seven."

"Yes. I remember being taken out of school often because of them."

"Hmm. And what about since your sessions with Mr. Jabez?"

"I'm having a hard time focusing my eyes, like I'm looking out from behind a layer that's between me and the outside world. It's very odd. Maybe from fatigue? I can't sleep—not for more than a couple of hours at a time, and that's only if I keep the lights on. My eyes burn because I'm so tired, but I can't close them for fear of flashing images in my head."

"What do you see?"

"I'm not sure. They pass by so fast."

"Memories?"

"They don't feel like memories. Although, usually if I don't have a tangible object associated with a bad memory, it vanishes." Rella smiled. "I like it that way."

"How is your memory in general?"

"It's . . . it's cut, until it's pasted."

"That's an interesting way to put it."

"Sometimes something will bring the memory back. Some memories have no beginning or end, only a middle, as if I'm dropped into the moment. And many times, I still don't remember, despite a description of the event."

"These symptoms are what prompted you to see Mr. Jabez in the first place?"

Rella twisted the tissue. Pieces of white crumbled in her lap.

"My mother recently tried to commit suicide, possibly. She hasn't been well for a long time and can get very confused. My older sister, Morgan, told me horrible things, about how our mom grew up." Rella reached for another tissue. "Abuse. From her father and brother."

"Sexual?"

Rella nodded. "Morgan thought maybe something had happened to me."

"Why would she think that?" CJ asked gently.

"All my health issues. She said it just didn't seem normal."

"And did you find anything out?"

Rella cried. Nodded. She blew her nose. "Seth somehow got me to see who did it." She told CJ about the photo album. "I never would have believed it could be true. How could something so *horrifying* have been blocked out so completely?"

"Sometimes it's necessary to erase certain experiences," CJ explained. "Otherwise, we would die, in a sense. It's a protection. Some events are so traumatizing, the brain simply can't understand them or place them, even more so at a young, formative age, so, it buries them. You may forget, but the body doesn't. No memory is ever absolutely gone. And it can manifest as a pain, behavior, or aversion."

Rella's eyes filled with tears.

"I'm so sorry for what happened to you, Rella."

"My life feels like a lie. I don't know what to believe. I never wished to unearth any of this. It was pointless. The brain forgets for a reason. I feel ruined."

"There is definitely a right and a wrong way to approach healing. The brain validly puts up protections. They need to be respected and handled carefully. What are some other repercussions you've incurred since going to Mr. Jabez?"

"Food I used to tolerate repulses me now. But then I feel sick from not eating. So, I try an apple, steamed vegetables, and my stomach expands like I'm three months—you know."

"Pregnant?"

Rella looked disgusted. "Yes."

"Is that a difficult word for you?"

"Yes. I cringe when I see a—pregnant—woman."

"Does it make you feel a certain way?"

"Trapped. Angry."

"And this is new too?"

"No. But my own stomach has never expanded before. If I eat, this drowning murkiness collects inside. I'm vomiting nearly every day."

"Sometimes, vomiting is the brain rejecting what it can't accept," CJ said.

"Huh. I never thought of that."

"The part of the brain highly affected with trauma, the hippocampus, has direct links to the digestive system. We could try an approach today, to address the stomach."

"I'm not ready for TDT."

"Oh, no, I agree. I'd like to get to know you better, and only use what is appropriate. Perhaps TDT isn't for you at all. This is a visualization, a preliminary scan, looking internally into the body. You just describe to me what you see. You can even keep your eyes open. Oftentimes, our body can tell us things, but our busy lives prevent us from seeing or hearing what is being expressed."

"Okay."

"You're going to journey in a capsule. This capsule is clean and safe, it has a big viewport, and you can exit it whenever you want. Sound okay, Rella?"

The word "capsule" made Rella think of a pill she had to swallow. "I'd rather take a glass elevator."

"Perfect. A glass elevator."

Rella rested her gaze on the floor.

"I want you to go down the throat, traveling to the stomach."

Rella descended her esophagus.

"Can you describe to me what you see?"

"It's red, raw, shredded."

"You mentioned having sore throats, right?"

"Yes, from a young age. At times I can barely swallow.

124

They've been better since moving to California."

"Ask the throat what it needs to feel better."

Internally, Rella asked. She didn't get an answer.

"Water, perhaps?"

Rella shook her head. "The stomach doesn't like water."

"A salve?"

"No." Rella looked up, figuratively. "I see a trapdoor. Over the throat."

"Can you get through it easily?"

"No. It's heavy, made of metal."

"Can you continue down?"

"Yes." Rella did. "I'm at the stomach. The outside is pink and healthy." Rella orbited around the organ. "Oh! The bottom part—it's slashed."

"Can you go inside?"

Rella discovered that she could. The little elevator was quite handy.

"It's full of a tarry substance."

"Can you help? Clean it, perhaps?"

"It's thick, sticky. I don't want to do further damage."

"Maybe you can think about why the tar is there, and the trapdoor."

"Mm." Rella made noises of discomfort.

"Rella, let's travel upwards now, away from the stomach, out of the throat."

Rella ascended from the viscera.

"Can you feel yourself back in the room?"

Rella pulled her legs up into the chair.

"Rella, let's do some grounding. Do you see the mantel?"

Rella slowly raised her eyes.

"Could you pick out an object that's on the mantel and describe it to me?"

"I see a vase. It's small, round."

"Can you describe what is happening for you?"

"A plummeting feeling. Watching. Then, an evil face pops out."

"An evil face?"

"A mask, actually. It forms a slow, depraved smile."

"This has been happening since you saw Seth Jabez?"

Rella nodded. "At first, it only dropped in front of me when he did the TDT. It just hung there, suspended. Now I worry I'll see it in windows, after nightfall. I'm afraid to look in the mirror, mainly at night. And lately, I see faces changing into the evil face."

"Whose faces? Strangers, or people you know?"

"It could be anyone. Their face is normal at first, then their expression morphs into a malevolent grin." Rella paused. "Ever notice how malevolent is one vowel away from being 'male-violent'?" Rella pressed her hands on her legs. "It's taunting me. Out to get me."

"Does it want to hinder you from eating?"

"No. It's more than that."

"Have you ever had difficulty with eating before?"

"A long time ago. I shunned food almost entirely."

"Anorexia?"

"Yes."

"How old were you?"

"Seventeen or eighteen. It's strange. I remember sitting

down one day and seeing my thighs, but I didn't recognize my own legs. They looked bigger to me. I hadn't gained any weight. I've always been thin."

"How long did it go on for?"

"Five years, I think."

"And what made it stop?"

Rella shrugged. "One day, it just did."

CJ's eyes lingered on Rella, as if finding this statement important.

Rella sat forward.

"Nearing the end, something impelled me to document the experience, or it would be lost forever. I didn't want to do it, so I wrote fast. I actually had to, because the memory bubbles were bursting quickly. I finished, put it away, and didn't look at it again until a few weeks ago."

"How did it feel reading it?"

"I couldn't get through even the first page. It felt like I would be opening a file whose contents I wouldn't want to see or be able to handle."

Fresh tears arrived. Rella dabbed her eyes.

"In one of the later sessions with Seth, this scene unfolded, from when I was little. A link to the eating disorder." Rella took a breath. "I was sitting at the dining table, at my grandparents' house, and my grandmother was forcing me to eat. I wasn't hungry. I was . . ." Rella stopped. "Traumatized. My grandfa—he was staring at me, tauntingly so. I think something must have happened just prior. Something he did to me. He knew I didn't want to eat because of it. I felt forced. Forced by him, then forced by her. Each mouthful like swallowing bitter, sour pain, secrets, lies. And I sat there and pretended."

Rella felt nauseous. She looked up at CJ.

"I had no memory of this. I still don't—not really. All the scenes that came to my mind in my sessions with Seth, I felt like I was just watching them unfold, not recalling a memory. Just like what I had written all those years ago. Anyway, going to him did nothing but thrust me into a spiral of torture I can't escape from. I need to get my life back. Can you help me?"

"I will certainly try. I use a gentle approach, and we will do this step by step."

"Good, because I can't handle much else." Rella folded and unfolded her hands. "There's more I should tell you, I guess."

"Okay."

Rella recounted what she could remember about the night she went out to the garage and started the car.

"I've never thought of killing myself before! Even then, I felt more like an observer being led."

"What stopped you?"

"A ladybug saved my life."

"A ladybug?"

"Yes. I saw it and didn't want it to be hurt. The thought made me overwhelmingly sad. I turned off the car and opened the garage door and sat there until it flew away. Ironically, I slept well that night."

"Do you have any inclination to do that again?"

"No, not at all."

"Good. What else?"

Rella inhaled. "I don't want you to think I'm losing it." Rella described the night she saw the wraithlike creature. "She wasn't *literally* there, of course. I know that. But it wasn't a pleasant sight. She kept opening her mouth over and over."

"You've never had an experience like that before?"

"No." Rella's forefingers went to her temples. "Shadows walk around in my head. My mind talks to itself, but I am kept out of it."

Nineteen

In their next session three days later, CJ picked the clipboard up off her desk and held it out to Rella.

"Rella, this is a questionnaire I'd like you to fill out. There are thirty-five questions. Please be as accurate with the answers as you can. Take as much time as you need. I'll leave the room. Come out when you're finished."

Rella watched CJ close the door. She looked at the papers, uneasy, but unsure why. She read the instructions.

The following questionnaire pertains to things you may experience in your daily life, not under the influence of substances such as drugs or alcohol. When responding to each question, please mark along the scale where you fall, with 0 meaning you never experience this, and 10 meaning you always experience this. There are four sections.

Rella picked up the pencil.

Interactions with others

1. There have been times I have not recognized friends or close members of my family.

No.

2. I've had people come up to me who call me a different name, or people I don't know saying they know me.

Never.

3. When listening to others speak, I sometimes realize I haven't heard all or part of what was said.

Sure, if her mind was preoccupied, or the person wasn't saying anything worthwhile or interesting.

4. When speaking with others, it can sometimes feel that the words coming out of my mouth are not my own.

Yes, eerily enough, this had happened often.

5. I've been accused of lying when I know I have not lied.

Perhaps a few times, when she was younger.

6. There have been times, in some situations, that I have acted very differently than I have in other situations.

That didn't seem unusual.

Location

7. At times I have found myself somewhere, with no recollection of how I arrived.

Definitely not.

8. When driving or as a passenger, I sometimes realize I can't remember part of the trip.

Rella sometimes spaced out a bit while driving.

9. When driving, I find myself in a place I hadn't intended to go.

No. She'd taken a wrong turn here or there, but didn't everyone?

10. There have been times when familiar places suddenly feel strange and unfamiliar.

That's exactly what she experienced after returning to California from Atlanta. Her anger flared at what she had gone through in an effort to get help. She pushed the feeling aside.

Memory

11. I've forgotten important life events, both happy and unhappy, such as a wedding, or death in the family.

Yes.

12. I have found myself dressed in clothes I don't remember putting on.

Never. She always chose her attire carefully.

13. I find articles around the house I don't remember buying, or in places I don't remember putting them in.

She had come across a few forgotten purchases and had chastised herself to be more discerning in her shopping.

14. Sometimes, I don't know if I really did something, or if I just think I did, or dreamed that I did.

Maybe, sometimes.

15. Sometimes I'm not sure if I've really had an experience, or if I just think that it happened.

Not common, but yes.

16. I have found evidence of doing things I don't remember doing.

Didn't everyone?

17. I have found things written on paper, such as notes or drawings, that I don't remember doing.

She supposed so, once or twice.

Self

18. When alone, I sometimes talk to myself out loud.

Sure.

19. I have experienced feeling I am watching myself, as though I were looking at another person.

She recalled an experience she would never forget.

She was nineteen or twenty at the time, exiting the gas station, her mother in the passenger seat. One minute she was turning the steering wheel, the next, floating above. She could see the top of her head, the top of her mother's head. She no longer felt the wheel under her hands or the gas pedal under her foot. The voices of her and her mother echoed as though far away. She saw the car pull out onto the avenue. In seconds, she was back in her body again. She had never told that experience to anyone.

20. At times, I've looked in the mirror and was surprised not to recognize myself.

No, but she feared seeing a face different than her own looking back at her.

21. There have been moments when the world, objects around me, people, or pets, don't seem real.

She recalled this happening a lot when she was younger, but it had lessened considerably.

22. Sometimes, my body does not feel like my own.

Yes.

Rella started to wonder what this questionnaire was for.

23. There are times I can completely ignore pain, as though my body isn't feeling it.

She wished she could.

24. I find myself sitting for long periods, doing nothing, staring, unaware of the passage of time.

She would find that a waste. No.

25. I can daydream or fantasize so realistically it seems as though it's really happening.

Yes. She had an animated imagination.

26. There have been instances where I've been able to do things quite easily, that I might have thought difficult.

She wasn't sure how to answer this one, if "difficult" meant "new," or "daunting." She liked challenges.

27. My tastes vary widely.

Yes.

28. I get sudden bursts of emotion, that don't seem to have a source.

Yes, after seeing Seth Jabez. And, yes, perhaps earlier than that too.

29. I have sudden impulse behaviors, that seem unlike me.

Maybe, at times.

30. I can name a few instances when I felt like an onlooker, unable to control what I was doing.

A chill went through Rella when she thought of smashing the cutting board and starting the car in the closed garage.

31. At times my body feels smaller or bigger than it should.

Rella's pencil hovered. What *was* this questionnaire for?

32. At times I suddenly feel very happy, and at times extremely sad, without a reason I can perceive.

Rella recalled this happening in grade school, experiencing random surges of happiness. Lately, however, she succumbed more to sadness.

33. Conversations go on inside my head, perhaps voices telling me to do things, or making comments on what is going on at the moment.

Before the sessions with Seth, she would have answered "never" without hesitation. But her brain had changed. She couldn't say there were voices, but there was—something.

34. It can feel at times that my vision is unclear, as though I'm looking from underwater or through a fog.

Yes, the bothersome film over her eyes. Some days, it clouded over her sight, while on others, she hardly noticed it.

35. I can't say I always understand why I feel and act the way that I do, which at times seems out of character for me.

She supposed this could happen to anyone.

Rella re-read all the questions, then sat for a few minutes with the clipboard in her lap before rising. She opened the door to find CJ, who was standing in the hall. CJ smiled and walked back in the room. Rella handed her the questionnaire after she sat.

"This was a strange questionnaire," Rella said. "For some of these questions, anyone could answer yes, at times, right?" She paused, looking CJ in the eye. "What is this for? What's my score?"

In Rella's scholastic world, a high tally was a good thing. She had deduced that might not be the case for this test.

"I'll look it over for next session," said CJ.

Twenty

Rella's legs swayed in the chair. "So, what did you learn from the questionnaire?"

"It's never good to jump to a conclusion, so I'd like to work with you a bit more first."

"All right."

"Before beginning deeper work, it will be important to establish ways to keep you grounded, so to speak, so you don't get lost and scared."

"Pitched into a labyrinth. That's how it felt with Seth."

"With trauma, the brain isn't always living in the present. This can instill a sense of unsafety. I thought it might help to write the year on this big piece of cardboard, and we can place it in plain sight across from you, on the mantel."

"Someone might come in and change it," Rella said, immediately perplexed by her own words.

"Okay, we won't do that."

Rella rubbed her forehead. "Bad migraine day," she said, briefly closing her eyes. The pressure expanded and a violent image flashed before her. She cried out. "The minute I let my guard down, there it is. The evil face. It was so close this time."

"The mask might represent a memory," said CJ. "Part of you may want to protect you from healing. We aren't sure why yet. But it needs to be honored. It has brought you this far."

Rella thought this statement a little odd.

"You've been good at keeping your mind occupied your whole life."

"Yes."

"It's a way not to have to think about things."

"I'd never known there was something I shouldn't be thinking about."

"I realize that. Concealed memories are unclaimed baggage, going around and around in the terminal of the mind."

"I want them back in the lost and found. But not found."

CJ smiled. "I can understand why. Do you ever check out during the day, for whatever reason?"

"Check out?"

"I've seen a change in your eyes a few times. You leave."

"Leave?"

"Mm-hmm."

"My mind wanders easily."

CJ nodded. "Since you'd prefer not to have the year displayed, take a look around the room, and get yourself familiar with the objects. They will represent the present. I may ask you at different points in session to describe an object or two to me, to help bring you back into the room."

Rella's eyes toured the space.

"There is something I'd like to try today, called ego state therapy."

"It's not hypnosis, right?"

"No. It's a technique to explore the different roles we play in life, depending on the situation."

"I can try it."

"Relax your eyes."

Rella looked at the floor, hoping the evil face would leave her alone.

"Picture yourself going down a staircase," CJ guided.

Rella shrank back into the chair.

"Okay, not a staircase," said CJ. "How about down a hallway?"

Rella pictured a cold, sterile hospital. "What about a path outside?" she suggested.

"Perfect," said CJ. "As you walk down this outdoor path, I'm going to count backwards from ten to one, and with each step, envision turning more inward into yourself."

Rella took a breath.

"Ten. Nine. Eight."

Rella remained in the chair, in the room.

"Seven. Six. Five."

A new realm of atmosphere unfolded. Fragrances of vegetation entered her nose. Sun caressed her skin.

"Four. Three."

The crunch of gravel beneath her feet.

"Two."

Pastel flowers sprouted in a garden, muted colors of lilac, ivory, and goldenrod, under a sapphire sky.

"One."

Peace.

An undisturbed place, beyond boundaries and latitude.

"You have come to a conference room." CJ's voice sounded beyond the image as though through a low speaker.

Rella noticed an apex of a structure among the trees. She continued up the path, a genial turn to the right like a welcoming, open palm. "It's a greenhouse," Rella said. "White and broad, with walls and ceiling made of glass."

"A greenhouse," CJ amended. "Is there a door?"

"Yes."

"Go ahead and step inside. How does it feel?"

"Fine."

"Describe it for me, please."

"It's warm, and I can see through the walls to the outside."

"Can you see a table inside?"

And suddenly, Rella could, long and rectangular. She nodded.

"How many chairs are around the table?"

Much longer than it needed to be, it more than accommodated the three chairs on each side, and one at the top. Rella explained what she saw, adding, "The rest of the room is empty."

"At the other end of the room is a door. Can you walk to it?"

"Yes."

"This will allow you to invite people into the conference room."

"Greenhouse," Rella corrected.

"Yes, I'm sorry. Greenhouse. Could you open it now?"

Part of Rella didn't want to, but she turned the knob. A corridor lay beyond, lined with closed doors. She didn't move past the threshold.

"Anyone coming in?" CJ asked.

Rella stepped away from the door, to the side, ill at ease with what she might confront.

A minute later, as if cut out by light, an outline of a person, tall and somewhat muscular, with mussed jet-black hair, wearing jeans, a white top, and black biker jacket, appeared. He ambled past Rella without recognition.

A second person arrived, a young boy, with short brown hair, smiling.

"Rella?" CJ asked.

"I see a young boy."

"How old is he?"

"I think twelve. And someone else came in first. A boy too. Maybe eighteen or nineteen." She wondered how she knew their ages.

The young boy took a seat. The taller one followed, sitting to the left of him. He straightened his long legs, making arcs back and forth in the swivel chair.

"Anyone else?" CJ asked.

A form, in the corner. "A little girl. Sitting on the floor. Her face is turned away from me."

"How old is she?"

"Six? No, four. I think she's four."

"Do you want to go over to her, make sure she's all right?"

In her mind, Rella approached the little girl. Like a frightened animal, the child whipped around, face contorted, mouth wide, baring teeth. She jutted out a hand, her fingers shaped like claws.

"She doesn't want me near her. She looks really mad."

"And I'm sure she has a right to be. We will leave her alone for a while. Is anyone else waiting to come in?"

Rella peered down the corridor. Empty. "No."

"Okay. Go ahead and take your seat."

Rella eyed the two, the smiling young boy with his hands folded on the table, who seemed to be in a convivial mood about the meeting, and the older boy who sat with crossed arms and narrowed eyes, deflecting his gaze.

"I am going to address everyone in the Greenhouse now. Hello, my name is CJ, and I am the counselor working with Rella. You can hear everything being said and you can also talk if you want to. If you are not ready yet, that is okay too. We are here for an open discussion. Who would like to go first?"

A couple of minutes passed.

"No one is volunteering," Rella said.

CJ gave it a little more time, and Rella sat patiently, but the room remained silent.

"I want to thank each of you for coming," CJ conveyed. "This space can serve as a forum for communication, if you so desire, in the future. Before we end for today, let's make sure each person is in a safe place. It's a process sometimes called 'tucking in.' "

"I don't like that expression," Rella interjected. She pictured a child being hemmed into bed so tightly they couldn't move.

"We don't have to use it. Is there a place each of you prefers to go until the next time we meet?"

Rella waited for the answers. They came surprisingly fast, clear, and distinct.

"The young boy likes the desert. I see him in front of a campfire."

"Great, we will leave him there until next time. And the other two?"

Right before her eyes, the older boy sat, his back to her, at a counter of a diner. The little girl was positioned on green grass under a tree, in its shade, her face still turned away.

"Each is content in these places?" CJ asked.

"Appears that way."

"Before we close up the Greenhouse, is there anyone else inside?"

"No," said Rella, "but . . ."

Her eyes went to another corner. As the shadows fell away, Rella saw the same wraithlike figure that had shown herself in the dining room, sunken into the corner as much as her flesh had into her bones. Her head was cast down. Rella had the notion the creature wanted her presence known but was afraid Rella would not want her there.

"It's the girl, from the other night, the one I told you I saw in my house."

"Does she have something to say?"

"Her mouth is closed."

"Let's settle her into a place where she can be comfortable."

Rella knew immediately: a sprawling country house with generous rooms and a front porch. The kind of house she'd longed to live in as a child.

"She's tired. She wants to lie down." Rella pictured her retiring in a cozy bedroom of the farmhouse, a quilt over the bed, homemade curtains on the windows, tied back to reveal endless green pastures outside.

After the Greenhouse was empty, CJ had Rella come back to her office, in the present moment. "This is an important process," CJ said. "Otherwise, you could have emotional distress later."

"Seth didn't do any of this."

"It doesn't sound like he was cautious at all."

"I should have walked out after the first session and never gone back," said Rella. "Do you know he actually had the nerve to keep answering his phone during our sessions?"

"What?"

"I waited too long to speak up about it. But I was fuming inside."

"Incredible."

"I don't know why I stayed there. I really can't figure it out. And now I see how completely unqualified he is. Well, I know people are mistreated by those in the medical field all the time. My mother surely was. Anyway." She looked down, then back up at CJ. "What we did today—who are those people? I have never seen them before. Where is this information coming from?"

"I think we will learn more in our upcoming sessions," CJ said.

Rella couldn't get the Greenhouse out of her mind on her drive home that day.

CJ had called the process "ego state therapy." Did that mean these people represented her personality? The older boy wanted to go to a diner. Diners were far from Rella's choice for an eating establishment, with their greasy food, tattered furnishings, and outdated decor. But they were often located on long stretches of highway, between destinations. That appealed her. Travel and anonymity also came to mind. This mysterious boy stayed hunched over the diner counter, a cup of coffee around one hand, talking to no one.

The younger boy had also chosen to be alone, in the desert, self-sufficient. She saw him heating food over a fire, under a sky twinkling with stars. A familiarity about him crept up from behind, prickling her neck.

The defensive little girl sat in a grassy clearing, under a tree, sun in the periphery, enclosed by shade.

Lastly, the cryptic creature on the verge of being skeletal, gray and injured, had reappeared. Initially, in the dining room, she'd repeatedly opened her mouth. Rella now wondered if she had wanted to eat.

In the middle of the night, Rella woke with a clearer image of the little girl under the tree in the clearing. She had blonde hair, in pigtails, and wore a white dress.

"Have you heard of Life Map therapy?" CJ asked Rella at their next appointment.

"Yes. A counselor I was seeing a few years ago when I first arrived in California tried it on me. I had confused her."

"How so?"

"In one session, she had me scan my life, as though it were on a line, checking for an age that stands out. Seven and three came to mind; I have no idea why. She asked me to go back further. I told her the line frayed, going in all directions."

"Curious."

"She'd never had anyone describe it as anything other than one straight line," said Rella.

"How many branches did you have?"

"I don't remember. I wasn't sure at the time, either."

"And the branches formed at age three?"

"Perhaps."

"What led you to make an appointment with her?"

"When I first came to California, I stayed a couple of months in a rented room until I found an apartment. The bathroom there bothered me, the shower in particular. It was in a tub with a curtain. While showering, I grew convinced someone was standing outside the curtain. No one was there, of course, but the phobia worsened. I would check three, four, five times a shower. It got to the point where I couldn't close my eyes, even to shampoo my hair, because I was certain when I opened them, someone would be standing there. I knew if I went to a doctor, they'd push an antidepressant. I'd met Serla—that was her name—at a bookstore where I'd study sometimes."

Rella remembered the kind woman fondly, her long, flowing skirts, white hair falling as it pleased around her shoulders, and wrists lost in plump, doughy arms.

"Do you get a sense this person wants to hurt you?" Serla asked.

"Sometimes yes, sometimes no."

"Are they male or female?"

"Male." Rella's hand went to the left side of her neck.

"Are you okay?"

"Just my neck pain."

"What emotion would you say is related to it?"

"Anger," Rella replied, without forethought. Then, unexpectedly, she felt angry—something she didn't experience very often.

"Do you think this pain is trying to tell you something?"

The question left her with the sensation of someone perched in the spot between the top of her scapula and the base of her neck, on the left side. She shivered noticeably.

"All right?"

"Fine," she replied, a response often given when a person wasn't.

"Memories talk to us, from inside, communicating in different ways—through pain, for example. Until I see you next, tune in to that part of your body. See if it has anything to say."

"I'm afraid it will scream at me."

"Ask the pain if it could whisper what it needs in your ear."

Rella found that creepy.

Later, in the shower, as soap and water converged in a whirlpool around the drain, the familiar apprehension arrived, stronger than ever. She couldn't bring herself to look outside the shower curtain.

She toweled off, dressed, and sat down to read.

The pain in her neck returned, gnawing, clustering.

Maybe it *was* trying to tell her something.

In CJ's office, Rella had an abrupt realization. The person outside the shower had been a boy, a child of maybe twelve, one who looked a lot like the younger boy she had seen in the Greenhouse.

Twenty-One

Early March 2017

She'd never been lax on the job.

In all her years, files had never been breached. This blindside, this unanticipated assail, had delivered a momentous impact to the substructure.

There had been no way to intercept it. She had to execute serious damage control.

She didn't know how many had been affected, or what repercussions would be coming her way. Most of them didn't live in the now. She did. And *she* did. The one she was responsible for.

She carefully controlled every particle in her life and made zero attachments. No favorite clothing, mementos, or time of day. No friends, pets. Always ready to live without.

She was the opposite. *She* created a life of cushions spun from stability and stuffed with happy thoughts, where security couldn't evaporate in an exhale.

How could she have been so careless?

She had always maintained, with concrete confidence, that if she were the one in charge, preserving control, chaos simply could not ensue.

She went to the window to assess the situation.

Crumbling.

She bit her lip. An inferior habit; her only one, but it showed weakness and could be seen on the outside.

Opacity. She still had that. It would never, could never, be completely revealed. She held on to that assertion.

If only what was seen could be taken back.

She straightened her posture and raised her chin. She was up to the task. She was always up to the task.

Even if the memories snowed in *her* brain, blizzarded, to the point of collecting on a ridge, portending an avalanche, she would remain, at the foot of the mountain, in the zone of jeopardy. It was her job. Where she had always existed.

"How are you, Rella?"

Rella sighed. She wanted to say "Better," wished for one small glimmer of improvement, even a minor alleviation of a symptom, to show that the abrasions to her memory had been worthwhile. Tears streamed down her face.

"This vile world. How many are being abused as I say these words? I see a child, and hope they are safe, loved. I wonder what they have forgotten. Were they harmed in some way? Children should have happiness, kindness, an upbringing as weightless as a leaf in a stream." She could never understand how one person could take the life of another. There were those who stole lives without killing. "These thoughts repeat over and over and over." Tears flowed down her throat, into her stomach.

"Let's see if we can ease them for you."

"Excuse me." Rella ran out of the room down the hall

to the bathroom. She lifted the toilet seat quickly. Deeper, undigested gunk needed to come out, but only mucus surfaced.

She returned to CJ's office, paper towels in hand, just in case.

"Do we need to conclude for today, Rella?"

Rella shook her head. "I'm not going to feel any better at home."

"Maybe we can lighten this burden, or perhaps replace the images so you're not so inundated. Fix your gaze for me, please. Breathe in, and then out."

Rella did. She continued for a few minutes.

The tears dried up as if a switch had been flipped.

"This is a waste of time."

"Oh?" CJ asked.

"It all has been." She sat up straighter in the chair, stiffly, pursed her lips.

"It all has been? Do you mean here?"

"He was an idiot. Incompetent. That's what started this. Men are useless and can't be trusted."

"All men?"

"Things need to return to the way they were."

"How is your headache?"

"I don't have one."

CJ was quiet for a moment. "Who am I talking to?"

Rella felt a *whoosh*, landing in the chair. She realized that a face had been next to hers, female, close enough to nearly brush cheeks. CJ's question caused the visage to dissipate into vapor.

Tears rolled from her eyes. She curled up in the chair.

"Rella?" CJ asked, as if unsure. "Are you here?"

"Of course, I'm here. Where else would I be?" Rella had a strange sensation of missing time. Her hands shook. "I don't like this."

"Let's make sure you're completely in the room. Describe an object on the mantel for me."

She struggled, sight ill-defined. "The painting, above the mantel. There's an orchard, blue sky, clouds."

"Good," CJ said. "Did you feel absent from the room at all just now?"

"I—I have a blank. I remember you saying, 'Who am I talking to?' " Rella shivered. "There was a face, next to mine, *breathing*. I don't get it. What's wrong with me?"

"Nothing is wrong with you. You have a coping mechanism, formed when you were young. It extricated you. Trauma can be incomprehensible, so much so that the person goes somewhere else. Different parts develop, to deal and manage."

"Parts?"

"Yes. To preserve you, keep you separate. It's referred to as a dissociative disorder."

Rella shook her head. "I don't understand."

"There are different levels of dissociation that can occur."

"What level am I?"

"I believe you have what's called dissociative identity disorder."

"Never heard of it."

Rella sat for a minute. Dissociative *identity* disorder.

"Wait." She laughed. "Are you saying I have multiple personalities?"

"That term isn't used anymore."

"It doesn't matter what the *term* is."

"This probably is not what you expected to hear."

"Uh, no. I don't have multiple personalities."

"It's a condition that can go undiagnosed for a long time. And you, Rella, are not a typical case. You're quite high functioning. You've hidden it from everyone, from yourself, all this time. And you do it extremely well. It's so subtle, unless someone was paying heed, they wouldn't see it."

CJ announcing a herd of elephants taking over the parking lot would have been more plausible.

"So, that questionnaire you had me fill out, that was to check for this?"

"It is one screening tool."

"And the Greenhouse?"

"That technique has other purposes, but yes, it can be useful to identify dissociation. It's a way to create a safe space where the different parts can talk if they want to."

"Parts."

"Yes, parts of you."

"They aren't me." Rella had seen them. They were distinct people! They weren't her age or likeness, and two of them were even boys!

Rella held her head in her hands, her mind spinning. This wasn't the answer. "I didn't even think multiple personalities— dissociative identity—was real."

"Movies and TV and books tend to sensationalize it. In reality, it's a defense mechanism to contain certain memories, time periods, difficult or harmful information. Look at all you've accomplished. Your mind created a way for you to forget, so you could go on and live a fulfilling life."

"I was perfectly fine before I went to Seth!"

"Your body was alerting you, in different ways."

"Maybe. But these thoughts are so much worse!"

CJ nodded. "One of the first and most important steps before administering TDT is to screen for any dissociation. If it's suspected or found, the practitioner needs to have experience with it. Certain guidelines must be followed, and protocols adjusted. Even then, there is always a risk. Your memories are encoded, Rella. Elaborately. You have been compartmentalizing all along, so you could get through your life. What Seth did eroded your system. Your mind got flooded."

"How—how could it happen so fast? You're saying I've had this condition, who knows how long, and he was able to do all this damage in just a few days?"

"Think of it this way. Imagine a wrecking ball. If it hit a critical support area of a building, how long do you think it would take before the structure is no longer stable?"

"Well, it would be immediate."

"Exactly. One blow could take down, say, a quarter of the building. Maybe more. I'm not well versed in construction; that's your area of expertise. But I've studied dissociation extensively, and TDT, in your case, was a wrecking ball."

Two days later, Rella returned. She sat with her arms crossed.

"I don't think I have this condition, but regardless, I need to get better, so I will continue."

"I prepared a printout for you to read. It's quite long, but I highlighted key areas. I thought it might be helpful for you to understand what happened."

Rella leaned forward and accepted the stapled packet.

"TDT is powerful," CJ explained, "which is why caution is paramount. In some cases, TDT may be completely contraindicated. That packet goes into further detail on recommended guidelines, and it's clearly stated that use of TDT in someone with unrecognized dissociative identity disorder can result in unintended breaches, abrupt emergence of parts, and rapid destabilization. Seth Jabez went in with a sledgehammer, dismantling barriers your mind had put in place for a reason, protections that had safeguarded painful information for years."

"Thank you for this."

"I know having this information doesn't fix it."

"*Can* it be fixed?"

"We will keep exploring. Can we continue to use the Greenhouse?"

"Yes, that's fine."

Rella walked down the trail to the Greenhouse. It was a nice day there, the sun shining, the herbage a bright green.

She reached the structure.

"I'm here," she told CJ.

"Would anyone like to come into the Greenhouse?" CJ asked.

Minutes passed. CJ repeated the question.

"I don't see anyone," Rella said. "The room is empty."

"Let's try this. Rella, I'm going to have you exit the Greenhouse and go back down the path you took to get there. Find a place you can settle into."

Rella walked. She discovered another path, which led to a secluded beach.

"I'm at the ocean," she said. "It's warm, quiet, peaceful." A lone tree reached out over the sand. Gentle waves arrived upon the shore. "I'll sit here."

Rella situated herself in a place of no memories, where pain, cold, or harm couldn't abide. In the distance, CJ talked about the Greenhouse. A sensation of absence unplugged her.

The Greenhouse awaited.

Twenty-Two

"Do you know Rella?"

"Yes."

"My name is CJ."

"I know who you are." The voice, monotone.

"Great. I'm here to help. Did you speak during the last session—saying this was a waste of time?"

"Yes."

"So, you have been listening in."

"Yes."

"You must have concerns."

"I don't have time for idle chitchat."

"Do you often speak for Rella?"

"When needed."

"Are you ever in Rella's place?"

"If necessary."

"Do you put Rella's interests ahead of your own?"

"Of course. This isn't going to help her. I am the only one who can."

"Your confidence is commendable. It's a big job."

"I can handle it."

"Do you get tired?"

"No," her reply, tinged with indignation.

"Rella has been in pain for a long time. Do you have any physical issues?"

"My neck muscles get tight."

"Does it bother you?"

"I don't let it."

"Do you hold the memories Rella has forgotten?"

"No."

"What is your role?"

She paused, compressed her lips. "I oversee."

"Can you tell me what that means, please?"

No answer.

"Could you communicate one aspect?"

"I am the keeper of the files."

"The files. Do files mean secrets?"

"Files mean files."

"Can you tell me about these files? Where are they?"

"In my office."

"How thick are the files?"

"Some are thick. Some are thin."

"Are there a lot of files?"

"Yes."

"Can you describe your place of work to me?"

"I don't see why that matters."

"Humor me."

She vented a tempered exhale. "There are three rooms. The front one has the file cabinets."

"Are there any windows or doors?"

"No windows in the file room. One door."

"Is this the main door to enter and exit?"

"Yes."

"Is it locked?"

"Yes."

"Do you have the key?"

"There is an access code."

"I see. And you know this code?"

"Yes."

"Does anyone else?"

No answer.

"Tell me more," CJ said. "What kind of flooring do the rooms have?"

"Carpet in the file room and middle room."

"Sounds quiet."

"Soundless."

"Tell me about the middle room."

"It's smaller. There are two paintings, and a wooden table in the center, with flowers. Not fragrant ones. I have allergies."

"Does Rella have allergies?"

"No."

"Has Rella ever suffered allergies because you have them?"

"Yes."

"What are the paintings of?"

"A ship. A house."

"Is the ship in calm waters?"

"No."

"Where is the house?"

"In the countryside."

"Has Rella ever lived there?"

"No."

"Back to the file room—what are the cabinets made of?"

"Wood."

"They sound sturdy. Are they locked?"

"Yes."

"And you have the key?"

"Yes."

"Why do you keep the files locked?"

"I never said I keep them locked. They are just that way."

CJ made a note. "Do you put the files away?"

"Yes." She paused. "I do now."

"You do now?"

"Yes."

"There was someone before you?"

"I think so."

"Why do you think that?"

"It was in complete disorder when I arrived."

"Can you describe how?"

"Dusty, dirty. The cabinets were old, dented. Rickety. Made out of metal. Unattractive. Difficult to open and close. Terrible grating sound."

"What about the decor?"

"The floors were cement, the walls gray. I don't think the person wanted to be there. Or maybe they were being punished."

"Punished? That's an interesting word to choose."

"I certainly wouldn't have stayed under those conditions."

"So, you did all the work to clean it up, and make it nice."

"Yes."

"You must spend a lot of time in your office."

"Yes."

"You mentioned there are three rooms. What is the third one?"

"My living quarters."

"I see. And you live alone?"

"Yes."

"Have you always?"

"Yes."

"How were the living quarters when you first arrived?"

"There weren't any."

"Where did you sleep?"

"On the floor."

"On a cement floor?"

"Yes."

"Doesn't sound very humane."

"Humane. Such an incongruous word. Used to describe what should be normal, civilized compassion, but frequently utilized to accentuate when it is so, as if it is usually not."

"I never thought of it that way."

"Most people don't think. In any case, it's what was expected of me."

"Maybe that's why you have neck pain and stiffness."

"Perhaps."

"How are the living quarters now?"

"Fine."

"Where do you sleep?"

"On a couch."

"Is it soft?"

"Soft enough."

"We are about out of time, so I need to get Rella. I'd like to get to learn more about you. Can we talk next session?"

No response.

"Could I know your name, to address you properly?" CJ

waited for a reply. "Well, perhaps another time."

She pursed her lips.

"I gather you don't want to be here."

"No."

"And you did not want to come out, at all."

"No."

"Am I the first person you have met, as you, not as Rella?"

"Yes."

"Well, I am honored." CJ kept her thoughts to herself—about what a lonely existence it must be for this person. "I'm sorry for all the disruption lately."

"Not your fault."

"I assume you weren't the one who called me, initially I mean, to make the first appointment."

"No."

"Was it Rella?"

She hesitated. "No."

"All right. So, I will get Rella at the beach now. Is there a place you'd like to go?"

"I'm always in the office."

"It's a beautiful day outside today."

"I don't go outside."

"Never? Can you see outside?"

"There is a wall of windows in the living quarters. They don't open."

"Is there daylight or darkness from the windows?"

"Both. Usually daylight."

"What do you see outside of the windows?"

"Other buildings, other windows."

"Where is your office located?"

"In a high-rise building."

"I will let you settle back into the office."

CJ spoke to bring Rella back.

Rella's tranquil view drifted away as she heard CJ's words, the features of the beach dwindling. She became aware of her fingers, hands, arms, legs. She rubbed her forehead.

"Rella?"

Between existences.

"Rella?"

"Yeah?" She rubbed her forehead again.

"Are you here in the room?"

"Yes, I think so."

CJ gave her another minute. "What do you remember?"

Rella searched her mind. "The beach," she said. "I'm dizzy. My vision is unclear."

"What's on your schedule for the rest of the day?"

"I don't plan much on session days," Rella replied.

"Reasonable. How are you feeling now?"

"Fine." Rella collected her things. "So, we are good for next Tuesday, then?"

"Yes, all set. I have us down for twelve to two, both Tuesday and Thursday."

"Great. See you then."

Rella's pace slowed as she walked to her car, the world peculiar, though not in a scary way. And maybe she even felt a little—better.

Rella pulled up to the house. Still in the car, from behind the windshield, she saw her. In the driveway, composed, motionless. Unreadable expression on her face. Thin, dressed conservatively in slim pants and a matching blazer of gray, white shirt, plain shoes with a sensible heel, dark hair in a bun.

Her presence didn't upset Rella. She wondered who she was.

At the start of their next session, Rella told CJ about the woman she had seen.

CJ didn't seem surprised. "What is her name?"

There's a name? Rella thought, a cold sensation overcame her, as one had when the woman's face first appeared next to hers.

"Take a minute. There's no rush."

Without any effort, the name came, as if she'd known it all along.

"Margaret. Her name is Margaret."

Twenty-Three

Late March 2017

Ginnie had flown back to her home state for a visit, and many of the local bars and restaurants were boisterous and overcrowded with spring break partyers. Rella kept to herself, lengthening her walks outside, taking the time to reflect on all the information whizzing at her. So bizarre, this light shining into other universes never explored. She hadn't known they existed. The effect had her feeling she'd left gravity, suspended in the unchartered. Rather than overthink it, she decided to hand over the controls and embark on the ride as a passenger with an open mind. So far, she hadn't gotten any worse.

She looked up to the sun. Ninety-three million miles away, it took just over eight minutes for its rays to reach the eyes. It was like seeing the past.

"Anna," Rella told CJ in their Thursday session. "She's the thin, sickly creature who showed up in the doorway that night at home. Only she doesn't look that way, in actuality. I don't like the way she first introduced herself to me."

"Understandably," CJ said. "Perhaps she used to look that way."

"It's strange, all this information I now have. It's only

been a week since I 'met' Margaret, and now I'm finding out about Anna."

"Tell me about her."

"She's tall, runway-model height. Nothing like my stature or build. I always thought my body looked more teen than adult. She has long, thick, straw-colored hair, usually wears it down, but sometimes pulled back. Pale skin, doesn't get outside much. No makeup. Loose-fitting clothes. Sleep gives her a break. She's used to the rain but prefers the sun."

CJ directed Rella to mentally visit the beach. Shortly afterwards, Rella's demeanor quieted, to the point she looked drowsy, before her body straightened.

"Anna is reckless. She always thinks her way is right. Wants Rella informed."

"Is this Margaret?"

"Yes," she replied stonily.

"Thank you for coming today, Margaret," CJ said. "It's nice to know your name. So, you are conversant with Anna, then?"

"Of course."

"Sounds as though you don't agree with her actions."

"Certainly not. Anna thinks only of herself. She's gone so far as to sneak into the file room, I suspect. She might have gotten hold of the code, a key. I am the only one to do this job. I am the one put in charge. I take everything into account."

"Maybe if matters were more out in the open, so they could be handled, it would be easier on you. You could rest."

"No. It would be much worse. Information could get to the wrong person. I would never rest. I would never rest again."

"There were a few others in the Greenhouse, our first day visiting there."

Quiet.

Telescoping away, Margaret dissolved, and someone else came. The posture not as firm, the arms relaxed, the fingers loose in the lap.

A sigh departed from their lips.

"Hello," CJ said, in greeting.

The person took a minute to respond. "Hello." The voice softer, fatigued.

"Who am I speaking with?"

"Anna." She spoke with effort, as if out of breath, or in pain.

"Hello, Anna. It's nice to meet you."

"It's nice to meet you, too." Each word bore strain.

"Are you okay, Anna?"

"I don't feel well. I never do."

"I'm sorry to hear that."

"I'm used to it."

"Was Rella correct—you were the one she saw that night, the emaciated creature?"

"Yes."

"May I ask why you presented in that way?"

"To get her attention."

"I see. Well, maybe from now on, come as yourself, and not in a disguise. Rella didn't like it."

"I'm sorry."

"Thank you. Anna, I understand you and Margaret do not see eye to eye."

"We never have."

"She thinks Rella cannot handle information. What about you?"

"I'm not sure. But we need change."

"Were you the one that called me, Anna? To make the first appointment?"

"Yes."

CJ nodded.

"Margaret will not be happy I am out."

"Are you in pain like Rella?"

"Yes."

"What kind of pain?"

"Headaches. It's hard to hold my head up at times. Nausea. Menstrual cramps. All the time." She doubled over.

"Anna?"

The person made small grunting noises and rocked.

"Who's here now?"

The rocking grew faster, then slowly ceased. CJ waited.

Minutes later, the posture elongated as if raised by a string from the head.

"Margaret?" CJ asked.

"Yes."

"Margaret, who was that? I get the sense it wasn't Anna."

"No."

"Could you tell me who it was?"

No answer.

"Margaret, we need to finish up for today. Do you know if there is anyone else in the Greenhouse?"

"You can't talk to Katie."

"Was that Katie, who came after Anna, the one who was rocking?"

The posture gave way, signaling Margaret was no longer there.

"Rella?"

Rella heard the voice, far away.

"Rella?"

She fought to get back, unsure of time and the minutes that had passed.

"We need to leave the Greenhouse now. Can you make sure no one else is in there? Check behind the chairs, in the corners. We want to ensure no one is left behind."

Through the froth in her mind, Rella found herself in the Greenhouse. Unexpectedly, she spotted a figure. "There is someone small, cowering in the corner, frightened." Rella's head shook. "I can't say it."

"Say what? Can you write it down?" CJ grabbed notebook and pen and held it out. Rella took them.

Tears from an unsung place spilled onto her face. She hesitated, as if whomever she wrote for wasn't sure it was allowed.

Help me

"Tell me what you remember from last session," CJ asked Rella.

"Umm, Margaret and Anna were here."

"Yes. And I think a third person came after Anna."

"You can tell?"

"Quite clearly."

Pushing aside the notion that they were actually talking about her, Rella asked with curiosity, "Can you describe them to me?"

"Margaret has flawless posture."

Rella laughed. "Are you saying I don't?"

"Well, it's a quality we all can work on," CJ said diplomatically. "Except maybe Margaret," she added, a smile curving the corners of her mouth. "She's terse, doesn't respond when she doesn't want to. But I get the sense she always tells the truth. Puts her job ahead of herself. Tension skimming her muscles. She speaks with little to no emotion in her voice, no volume changes."

"Mechanical?"

"Her face holds a form. Which makes sense. When you have a job to do, you have a certain face."

"What is her job?"

"I am still learning about her. She has said that she's the keeper of the files." CJ explained what Margaret had told her about the office and what she does there. "Can you remember what it looks like, Rella?"

Rella thought about it. "Yes, I can." She sat in fascination as it mentally reconstructed around her. "This is weird. All this detail that's always been there. But not. What can you tell me about Anna?"

"She's tired, and has a lot of pain. She's in support of therapy, while Margaret wants restoration back. She thinks

Anna is impetuous. Anna did confirm she was the one there in your doorway, as you suspected. I told her not to use a tactic like that again. She was endeavoring to get your attention. I asked her if she was the one who initially called me for an appointment, and she said she was."

"*She* called you?"

"I could tell once I heard her voice."

"Wow."

"Did you ever see a counselor as a child?"

"Yes, actually. Compulsory sessions after my mother's first hospital admittance."

"Do you recall them?"

"Not really. I didn't say much. I tried to maintain a veneer of normalcy. I've always had a hard time talking."

"I see. How old would you say Anna is?"

"I don't get an exact number. Between eighteen and twenty-one."

"Are those the ages when you had the eating disorder?"

"Yes, about. You'd asked me before what ended the eating disorder, and I'd said one day it just stopped. Was that one of your clues, too, to this condition?"

"Yes."

"I mentioned that I felt a sense of urgency compelling me to record the experience, as though I had a finite amount of time in which I'd be able to remember. Do you think someone else wrote that account?"

"That very well could have been the case."

"Huh. Do you think one of them stopped the eating disorder?"

"I think it is highly likely."

"Why?"

"What affects you affects them. If you had died, they all would have. The other possibility is that the part of you that turned to the eating disorder, out of a need to control, went away."

"But I had it for years!" Rella said with surprise. "I was someone else for *years?*"

"Perhaps."

Rella had assumed these different people came briefly. She wondered who she had been during school hours, with her family, at happy times. Who was she now?

Rella put her hand to her throat.

"One day, in my early twenties, I asked myself when I last felt good. Physically. No pain, no migraines, no nausea, no sore throats. I couldn't remember. I'm a different person than I would have been." She sat quietly for a moment. "And this diagnosis—it's surreal."

"I treated a client with the same diagnosis, and for three years she kept thinking she was making it up, that it wasn't real. But it is real," CJ validated. "Do you remember the end of our last session?"

"Vaguely."

"Two words were written down. I believe by a person we haven't met yet." CJ handed her the paper.

Help me

It wasn't her writing. Rella wondered who was continuing to pay the price for her years of nescience.

Twenty-Four

Colorado—Late March 2017

"Hey, Morgan, I'm here!" Trevor called out from the entry of her apartment.

"Coming! Just looking for my purse," she replied from the bedroom.

"I see it here on the couch!"

Morgan entered. "Oh yeah." She picked up the bag and rifled through it. "Okay, I have enough cash. Let's go."

"I can drive if you like."

"That'd be great."

In the car, Trevor said, "I'm thinking of starting my own construction business. I need to build something for myself."

"Great. You can hire me as your secretary. These hospital shifts are killing me."

"Working for someone else is killing me. Have you heard from Rella?"

"No. I call, and she doesn't answer, or when she does, the conversation is short."

"Yeah. Something's different with her the last couple of months. Must be busy with the new job and all."

Morgan pressed her lips together. Rella had made her promise not to tell Trevor that Morgan's hunch she had been abused was correct.

"Let's call her," Morgan suggested. She pulled out her phone. "Do you have Bluetooth?"

"Not in this bucket."

"I'll put it on speaker, then." Morgan hit Rella's number. She answered on the fourth ring.

"Hey, Morgan."

"Hey, Rella! You're on speaker. Say hi to Trevor."

"Hey, Sis!"

"Hey, Trev. Where are you two headed?"

"The movies," Morgan answered.

"Wish you were with us," Trevor said.

"A movie day does sound nice," Rella agreed.

"Remember when you were a teenager and I'd take you to the Cineplex 10 over school breaks and we'd spend the whole day there, watching movies and playing video games?" Trevor asked.

"I do remember that!" Rella said. "You'd always beat me in the Grand Prix car race. I can still hear the buzzing of the digital engine as I went around the track—so nerve-wracking—and smell the popcorn from the concession stand."

"You won a few times too," Trevor pointed out.

"At Big Choice, maybe."

"Right, the claw game! You amassed quite a pile of stuffed animals from those winnings."

"Rella, what have you been up to?" Morgan interjected.

"Same. Lots of work, which is good for me."

"Anything else?" Morgan pressed.

"Not really."

"We're just pulling into the theater parking lot now," said

173

Trevor. "I'm glad you answered, Rella."

"Me too," Rella said. "Enjoy the movie!"

"I've got more information to share." Rella sat in her usual chair across from CJ.

"Let's hear it."

"The young boy of about twelve, one of the first to appear in the Greenhouse, I think he might be the boy I'd see outside the shower when I first came to California. I have his name. It's Dustin. These names come in such a way that I'm sure they are correct. I think he had a reason for letting me know about him; I'm just not sure what it is."

"Sounds like you have been giving more thought to Dustin."

"It's more like the thoughts come to *me*. Like this one: Dustin doesn't like secrets. Just popped into my head the other day."

Rella toyed with the fringe on her shirt.

"The life line I'd drawn for Serla during therapy was a sign. All those branches. Someone was trying to tell me they were there." Rella rubbed her hands. "If they need to say something, I should be strong enough to listen. But I'm not."

"One step at a time, one thought, one wedge of information. Rella, Margaret has mentioned someone named Katie. Do you know who Katie is? I don't think she's the one who wrote the note on the paper. What do you think?"

Rella asked inside. Sometimes the answer came clearly. She shook her head. "No. I don't think she wrote on the paper."

Katie doesn't ask for help. The thought arrived in confirmation.

"Margaret asked that I not talk to Katie," said CJ.

"I wonder why," said Rella. Her mind went back to the first day she had been in the Greenhouse. She recalled the little girl in the corner who had wanted to be left alone and had lashed out at her when she'd ventured too close.

Then her mind replayed part of a session with Seth. The four-year-old with the blonde pigtails in the white dress. *No one is going to save me.*

"I know who Katie is," Rella said.

"Oh?"

"Ow!"

"What is it?" CJ asked.

"Pain, in my foot. Blocked. Trapped." Rella's mind flashed to bedsheets. She twisted in the chair. "Ow!" Her right hand flew to her left side as though she'd sustained a knife wound. "A grip on my shoulder, my neck, my throat," she managed to get out. The stabbing shot to her back, her lower abdomen, intensifying. Her body stiffened. She curled into a protective position.

"Rella?"

The moaning amplified into short grunts. She pummeled her legs, angrier with each blow.

"I need this to stop, please," CJ said.

It continued.

"I'll have to get Margaret to come in and help."

Slowly, it lessened.

"Is this Katie?"

She tilted her head back, as if it were not attached to her neck and could fall off. She raised her upper lip, exposing teeth.

"Katie, I was asked not to talk to you yet. And I don't want to upset you. Is there a place you can go and rest for a while?"

Katie writhed as though restrained.

"Margaret," CJ called, "could you come and help? Margaret?"

The person slouched in the chair, stretching the legs out. "No, this ain't Margaret."

"I'm sorry."

"She doesn't let anyone near her."

"Do you mean Katie?"

"Yeah. And she doesn't like Margaret. Doesn't like anyone."

"I appreciate you coming to help. And what's your name, please?"

"Max."

"Max, it's nice to meet you. Were you by chance in the Greenhouse the first time we were there?"

"Yeah."

"What's your take on the work we are doing here?"

"I'm with Margaret. Not gonna do any good." He shrugged. "I'm stuck. We all are."

"Where would you like to be?"

"Outta here, on the open road, alone."

"Are you the only person that can be near Katie, calm her down?"

"Yeah."

"It's nice you stay around to help her."

He shrugged.

"Can I ask you what year it is, for you, Max?"

"Yeah, it's '95."

"So," CJ calculated, "that makes you around seventeen, right?"

"Yup."

"Max, it's not 1995. It's actually 2017."

He didn't respond.

"I have a newspaper here." CJ turned to reach for it.

"Who are *you*?" a high-pitched voice demanded.

"Oh! Hello. I'm CJ. And you?"

"Katie!" she yelled.

"I'm sorry, Katie, yes. Do you know where you are?"

"No!"

"Well, we are in my office, having a session. Maybe soon we can talk, but for today, I need to get Rella back."

"I don't want to be here. I want to go home!"

"Okay, let's get you home. Would you like to be tucked into bed?"

"No, no, no!" She hit her legs harder with each objection.

"Right. Sorry. Katie, let's not do that. Let's get Max to come and help you."

CJ waited for Max to help Katie.

Eventually, Rella came to. She rubbed her forehead, new information loading into her brain.

Katie didn't have anger; she had rage. Boiling in a vat. Rella's legs bore the brunt, sore and bruised after Katie showed. At first, Rella assumed Katie pounded out of fury, or to hurt Rella. But then Rella realized she had only ever seen Katie sitting, never standing. She wondered if for some reason her legs didn't work, and it frustrated her. At times Rella could almost hear words in Katie's head. *Get off me.*

At their next session, Rella noticed a new addition to CJ's office: a basket piled with decorative pillows, an effort in response to Katie, perhaps.

"How do their ages work?" Rella asked CJ. "The year they are now is how old I was at the time they first came?"

"That could be the case," CJ replied, "or not. They can be in another year, another time, and hold the memory and sensations of that earlier time. Perhaps they are stuck there. Sometimes older ones are here to help the younger ones."

"Like Max."

"Like Max."

"He stays for Katie. It's a sacrifice."

"Yes, it is," CJ agreed. After a pause, she asked, "How old would you say Margaret is?"

"Twenty-seven? But she seems to exist in both the past and the present, so she would have to be older."

"I think Margaret has been around a long time."

It wasn't the words, but the *way* CJ uttered them.

"Margaret may have a distinctive role," CJ revealed. "As a gatekeeper."

"A gatekeeper?"

"Yes. It's quite a comprehensive job. This person controls access to the front, to you. You can imagine how chaotic it could get if someone didn't manage that."

"Access to the front. Sounds like a battle line."

"In a way, it is. Life becomes a war after abuse. The body is jammed on alert mode, and minor disturbances are amplified because the subconscious holds a catalog of stimuli the conscious mind is unaware of."

"What if this starts happening in my life, outside of here?" Rella asked. "Something could provoke them I know nothing about. It's unnerving."

Another thought entered her mind.

"What's it called when they come out?"

"Some refer to it as switching."

"It's the switching that makes me dizzy, right?"

"Yes, that's likely."

"I'm dizzy most of the time these days."

Twenty-Five

Curious about the job of "Gatekeeper" CJ had mentioned, Rella opened up a web browser to search for the term in relation to dissociative identity disorder.

The Gatekeeper controls switching and access to the front, to certain alters, or to memories. The Gatekeeper is highly stabilizing for a system and can deter unwanted switching. They can help prevent traumatic memories from bleeding from those who hold them to those who could not handle them.

Alters. The people she was meeting.

Bleeding memories. Rella wondered how it was decided who could handle traumatic memories, and who could not.

Rella reflected on this vast job. If Margaret had been brought in to instate order, she had likely arrived at a time when there had already been Others.

They are often or always near the front, so may witness what happens to the system. As a result, they may present as ageless and emotionless, as a way to process and cope.

"Whatcha doing?" Ginnie had come up behind Rella.

Rella jumped and slammed her laptop shut. "Nothing. Research."

"Research." Ginnie nodded slowly. "I love how secretive you are. So mysterious."

"Am I? I guess I'm used to being alone a lot." Rella realized how paradoxical and untrue that statement now was. "I'm going rollerblading tomorrow. Want to join?"

"Rollerblading?" Ginnie threw back her head and laughed. "Haven't done that since I was a kid. I'd look like an ostrich on wheels now. But what the hay, why not? Do they rent them, or should I get some?"

"Hmm . . . I'm not sure." She looked down at Ginnie's feet. "I have an extra pair."

"There's definitely no way I'd fit into yours. Your feet are tiny! I don't mind purchasing. If it goes badly, I'll just donate them."

The next day, outfitted with blades, elbow guards, knee pads, and a helmet, Ginnie made her debut on the Huntington Beach path. Rella giggled as Ginnie floundered at first, but within fifteen minutes, her friend had developed an easy glide.

"You're a natural!" Rella exclaimed. As they weaved in and out between bikers, skaters, and runners, Rella thought about CJ's office, not far away from where they were, and all that had transpired in just a few short weeks.

"Am I talking to Margaret?" CJ asked, at their next session.

Rella felt herself thrust forward as Margaret pulled away. She held on to the armrests of her chair.

"Why did you ask that question?" Rella said, more demand in her voice than warranted.

"It was the way your voice changed—no inflection."

"I don't like this," Rella said, freaked out. "Margaret *spoke* for me."

"You've been doing it all your life. You just never realized it."

What if she became Katie, and stayed that way? Or Margaret? Or someone else?

"What if I can't get back?" Rella asked, more to herself.

"So far, you've always been the one to leave the office."

Rella didn't consider this an answer to her question.

"Why did Margaret show up?"

"Maybe I was asking questions she didn't want you to answer, or hear."

A sentence repeated inside her head. *Nothing goes to her that hasn't gone through me first.*

"She's good," Rella had to admit.

"Yes, and strong." CJ put her pen down. "There's a term used with dissociative identity. It's called ANP. Apparently normal parts of the personality."

"Apparently *normal?* What?"

CJ laughed. "I guess it's not the most endearing description. Basically, it's appearing 'normal' in the sense of not continuously living in a trauma-state. One of the major functions of an ANP would be to pass themselves on as the host, acting like them, answering to their name, and thus deflecting detection. Parts of you have been exemplary at this."

"Host. I sound like a science-fiction movie."

CJ smiled. "One of the core objectives of dissociative identity is to remain hidden, undetected. Last session we talked about you being the person in the front, dealing with

182

the day to day, apparently leading a normal life, to yourself, to the outside world. A little like a blank slate, without the burden of the memories of the past, able to fully function and work and be productive, while others contain the bad stuff."

"It's astonishing that I had no idea whatsoever."

"You were masterful."

Rella wondered if she were even Rella, the same person who was born in July of 1978.

"This job is more difficult with all of this refiling."

"What if we left the files out, Margaret?" CJ asked.

"Then I'd think about them all the time."

"We could keep out one file, see how it goes."

"She doesn't know where the file room is."

"Who doesn't? Rella?"

Silence.

"Margaret, can you see, in the file room, if there are any files on someone younger than age four?"

"I'm not sure. Some drawers have been stuck since I arrived."

"Who put those files there?"

"I don't know."

"Margaret, what is causing the pain in Rella? Are you?"

"No."

"Someone else?"

CJ repeated the question.

"I can't talk about it," she finally replied.

"Are you in control of everything, Margaret?"

She didn't answer.

"If you are, then you are in control of the pain."

"I'm not," she conceded.

"Then who is?"

She paused. "He is."

"He? Who is *he*?"

No answer.

"So, you are second in command?"

Margaret nodded slowly.

"Then, he is controlling the pain."

"Maybe, maybe not. I'm not told every detail. I was hired to clean up and put the files away and maintain organization."

"Does he have a name?"

No answer.

"Are you fearful of him?"

"No."

"Has he ever treated you badly?"

"He hit me once."

"Why? Had you looked into a file?"

"Yes."

"What did it say?"

"I don't remember. But it was shocking."

"Has he become angry at anyone else?"

"He yelled at Max."

"What did Max do?"

Margaret didn't answer.

"And what about Anna? You mentioned she can be contrary."

"She recognizes his power. Mostly adheres."

"Is he always listening?"

No answer.

"Always watching?"

No answer.

"Is it fair to say he has access to the others? Do they adhere to his rules?"

"There are files all over the floor now," she criticized.

"I am pulling out the files and you have to put them away again," CJ acknowledged.

"Yes," Margaret replied, irritated.

"And he is not pleased."

"No."

"Does he have a key too?"

"He doesn't need one."

"Does he cause pain to anyone?"

No response.

"Does anyone other than you know about him?"

"Yes."

"He can influence them?"

No answer.

"Was it his request I not talk to Katie?"

No answer.

"Well, perhaps you can tell me more about Katie. What is she doing right now?"

"She sits under the tree."

"Can you describe Katie to me?"

"She has blonde hair, wears a white dress. She hates the dress."

"Can she change? Perhaps we can use a changing room."

"She won't go in. She doesn't like walls. Only open spaces."

"Is her dress clean or dirty?"

"Clean."

"Margaret, I have an important question. Is Katie separate from Rella?"

"Of course."

"Could she sit in that chair over there?" CJ pointed to the one adjacent.

"Yes. But she won't."

"Why?"

No answer.

"Could she sit on the floor, right now, away from Rella?"

"Yes."

"And I could see her?"

"Yes."

"So, you view her and Rella as different people."

"Of course."

"Am I trying your patience?"

"Yes."

"I'm sorry. I just wanted to establish something. Moving on. Does Katie like to play with toys?"

"No. She is obstinate."

"Is she in pain?"

"She stabs."

"She does? People?"

"No."

"She may lack reassurance and love. Children look for their needs to be met."

"I am not her mother."

"No. Has Katie ever been scared, or felt alone?"

Grunting flared, hitting of the legs.

CJ's eyes shifted to the basket on the floor. Rella hadn't taken a pillow.

"Katie, please calm down," CJ said. She reached for one of the cushions. "You could hurt Rella. Can I put one of these on your lap?"

Katie hit harder and made more forceful noises.

"Katie, there is nothing here to harm you."

Katie alternated between putting her hands over her ears and beating her legs.

"I'm sorry if I upset you."

Katie calmed.

"Would you like me to ask Max to take you to your tree?"

She dropped back against the chair. Her eyes rolled upwards.

"Katie?" CJ asked.

The posture changed, straightened.

"She is hard to control—especially now," Margaret said, lowering her gaze to meet CJ's eyes.

"We're not aiming to control her. Just understand her."

Margaret didn't answer.

"Margaret, I'd like to keep talking about the pain. Is there a file on headaches?"

"Yes."

"Whose names are on it?"

"Rella's. And Anna's."

CJ noticed a subtle agitation. "What? Is there another name?"

Margaret bent her head ever so slightly.

"Can you tell me?"

"He might get mad."

"I don't want you to get punished later."

Margaret's hand went to her head.

"Margaret?"

"I'm fine."

"Is someone inflicting pain on you?"

Margaret winced nearly imperceptibly. "It's a girl's name."

"Katie's name?"

"No. I have never seen this name before."

"You don't know who this person is?"

"No."

"I'll leave it up to you if you want to tell me. I don't want to make anyone mad."

Margaret pursed her lips. "This is ridiculous—files popping up all over the place." An air of defiance in her voice, she said, "I'll take my chances."

CJ waited.

"Lisa."

"Lisa," CJ restated. "Margaret, how many of you are there?"

No answer.

Twenty-Six

In a cramped two-bedroom apartment located above Pazzi Pizzeria in the heart of Brooklyn, on a stifling day in August of 1972, Lena Laurino's water broke—the same day the family car conked out.

Her husband patted her hand throughout the contractions as she laid into him with every toiling push—at having a busted car the day she went into labor, at how repulsed she was with the smell of garlic from below.

Two hours later, Chiarina Jovanna Laurino kicked up her own ruckus as she entered the world. Her mother gazed down at her, sweat glistening her brow and chest, a loving smile on her face. She told Mr. Laurino to order her up an olive, pepper, and broccoli calzone, with a side of hot sauce.

Her mother, Lena, loved telling the story.

By the age of six, it was clear Chiarina was her mother's daughter, outspoken and opinionated.

"It's stupid to have concrete in a playground," Chiarina said as she examined her injured knee.

"You think everything is stupid," a boy classmate scoffed.

"I certainly think *you're* stupid, Dino Moretti!" she retorted.

No newcomer to schoolyard tussles, she was sent home with a note from the principal and an additional skinned knee.

"Do you hear this, Stefano? Do you hear what your daughter did?" Lena said from the kitchen as she fed the three youngest.

Chiarina and her father exchanged devious smiles. She ran over to him and jumped in his lap.

"That Moretti kid had it coming!" he whispered in her ear.

Chiarina grinned broadly.

"What are you saying to her?"

Stefano squeezed his daughter's hand and spoke loudly enough for Lena to hear.

"Now, CJ, school prepares you for life. Better to be nice—when you can."

"Her name is Chiarina Jovanna. *Not* CJ," Lena reproved.

"I like CJ. It's *my* name, after all!" CJ pointed out emphatically.

Her father laughed.

Lena threw her hands up in the air. "I make a good pie, I make a *bellissima panzanella*. I make a risotto that puts Mrs. Esposito's to shame. You, your father—you make noise."

"You don't make noise, Dad," CJ said softly.

In truth, he seldom uttered a peep. While both of her parents worked equally hard, CJ felt sorry for her father. He would rather be home, in the kitchen and with the kids, than running all over Brooklyn in a temperamental relic, delivering restaurant supplies. He made a lot of sacrifices for his family.

Twelve years later, when CJ finished high school with honors, her father stood taller and clapped louder than any other parent present. Despite his humble profession, he'd accrued more than a modest sum, which he presented to her as a surprise. CJ refused, her own pile of pennies earned from after-school jobs stashed in the bank, but he had insisted. She'd used only what was necessary, keeping the rest safe should any of her family members need it.

The day she left for the west coast, having been accepted at a university in Washington, her mother had cried enough tears to fill the Hudson, while her father held his in. Lena had folded her classified recipe for ribollita into her daughter's hand, as if worried she would never eat again.

"Bread and vegetables," Lena had said. "Easy to make."

CJ had not foreseen a career as a licensed clinical social worker, but after taking two psychology classes as part of the minimum core requirements, she added more, quickly realizing her enthusiasm for the complexities of the human brain far exceeded her preliminary interest in analyzing enterprise operations and performance evaluations. She changed her major from business management to psychology, followed by a move to California for a master's in social work.

The Golden State flaunted contagiously perky people and oodles of intoxicating sunshine compared to the irascible inhabitants and cramped sidewalks lined with brownstones of her hometown in the Northeast. CJ strolled the boardwalk on free weekends, surfers dotting the Pacific like seals, the scent of pasta primavera beckoning from trattorias brimming with outdoor diners. It was a lifestyle hard not to love.

She'd found another unexpected love in the form of a man named Kyle Deter, a newly appointed professor who taught instructional planning and educational assessment to aspiring elementary-grade schoolteachers. They'd met at a mixer CJ had been dragged to by a friend, said friend having quickly abandoned her the minute she'd found her target professional contact.

CJ wouldn't describe it as love at first sight, as Kyle did, for such nonsense didn't exist in her mind. It had taken Kyle multiple efforts and some innovative planning before CJ had agreed to a date.

Five months later, CJ had casually invited him to New York over one of the school breaks, to meet her parents, stipulating that he would have to secure his own accommodations. He willingly and earnestly accepted.

CJ's black locks and Italian skin tanned by the Pacific coast sun provided a striking contrast to Kyle's blond hair and Oregon complexion. Her mother had eyed him suspiciously as he'd sunk his fork into her lasagna. Anyone that skinny couldn't appreciate good food, she had surmised, but when he'd not only finished the first robust portion he'd been served, but then asked if he could have seconds, Lena's 96-degree setting warmed up to 375, and she heaped three more scoops onto his plate.

Kyle later confessed to CJ that he'd been unable to eat for two days after the meal, but it had been worth it, to make her mother happy.

She married him six months later.

Years had passed, and at times she still missed the nip of winter winds racing around ruddy brick buildings and good old-fashioned Italian arguments over faulty politics and pepperoni.

In Brooklyn, there was no pretense. People said what they meant, didn't mince words; they didn't add water to the marinara. They dished it out straight.

Many of the people she'd met in California were soufflés—more hot air than substance. Once in a while she'd mention the idea of leaving to Kyle, but their lives and that of their son, Bryce, were stirred into the pot of Southern California.

Huntington Beach—April 2017

CJ arrived at the Shipley Nature Center at promptly 8:55 a.m. on a Wednesday morning, five minutes prior to opening time, before any possible crowds, the sun high in the sky.

"Mornin', CJ."

"Good morning, Alden," she replied, dropping five dollars in the donation box, more than the suggested amount.

"Enjoy your promenade." The elderly gentleman tipped his hat.

"See you in a couple of hours."

CJ went left on the loop, passing a reproduction Native American reed hut. She made her way over the footbridge, past willows, entering the Southern Oak Woodland habitat.

CJ appreciated the normalcy and intelligence of trees. They recorded history in their rings, and had eyes and ears in a different way, sharing knowledge and nutrients, communicating with each other through an underground system in the soil. She thought about internal human functions, how much they operated out of sight.

As CJ neared the meadow, she wondered if it resembled the one where Katie's tree was planted.

Rella's mind had done an absolutely thorough job of sealing her memory. If CJ were to liken Rella to a tree, it would be a birch. White, thin, and unassuming, it still withstood the toughest winds.

While volunteering for two summers at the Angeles National Forest, CJ had learned that adversarial wind gave a tree its strength. Trees exposed to the pressures of the wind compensated by forming reaction wood, or stress wood, composed of a different structure of cellulose.

Children were saplings planted in a world where the wind could be vicious rather than constructive. Instead of making them stronger, it broke them. At times, irreparably.

In addition to wind, trees also needed light, and they would stretch and grow as needed to reach it. Katie was denied this element. Confined to the shade, she couldn't reach the sun. She seemed unable to stand, pummeled her legs.

CJ believed there was a connection. Katie had not been allowed to grow up. She was consigned close to the ground, like stinging nettle, a weed avoided for the sharp hairs on its leaves that released pain-causing chemicals when coming into contact with skin. Its defense mechanism, to repel.

She wanted Katie to believe she could run, play, smile. She could leave her spot under that tree. She was no longer in the situation that had rooted her in forsaken, lifeless earth.

CJ pulled up to the school entrance. First graders poured out of the building, their lively chorus chiming in the air. Her fingers tightened around the steering wheel, thinking how not all children were able to join in such carefree song. She loved her job, but it wasn't easy. It left a sap-like residue that never came off.

She exited the car.

"Mommy!" Bryce ran towards her.

"Hey, B!" CJ knelt, wrapping him in her arms. She'd make sure her little tree received all the sunlight, water, and care he needed, and hoped he would only confront the kind of wind that made him solid, not splintered.

Twenty-Seven

Laguna Beach—Early May 2017

Rella headed out into the sunshine to pull weeds, the simple task helpful after sessions, satisfying, the soil between her fingers therapeutic.

To her tremendous surprise and delight, she stumbled onto a strawberry patch in one corner of the yard, partially hidden among the brush, bounteous with fruit.

She excitedly ran into the house for something to put them in. Gathering the bright red strawberries brought a joy she'd not experienced in some time.

By the time she was done, the yield overflowed three containers.

She rinsed some and put them in a bowl. They were soft, perfectly ripe, and bursting with flavor. After months of struggling to eat and keep food down, she appreciated and savored each morsel, feeling good afterwards rather than sick.

"I can live on berries!" she announced happily.

The next day, Rella returned home from work, eagerly anticipating another bowl of freshly picked berries.

Walking up to the patch, she found it completley destroyed.

I must have the wrong area, she thought.

She circled the yard, ending back at the deathbed that used to be the strawberry patch.

"This can't be!" she said aloud. "Who would do this?" Tears filled her eyes.

She spotted the gardener's truck leaving. She ran over.

"Hey, miss," one of the guys said.

"What happened over there? Did you do that?"

"We had to cut the grass."

"Didn't you see the strawberry patch?"

"It was easier to mow the whole yard. It will grow back."

Rella had precious few crumbs of happiness in her life at the moment. Just as she was about to shrivel in dismay, emotional apathy coursed through her like an IV.

Her tears dried up, and her posture lengthened.

"You're fired," she stated coolly. "Don't expect payment, and don't ever come back."

"But, miss—"

"Leave this property at once."

It wasn't until she went outside the next morning and glanced in the direction of the yard where the berries used to be that Rella remembered what had happened, and she dissolved into tears.

"You look down today, Rella," CJ said with concern when Rella arrived for therapy.

Drenched in sadness, Rella told CJ what had happened.

"I'm so sorry, Rella," CJ empathized.

Rella nodded a thank-you, reaching for tissues.

"Do you want to talk about it?"

Her head lowered. "I just want to find a place where no one will bother me."

CJ took a moment. "This may sound like a silly question, but who am I talking to?"

Rella's body became tingly and alert but desensitized at the same time. A presence. Then Rella was gone.

The feet swayed, not touching the floor in the oversize chair.

"As soon as I'm happy, something *ruins* it." She gulped, then let out a sigh.

"Who am I talking to?"

Her head dropped further. "Lisa."

"Hi, Lisa, I'm CJ. It's nice to meet you."

"Nice to meet you too," she replied, in a sweet child's voice.

"Lisa, are you talking about the strawberry patch?"

"I loved the strawberries! It was mean! It was just mean!"

"Something was taken away from you that you loved."

"It was so beautiful, and they hurt it. I don't even like to see a broken flower. I don't want it in my mind anymore. Make it go away."

"Lisa, I'm very sorry that happened. You're right. It's not fair."

"It's not fair—it's not fair!"

"We could change the topic, if you'd like."

Lisa rubbed her nose with the back of her hand and shrugged.

"What do you like to do, Lisa?"

"Be in my playroom and color in my books at my table and play with Strawberry Shortcake!"

"Are you in your playroom now?"

"Yes."

"How old are you, Lisa?"

"I'm seven," she stated proudly.

"Seven, wow. What school do you go to?"

"I don't go to school. My mommy loves me so much she wants me with her. All. The. Time." Lisa's head tipped right to left.

"Are you working on something right now?"

"Oh, yes. I always am. I must pick the right colors and always stay in the lines!" she said, emphatically shaking her forefinger in the air. "Powder blue for the sky. Have to be careful not to mix the blue and the green."

"What are you wearing, Lisa?"

"I have on my *crisp* white shirt and a blue smock, so I keep neat and clean."

"Are your legs covered?"

"I don't like pants. I want my legs free!"

"I don't blame you. What's on your feet?"

"White socks and black shoes." Her legs continued to sway.

"Lisa, do you get headaches?"

Lisa grimaced. "Yes."

"Did your headaches start before you turned seven?"

Lisa scrunched her nose.

"How often does your head hurt?"

"I don't like the house! I don't ever want to go there again."

"What house, Lisa?"

"The house, the house. Where's the purple crayon? Here it is. Blue and purple are my favorite colors."

"If I went by this house, would it look like a regular house to me?"

Lisa didn't answer. Instead, she said, "Raspberry Tart's hat is purple."

"What does the house look like to you?"

"Yucky. Ugly. With teeth and eyes." Her hands stretched. "Yellow for the sun!"

"Could you draw the house for me?"

"I don't draw so good."

"That's okay."

"I don't want to draw it. I want to burn it down so nobody else goes in there."

"I'd like to see what you see."

"Fine," Lisa mumbled.

"Here, I have paper and a pen."

Lisa took the materials and began. Pausing, she looked at the drawing, fisted the pen, and scribbled all over it.

"Lisa, is your playroom in this house?"

"No way!"

"Lisa, can I tell you something?"

"What?"

"Rella is thirty-eight years old. It's thirty-one years later."

"Later than what? And who's Rella?"

"It's 2017, Lisa."

"You don't make any sense."

"I will explain it to you sometime," CJ said.

"I don't want this anymore." Lisa handed over the notepad

and pen. "I don't want to see that picture. Make it go away."

CJ took the paper and pen.

"I'm going back to coloring. It's much *nicer*. I like *nicer*."

"I can understand."

Lisa inhaled slowly and exhaled in one short puff. "I should tell you, and you should know—Anna and Margaret fight."

"Ah."

"But I'm no tattletale!"

"No, of course not. Thank you for telling me, Lisa."

"Mm. Anna talks and opens drawers. Margaret scolds. Wants it or-der-*ly*. Anna knows things," she said conspiratorially, lowering her voice. "Margaret doesn't."

"I see. How about you?"

"I stay in my playroom."

"You must like to run and play outside too," CJ said.

"I used to. But I can't run anymore."

"Oh? Why is that?"

"My legs have turned to wood! Wood is dead."

"Do they hurt?"

"Yeah, kinda."

"Lisa, maybe we can help your legs."

Lisa shrugged.

"I could demonstrate—that way I don't have to come close."

"Sure," she said unenthusiastically.

"Cross your arms over your chest, like I'm doing, see? Now, lightly pat where your fingers are. How's that?"

"Fine."

"Good. Here is what we are going to think about."

Lisa appeared hazed, fading. Her legs slowed their swinging and her hands dropped.

"Lisa?" CJ asked.

Her breathing seemed to momentarily stop.

"Lisa?" CJ repeated.

"Where am I?" The voice was soft-spoken.

"Hello." CJ waited a minute, observing. "I can see this isn't Lisa. I'm CJ. Have we met before?"

"I've heard of this place."

"What year is it for you?"

"There are no years."

"How tall are you?"

"Like a normal person."

"What is your name?"

"Name?"

"Could Margaret tell us?"

She slowly shook her head.

"She can't, or she is refusing, or you are refusing?"

Her head swayed like a pendulum in a thick breeze. "I don't feel my body."

"Where is it?"

"It disappears."

Rella left CJ's office after that day's session with, as usual, little memory of what had transpired when someone else took her place. Faint sensations lingered in her body. Her right ankle tingly, cold. The feeling climbed, looped up one leg, circled the other, diffused into both knees, erasing them away.

She made it to the car just as her legs became unsteady. She sat, with the door open.

Fragmented details of the sessions would often filter through on her drive home. She readied her voice recorder, waited for the blood to return to her lower extremities, and drove away.

On the way, she spoke aloud whatever thoughts came, in whatever order they arrived, even if they didn't make much sense. By the time she got home, most of the session had left her memory.

Exhausted, Rella turned down the bed. She'd graduated from keeping the bedroom completely bright to using a lone, small lamp on the floor near her.

Two hours later, she woke, sensing a presence in the room.

At the end of the bed was a shadowed shape, with the height and build of a child. Her long hair hung in strings around her head, and she had old, dried, brown blood caked on her clothes.

Rella reached for the light on the floor, raising it, vanquishing the girl to a silhouette in her mind.

"Who is she?" CJ asked Rella at their next appointment, after she'd recounted what happened that night.

"I couldn't see her face."

"Is she someone we've met before?"

Rella shook her head. "I don't think so." Rella sighed. "I feel terrible. All these people—I should have known and acknowledged them a long time ago." She looked up at CJ.

"Thank you for helping me—and them—for creating a place they felt they could come out, safely, after all that's happened."

"Of course."

"All right. We keep going."

"Let's look inside," CJ suggested.

Once Rella went "inside," she stepped away from any control she had over her mind. In CJ's office, it had become nearly effortless, like gliding outside on ice on a still, gray day.

A few moments later Rella whispered, "I see her."

"What is she doing?"

"Standing quietly, hands by her side, head down."

"And it's not Lisa?"

"No."

After Lisa had first come forward, Rella later saw her clearly in her playroom, sitting at her table, working on projects.

Lisa was different from the others.

The Others. They were real people to her now.

Lisa had no job, as Margaret and Max did; no engulfing pain and fatigue like Anna; no eruptive emotions like Katie. She gave the impression of a merry, friendly, well-adjusted kid.

This poor little girl looked as though she'd known only horrors. Her shadow was white, her body nearly see-through. Rella wanted to cradle this broken doll.

"What is she wearing?"

"A dress, long, baggy, like a sack worn by impoverished children in the olden days, dull white, covered in dried blood. Her shoes are tall, old-fashioned, swallowing her ankles."

The only flesh visible was at her neckline, and her stick-thin arms. Ethereal.

Her eyes met Rella's.

"Oh!" Rella cried out, pained by their imploring.

"Rella?" CJ said.

She cleared her throat. "She doesn't have a voice," she replied evenly.

"Is this Margaret?"

"Yes."

"Who doesn't have a voice? This little girl? Do you know her name, Margaret?"

"Abigail."

"Abigail." CJ wrote it down. "Did Abigail write on the notepad the other day? The words *Help me?*"

Margaret didn't answer.

"I like to be in my playroom!"

"Lisa?"

"Yes, it's Lisa."

"Lisa, is Abigail there with you, in your playroom?"

Lisa sighed. "Yes. She is standing here at the table. Staring. She smells funny."

"She hasn't been taken care of for some time," CJ told her.

Lisa didn't look up. She wanted to stay absorbed in her project.

"Abigail can change her clothes, put on something fresh and clean. You like things nice. Maybe she would too. There is a dressing room, right behind that curtain. Do you see it?"

"I don't like curtains," Lisa informed her. "And Abigail doesn't either."

"But it's a magic curtain. She can see out of it, but no one else can see in."

Lisa rolled her eyes. "There's no such thing as magic."

CJ chuckled. "You're right."

"She can wear a pair of my shorts and a shirt from my drawer, if she wants, but I'm going to keep coloring."

"That's very nice of you. I'm sure she will appreciate that."

CJ waited a few minutes. "Has she come back to the playroom in the new clothes?"

"Yes."

"How does she look?"

"They're really big on her."

"How does she seem? Happier?"

Lisa shrugged. "I'd be glad to be out of that yucky dress. But her hair is still icky."

"Can you fix it for her?"

"We need to wash it," Lisa appraised the situation authoritatively.

Abigail sat motionless as Lisa tended to her hair, rinsing away years of neglect, then gently scraping a brush through the knotted strands. She looked like a different girl when Lisa was done, though her straw-colored hair remained listless compared to Lisa's glossy near-black locks.

Lisa sighed in irritation.

"What is it?" CJ asked.

"She wants to hurt her arms."

"She does?"

"She wants to cut up her arms and see the blood. She's weird."

"Abigail needs to cut herself in order to feel," CJ explained. "I know that probably doesn't make sense to you."

"No." Lisa liked to stay in her playroom, minding her own business. She didn't want outsiders, and she didn't want mess.

"Are her old clothes visible? If she wants, she can look at the blood there; she doesn't have to create any new blood."

"She doesn't look convinced," Lisa said.

"Perhaps you can keep her occupied. Is she still with you?"

"She's standing at the end of my table, staring at me."

"I'd like to talk to Margaret. Will you two be all right together?"

"I suppose."

"I will leave you both in the playroom, then. Margaret, could we speak?" CJ waited.

As if tossed overboard, she sank. *Look up, look up.* Pressure on all sides, the sky unreachable.

Abruptly, she swam up out of it, her head suddenly above water, in a vast sea. Waves of nausea timed with the current, up and down.

"I feel sick."

"Who is this, please?"

"The rocking. I hate the rocking."

"Where are you?"

"Get me off this boat."

"Who is this?"

From somewhere within, she heard *Rella.*

It took longer than usual for Rella to return to the room, and she felt queasy for the rest of the day, as if the ground were moving unremittingly beneath her.

Twenty-Eight

Since the devastating death of the strawberry patch a few weeks ago, Rella couldn't bring herself to pull weeds after therapy sessions anymore, so she turned to puzzles instead. It gave her satisfaction to work on something she had the ability to solve. Jigsaw puzzles were a relatively easy undertaking—a fixed number of pieces; no surprises.

Therapy resembled an upside-down puzzle with backwards pieces, secrets scattered in the words of the Others. Each session sprinkled droplets, clues, but how to connect them stayed out of reach. There was no cardboard box with the picture of the end result.

Rella wondered if she would need to be able to see all the pieces in order to be put back together again. She hoped not.

It still didn't feel like *truth* to her. If she couldn't remember it, it didn't happen.

Darkness encircled the perimeter, a spotlight illuminating only what she was permitted to see. Lisa concentrating on a current project, her bangs framing—but also slightly shielding—her face.

Rella felt like an intruding spy. She squinted her eyes to see the surface Lisa was working on, a small table similar to the one Rella remembered having in *her* playroom. She'd spend hours there, drawing the day away. She had been Lisa's age at the time.

A shiver went through her.

"What is Lisa doing?" CJ asked.

"Drawing, coloring." She was a little chubbier than Rella at that age.

"Is Abigail there too?"

"No."

"Have you seen Abigail since?"

"Yes."

"Is she still in the clean clothes?"

"No. She is back in the dirty dress."

"Hmm."

To Rella, it seemed permanent change wasn't possible for any of them. She had wondered more than a handful of times if the sessions were just taking a needle and thread to air.

"What else do you see?"

Rella continued to allow Lisa's world to unfold, wondering if Lisa had created it, or if it had been created for her. Through the walls of the playroom, she saw a kitchen. A young woman prepared lunch, whirling happily around the room.

"I see someone else. Her mother. Lisa's mother. She doesn't look like my mother. She's in a spotless kitchen with shiny, old-fashioned appliances, wearing an apron and a full-circle swing dress. Looks like it's right out of *The Donna Reed Show*."

Lisa needed this mom, one who made her favorite sandwich daily. Lisa liked order and consistency. She liked routine.

"Let's ask Lisa if she knows about the abdominal pain," CJ said.

Lisa's head shot up, but rather than Lisa's face, Rella saw the evil one.

"Uh!"

"What happened?"

"Why do I keep seeing these masks? Why would Lisa be wearing one? Why would she want to scare me?"

"Sometimes different parts of your personality wear masks to frighten, as a protection. For themselves, and, maybe in this case, for you."

"To keep me in the dark?"

"Yes, perhaps. Something is obstructing you from healing," CJ said. "If you could describe pain, in general, what words would you use?"

"It's black and tall and oval. A gravestone. Marking the buried. Holding ground. Solid, immovable. A muscle's scream." Rella's own description intrigued her. "The mask is someone other than Lisa, bullying me. It's like he has control, and relishes taking it away from me."

"He."

"I'm not sure where that sentence came from."

"Margaret has mentioned a 'he' also."

It's not one of us wearing the mask. It's a memory. Her memory. Only she and Rella can see it.

Somewhere Rella heard this sentence in her mind. Maybe the 'he' was the last deadbolt to be unlocked.

"Let's try again." Rella softened her eyes. Her head tingled as she slipped away.

A smug smile curved the lips.

"Hello. Do I know you?" CJ asked. "Do you not want Rella to have any information about the abdominal pain?"

The smirk widened.

"Do you enjoy hurting Rella? Have you hurt her before? Have you kept information from her?"

Rella's body jolted forward, as if someone had pushed her from behind.

"Rella?"

"Unacceptable."

"What?"

"This mask business."

"Margaret?"

"Yes."

"Hello, Margaret. We are being blocked from learning more."

Suddenly, she doubled over.

"Ow, ow, ow."

"What's going on? Is this Rella? Who is feeling this pain?"

"It's so sharp. Piercing." The person rocked. Sipped breath.

"Who is here now?" CJ asked.

"It's Anna."

"Anna. Hello."

"Hello," Anna returned, voice constrained.

"Anna, maybe I can help with this pain. It seems severe."

"Debilitating. I get through it somehow."

"Let's get you into the present. Do you know what year it is?"

"Yes, yes. I have been following all along. I want her to get better."

"Have you been behind Rella seeking help before?"

"Yes."

"If you were to go back in time, Anna, when would you say your pain first developed?"

"I feel I was born with pain."

"That is entirely possible."

"I see a hospital sometimes. White sheets. A girl. I hear screaming." Anna continued to rock, holding her side. "I need to get away from here. It's best when I only observe. I never mean to cause Rella pain."

"I don't think you are causing Rella pain. Who is?"

"Pain obliterates thought. All you can think of is pain."

"Where is the pain, Anna, exactly?"

"Inside, outside. Attacking the uterus."

"Attacking? Who would do that?"

"Katie."

"Katie?" CJ said, surprised. "Why would Katie do that?"

"She thinks she is pregnant."

"Why would a four-year-old think she is pregnant?" CJ asked through gritted teeth.

The body languished, as though a heavy weight had descended upon it.

"Oh, this is horrible."

"This no longer sounds like Anna," said CJ.

"Sinking. Fog." The person started to cry. "Ending."

"Who is this, please?"

She bent forward, arms wrapped around her waist.

"Uh," she moaned.

"Anna?"

"Yes."

"Anna, what happened just now?"

"I was gone. I'm not like the others. I don't take over. It's not right. It's her body, after all."

"True."

Holding her side, she bent to the right. "I have information that Rella may not be able to handle."

"Were you ever in control of the file room, Anna?"

"It was so cold. The cement floor. So dusty. I was there too long. It weakened me. I'm always so tired. I need to lie down."

Gradually, the hands fell away from the body.

The posture straightened.

"Margaret?"

"Yes."

"How is Anna doing?"

"I don't check on her."

"A person came for a few minutes who was not Anna. Do you know anything about that?"

Margaret did not answer.

"Margaret, if we thought of a labeling system, where green-tabbed files are nonthreatening, neutral, or happy information, yellow files could be considered to contain possibly hurtful information, and red files are high-risk, what color are most of the files?"

"Yellow or red."

"You mentioned some files are thick, and some thin. What color are the thin files?"

"Green."

"And the thicker files? Those are yellow or red?"

"Yes."

"Are pages ever missing out of any files?"

"Yes."

"Who takes them?"

"Maybe Anna. She's always causing trouble. But," Margaret paused, "that wouldn't make sense."

"If all the pages of a green file were restored, would it change color?"

"Yes."

"What color would it become? Red?"

"Possibly."

"Rella hasn't met many of the people coming forward. Does each have their own file?"

"She doesn't like the information."

"Does Rella remember anything after the sessions?"

"Some. Most of it is wiped."

"Wiped?"

"From her mind and put into a file."

"How big is Rella's file?"

Margaret pursed her lips. "Thin. Almost empty."

"That might not be so helpful anymore. She is getting to know the parts."

Margaret frowned.

"What's wrong, Margaret?"

"Parts. We aren't a car."

"I apologize."

"My job is to keep her mind clear."

"Rella is putting in a lot of effort."

"She never felt crazy before all this."

"She's not crazy."

<hr />

Another session.

The body was unfamiliar. A scar at the top of the right knee. She wondered how it had gotten there. She rotated her hands slowly.

"Who is with me?" asked CJ.

With her, *was* her.

"Rella?"

Rella returned, grabbed the armrests. "Whew, I feel . . . seasick."

"Seasick?" CJ wrote that down.

Rella opened and closed her mouth, her saliva pasty.

"I think a new part—person—came," CJ said.

Rella had learned how to tell when someone she already knew had been out. It didn't feel like that now. "Yes, I think so."

"Are you back?"

"Mostly."

"Tell me what it's like for you, as you're—leaving the beach, so to speak."

"A dream waking up from a dream. Layers . . . levels of water in an ocean. From the shallow to the subterranean and in between. The closer I am to the top, the more I remember.

But the deeper I've gone—those thoughts and what has transpired, stay there. They don't come back with me."

"Levels of water in an ocean."

"Sometimes I'm between people. In gray shadows with ambiguous borders, a limbo state—not me, but not anyone else I can determine. At a loss for words and thoughts, muddled between minds."

"Sometimes I can tell when that happens," said CJ.

"I wasn't feeling any internal pain earlier today, before coming here—the period-like pain. Now I do."

Rella would have much preferred a simple, uncomplicated body, minus all the parts that brought grief.

Growing up, she'd been a tomboy, wearing mostly boys' clothes, choosing GoBots over Barbie, preferring blue rather than pink. She'd never played house, pretended to be a mother, or had a baby doll. Instead, she'd daydreamed about escaping for a month or two to hike in the woods, carrying only a backpack and art supplies, camping wherever she ended up, warming herself by a fire at night, and sleeping on the forest floor.

But it always came back to the big red X permanently defiling her calendar.

"The average woman spends ten years of her life having a period."

"Ugh," CJ commiserated.

"It's disgusting. Girls as young as eleven, twelve, thirteen having to deal with that nonsense. They are still children. Makes me so angry."

Her fists clenched.

"Who do you feel right now, Rella?"

"Katie," she said, teeth gnashed.

"Try and stay in the room."

Rella thought of work, babbling streams, the sound of wind. Katie subsided.

"Good," CJ said. "How's the pain?"

"Still there. I want to go back to the way I used to be." The statement stung a little. She didn't wish to negate the Others. "The pain was the same, and at least my mind wasn't tormented."

"You aren't going to want to hear this, but things will never be exactly how they were formerly."

Rella knew this. *Lifelong condition.* She'd seen it online when reading up on dissociative identity disorder, learning that the therapy process for DID was "long and slow."

"I can barely drink water anymore. It turns to sludge in my stomach. I want to get something out of me, throw it up. But thoughts, dreams, feelings, they're not in the stomach. I can't reach the bottom." Rella sighed. "I'm not me anymore. And I can't get back. I'm exhausted."

"This takes more out of you than you realize."

"I never would have known if I hadn't had gone to see Seth Jabez."

"Considering how many years had passed, I tend to agree. You may have just continued living your life in the same way." CJ paused. "If you really think about it, are there any signs you can recall from your past, even recently?"

Rella closed her eyes for a moment, then opened them to look directly at CJ.

"My ability to unplug from feelings, emotions—how at times, if I hear or see something upsetting, I completely forget about it, unless something triggers a reminder. Is that Margaret?"

"I think so."

"Huh." For the first time since her diagnosis, Rella recognized interceding assistance. "Is Margaret always listening?"

"I would imagine, to some extent."

"An overpowering urge came over me that night I was so scared in the house; I wanted to hurl heavy objects. I searched the cupboard for cans, anything heavy. I'd forgotten all about that until just now."

"Kind of sounds like Katie."

Rella sat, knitting her thoughts together.

"That was before I went to Atlanta. Before I saw Seth."

CJ nodded slowly.

"Margaret and Katie—they came out before the TDT."

"Yes."

"How long have I had this condition?" Rella nearly whispered.

"I would imagine since childhood."

A chill coursed through Rella.

"If you were to scan your life, what you can remember, you might see evidence of it from even the earliest chapters."

Twenty-Nine

Rella took a drive up to Old Towne Orange, finding a parking spot adjacent to the Plaza Square Park. The fountain in the center bubbled over into a basin of bright blue-green water.

Where she lived by the ocean, homes were newer, and she enjoyed stepping back in time as she meandered along the sidewalks, the assortment of architectural styles a delight. The spiraling towers of the Victorian. The low roofline of the Prairie. The white stucco and orange roofs of the Spanish Colonial Revival. She imagined what the town had looked like in 1871 when founded, momentarily closing her eyes to transport there.

She turned a corner and faced a gabled two-story with wraparound porch and matching fence, similar to the kind of house she pictured Anna in, when she retired to her country bedroom, in the solace of green hills, no other houses in sight.

An image of a horse and buggy trotted through Rella's mind, riding away upon the sound of a car's horn. She continued on, humming, enjoying the pleasant May day.

After surrounding herself with artifacts from bygone eras in the many antique stores, she headed for a darling, somewhat health-conscious, restaurant, located in a historic bungalow.

"How many?" the hostess asked from her outdoor station on the patio.

"Just me," Rella replied.

"Inside or out?"

Although Rella loved being outside, the charm of the interior beckoned. "Inside, please."

"All-righty."

Rella followed her up the path to the entrance, puffs of pomegranate-hued rhododendrons and sunflowers edging the way. They moved through the rooms filled with chatter and bric-a-brac decor.

"Here we are." She dropped the menu and skittered away.

Rella sat, her back to the wall, facing the room, where she could see everything.

A smiling waiter placed a cup of water on the table. "Need a few minutes?"

"No, I'm ready to order."

"Tell me."

"Grand Salad, no celery, with lemon and tahini."

"Anything else?"

Rella wondered if she should chance it. "Super Seed Spinach Wrap, no corn, extra carrot ginger dressing on the side," she added, smiling. Having a hearty appetite was exciting.

"Super." He put the pencil in his ear, removed the menu, and headed away.

Minutes later, she looked up. Her shoulders slipped back; her chin slightly raised. She carefully unrolled the thin paper napkin, revealing the cutlery. She raised each utensil. Thin.

Unpolished. Simple. What a vagabond might use to dine. She was not fond of it.

Her eyes canvassed the room, landing on a shelf of tea sets on display.

"Banal," she uttered aloud.

" 'Scuze me?" the waiter said, placing a bowl down.

Rella blinked. "What?" She noticed the salad. "This looks wonderful, thank you."

"The wrap will be out shortly."

"No rush." Rella picked up the fork and gathered leaves. She chomped, enjoying the crunch.

A bell tolled in the distance.

CJ saw a change come over Rella, an expression of confusion clouding her face, eyes surveying the room, then looking down at the body, pulling at the bottom of her shorts as if wishing to make them longer, hands wrapping around the arms, covering them.

"Hello there," CJ said.

The person examined the thin, silver bracelet Rella often wore around her right wrist, then felt the hair, looking alarmed when grasping its length.

"I'm CJ. May I ask who you are?"

The person continued to examine the hands, as if seeing them for the first time.

"Well, this is peculiar," the voice finally said, an airy female one, slow to speak, with a hint of an accent CJ couldn't place.

"Could you explain?"

"My hands. And these clothes! Dreadful! I certainly would never dress in such attire."

"Who do I have here with me?"

"How did I arrive here? I am simply not supposed to be here," she said. "And I do not *choose* to be here." She said each word as if she were tiptoeing over pebbles. "Dissatisfactory, I must say."

"Do I know you?"

"No."

It was the most agreeable sounding "No" CJ had ever heard.

"I wish to leave and go back."

"Where do you come from?"

"Rather bold of you to assume I would disclose information of such a personal nature to a perfect stranger."

Her elongated manner of speaking and the way she said "stranger"—as if the word had a "y" after the "a"—made CJ think it was a Southern accent she detected.

"Perhaps we can get Margaret to come forward and help."

"I am unacquainted with anyone called Margaret," she replied, stretching out her syllables as one does their arms in the morning.

"Well, I'm CJ, and this is my office."

"*Your* office. How re*fresh*ing."

CJ contemplated this. "Yes, it's not uncommon, in 2017."

"Two *thousand* seventeen. Indeed? How *in*teresting."

"What year is it for you?"

"Nineteen-oh-two, of course."

A sound of a car alarm went off outside, and she was gone.

"The first sketches I made as a child were of Victorian houses," said Rella. "I remember feeling misplaced—that I didn't belong in this time period—and I yearned to be back there. The pull is strong. I've gone so far as to scrutinize old photos hanging on museum walls, searching for clues. It's never made sense to me, to miss a world I've never lived in."

"You've said those words repeatedly in our sessions—that you 'want to go back,' in different contexts. You can see her?"

"Oh, yes. Clearly."

"Can you describe her for me?"

"She has long, wavy, blondish light-brown hair," Rella said, gathering her own hair in demonstration, "more copious than mine, usually in a loose updo, how women wore their hair back then." She let hers fall. "Sometimes I see her with concern on her face, looking over her shoulder."

"Do you know her name?"

For the first time, a name came to Rella while she was still in the office with CJ rather than after leaving, or through Margaret. "It's strange, but her name is Anna too."

They discussed this new person further at a later session.

"Does Victorian Anna have pain?" CJ asked.

"Physical pain, I'm not sure. Emotional, definitely. I've wondered at various times in my life if my pain was linked to someone else's pain, who'd come before me. Locked in my cells. Memory pain. Not a reincarnation thing—more like genetic heritage, because I seem to have such a connection and longing for the past."

"What brings Victorian Anna out?"

Rella thought for a minute. "The bells."

"Yes. There's a town hall nearby."

"I see her, standing, in a black cape, head down, bells above in a tower, hinging their weighty bodies side to side. She's at a funeral."

"Who is it for?" CJ asked.

"I think her sister. When Victorian Anna first came out, she divulged it was 1902, right?"

"Right."

"I think this is later, maybe 1908 or 1910." Rella sat forward in the chair. "The pages of her story have come to me over the years, in clear images in my head. I've never known what prompted them—pictures of her in town, streets lined with horses and carriages, few automobiles. Anna entering a store, her little sister trailing behind, clumsily navigating the sidewalk. Anna had told her to be careful and keep up. Anna is much older than her sister. She had a nickname for her." Rella looked thoughtfully into the air. "Starts with a D? Didi, maybe?"

"What else about them?"

"They were from America—Louisiana. Their parents died, after which they went to France. I'm not sure why. They didn't have a lot of money. I'd never known her first name before coming to see you, but something tells me her last name was Martin. Anna met a man, Marchand was his last name, I think, older, but they fell in love and married. He was super wealthy, with an immense manor, lots of servants, and a vineyard. He became sick soon after they wed and died shortly thereafter. It was quite a shock to her. But with her parents' early death, she was used to assuming charge. She took over the vineyard and household. It was the talk of the town, I guess because women weren't in those types of positions back then. She never held to social norms or gender impediments. She didn't care what other people thought." Rella laughed. "I can see her wearing pants, riding a horse through town, riling up disapproving women."

"She has gumption."

Rella smiled, her eyes wandering. "She was adept at running the business and estate, and the servants loved her. I see her strolling the fields, her face to the sun." Rella tilted her own upwards. "I receive little snapshots of her at different times in her life, in haphazard order. Sometimes she is joyful and young with her sister, sometimes alone and grieving."

"Losing both her husband and sister, after her parents at a young age, she has every right to be grieving."

"How do I know all of this about her? Where she lives, her life, her background? It unfolds as if it were my own experience. Paintings from that era resonate with me. I hear the clacking feet of the horses on the street, ladies' heels clicking along lush tree-lined boulevards edged by grand houses. I see elegant men in top hats, with canes. When Anna enters a store, the bells over the door jingle in my ears, too. Smoke from the wood-burning stove in the corner reaches my nose. The cumbersome swishing of her long skirt gathers around my ankles, as she roves among rows of vines, pausing to cradle baby grapes doused in sun. She receives callers in the drawing room, thick tapestry curtains trimmed in gold suspended over giant windows. I gaze out over the view through these windows. These vignettes have played in my mind for so long. She shares Modern Anna's name, but I don't believe there's any other connection. And she's the only one I see at different ages. Is it common to have Others from different times?"

"No."

"What could this mean?"

"I'm not sure. I am consulting with someone on it."

"I don't believe in past lives."

"I don't either."

"There's another riddle," Rella revealed, "related to her."

"What's that?"

"If I go on a boat, I hear screaming."

"Screaming?"

"Yes. In my head, like a memory."

"When did that start?"

"Since moving to California. Prior to that, I'd only been on a boat once or twice, when I was much younger, and I was fine. But this was awful. Impending doom shrouded me. I tried to shut out the noise of the boat engine, the wailing, pretend I was somewhere else, but then images came, of the boat sinking, people scattering, and I was helpless to save them from drowning. I ran into the bathroom because I was crying and didn't want people to come over to me or think I was nuts."

Rella paused a moment before continuing.

"A few weeks after that initial boat experience is the first time I saw Victorian Anna. Maybe being on the boat is what brought her out. I saw her standing at the rear of a ship, gloved hands on the rail, looking out over the water, dressed in black. An older woman next to her. Maybe they knew each other, or had met on the boat. It was clear to me that this scene was from the past, the late 1800s, early 1990s, the time period I've always been drawn to. There was a sinking. Victorian Anna survived. She feels responsible."

"Responsible?"

"For the deaths. She laments that she couldn't do more for those aboard."

"Her husband died before the sinking?"

"Yes. Long before. Her sister too. I think she was on the boat to get away, distance herself from the pain."

"How many times have you been on a boat since moving here?"

"Three crossings to Catalina."

"And it happened each time?"

"Yes. By the third time, I heard the screaming even as I approached the boat, the sway of the dock underfoot. I don't go anymore."

"The sway," CJ echoed. "Rella, do you remember the new person who'd come a couple of sessions ago, the one who seems to be adrift on a boat?"

"I was the wooziest I've ever been after that session."

"Do you think there is a connection, or a relationship between that person and Victorian Anna?"

"I don't think so. The person in the water is—banished, in a sense."

"Banished. Hmm. And what about Victorian Anna's sister? Does she seem connected to anyone else?"

"She's only associated to Victorian Anna, that time period."

"Okay."

"None of this makes sense."

"Maybe at this point, rather than striving to figure it out or assign meaning to it, you could write down her story. See what comes."

Walking back to the car, Rella passed a vintage clothing shop. She stepped inside. *Put on your old gray bonnet with the blue ribbon on it . . .* The early 1900s song by the Haydn Quartet played from a distant speaker. The cheery horns lightened Rella's mood. She bounced to the rhythm as she browsed.

She came upon a collection of shapely, sumptuous hats, ornamented with flowers, netting, feathers, and cameo clips, the kind that curtained a lady's face with a tilt of the chin.

Rella lifted an ornate, puffed, cream one, trimmed in lace, embellished with blush silk roses, and set it upon her head, the flowy train curling around her shoulders like a feather boa.

"Oh my, that hat was made for you!" a shopper exclaimed.

Rella twirled, catching her blurred reflection in the mirror, reminiscent of an Impressionistic painting immortalizing a moment with palette and frame, a rendering perhaps of what Victorian Anna looked like.

Thirty

June 2017

The sound of the bells tolling near CJ's office prompted the change.

"How are you today?"

"Apparently here, for some reason."

"I've learned a bit about you since your last visit. I hear you are good in the vineyards. Do you garden?"

"Oh, yes."

"Do you have strawberries, by chance?"

"No. Vegetables. Lots of vegetables. I do enjoy that word. Vegetables." She turned the four syllables around in her mouth. "There are servants, of course, to grow all the food." She flared her fingertips out in front of her. "Though, I must admit, the tillage is most glorious, and I sinfully enjoy earth under my fingernails." She released a quick sound of amusement that sounded like a musical note.

"I've been known to turn a spade myself. Are you in the garden now?"

"No. In town."

"Visiting a friend?"

"Heavens, no. The women here are utterly insufferable. I prefer to occupy my mind prosperously, not yatter away on meritless gossip. I'm in a park, reading about recent innovations. I do love sophisticated inventions. I have a few of my own that I've employed in the vineyard."

"I understand it's harder for women in your era to be valued and taken seriously, recognized for what they can do."

"Daft men. Feathers for brains. And the women, too, who accept it. I never let anyone define what I can or cannot do."

CJ smiled. "It might please you to learn that in the present time, my time, and Rella's, it is much better for women. Not perfect, but better."

"I'm not sure how that pertains to me."

"Well, keep it as a tidbit."

"Knowledge is delicate." The digits of her right hand strummed, as though playing a harp in the air. "Like fine porcelain dishes, prone to chips or breakage if mistreated. And it should only be presented during choice occasions."

CJ's pen moved swiftly to capture the words, as it often did when the Others spoke.

From a clinical standpoint, they were all Rella. All branches from the same tree. But she equally acceded that in distinct visible, and audible, ways, they were different people.

"Rella wishes she could meet you," CJ said to Victorian Anna.

"I am indisposed to making any new acquaintances."

"She loves the time period you are from. She senses a need within her to go back."

The change happened fast, the head pitching down to the right at an unnatural angle, like an invisible noose around a snapped neck.

"Hello. Is this someone I have not met before?"

The arms lay limp by her sides.

"Who is with me now?"

The body position dwindled further, the eyes not making contact.

CJ was still for a minute. "Is this Abigail?"

The head bent further inward, in shyness, or shame.

"Hello, Abigail," CJ said quietly.

Abigail's eyes remained averted downward.

"I'm pleased to meet you. Could you share how old you are?"

Slowly, she raised five fingers on her left hand, three on the right.

"Eight years old. Wow. Thank you for sharing that."

Abigail's fingers curled back inward.

"Is there anything you'd like to say, Abigail?' CJ asked.

Abigail sat silent, head down.

"It's okay to talk in here."

A tear fell.

"You're sad, Abigail?"

Tears streamed.

"Do you want to tell me why?"

Then it hit CJ. She felt foolish, remembering that Margaret had told her Abigail didn't have a voice.

"Abigail, I have some paper here." CJ retrieved a clean sheet. "To write on, if you wish. And a pen."

Abigail's head stayed sharply angled.

"You can take them," CJ prompted.

Abigail opened and closed her hands, elbows cinched to her waist.

"Maybe these are difficult for you to reach. Here, I'll place them on your lap for you, if that's okay."

Abigail made a sideways up-and-down motion with her head.

"Here you go."

With the laboriousness of a stroke victim, Abigail drew the pen in and pinched it next to her forefinger.

After a moment, she wrote:

I want

She crossed it out.

"Did someone tell you not to write? It's okay, Abigail. You can write what is needed. It's important to be heard."

After a minute, Abigail slowly picked up the pen again.

want the clean

want to be clean

Each word an effort. Her fingers loosened from the pen.

"May I?" CJ asked, leaning forward, glancing at what was written. "Ah. Abigail, remember when you were in the playroom with Lisa and you were able to change your clothes and she washed your hair for you? You don't look like that anymore?"

A meager shake of the head.

"Who changes the clothes back?"

happens

"Is there anyone who helps you, sees you, talks to you?"

She shook her head.

"Why not?"

I'm dead

CJ was silent for a minute. "Do you feel dead inside?"

Abigail nodded.

I no person

want to be clean want the sun

"Why can't you be in the sun, Abigail? Are you under a tree?"

She shook her head.

"Where are you most of the time?"

Her head declined further.

"It's important to find you a safe place, comfortable for rest."

can't sleep

"Why is that?" CJ asked.

Abigail gave no response.

Rella stood in the corner of her kitchen, fists closed, staring. Sadness had engulfed her midday, followed by the inability to proceed with any of her normal tasks.

Blinking her eyes, she slowly returned to the room, unsure of how long she'd been standing there. She noticed an untouched bowl of cooked vegetables and a multigrain roll on the counter. She located her phone to check the time. It beeped at the exact moment she lifted it, indicating a voicemail, from her mother.

Rella hadn't talked to her in a couple of weeks—not because she hadn't wanted to, but because she knew it would entail an act, likely similar to one her mother had needed to put on during difficult mental-health moments, painting over the past for the sake of her children.

"Hi, Mom."

"Rella! Oh, honey, how much I miss you. What are you doing? How are things?"

"Same ol'. Not much to report. Nice to hear your voice."

"Nice to hear *your* voice."

"How are you?"

"Better now that I'm talking to you. So, I have something to tell you."

"What's that?"

"I was thinking of getting a fish. But you can't hug a fish, or cuddle with it. So, I scratched that idea." She laughed. "My place doesn't allow any other kind of pet."

"Do you like it there?"

"Oh yes. It's spacious. Everyone is friendly."

"That's good."

Rella could hear the influence of her mother's medication, a slow, slight slurring as though she spoke with Novocain lips, words moving through clay. She didn't drink anymore, except the occasional glass of wine, but her psychiatrist did have her on mood stabilizers. She'd never been the same after the electroshock therapy. That one "treatment" had changed everything.

Seth's "treatment" had permanently changed Rella. But she was determined to work hard at making sure she restored herself and her life, and not allow another maltreatment to disable her.

"I feel empty."

234

"Who is speaking, please?" CJ asked.

"It's foggy."

"Have I talked to you before?"

"Ugh. I feel so sick."

"Where are you? What do you see?"

"Water, all around. Waves up and down. Ugh, it's making me sick."

"Are you the person on the boat?"

"I hate this boat."

"Could you tell me more about yourself?"

"Up and down. I hate it. What did you give me?"

"Give you?"

"Drugs. Was it morphine?"

"No."

"Spinning. Waves crashing. In my stomach, my head. My mouth hurts. My face hurts. My teeth hurt."

"Did someone hurt you?"

"Ugh."

"Is someone causing the waves?"

Her head circled once. "I hate this boat. Get me off of this boat."

"Look down at your feet. Can you see the ground?"

"There's no ground. I don't see my feet," she said hoarsely.

"Where are they?"

"Covers. Tight. Restricted." The body wrenched.

"Can't sleep. Can't sleep," a voice whispered.

"This sounds like someone else."

"He will come in."

"Who?"

"I have to stay awake."

"Where is this?"

She made sounds of discomfort.

"Look around the room. You are here, not there. See the light coming in through the window?" said CJ.

"That door. Light from the other side. It's brighter. In my face!" She threw her hands up.

"Who is this?"

"Don't come near me!" The voice turned much younger. "Don't touch me. I'll kick you. I'll punch you. Don't look at me. I'll stab your eyes!" She used the air as a punching bag. "You lie. You lie. You lie. You're a liar. You're a liar."

"Who is this?"

"You know."

"I'm sorry; I'm not sure."

"Maybe if I hit you, you would. Leave me alone. Leave me alone. I don't like you."

"Katie?" CJ asked.

She slapped her legs. "I'm gonna get back. I'm gonna get back."

"Get back where, Katie? Are you still on the boat?"

"You think you're a know-it-all. You're wrong. You're wrong."

"I'd like you to stop hitting your legs."

"I like to hurt. I like to hurt."

"Four-year-old girls don't like to hurt."

"I like it. I like it."

"Katie, you share that body with Rella. You're hurting her too."

"I do not!" she screeched.

"Max? Are you around?"

"I'll take her to the tree. It's okay, Katie," Max said gently.

The hands gripped the armrests. "Oooh." The voice different again. "I don't like this." The whole body tensed. "Oooh, I don't like this."

"What is going on? What don't you like?" CJ asked.

The feet rubbed together as if resisting being pulled apart. "Held down. His face. Breath."

"This is someone different. Who am I talking to?"

"Lisa," she sputtered. "I don't like this; I don't like this."

"Lisa what do you see? Where are you?"

"Make him disappear."

"Who is there, Lisa?"

"Make him disappear. Make him disappear. Make him disappear. Make him disappear."

"Lisa, can you look at me, see where you are?"

"Make him disappear. Make him disappear." Her voice grew hushed.

"Lisa?"

Her eyes closed as she continued repeating the three words until she only mouthed them. "I did it," she said softly. "I made him disappear."

"How, Lisa?"

"I go away."

"You go away?"

"Yes. Oh, that's better."

"Does Margaret help you, Lisa?"

"I like Anna."

"Lisa, can you tell me more about what just happened?"

No response. Lisa was pulled away. CJ could almost see it, Rella's body emptied, and she wondered if this was what it looked like on the outside, what Rella had described as being "between people," in a "limbo state."

"I don't have Rella back. Who do I have?"

A thin smirk drew across the lips like black ink from a fountain pen.

"Are you the one who causes pain?" she asked.

A self-satisfied expression of superiority.

"I need to get Rella now. Can I talk to you next session?"

"Maybe."

CJ imprinted the new voice in her mind, with this one word, as it was the first time the person had spoken. She wasn't sure if it was the "he" that had been mentioned, but she imagined so.

The smug look faded. The eyes closed and then opened.

"This is strange." Victorian Anna's mild demeanor was welcome. "Why does this keep happening? I'm disinclined to such disruptions."

"Let's get Rella back," CJ said.

"I hear traffic noise."

Victorian Anna heard this person called "Rella" utter those words several moments later.

She left the office with this Rella, exiting onto a street. The buildings were hideous, the automobiles nearly unrecognizable. The drab gray smear overhead disgraced the sky, a far cry from the radiant blue dome where she was from. Droves of people brazenly strolled by in unsightly clothes, some of the women practically on stilts!

Even though Victorian Anna unequivocally preferred her own time period, she observed from an arm's length, an inadvertent passenger, until she was no longer there.

Thirty-One

CJ checked on the simmering tomato sauce with a wooden spoon. Not a recipe her mother would rave about, but decent. She added another sprinkling of fresh oregano. Re-covering the pot, she walked into the dining room.

"How's it going in here?" she asked Bryce, noting the incomplete papers on the table.

"Math stinks." He dropped his forehead into his palm dejectedly.

CJ pulled up a chair next to him. "Sometimes we have to learn things we don't want to."

"But I don't *need* to."

"Well, let's examine that. Imagine you went to the store, and you gave the person a one-hundred-dollar bill—"

"Wow, a hundred-dollar bill?"

"Yes. And they cheated you, because you couldn't calculate the change."

Bryce creased his face. "That's not nice."

"No, you're right. But not all people in this world are nice." CJ's profession, helping others cope with the aftermath of trauma, abuse, and exploitation, mercilessly demonstrated that.

"Mommy! You're not listening!"

"I'm sorry, B. My mind was elsewhere."

"Where? Madagascar?" His eyes widened.

CJ laughed. "If only it were that easy." She thought of Rella. Her mind had provided escape, shielding her on a plane with no other passengers, floating her away from harm in a sky empty of memory. But planes weren't impenetrable. Turbulence rocked. Engines failed.

"I wish my math problem was about Madagascar. That would be more fun."

"What's this obsession with Madagascar?"

"We're learning all the countries of the world. Do you know what the capital is?"

"Actually, no, I don't."

"Antananarivo!" he exclaimed. "Say that three times fast. Antananarivo. Antananarivo. Antananarivo!" He giggled.

CJ looked at Bryce with fondness. She hadn't ever thought she'd want a child. Kyle loved children, and wanted five, but she had agreed to one. Now, she couldn't imagine life without her B.

The children in Rella's life, Katie, Lisa, Abigail, and Dustin, and perhaps others, were just as real as the little boy sitting in front of her, though locked in static moments and states of time. Rella had come a long way, in even being able to meet and interact with the Others. But her path to each of them was still narrow, winding, treacherous, and long.

CJ heard Kyle finishing up in the kitchen before he headed upstairs to check on Bryce.

A few minutes later, he came to find her at the computer.

"Cup of tea?"

"No, I'm set, thank you." She smiled appreciatively at her husband. "I'll be up soon. Doing a little research."

"Okay. Be careful not to read anything disturbing." He squeezed her shoulder before leaving the room.

She returned her eyes to the screen. "Nothing disturbing," she murmured. She'd never had nightmares, but her work had proven the worst horrors occurred during waking hours.

"A lot happened last session," CJ said.

"I felt pretty drained. And my legs are sore. I have bruises."

"Yes, I can imagine."

"While she's hitting, I don't feel it. And later, to be honest, I don't mind the soreness. Katie has a power inside her; it came from when there was still fight in me, I guess."

CJ wrote that down.

"I can see why Katie wants to stab and destroy, because trust was demolished for her. She doesn't believe in happiness or protection. Her rage is justified." Rella paused. "Huh. My mind went to Max. He hates injustice. I wonder if there is a connection there."

"There could be. I'm not confident we secured everyone at the end of last session."

"Victorian Anna was with me when I left your office last time. It was strange, showing someone else a world by sharing my own eyes. She didn't stay long. I felt her leave about halfway home."

"Let's talk about what we can do to bring you back more easily. Last session I tried for about twenty-five minutes."

"Really? Wow."

"Maybe making a small noise in the room, flipping on the air conditioner?"

Rella shook her head. "I don't like air conditioners. The kind in the window—" She shuddered.

"We definitely don't want any triggers. What do you suggest?"

Rella thought. "I love my work. Maybe if you asked me about it, requested specific details."

"An intellectual prompt."

"Yes."

"Got it."

CJ wanted to talk to Margaret, so Rella went to the beach.

"Can you tell me what happened last session?" CJ asked her.

"No."

"You weren't here?"

"No."

"What about after Rella left the office?"

"I have no idea."

CJ had been under the perception that Margaret was always present in some capacity. She adjusted this supposition.

CJ noticed a change in Margaret's face. "What? What are you seeing?"

"There's a small boat on the table in the file room."

"How did it get there?"

"How should I know?" Margaret pursed her lips, her characteristic signal of displeasure or disagreement.

"What is it?" CJ asked.

Margaret hesitated. "There is another file room."

"Another one?"

"Yes."

"Where is it located, in relation to the other rooms in your office?"

"Behind a wall."

"How do you get to it?"

"There's a door I've never seen before."

"Can you go inside?"

"If I must. I prefer not to."

"Are you not supposed to?"

She didn't answer the question. "I am inside." She made a face of distaste.

"What's wrong?"

"It looks the way my office did when I first arrived."

"Can you describe it to me?"

"Small, cramped. Poorly lit. A single dusty bulb hanging from the center of the ceiling. The corners of the room are unclear. No windows, merely a vent. I don't think anyone has been here in a long time."

"What is the temperature like?"

"Cold."

"How many file cabinets are there?"

"I don't know."

"Are they metal ones, like what you used to have?"

"Yes. Ugly, old, dented. Covered in grime."

"What is the difference between the files in this room and the other room?"

"These are old files. I didn't put them here."

"What do the files in this room contain?"

"Your questions are tiresome."

"Rella's childhood?"

No answer.

"Are there any files out in this room?"

"No."

"Are there locks on these cabinets?"

"No."

"Can you get a sense of how many files there are?" CJ asked.

"It's undusted in here. Making my allergies worse." Margaret slid her left fingertips over an eye and rubbed the bridge of her nose.

"Do you wear glasses, Margaret?"

"Yes."

"Margaret, maybe you can take over this room, too. You've done such a thorough job with the other file room, perhaps you can also be in charge of this one, clean it up."

"I don't have the authority to make that decision."

"Does 'he'?"

"I am not to clean the room." Her lips pursed.

"Who ordered that?"

"I should be exempt."

"Margaret, did the boat come from this room?"

"Don't ask me."

"Do you see any other objects?"

Margaret's head slowly rotated. She twitched. "A mask."

CJ held in a shudder.

Thirty-Two

July 2017

"I have two words for you," Ginnie said Friday afternoon.

"Tell me," Rella replied as she entered calculations into her program.

"Sawdust Festival."

"Sound intriguing. What is it?"

"Only the best part of Laguna Beach. Art, music, drinks, food—well, you probably wouldn't eat the food—but it's super fun, outdoors, and I know you'll love it. You can watch glassblowing, which blows my mind every time, no pun intended, and every booth is so different, depending on the artist. It's a browser's paradise. There's a girl that makes the most beautiful earrings. I buy a pair every year. Tomorrow they are having a mixed media art class, and it's totally free!"

"Sign me up!"

Under the shade of eucalyptus trees, woodchips below their feet and paint under their nails after class, Rella and Ginnie strolled the aisles of the outdoor festival in a leisurely fashion, spending as much or as little time at each open-air hut as they desired, occasionally pointing out something to one another. The whimsical variety in the shapes and styles of the roofs made Rella feel she was in a fairy tale.

"Check this out!" Ginnie said. "This booth is like a storybook treehouse." She settled a small crown of dried flowers atop her head. "What do you think?"

"It looks amazing on you." Rella looked up at the strings of pearls hanging from brass candelabras. "Imagine sleeping in a tree? One with moss, so it's soft," she said more to herself, as Ginnie inquired further about the dainty headpieces.

Rella felt a presence. One of the Others stepped out. Lisa. She looked up at the displays, wonderment in her eyes. Rella tensed, as though Ginnie, or anyone else around, could see her.

Lisa's gaze turned to Ginnie, who tried on variations of the crowns in front of the small, hanging mirror. She started to walk over to her.

Rella's eyes widened.

Stay with me, Rella said internally.

"I've decided!" Ginnie announced, spinning once, sashaying to Rella, the ribbons of the wreath flowing behind. "I've never felt like a princess, but this helps. Find anything?"

Rella felt Lisa leave. "Discovering new things all the time."

"Lisa wants to meet Ginnie," Margaret said.

"Oh? Perhaps I can talk to Lisa about that," said CJ.

Lisa didn't have a problem asking for what she wanted. She had become more and more interactive, at times coming out at sessions to see what was going on.

"Lisa, I understand you want to meet Ginnie."

"Yeah."

"Would you agree that this is a decision for Rella to make?"

"But I want to meet her," Lisa asserted stubbornly.

"Why?"

"She seems nice."

"Yes, she does sound nice."

"And she likes art, like I like art."

"Why don't you draw a picture for Ginnie, instead?"

"I suppose."

"For now, you can just observe quietly, until perhaps Rella makes a different decision. This is hard for Rella, too. What do you think might happen if everyone talked when they wanted to, maybe all at the same time?"

"No one would be heard," Lisa said.

This insightful answer surprised CJ. "Yes, that's right, and very astute of you to say."

"I just want to tell her I'm not a bad girl."

"Why would you be a bad girl?"

Lisa shrugged.

"Did someone tell you that once?"

Lisa didn't respond.

The fact that Lisa didn't reply to this question stayed with Rella, even hours later. Lisa couldn't stand the thought of people thinking less of her. She felt personally wounded by criticism or red correction marks on her school paper, just as Rella had. As a child, if Rella had overstepped or disobeyed, all Leah had to do was look at her with disappointment and it crushed her. Lisa shared those characteristics. Lisa couldn't handle disapproval. She strived to be perfect.

Lisa loved animals, couldn't bear to see bugs hurt, and wanted all living creatures to be safe. Rella was sure she stayed in the playroom because it served as protection, an asylum against the world, where she could distract herself with drawings and coloring.

<hr />

At their next session, CJ asked, "Do you have any happy memories, Lisa?"

"Yes, I have lots of happy memories."

"Can you tell me some of them?"

"Every day I spend at my table in my playroom, when my mommy makes me my favorite lunch."

"You're in your playroom every day?"

"Uh-huh."

"Did you ever go to school with Rella, when she was younger?"

Lisa's eyes skirted sideways. "Maybe."

"What is your favorite lunch, Lisa?"

"Peanut butter sandwich!"

"No jelly?"

"Jelly? Yuck!"

CJ laughed. "What else do you have?"

"An apple. I love apples."

"Does your mommy let you have candy?"

"No. She's a good mommy. And I don't care for it anyway," she said, head held high.

"I don't think I know any kids that don't like candy."

"Well, you do now!"

CJ smiled. "What other happy memories do you have?"

"Just that one."

"I thought you had lots."

"I do. Lots of that one."

"So, your lots of happy memories are all the same memory?"

"Yup."

"Hmm. Okay."

"Well, there is another one. Kind of."

"Tell me about it."

"I was in my playroom and it wasn't lunchtime yet, but the daddy came to the playroom."

"The daddy?"

"Yes."

"Whose daddy? Rella's?"

Lisa shrugged.

"So Rella's daddy is not your daddy."

"No."

"And is Rella's mommy your mommy?"

"I pretend she is, but I make her a little different."

"Different how?"

Lisa didn't answer.

"What happened the day Rella's daddy came to the playroom?"

"He came to take her to the store to buy a bicycle."

"Fun. Did you go along?"

"Yes."

"Did you learn to ride the bike?"

"It was scary!" Lisa scissored her dangling legs vigorously.

"Lisa, do you decide when or when not to be with Rella?"

Lisa shook her head.

"I have an idea. Do ever write stories?"

"Oh, yes."

"I'd like you to write about the bike, but in a specific way. In the first person. Have you heard of that?"

"I write like me talking."

"Yes, exactly. Instead of saying "she" you say "I." You tell the story from your point of view."

"I can do that."

"And one more thing—I want you to write in the present tense, as though it is happening to you right now."

"Ooh, sounds hard."

"Picture that day. Take yourself there. Can you see it?"

Lisa squeezed her eyes. "A little."

"Good. Take a few minutes, and when you are ready, you can write the story."

Lisa sat with her eyes shut for a while before taking the pen and paper CJ had placed on the table between them.

It's a sunny day. I am going on a bike. It is blue. Blue is my favorite color. Not pink. Why always pink for girls? The seat is white and squishy. The bike is big and wobbly! I'm going to fall! The daddy says go faster. I feel shaky. We are moving forward. My heart is going really fast, but I like the wind on my face. Look out world, here I come! But the daddy's holding on. How far can I go with that? But then I hear him laugh and say, "You got it," and he sounds far away—and he is! He let go! He knew we could do it. But now, how to stop?!

Rella unlocked the door, keeping the lights off on the first floor. She'd be the only one in the office that day—or so she had thought.

Once upstairs, Lisa appeared, child's briefcase in hand. It surprised Rella, and she would have freaked if Garrett hadn't been away on vacation and Ginnie hadn't gone to a seminar in La Jolla.

Lisa put her case down on the floor and walked about, over to Garrett's fastidiously neat workstation, and then to Ginnie's desk, her nose turning up at the sight of the coffee cups Ginnie had left behind.

She studied the framed drawings and blueprints on the walls, tipping her head right to left as she tried to make sense of them.

After lunch, she stayed close to Rella, observing what she did, picking up lining pens and mechanical pencils, twirling her compass, and turning on Rella's desk lamp when she thought she needed more light.

She giggled as she struck her knees with Rella's T-square as though it were a rubber tomahawk.

Rella saw her eyeing the drafting chair, thinking about spinning 'round and 'round in it, but Lisa maintained self-control, recognizing Rella's place of work was not for play.

Lisa pitched in at the end of the day, wanting to organize and rearrange the papers on top of Rella's desk, and roll up the tracing paper.

Rella had had one babysitting job, when she was fourteen, which lasted all of three nights. She hadn't liked watching kids and decided she'd do any job other than that.

She couldn't have fathomed that over two decades later she'd be babysitting herself. The experience had been both interesting and exhausting.

"All right, Lisa. Done for today. Time to go," Rella said aloud.

As soon as she got into the car, Lisa was gone.

The golden light of the sun had passed its summit and the day relaxed into early evening. Rella drove to one of the quieter residential parks.

She had gone to the playground alone often when she was younger, a large one used by several communities, with tennis courts, a baseball field, and a sprawling jungle gym area. She'd spent the majority of time on the swings.

Rella picked a swing and sat. She pushed back and let go, straightening her legs, then bending them, gaining momentum. She liked when no one else was around, the motion of the rocking lulling her mind into creative thoughts. She developed some of her best architectural plans while on the swings.

A little girl rode by on her bicycle, her dark hair trailing behind. She looked close to Lisa's age.

Rella's mind drifted to what Lisa had written in the last session. Rella remembered when her father had taught her how to ride a bike. She never imagined that another little girl had learned alongside her on the same day—the same seven-year-old who had gone to work with her today, thirty years later.

Thirty-Three

A dense fog seeped inside the Greenhouse, blocking out the windows.

Abigail's diaphanous body materialized in the opacity. Modern Anna came up behind her, laid her hands on her shoulders. The gentle gesture and Abigail's stillness gave Rella the impression she'd been supported by Anna before, as one would aid a small animal feigning a death-freeze response until able to get away from a predator.

"Abigail doesn't want to eat," said Rella, "doesn't want to exist."

"When you struggle with eating, it might be a time to check in with Abigail," said CJ. "She may be having difficulty. Or, trying to be helpful."

"Helpful?"

"She might reason that if she doesn't eat, she would fade away, as would you. In this way, you couldn't be harmed anymore; no one could."

"I never would have thought of it that way," said Rella. "So, my physical symptoms could be coming from them? That's why one day I can eat, and the next, I'm bloated and ill, from exactly the same foods?"

"Very probable."

"This is tricky."

"They are all here for a reason," said CJ. "Each action and reaction they have, all the aspects of their personalities—they have all come about to aid you in some way."

"What Abigail endured consumed her." Rella wiped away a tear. "I wish I could have saved her."

Rella had begun to take notes on each of the Others, creating separate files with their names, jotting down information as she received it. Maybe in doing so, she could find ways to ease their pain, and make connections to help hers.

Brushing her teeth, her mind went to Max. He wasn't happy. She felt his strain and longing to break free. She pictured him sitting in the diner, his back to the open road he hungered for.

Max, you don't have to stay in the diner, she said internally. *Ride. Take your bike on those long stretches of road through the desert. Even cross into another state if you want to.*

He needed to stay close to Katie.

We'll take a drive up the coast, and maybe Katie can come.

Later that week, for about two glorious hours, Rella's left eye cleared and she could almost see normally. Her head calmed; the haze lifted. Her stomach settled, and she didn't have the urge to vomit. The dizziness receded.

When she had first arrived in California, busy and fired up, those had been the happiest days of her life. She didn't know if she could ever get that back again.

It was 11:30 p.m.

Rella was lying in bed, awake. A thought intruded.

Waterbed.

In the minutes that followed, she saw Abigail.

Rella felt her presence the rest of the night, in the room, and she didn't sleep well.

She woke up with a headache and tight neck.

Rella related the Abigail incident to CJ at their next session, along with her reaction to Ginnie's waterbed during the sleepover.

"Of course, no tangible memory or experience comes to mind. My mother had a waterbed, but that's all I recall. I've been thinking about links and connections, though. I made a list related to this. Can I share it?"

"By all means."

Rella picked her small notebook up off the table.

"One of the images I had during my sessions with Seth was of a little girl in a bathtub, which was likely me. I have had trouble drinking water ever since seeing him. Throughout my life, dreams involving water have trickled into my sleep, tsunami towers and drowning dangers. Victorian Anna has a connection to water, that boat I see her on. Then, there's this unidentified girl seemingly stuck out in an ocean."

Rella looked up at CJ.

"I decided to call her Water, since I haven't been given her name."

CJ jotted on her pad.

"I feel she holds important information, but in riddles, metaphors. Hidden, deep, like what's contained by the sea."

"Interesting," said CJ. "And Abigail showed after you thought about a waterbed. Do you feel any association between her and Water?"

"No. The opposite, actually. I feel she can't go near water, the substance, for whatever reason. She's stuck in that dirty dress. She feels dirty. She can't permanently change out of her clothes because she can't take off the feeling. It wears her. She can't speak. I think she was threatened not to. I believe she came not just to protect me, but Lisa as well. I don't remember terror, but Abigail does. I tell her, 'It will never happen again, Abigail,' but I'm not sure my words reach her ears."

"Did anyone else show other than Abigail?"

"No. In my research I read that someone could switch as things are revealed because each one doesn't hold the same memories, experiences, feelings. But these appearances—they must mean something, too."

"Certainly. Each can have different memories, or lack of memories, or one memory. Some can hold only a sound, or a smell. But each one is there as a protection for you."

"Even after the—bad—stopped, some could have come later?"

"Yes."

"Will I ever meet all of them?"

"Perhaps."

Rella thought about this for a few minutes.

"There's a force under my skin; I feel them wanting to come out."

"They are being recognized after all this time."

"Lisa came with me to work the other day."

"She did?"

"Thank goodness no one was there!" Rella said.

"Margaret mentioned that Lisa wants to meet Ginnie."

"It can't happen. No one can know about my condition!"

"Lisa and I had a talk about it. I told her it's always your decision."

"Ginnie's been asking to get together since returning from her seminar. I'm afraid now. But losing her friendship would be heartbreaking."

"Lisa agreed to color a picture for Ginnie, in lieu of meeting her."

"That's cute." Rella's grin became sheepish. "In the store the other day I passed the arts and crafts section and saw crayons. Lisa wanted them. I bought them for her. I pulled out my old coloring books and colored. She was there with me."

"What a wonderful and nurturing thing to do."

"I enjoyed it too. I wish I could do more for them."

"Little by little, you will know how," said CJ. "Now that they've come out, it's important for you to hear them. In order for them to heal—for *you* to heal—you could listen more often, perhaps granting small wishes, within reason, of course."

"Sometimes it's strong at home, their desire to come forward."

"That's because it's a safer space for them to step out. They are no longer obscurities. They have forms and memories and needs."

Rella saw each individual as though they were standing in front of her. "They are real people. They have shadows too."

Thirty-Four

August 2017

"Did the bad happen at ages four, seven, and eight?" Rella asked CJ, the ages of the three youngest, Katie, Lisa, and Abigail.

"Have you asked internally?"

"Yes, but I'm not sure. Only a year separates Lisa and Abigail, yet their personalities are so different."

"Yes." CJ paused. "I am curious if you ever feel the presence of anyone younger."

"No. But that makes sense. If Katie is the first one, doesn't that mean that's when this started?"

CJ's lips became taut as she folded them inward. She had wanted to broach this subject with Rella for some time. "You might think so."

"The look on your face says otherwise," Rella worried.

"People don't disassociate into others after the first event."

Rella's expression didn't register comprehension.

"Dissociation, as a mechanism of escape, is, it happens after . . ." CJ hated her job sometimes. "After more than one event. Usually, repeated, sustained offenses, from an earlier age than when the first dissociation occurred."

The words hung in the air like an ax that took a minute to fall. The implication struck.

Rella's expression turned to one of revulsion. She put her hands over her ears.

"Rella? Are you still with me?"

She rocked. "I have a bad feeling. I have a bad feeling. Mm."

"Rella—Rella, come back into the room."

"I want to go home," a child's voice sobbed. "I want to go home."

CJ asked her to describe objects in the room. She scrolled through the list of subjects they had compiled together, to use in the event of an emergency.

"I need to speak to Margaret. Margaret, I need your help. I need to bring Rella back."

"I'm trying," a different voice said, as the rocking slowed. "She's asleep. I'm shaking her. She's not moving."

"Who is this, please?" It sounded like Modern Anna's voice.

"Anna."

CJ nodded in confirmation. "Anna, can you get Margaret to help?"

"She's just arrived."

"Margaret, can you pour cold water over Rella's feet?"

"I don't see what good that will do. She has shoes on."

Rella's right cheek was slapped.

"Margaret! We don't have to resort to slapping!"

"I didn't slap her. Anna did."

The body went lifeless.

"Rella, are you with me?"

"I feel strange."

"Who is this?"

"I don't remember coming here."

"My name is CJ. I'd like to help."

The rocking and crying resumed, then slowed.

The shoulders straightened. The tears dried, the eyes methodically wiped.

"Margaret?"

Her eyes solidified. "Stop digging."

"Thank you for coming, Margaret."

"This needs to end. She can't handle it. She is tortured all the time now. This has not helped. She is worse."

"I agree, this is a difficult session."

"They all are."

"How do you handle them, Margaret?"

"Remove. File."

"Do you have anything *you* don't want to remember, Margaret?"

Margaret hesitated. Then she said something CJ hadn't expected at all.

CJ did a poor job of hiding her surprise. She was supposed to be more like Margaret. Receive, process, file. Sequester emotions.

"Thank you for telling me, Margaret. I'm sure it was difficult for you."

"It is more difficult for her. Can't you see this is damaging?"

"Rella came to me for help. It's my job to try."

"Anna started this whole mess."

"She has advocated for change, and yes, with some consequences. Margaret, was Anna the original Gatekeeper?"

"You therapists and your titles."

"So, that's a yes? Is that why she is so tired all the time? Did the job exhaust her?"

"*You* are tiring."

"I'm sorry you feel that way. It's time to bring Rella back anyway."

"I'm not exposing her to any more today."

"It's just to conclude the session."

"She is not returning."

"Margaret."

Margaret raised her chin. "I am perfectly capable of getting her home."

"I would prefer to end with Rella."

Margaret did not respond.

CJ looked at her watch, something she despised doing when with a patient. "Margaret, I only have a few minutes before my next appointment arrives."

"I'm not the one who began something I couldn't finish."

CJ looked into the deadpan eyes, devoid of the emotion and warmth of Rella's. "Why don't you have a seat in the waiting room, and we can talk more in about an hour?"

CJ led her out. "Hi," she greeted her next client. "Please go on in," she gestured. "See you soon, Margaret."

When she emerged from her office an hour later, the waiting room was empty.

Margaret drove Rella home, eyes level, hands steady at ten and two.

"Rella, do you remember leaving here after our last session?"

"No."

"I wanted to talk with you about it, because I need to make sure you're safe."

"I've never driven when I didn't feel capable of doing so."

"We just need to make sure it's always an adult behind the wheel, and never a younger one."

Margaret nodded internally.

"Margaret accepts," Rella said. Her eyes settled on the back of her hands. They'd always looked so much older than her face. She pictured Margaret's fingers, Margaret's skin, Margaret's hands, supportive ones still guiding.

"If—*when*—I try and remember sessions," said Rella, "I sit down at the computer, with no idea of what will come out. My fingers start moving. I think it's Margaret writing."

"How long after being home this time did *you* return?"

"It was a long, slow process—pieces of me and pieces of Margaret dropping in, dropping out. A call came in from Garrett. My mind saw Margaret answering the phone! I worried she'd say, 'Rella will get back to you.' I didn't pick it up, and I put the phone away for the night."

"Sensible idea."

"I didn't recover 100 percent of me until right before bed. I sensed Lisa, checking on me."

"How did that feel?"

"Comforting."

"Rella, Margaret spoke of a memory last session."

"A memory?"

"Yes."

Rella concentrated hard. She had no idea what CJ was talking about. "I don't remember."

"She said someone was on top of her."

"What?"

"Yes."

"I never would have remembered that."

Rella felt horrible. All of the Others had suffered. Not even Margaret was immune.

Thirty-Five

"Hey, Rella, sorry, I'm a smidge behind," said Ginnie. "This project is as full of little snags as a well-worn sweater. But, my computer's on eight percent and I'm down to ten myself, so I'm finished for tonight!"

"No worries. I'm home getting a few things done."

"What do you need me to bring? What do you have there?"

"Botanical gin and potatoes," Rella replied.

Ginnie laughed. "I knew I liked you. It's Wednesday. I'll pop over to the outdoor farmers market, grab some green beans and strawberries. Then we'll have all four food groups."

"Let's make it blueberries," Rella said.

While waiting for Ginnie to arrive, Rella pushed back the folding doors and stepped out onto the patio. A gentle breeze weaved its way up the hills from the ocean, humming through the pines. Rella soaked in the soothing, calming tones.

Lisa hadn't shown up at work again. No one else had pushed to come forward while other people were around. The night would go just fine.

Ginnie gusted in twenty minutes later. "I'm here!" she sang, arms full of groceries, red hair spilling out of her clip.

"Let me help you." Rella rushed over. "What happened to just green beans and berries?" Rella saved a stray rolling pear heading for the edge of the counter.

"Fruit is irresistible! And," Ginnie said, pushing curls away from her face, "I may have no maternal inclinations whatsoever, but I can do math. You, minus weight loss, equals the need for more food."

Rella wondered if Ginnie had noticed anything else about her in recent months.

"Ugh!" Ginnie grabbed a handful of tresses. "This hasn't wanted to stay in place all day. Guess hair gets tired too."

"Ginnie, you didn't have to do this. I appreciate it, though."

Ginnie tossed her hands in the air like a salad. "Oh, don't mention it. We'll have a real feast! I'm hungrier than a hornet, so if you get cleanin', I'll get choppin'."

"On it!" Rella grabbed some items and took them to the sink.

"Where's your cutting board?" Ginnie asked.

"Above the refrigerator, just there." Rella pointed with her head.

Ginnie opened the cabinet and Rella heard rummaging. "Huh."

"What is it?" Rella asked, filling a bowl with water.

Ginnie held up the two halves of Rella's former intact cutting board. "What happened to this? Unruly radish?"

The apples and pears fell out of Rella's hands into the bowl as she recalled the cutting board incident. She laughed shakily. "Guess I don't know my own strength."

"Hey, I always appreciate a good drop of red-haired temper," Ginnie said, chuckling.

Rella loosened with relief.

Thirty minutes later, the girls enjoyed lemon and blueberry

gin drinks and an assortment of fruits and vegetables on the back deck.

"Super dinner," Ginnie said, popping a grape tomato in her mouth.

"This is how I prefer to eat," Rella said. "Picnic style. In the fresh air."

Both took a moment to enjoy the surroundings.

Rella rolled a berry between her fingers. Part of her—a timid vote—wanted to share her diagnosis with Ginnie, but it was overruled by the gaveling of fears keeping her from saying anything that remotely resembled "I found out I have multiple personalities. Wait, now it's called dissociative identity disorder."

"Ginnie, I'm sorry. I haven't been the greatest friend lately, getting together sporadically, seeming distant at work some days, working from home more often. I just want you to know, I'm not avoiding you. It's not that at all."

Ginnie rested her hand on Rella's. "Hey, it's okay. We all have our own way of dealing with things. If you need space, then that's what you create for yourself. No one wants to be boxed in, even by sincerity. Just remember—I'm here if you need me!" she finished dramatically.

Tears of gratitude misted Rella's eyes.

"The longer I live with this awareness of my diagnosis, the more I see how it will always impact my life. Are there any other health conditions that could result from DID—serious ones, I mean?"

CJ opened her hands. "I do believe such horrible repeated trauma, especially when experienced young, can affect a person throughout their entire life, and could possibly even result in a disease like cancer."

Rella wished that each time a man selfishly imposed himself on another, *he* would get pain. *He* would get migraines. *He* would vomit after eating. *He* would scream soundlessly in the middle of the night. *He* would suffer nightmares. *He* would get cancer.

Rella looked down at her hands, resting on her abdomen. People associated emotion with the heart, but other organs had to feel them too.

"Cysts," she said.

"Hmm?"

"Uterine cysts. Can they be caused by trauma?"

"Yes, I would imagine so."

Rella's eyes dropped down. CJ's recent disclosure—that Rella's abuse had to have started when Rella was younger than four—had curdled her insides. She'd tried not to think of it.

"I had a scan, several years back, seeking a diagnosis for my excruciating menstrual pain," Rella began. "I didn't expect anything to be found. But something was. A cyst, of a pretty substantial size, like a grapefruit, the doctor had said. I had asked him how long it had been there, and he'd said it must have been since the age of three."

"Oh, Rella."

"I had the surgery, laparoscopic. Didn't help the pain at all."

"There's the manifestation, but first the cause," CJ said quietly.

"Violation of any person . . . it's unthinkable to me. But to a child . . ." Rella's intestines twisted. "Silent screams are the only ones I know—that many victims know. The mind can't clean itself out. It continues to cry. There's always an old, dusty file room. Even when hidden from view, it's still there, in the cerebral folders. Affecting everything."

"You're right," said CJ. "The body knows. It remembers."

"It certainly does."

Late September 2017

Come for a visit.

Rella stared at the text from Morgan.

I miss you, and it would be good for Mom, too. Come next month!

She'd have to plan at least four weeks in advance to be fair to Garrett and Ginnie. She hadn't returned to Colorado in the colder months since leaving.

Thoughts of the autumn season carried memories of junior high years.

———

September-morning air entered through Rella's open bedroom window, clean and fresh. The first day of school brought out sweaters, excitement, and nerves.

She'd studied the schedule until nearly memorized, as though she'd be tested in homeroom, all the while wondering what the teachers would be like and who would sit next to her.

She situated the hardcover textbook in the top left corner of her desk as they were passed out in each class, peeking inside during roll call, running her fingers over the glossy pages of colorful pictures, enticed by the knowledge inside.

Once the year was under way, she went from being both comfortably and uncomfortably invisible, to feeling buried in eyes when she answered a question, the words exiting her mouth like a snowball cast down a hill, out of her control.

She always had the right response.

"Very good, Rella," the teacher would say.

Rella's cheeks would flush and she'd unwittingly smile, hoping she didn't look proud of herself. She'd never been picked on, and knew if she was more outgoing and responsive, she might have a lot of friends, but the effort was exhausting, so she folded into the crowd like a plain outfit little noticed.

The noise and chaos of crowded halls between periods left her disoriented, and she kept her head down going from room to room.

By the end of November, the novelty of the scholastic year had waned with the sun, and the chill of late fall curled around Rella's neck and traveled down the first few vertebrae of her thoracic spine.

Rella's body felt the absence of the earth's retained warmth acutely, pulling through her, draining vigor just as energy left a solar-powered battery.

The sky grayed. Bright leaves withered. Trees shed to conserve resources, leaving themselves exposed. With each day, Rella felt more porous and breakable, like osteoporotic bone.

Winter extended its icy fingers, further constricting her movement. She kept her arms down close to her body when outside, to conserve warmth, leading a mostly indoor existence for months.

It had been a big reason for her move to California. Like a flower, she craved the sun. Winter felt like living underground. Trapped. Dark. Buried.

"Spring is just around the corner" people would say, but she couldn't see the corner, let alone around it.

"Morgan wants me to visit," Rella told CJ at their next session.

"How do you feel about it?"

"I dread the thought of going back there, even though none of my family members live in Eastport anymore. After knowing what I do, I can't imagine ever going anywhere near that house again. That would be asking for trouble."

"I agree."

"But even so, I still have no control over this—my new existence, for lack of a better word. I dreamt last night that the Others came out when I was with my family. That simply cannot happen."

"We had Lisa's agreement for Ginnie. It went well, right? She didn't try to come out?"

"No. But going back to Colorado—I could be lighting a fuse. My sessions here incite their appearance. I'm not blaming you, of course," Rella clarified quickly. "I am so grateful for your caution, your care, your help. I have no idea where I would be otherwise. Thank you."

"Of course."

"There is one area where I'm feeling better, amazingly. My migraines, and the constant low-grade headache I've had nearly all my life—they are all but gone."

"Rella, that's wonderful."

"I hadn't told you yet because I was afraid to get too excited and happy about a gain that might just be taken away. You found the hidden reason behind it. That's why they're better. You were right: Memories are never entirely silent. They murmur in your cells, shadow the mind, knock at the door. The headaches were the Others."

Rella booked the flight to Colorado. The night before she was scheduled to leave, she sensed unease at the foot of her bed.

Abigail.

Internally, she consoled her.

Rella stared at the ceiling, wondering if she would be able to get off the plane when it arrived. Sleep elusive, she sat up and switched on the lamp, vanishing Abigail as she did so.

With courage, Rella turned on the bathroom light, slowly raising her gaze to face her reflection. She recalled something CJ had said a few sessions ago: *They have worked hard to mirror you.*

She saw them, as though staring into an infinity mirror, shadows stretching out behind her, and wondered who would step in when she needed it most.

Thirty-Six

Eastport, Colorado—1968

Leah sighed heavily upon returning to the small, second-story apartment, her roommates' breakfast dishes piled up in the sink. Mess and clutter reminded her of how she'd grown up.

She folded the clothes she'd brought back from the laundromat. She wished she could have moved out of Eastport altogether, but her job at the law office paid quite a bit more than other girls her age made and allowed her to shave off some classes in her paralegal training.

While not ideal, the living situation was far better than what she had left. No scrutiny from her mother. No overhearing bloody fights between her father and Lester. No one cornering her or overpowering her, causing her to wonder why she was ever born. No one coming into her room at night, except the occasional inebriated visit from Gretchen, the youngest of the three who shared the apartment, which Leah had quickly put a stop to by way of a simple padlock. Gretchen was a nice enough girl, but highly naive and wasteful, paying for the place on her parents' dime as she tripped her way through college.

Marin, the last of the trio, wasn't untidy out of laziness, but for the opposite reason—busyness. She worked multiple jobs, only getting paid for one, volunteering at any political campaign she supported, on top of going to school full-time. Marin fixed her future on Washington. Her heroine was Eugenie Anderson, a United States diplomat, and the first woman to serve as chief of mission at the ambassador level in US history. One of her first quotes to Leah had been from Clare Boothe Luce: "Because I am a woman, I must make unusual efforts to succeed. If I fail, no one will say, 'She doesn't have what it takes'; they will say, 'Women don't have what it takes.' "

Leah finished putting her clean clothes away, then continued her Saturday-morning chores by scrubbing the bathroom to glistening brightness, white tile by white tile. No black. No pink.

She tackled the dishes, washing and towel-drying every plate, fork, and spoon, leaving a large note in the empty dish drainer that read: *Use paper plates.*

Scheduled to meet Janet for lunch, she changed into a pale-yellow top and jeans.

"So, how are things?" Janet asked. "Tell me all." She wore a lilac dress and a big matching bow in her hair, which Leah thought looked ridiculous.

Leah situated herself in the booth. "Good. Lots of work. The night classes are long, but not very difficult. How about you?"

"Dating is a bore," Janet said, assuming a pouty face. "But how else will I ever find a husband?"

"Why do you need one?" As the question left her mouth

Leah knew it was one Janet wouldn't be able to answer. She sighed and changed her approach. "Stop looking so hard and maybe you'll find someone. Besides, it's better to take your time, get to know the person first."

"Well, how about you and *Remington*," Janet said, batting her thickened eyelashes.

Leah had been dating Rem casually for the past two years. While he would describe their relationship as serious, she wouldn't go that far. It wasn't that she didn't care for him—she did. He was a catch, after all: handsome, tall, well-groomed, respectful and considerate, and he came from a stable, supportive family—all virtues that led Leah to conclude he wasn't anyone she deserved.

Remington arrived promptly at seven p.m. on Saturday night, flowers in hand, passenger car door open. His grin widened when he saw Leah.

"You look so beautiful," he said, handing her the bouquet while planting a kiss on her cheek.

"I'm in a sweater and jeans."

"Clothes aren't what make you beautiful."

"You wouldn't ever care to see me in a dress?"

"Not if you weren't comfortable. Here."

"Thank you, Rem." Leah accepted the flowers and stepped inside.

They made their way to the drive-in movie theater located fifteen minutes out of town, the favorite Saturday-night spot for many, their weekend date a predictable played-out amusement park ride along a fixed track, with no roller coasters or Ferris wheels.

The car settled into its usual site. Remington asked Leah what she wanted from the concession stand, and while one week she would order Mary Janes, and the next licorice sticks, and the next Sixlets, there was no mystery as to what Remington would return with: a medium popcorn to share, and a plain chocolate bar.

"Don't you ever get tired of chocolate bars?"

"No," he replied. "They're uncomplicated."

He drove her home afterwards. Normally they ended the evening with a kiss, but tonight he took her hands into his.

"Leah, I'd like to talk."

Leah's heart quickened.

"We've been going steady now for, well, almost two years. I know we're young, but, I love you, Leah. My heart is steadfast. I want to marry you."

The merry-go-round Leah had been spinning on since childhood halted, reversing direction. She gripped the armrest on the car door.

"Rem, I . . . Rem, you are wonderful. You're handsome and attentive. You treat me with care and kindness, a true gentleman. Genuinely the perfect guy."

His expression faltered. "Whenever a fella's called 'the perfect guy,' it usually leads to a breakup."

Leah's eyes lowered. "I care for you deeply, Rem."

"But do you want to marry me, Leah? You gotta know by now. I love you. I want to take care of you."

Leah suddenly felt cold, exiled, standing outside a threshold she'd never crossed.

"I don't understand love, Rem."

"All right, all right." He loosened his hands from hers but didn't release them.

Leah wondered if half-love was better than no love at all.

"Maybe if you give me more time," she said.

"Will time matter?"

Leah looked down.

He perked up. "You want kids, don't ya, Leah? Or do you want to focus on your career? You've gone far in school. I'm so proud of you."

"Thank you, Rem. Yes, I do want kids. And my career, too. I want both."

"Swell! We could get a nice house and you could work, I could work, and we could raise a family together."

Leah saw his vision of the future as if it were playing on the drive-in movie screen. Cue the cheerful music. Pan to a two-story house with shutters and a cherry-red door. She saw herself arriving home from work after a successful day ensuring that justice was delivered, Rem and the kids welcoming her.

"We could, Rem. We could."

"I'm sorry to drop this on you out of the blue," Rem said, reattaching his hand to Leah's more firmly. "We can talk about it another time. Please forgive me."

"Rem, this is not your fault at all. Blame me." She squeezed his hand. "I want to be free, but my mind doesn't rest. I have to focus on what keeps me sane. You are good for me. I want to be good for you, too."

"You are, Leah! Truly!"

"Give me a couple weeks alone to think on this. Can you do that?"

Reluctantly, Rem agreed.

Three weeks later, on a Saturday night, Leah sat home alone in the quiet apartment, Gretchen at a party, Marin at a political rally.

An unexpected knock sounded on the door.

It immediately transported Leah back to when she was nine, the first time Cal had come into her room.

Cal is dead, she reminded herself. Leah wondered what had burned in his head during the moments leading up to his chosen time of death, if he'd ever once experienced mental persecution by what he had done to her.

She closed her textbook. "Coming," she called out.

"Rem!" she said with surprise upon opening the door.

"Hi, Leah," he said tentatively.

"Come in." She stepped aside.

"Thank you." He shifted awkwardly from side to side. "We agreed on space, but I just miss you so much. It's been three weeks . . . I hope it's okay that I'm here." He looked down at the coffee table. "I'm sorry, you're studying. I should have called first."

"Oh, I've been reading so much today I'm getting cross-eyed. Probably not a bad idea to take a break. Can I get you a cola? Water?"

"Whatever you're having is fine. Or nothing. I'm okay."

Rem's nervousness was evident, and she felt responsible.

"Have a seat." Leah gestured to the couch. She sat next to him, but not right next to him.

The chasm of silence between them spoke what neither wanted to say or admit. Leah had missed Rem, but not enough.

"How 'bout some music?" Rem said.

"Sure. I don't have a radio, but Gretchen does. She won't mind if I use it."

Leah fetched it and placed it on the bookcase in the living room.

"I think there's an outlet back here," she said, searching.

"Here, allow me." Rem jumped up.

"Thanks. I'll go get you that drink." Leah crossed the room to the kitchen nook as Rem tinkered with the dial.

"Hey, haven't heard this one in a long time," he said.

The tune was instantly recognizable to Leah. She froze, the image of Cal on top of her, his face, sounds, and smells suffocating, immobilizing.

The glass she was holding crashed to the floor.

"Leah!" Rem abandoned the radio and rushed to the kitchen.

Leah's hands went to her ears. "Turn it off, Rem! Please turn it off!"

He ran back to the bookcase, hurriedly slid the switch to the left, and immediately returned to her side.

"Are you okay? Did you cut yourself?"

Leah's hands pressed tightly against her ears, the song unrelenting in her head.

"Leah? It's off. I'm here. Can you hear me?"

Tension released in fractions as the present slowly returned. Her hands lowered.

"Leah?"

She looked around the room. A kitchen. Not a bedroom. Rem with her. No one else.

"Yes." She trembled. "Clumsy me."

Rem studied her. "Why don't you go sit on the couch, and I'll clean this up."

"Thank you." She walked stiffly into the living room. She heard Rem examining the floor for fragments of broken glass, wondering if he'd ever ask what had shattered her.

He returned to the couch. Leah sat staring at the floor. He reached for her hand. She flinched, pulling it away.

"I'm sorry," he said.

Leah responded a few moments later. "No, I'm sorry."

They sat quietly.

"Leah," he said gently. "Can you tell me what's bothering you?"

Leah felt numb.

"You know, you've never taken me to your parents' house. Whenever I ask about your family, you change the subject. I know you have your reasons. You don't have to reveal all. You have a hard time trusting me, getting close to me. And there's this unseen . . . I don't know, this length you keep between us. I've never brought it up before, because I wanted to be mindful of your privacy, but now, I think maybe there's a connection."

Leah didn't answer, which was answer enough.

"You can talk to me. I want to be here for you. No matter what it is, I will still love you."

Tears formed in Leah's eyes.

"I mean it. Every word."

She wiped her face.

"Please. Tell me. If this is what is keeping us apart, maybe sharing it with me can bring us together."

Part of her almost started to talk. She had never told anyone. Never said it out loud.

Leah's mind went to the day she'd sat at the ice-cream parlor with her fries, dumping ketchup over that horrible ad. She wished it was as easy as that. Wished she could smear out invisible wounds the same way.

Telling Rem what had happened couldn't and wouldn't change the past. It would only make her look weak.

She shook her head. "I can't say, Rem. I can't."

He asked if he could stay with her until one of her roommates returned. He offered to sleep on the couch all night in case she needed him.

She thanked him, hugged him, cried some more. But ultimately told him it wasn't necessary.

He drove away, Leah watching from the window, both knowing it was over.

Thirty-Seven

Eastport, Colorado—1970

Jack Cooper circled the gleaming 750, inspecting for scratches.

"Is that . . . ?" He licked his thumb and rubbed the chrome. "Nah, it's good."

He stood back and grinned at his most prized possession. He wasn't a property-driven fellow. The less he owned, the freer he was. It was the screaming deal he'd ridden away with that fueled his satisfaction. The well-to-do previous owner had become bored with the bike in six months, and Jack happened to be the first person to look at it.

Jack appreciated its sleek design, the tank and side panels in Sunrise Melon, and most of all, its speed. At 67 horsepower, 44 foot-pounds of torque, and maxing out at 120 mph, when he wanted to go, it went. He regularly took long, two-hour drives on back roads before breaking for coffee and a noon breakfast.

"I'll have the garden salad, lemon and vinegar on the side, and boiled potatoes."

The waitress stared down at her over her glasses. "We only have crinkle-cut."

Janet wrinkled her nose. "Fries? No thank you, then."

The waitress waited expectantly. "That all?"

"Yes."

"And for you?"

"Spaghetti with red sauce—extra sauce, please," said Leah.

Janet did not veil her disapproval.

"Make that extra spaghetti, too. And the biggest salad you have, with Italian dressing," Leah added, handing over the menu.

"I still can't believe you broke up with Remington," Janet said. "But that's no excuse to let your figure fall to pieces."

"I'm thin, and I'm starving," Leah retorted. "And I've scarcely eaten in days, I've been so busy."

"Remington Skye." Janet folded her fingers under her chin. "What a perfect name. It could have been your name."

Although Leah believed a girl had the right to keep her own last name after marriage if she so chose, if she ever got married, she planned on chopping hers off like a diseased tumor.

Their breakup had plagued Leah. She didn't feel remorse, but rather guilt and sadness, for causing him pain. The clouds had since parted in her sky, and she hoped they had for Rem, too.

"I'm sure he will find a wonderful girl to marry, if he hasn't already."

"Silliness on your part," Janet chastised.

"Are you ever going to quit?"

"I would hate to see you end up with the last name Schneider or Dunkel or Crabbie!"

Leah regarded her dubiously. "Crabbie? Really?"

"You haven't been very pleasant lately."

Leah couldn't argue with that. After finishing school, she'd been certain the legal office would promote her, with a raise. But a new supervisor had announced the appointment of her coveted position to a less qualified male, asking Leah to fetch him a cup of coffee in nearly the same chauvinistic grunt. She'd quit and joined Gretchen in her evening escapades, dancing away the disappointment.

"Even so, you made that name up."

"Did not! I saw it in a book. By a British writer."

"Since when do you read anything but crummy magazines? And besides, we don't live in England."

"We certainly don't. I would think the men there are far more civilized."

A loud voice broke the low din of the cafe.

"Hey, who owns the red sedan? You took up two parking spots!"

Nobody 'fessed up.

The two girls stared as the young boy shook his head in incredulity, a motorcycle helmet in one hand.

"Well, I tell you, such manners!" Janet huffed. "He has a horrendous last name, I'm sure of it. Don't marry his sort, Leah."

"I don't even know him. And you don't marry or not marry someone based on their last name anyway."

"Hmph. I think all criteria need to be considered," Janet contended.

Leah's eyes followed the boy as he took a seat at the counter.

The waitress arrived with the food. Janet used her utensil like a musical conductor's baton, orchestrating each bite to be small and ladylike, while Leah twirled heaps of spaghetti around the fork and into her mouth.

After their lunch, Janet skipped off to a nail appointment, giving Leah money for her portion of the bill and blowing a good-bye kiss from her hand.

Leah approached the counter to pay the check, walking past the boy with the motorcycle helmet who'd burst into the diner earlier.

"This doesn't have bleached flour, does it?" she heard him ask, holding up what looked to be rye toast.

"Actually, I think it comes from the bakery up the street," Leah offered. "Their stuff is pretty good."

He nodded and continued eating.

"Are you from around here?" Leah asked him.

"No."

"Oh. Just traveling through?"

"Where the work goes, I go."

"What do you do?"

"Tend horses."

"Horses? You like animals, then?"

He looked up from the plate, straight ahead. "Horses have something inside them. Deep emotion. Their eyes are honest. Too much injustice in this corrupt world. Not in horses. They are unrefined purity."

"Like unbleached flour."

He smiled, dropped his head back to the plate and slopped up a runny egg. "Yeah, I guess so."

"I've never been on a horse."

"They can shift temperamental. But also, be your best pal. Horses get me." He shook his head. "People never seem to."

"I'm Leah."

"Jack Cooper."

"Cooper, did you say?"

"Yeah."

Leah smiled to herself, at how she would rub this in with Janet later.

"I could show you around town, if you like," she said. "Be a friend in the area."

He looked directly at her. His fluid blue eyes had a mercurial nature to them, like an unsettled tide.

"Sure," he responded.

Part Three

Winter is on us
Winter is watching us
Cutting and quiet
Winter is all over me
— Tanya Donelly, "Clipped"

Thirty-Eight

November 2017

Rella touched her fingertip to the small, round window, peering into the night at the lights sparkling below.

"I hope you enjoyed the flight, miss," the flight attendant said with a smile, pausing at Rella's seat. "Hot towel?"

"No, thank you," Rella replied.

The lights dimmed. The attendants strapped in.

"Ladies and gentlemen, this is the captain speaking. We'll be touching down in about ten minutes. Local time is 9:25 p.m., temperature a balmy thirty-five degrees. Welcome to Colorado."

Rella braced herself—not for the imminent landing, but for everything to follow.

The next morning, Rella exited the Craftsman bungalow she'd rented and headed down the quiet street. The watered-down sky made the scraggly, stripped trees more forlorn, their thin, brittle arms hooked in search of sun. Eastport, only an hour away, clawed at her too, like phantom pain. She walked faster.

Trevor picked her up at eleven to take her to Morgan's.

"Snazzy outfit. 'Specially for us country folk," Trevor said, adopting a drawl.

Rella had on a long-sleeved tunic dress, tights, and flat-soled, knee-high boots.

"Thanks. Ooh, and nice and warm in here. Appreciate that."

"I knew you'd fancy a toasty chariot."

Morgan smoothed the lace tablecloth from the center outward before arranging the plates on top. She'd found it stuffed in the back of her buffet, glad she had something to spruce up the presentation. She knew how Rella liked things fancy.

She stirred the pot of beans, cauliflower, broccoli, carrots, and potatoes, covered the lid, and reached for three heirloom tomatoes. They'd cost three times the price of other organic tomatoes, but their bright yellow, red, purple, and green would add lively color to the dish.

While chopping, she thought about Rella, wondering how the conversation would go. Rella had said little to her over the last few months, but that wasn't unusual.

She popped a chunk of tomato in her mouth.

Trevor and Rella pulled up to Morgan's apartment complex.

"The guest parking is a bit far," said Trevor. "I'll drop you off, so you don't get too cold. Number 220. She told me she left the door open since she might be in the kitchen, so just walk right in."

"Thanks, Trevor."

She climbed the outdoor staircase to the second floor.

Morgan had the end unit to the left. She knocked once and then walked in.

"Morgan?" Rella called out. She looked around the simply furnished room. Morgan had moved from her last place a couple of years ago, so Rella had never seen this apartment.

"Finally!" Morgan held out her arms and embraced Rella. "So glad you're here, Rella."

"Hi, Morgan. Nice place."

Morgan released her. "I still need to hang some pictures, choose paint. I know, you would have had it done in two days, not two years. Decorating is the last thing on my mind with these double shifts lately. But don't worry, I told them my sister was coming, so no overtime! And I got someone to cover for me today."

"Great."

"You settled in all right? I would have gladly taken the couch if you had wanted to stay with me."

"No worries. I found a cute bungalow nearby, in the center of town."

"I know you like to be on your own anyway."

"Yes." Rella stepped over to the sliding glass door. "I love the balcony over the green space, and the view of the mountains is gorgeous."

"I debated about getting a house, but I just couldn't make the commitment. Besides, coming home in the middle of the night as often as I do, I feel better knowing other people are around."

"I can understand that. The town seems pretty nice too, has charm. But where are all the mansions?"

"Yeah, well, there are no mansions in Mansion, Colorado, just like there are no ports in Eastport."

Landlocked, Rella thought.

"A historical tour would have been nice," said Rella.

"I know you like that stuff."

Rella unrolled her scarf.

"No coat?"

"I don't have one. Not needed in California."

"Well, I made us a great lunch. I hope you like it. All vegan, organic, so you can eat it."

"That was sweet of you."

"Where's Trevor?"

"Parking the car."

Morgan nodded. "Come on into the kitchen."

Rella followed Morgan down the hall. "Smells good." She noticed the white lace tablecloth. Her fists closed.

"I made it just a little spicy, but not too spicy," Morgan said.

Rella's eyes did not stray from the tablecloth.

"I brought some beer, Morgan," Trevor said as he entered, holding up a six-pack and heading for the fridge. "Want one?"

"I think I'll stick with wine, thanks. Rella, want a glass?"

Rella felt a separating from her body, drifting.

"Rella?"

Margaret, Rella spoke internally. *Keep me here.*

Slowly, she descended back into the room. Her left eye, which became watery and somehow felt higher than the right one when she disconnected, evened out and dried up. Rella worried that what she experienced on the inside could perhaps be seen on the outside. She rubbed her cheek. "Yeah?"

"You okay?"

She shook her hands out. "Sure. A little tingly is all. Not used to the cold, I guess." She pressed a smile onto her face.

"Darn it." Morgan tapped a serrated knife against the counter.

"What?" Trevor asked.

"I forgot the bread. Meant to run by the bakery after work yesterday."

"I'll go pick it up. It'll be better fresh, anyway."

"True. Thanks, Trevor."

"Rella, want anything?"

"I'm good, thank you."

"Be back in a jiffy."

Morgan reached for the bottle of wine after Trevor left, removing a corkscrew from the drawer. "Don't worry, I checked and it's a healthy one." She popped the cork. "Organic, biodynamic, all those wholesome words."

"That's nice of you—thank you. Morgan, do you mind if we go into the living room?"

"Sure." Morgan grabbed two glasses. She and Rella seated themselves on the couch. Morgan poured the wine. "So, how have you been doing?"

"Fine. Work is busy."

"How are *you* doing?"

Rella took a hefty sip.

Morgan folded her legs under her. "How's the therapy? You're still going, right? You haven't told me anything about it."

Rella studied the ruby-colored liquid in her glass. "I . . . it's . . . it's fine."

"Who are you going to?"

"A woman in Huntington Beach."

"She's nice? You like her?"

"Yes. She's been very helpful."

"Good."

"Other than the long shifts, how's the hospital?"

"They moved me to the children's ward. I really like it. The kids are so sweet. I just want to squeeze 'em."

There were times Rella wished she could hold Katie, Lisa, and Abigail.

Morgan tilted the wineglass back and forth. "I've actually been thinking about adopting."

"Really?"

"Yeah. I know you're not such a big fan of kids, and I didn't think I was either, but lately, I don't know, it would be nice to have one around. I think I have something to offer. I'd adopt one a little older, give them a good home."

"That would be an amazing thing to do."

"Maybe I just miss when you were little. At the time, I resented having to look after you so much, because of Mom. Now, I'd give anything to rewind back to then."

Rella noticed tears in her sister's eyes. "Morgan, I'm fine."

"I'm just so angry, I could throw this wine."

"I've never known you to waste alcohol."

Morgan laughed.

"Really, you don't need to worry about me."

Rella worried more for the Others than for herself. They

were the ones who remembered, who made fists and clamped teeth and pounded legs and drew in silence and doubled over in pain and cleaned up file rooms and stood hauntingly at the end of the bed. They were the ones who wanted to get away. And couldn't.

"I should have known, should have sensed something," Morgan said.

"Morgan, I want you to put those thoughts right out of your mind, today, and every day. Promise? And if not for you, for me. I don't want to think about it, talk about it, or dwell on it. Ever."

Morgan opened her mouth to respond just as a burst of cold air rushed in from her front door.

An image flashed into Rella's mind. A little girl on the floor of her grandparents' house, on the rug in the living room. The little girl had dark hair, like her. It wasn't Katie or Abigail. She was too young to be Lisa. She looked about three years old.

Rella saw the scene play out in her mind.

The floor tremored beneath her when the front door opened. The rattling contents of the metal toolbox in his clutch matched the insecure beat of her heart as it hit the floor.

The plastic comb to brush Pretty Pony's purple mane dropped from the little girl's hand. She kept her eyes low.

"Take your boots off," her grandmother said, coming up behind her, wiping her hands on a dishtowel.

"Get off my back."

"And leave your filthy clothes downstairs." She looked down at the little girl. "Into the kitchen, now."

White linen sat folded atop the table, its four corners sharp.

"Watch me," she instructed. "Lay it out proper."

She opened it up and smoothed the tablecloth. The little girl didn't like all the holes along the edges, empty spaces, like eyes watching her.

"What's that for?" her grandfather said, entering the dining room.

"Company."

"I don't want anyone over."

The woman didn't pay any attention and continued arranging place settings.

"No need to put on airs with this frilly nonsense and those puny dishes."

"Then you can eat downstairs. Or go hungry."

"I never go hungry." He fixed his eyes on the little girl, laughed, and went into the kitchen. He left out the back door, beer in hand.

"Rella. Rella!"

Rella blinked. Fingers were in front of her face, snapping.

"Morgan—sorry. I must have spaced." She noticed Trevor had entered, bringing the gust of cold air in with him.

Rella shivered.

"Sorry, Rella," Trevor said, shutting the door quickly. He held up the bread. "Baguette, and sourdough rye."

"You got back fast," Morgan remarked.

"No line on a weekday."

Rella kept her eyes down. She could feel Morgan looking at her.

"Everything okay?" Trevor asked.

"Yes, fine." Rella stood. "What can I do to help?"

Rella saw Morgan slightly frown, knowing she would have preferred to talk to her further.

"Well," Morgan said, hands on thighs as she stood, "most everything is done. Let's go into the kitchen."

Rella eyed the tablecloth upon entering the room. "Morgan, where did you get that tablecloth?"

"No idea." She checked the pot on the stove. "Like it?"

Rella's heart quickened and her stomach burned. She wouldn't be able to eat with that tablecloth there. She debated spilling wine all over it, but couldn't bring herself to ruin something of Morgan's.

"I wonder if we could take it off the table. I'm so clumsy, I'd be afraid to eat anything on it."

"Oh, I don't care."

"Umm, really, I would prefer it."

"Well, all right." Morgan shook her spoon like a scepter. "Trevor, can you take care of it, please?"

"Sure thing."

Rella faced the window as Trevor removed the tablecloth and folded it.

"Where do you want it?" he asked.

"Any drawer will do," Morgan replied.

Rella waited for the sound of the shutting drawer before turning around again.

Trevor drove Rella to the bungalow and walked her inside.

"Could we talk for a sec?" he asked.

"Sure."

He ran his hands through his hair. "Rella, I love you. I'm your big brother. I would do anything for you." He paused. "Morgan told me."

The words hit her like a stun gun.

"I want to . . . I wish I could make it right. Go back to when you were little and wrap you up and protect you. Be the savior, the knight in shining armor. All brothers and fathers should be protectors. And mothers. And sisters. And aunts and uncles, nieces and nephews. Wielding swords against anyone or anything endangering our loved ones. The very thought that—"

Rella wiped her eyes and composed herself. "You've never wronged me, Trevor."

"There is a big divide between not doing wrong and doing right."

"You couldn't do right about something you knew nothing about."

Trevor dropped down in front of her. "What can I do *now*? Tell me, and I'll do it."

Rella dropped her head. "Nothing," she said softly.

"Morgan told me you're going to therapy. I know all of this was yours to tell, but she's worried sick about you. She didn't let on today, because she didn't want to pounce on your first day here. She just cares."

Trevor paused, taking a deep breath.

"Rella, I've been thinking a lot, about this past year. What we found out, how you were scared that night when I came over to your place. I don't want to upset you; I never do. But there's been a change in you. You moved away years ago, yes, but I still had a connection with you, even across the miles. But it's . . . somehow, it's faulty now. I can't explain it, but part of you has gone somewhere else."

Rella stayed quiet.

"I'm here for you. You've always fended for yourself, but I want you to know, you don't have to."

"I know. You have always been a wonderful big brother, Trevor."

As Trevor drove away, her last words to him repeated in her ears. "If only our mother had had the same," she said aloud. Rella found it beyond comprehension that a brother would force himself onto his sister, or a father onto his daughter.

Why, why had Morgan said anything to Trevor? The devastating events from Rella's childhood was her information to tell, not Morgan's. It wasn't the first time Morgan had betrayed a confidence. Rella had needed at least the first day to go well.

Her mind swelled with bad images. Waves of nausea hit, along with thoughts of inky, black tarry sludge in her stomach.

Rella's breath caught in her throat. In rapid reverse, she transported back to her first visit with CJ, how she had described what she'd seen in her stomach: a tarry substance.

What she had been trying to vomit out. Knowledge. Stuck deep inside, under a metal trapdoor, what she'd had to swallow, endure, its weight the mass of an adult male body. A word she was loathe to utter, to think.

Raped.

Katie had been. Abigail. She didn't know about Lisa. She didn't know about herself.

She screamed, her voice hoarse, as though newly learning how.

She screamed again. A holler from the past, climbing out of her throat on its elbows, legs heavy with tar.

"Ahhhhhh!" she screamed, with as much strength as she could muster, a cry that had been entombed for decades.

Thirty-Nine

A soft rain pitter-pattered against the window. Rella gathered wood from the porch and brought it inside. She lit kindling and watched as the paper disintegrated and the logs ignited. She sat in front of the flames for several minutes before checking the time. Five minutes before her scheduled call with CJ.

"Hi, Rella, how's it going there?"

"Well, I'm managing."

"Anything happen?"

Rella's voice shook. "It's very difficult, living like this, not knowing what will jump out at me, whether it's an object that reminds me of something I can't even remember, or a new connection arrives, without warning."

"Want to tell me about it?"

"Maybe when I get back. I need to clear it away for now. I'm seeing Trevor in a couple of hours. How are you?" Rella knew it was a silly question to ask, but it came from a genuine place.

"I'm good. Dealing with learning a new phone. I miss the old days of flip phones."

Rella laughed. "I refused to text for a long time. Now, I can't live without it!"

"I know what you mean. So, what will you and Trevor do today?"

Rella used the poker to stoke the fire. "Actually, I was thinking about telling him."

"Telling him?"

"Yes. About my—condition."

"Oh. Quite a big step."

"Well, I feel like it might bring some relief, to talk about it with someone who's known me all my life. Maybe I could gain useful information. And if a—change occurs . . ."

"I see your reasoning."

"Thank you."

"What about Morgan?"

"I don't want to tell Morgan. She'd—I'm not up for it."

"It's your decision, of course."

"Yes." Rella studied the fire. "Maybe it's not a good idea. The Others may come out more easily if I tell him."

"That could happen. Whatever you decide, it's not necessary to go into details or relive everything."

"I agree."

"Also, some people, even well-meaning ones, may be a little *too* interested, ask a lot of questions, because of the nature of the condition, as it's not one ordinarily encountered. I wouldn't want you to feel like an object of curiosity."

Rella understood. But Trevor had never let her down or judged her. If there was anyone she would tell, it was him.

Miraculously, by the time she'd finished her call with CJ, the sun had come out, the clouds dispersed, and the air had warmed up a good 10 degrees. The bright rays beamed assurance, and she knew what she was going to do.

"Nice digs, Rella. I would have invited you to stay with me, but, well, my lone mattress is on the floor."

"When has it *not* been?" Rella ribbed.

"You got me there."

"Has your current apartment grown up at all?"

"Nah. What would be the fun in that?"

"Paper plates and no food?"

"Mustard packets. Does that count?"

"Plastic utensils next to the bottle opener?"

"Have you been spying on me?" Trevor jollied good-naturedly.

"I have a picnic lunch all ready. A *healthy* one. No fast food on my watch!"

"I've cut back, actually. Dumb of me to eat it for so long. And no more meat, either. Makes me heavy, sluggish."

"Wow. Who are you and what have you done with my brother?"

"I learned a lot when I visited you. And hey, I want to keep my boyish face and bod as long as I can, right?"

Rella smiled. "Right."

"Beer, though—can't give up the beer."

She picked up the bags containing their picnic lunch. "Why don't you drive us to a nice place where we can be outside?"

In the natural light of the inviting sunshine, Rella could almost forget she'd worn a scarf and hat to bed. The mountains were a beautiful backdrop to the meadow Trevor had taken them to.

They chose one of eight empty picnic tables.

"I'm starving," Trevor said. "You must be too."

"Mm," Rella replied vaguely. She needed to do her talking on an empty stomach. She reached for the bag. "Here—the first of three sandwiches I brought for you."

"Three?"

"You're always hungry. And one can generally eat far more when having vegan whole foods."

"Cool." Trevor accepted it, then put it down. "I'm sorry. You want to talk first?"

"Eat. Then we can talk."

Trevor unwrapped the sandwich and Rella wandered from the table to stroll the span of vivid green. She studied small wildflowers pushing up from the ground, alternating in yellow and white, with a few violet ones popping between. She thought of the Others, trapped beneath the terrain for so long, while she had been the only blossom in the sun. She wanted to give them each the opportunity to bloom. Maybe this was the first step.

Her heart rate intensified as she approached the table, where Trevor was finishing the last bite of his sandwich.

"That was delicious, Rella, thank you. What'd I eat anyway?" he asked, laughing.

"Tempeh, sautéed in a little tamari and fresh lemon, lettuce and tomato, and a dollop of mustard."

"A BLT, hold the bacon. More satisfying. And good for me." Trevor wrapped up the packaging and wiped his hands on his jeans. "Okay, I'm all ears."

Rella reached in the bag, retrieving two bottles of water.

Trevor studied her face. "We don't have to talk if you don't want to."

If she didn't do it now, Rella didn't know when she would—*if* she would. It wouldn't get any easier, and it wasn't going away. She was glad they were outside, in an open space, in the sun.

"I'm ready."

Trevor moved to sit atop the table, his feet resting on the bench. Rella remained standing.

"What I'm going to say, please promise not to tell anyone else. Not Morgan, not anyone. I don't want to be seen differently."

Trevor tilted his head, questioning, but kept silent for her to continue.

"The phone call I'd had with Morgan, during your visit, she had insisted I go for therapy, in an effort to address my health problems. She had suspected something happened to me, when I was young." Rella's voice trailed off. "And as you know, as she told you, something did. But what I went through while finding out . . ."

She outlined the course of events to Trevor, from Seth's office, to the perilous chute afterwards.

"Rella, I can't believe this. What an idiot!" Trevor vaulted off the table. "What did you say his name was again?"

She didn't want to get caught up in Seth and his gross incompetence, as it could result in her not continuing with what she needed to say.

"He was awful, yes." She shook her head. "There are no words." Surprisingly, she didn't cry, determined to say all she needed to, at this very moment. "He really messed me up. It's why I sought out another therapist, after months of living in the aftermath, to undo it. He shouldn't have done what he did to me—to anyone. But there's a specific reason he *categorically* shouldn't have done what he did to me."

Rella folded her hands together.

"He used something called TDT. It's a technique that's supposed to help people reprocess a traumatic event. Of course, I had zero memory of one. I'm sure I never would have recalled anything, either. Even though, based on my diagnosis, what happened to me would have had to have been—repeated."

Trevor's fingernails dug into the peeling wood.

"Let's not think about that," Rella said briskly. "That's not what I have to tell you. With TDT, the patient has to be screened first, for a certain condition, the condition I have. The new therapist did all the right screening. And . . ." Rella's heart pounded. "She found out . . ."

Trevor waited.

Just say it, Rella told herself. She swallowed.

"I have dissociative identity disorder." Rella exhaled. It was the first time she had said those five words out loud.

Trevor's face didn't register any recognition, which didn't surprise her.

She squeezed her hands together.

"Dissociative identity disorder. It's the name they give now to"—she swallowed—"multiple personalities."

It still sounded altogether implausible, so hysterical drama.

"Multiple personalities?" Trevor paused. "You mean, you

become another person or something? You don't have that, Rella. You've always been you!"

She'd initiated the reveal, but still had much to explain. Their conversation could continue for years.

"I think the new term explains it better. Dissociative identity. The person undergoes a trauma so horrible, more than once, that they have to find a way out. So, they dissociate—break off, switch into another identity. Then they don't remember doing so, because someone else lives it."

Rella looked at Trevor's expression.

"I know," she said. "I didn't believe it either. I mean, it makes no sense, right? All these years, you'd think I would have noticed, that you or Morgan or *anyone* would have. But I've come to see that it's true."

She described how Margaret had appeared. What it was like, that first time, in the Greenhouse. Meeting the Others.

Trevor had tears in his eyes when she told him about Katie and Abigail.

"No wonder I've always needed time alone. I had plenty of people in my head." She paused, smiling. "That was supposed to be a joke."

Trevor shook his head. "I don't want to laugh about it. I want to understand it. Tell me more."

As Rella did, she had to keep reminding herself what they were actually discussing. She couldn't believe how well Trevor was taking it, and how talking about it was far less scary than she had imagined it would be.

"This Max," Trevor said, after Rella described his relationship with Katie, "he sounds like an upright guy to me."

"Yeah. I can relate to him, too. I'd like to learn more about him. All of them. Sometimes I catch myself uttering words I later realize came from one of them, through me. I'm more attuned to their presence, in the background at times. Lisa wants to meet you. She wants to meet everyone!"

"I can't wait—when you're ready, of course."

"Thank you for saying that."

"I mean it."

The mention of her name kindled Lisa. Internally Rella told her it wasn't the right time.

"You can hear them talking?" Trevor asked.

"Not actual voices. But I'm given information, in small doses."

"Can you see them?"

"The ones I know, yes."

"Cool."

"CJ says they are all me, but I don't perceive it that way. They each have their own personality, mannerisms, emotions, physical appearance."

"Wow. Huh."

"The times when I completely change, I don't always remember what's happened."

"So, if one of them is here, it's like you're not."

"If I'm completely one of them, yes. Sometimes I can fight it—the change—and sometimes it comes so fast, with no warning, and I'm gone. I'd rather not change. But I don't always have control over it. I also can't summon them to come out, so to speak. It just happens."

"And how do you get back to—you?"

Rella sighed. "It can be a problem sometimes. Talking about my work helps."

"How often does it happen?"

Rella wanted to say, "Too often," but she didn't want to upset the Others, or alarm Trevor.

"It's best if I'm careful about any triggers. The predicament is, I'm still learning what those are."

"It must be hard."

"It's what worries me the most—the loss of control. I know you think your sister is calm and collected, but I've got firecrackers inside." Rella told him about the cutting board incident. "At the time, I had no idea what had come over me. One minute I was worrying about spoiled food, and the next, I attacked the counter. I needed to hit, needed the noise. I now know who did that, but it was quite the event to me when it happened. It literally felt like someone else had complete control over my body, and I was helpless to stop it—just an onlooker. A broken one, like the board. I'll always be like this now. No amount of Krazy Glue can fix it—*crazy* being the key word."

"You're not crazy, Rella. Not at all. Nothing is wrong with you. Wrong happened *to* you. And how you managed it shows . . . well, I see resourceful design. Not chaos. A remarkable function of the brain, not a disease state. Look how far you've gone in life."

"Funny . . . me splitting apart is what kept me together."

"It's astounding. I've known you all your life, and I had no idea."

"*I've* known me all my life, and *I* had no idea! CJ wasn't

311

even the person who revealed it. They were. The Others. I still don't remember anything congruent or clear, from the past, that is. Only vague images, shadows of memories. My therapist is a detective, with multiple witnesses offering separate testimony."

Tears formed in Trevor's eyes. "I'm sorry, Rella. Not about you having this condition, but for *why* you have it."

Rella knew she had been spared. The Others were the ones living in a time loop, where what had happened continued, over and over again, their entire existences tied to terror.

Trevor returned Rella to the bungalow.

"Thank you for telling me, Rella." He put his hands on her shoulders and met her eyes. "I'm honored that you did. And I won't tell anyone. Not because I feel it should be concealed, but because it's *your* right to decide who to tell. It's your secret superpower, your team."

"Thank you, Trevor. Thank you for listening."

"*That* you can always count on. Can I give you a hug?"

Rella nodded. In the reassurance of his arms, all the fears Rella had had about being judged, or seen as weird, or lying, melted away.

Forty

"Is that—no, it can't be. It *is*. Rella! Rella Cooper!"

Rella turned from the produce section. "Janet!" she exclaimed, in anxious surprise.

"I knew that was you. My, my, it has been a long time. Too long!"

Janet grabbed her, enveloping her in a smothering hug.

"Let me look at you. Still a pretty little thing." She brushed back strands of Rella's hair. "You look so much like your mother. I picked her up last week. She came with me to the salon."

"I was about to compliment you on your hairstyle."

Janet lifted her slick bob with the edge of her palm. "Never leave your looks by the wayside. So, what do you have in that basket there, besides apples?"

"Oh, more fruit, vegetables, nuts."

"Rella, you're ghastly thin. When's the last time you saw a doctor?"

"I don't go to doctors."

Janet's hand flew to her chest. "Then there *must* be something wrong."

"Janet, hey, how's it going?" Trevor said, walking over. "What are you doing in this neck of the woods?"

"Retirement allows change, and we grew tired of hearing

traffic noise. And it's better to be closer to your mother."

"That's thoughtful of you."

"Mm. Trevor, Rella needs to have a checkup. I know you two think youth is on your side, but just you wait until sixty comes."

"Rella's super healthy," Trevor said with a smile. "She'll probably outlive all of us."

"I'm calling Morgan first thing. I don't know about those New Age doctors in California, but we have the best of the lot here."

"I appreciate your concern, Janet, but I'm good, really," Rella told her.

"Trevor, give us a minute, please."

Trevor glanced sideways at Rella, who smiled slightly and nodded once. Trevor walked away.

"Now, Rella, you know your mother is not well. She'll never be right. She does her best, day to day. We've known each other since grade school. She's practically a sister to me. I'll always be here for her, and for you kids. I only wish there was more I could do." Janet closed her eyes and shook her head. "I was so young, then. I sensed something was wrong. Should have known. How she acted around her brother. The little clues she gave." Janet opened her eyes and patted Rella's hand. "She has you children. I wonder, though, why you had to move so far away," Janet said with a pinch of disapproval.

Rella didn't reply.

"All right, honey, I best be off. Earle's waiting for me. Maybe we can get together and have a nice lunch while you're here, before you fly off and leave us again."

Trevor returned. Rella stood stationary, alone, next to the Honeycrisp apples.

"Rella? You okay?"

Incessant thoughts plagued her mind since Janet walked away. Katie wanted to raise her hands and smash her temples with her palms to beat them out, but Margaret kept them lowered, knowing she was in a public place and people would see.

"Rella?"

Katie about to win, Rella fled the market.

Trevor found her in the lot behind the building.

"Rella!" he said, out of breath. He walked to face her.

She stood, rigid. Eyes impassive. Mouth set in a line. Stance fixed.

It wasn't Rella. It threw him, for he'd never looked at his sister and not seen *his sister* before.

"Rella, what happened?"

No response.

Dummy, Trevor admonished himself. He wasn't talking to Rella. He wasn't sure *who* he was talking to. Maybe that's what he should ask. As he was about to, an unseen truck backfired.

She scurried to the concrete wall and dropped, huddled, arms around knees, facing away.

"I'm sorry for that noise startling you. Can I sit down here?" Trevor kept his distance. "So, I'm Trevor. Rella's brother."

Then, it came to Trevor, what Rella had suggested to help bring her back.

"Rella's a designer—an architect." His sister had worked so hard for all she had, despite her condition. "Are you familiar with her work?"

No response.

"I wish I could say I knew more, too. It's complicated. Lots of math, but creative at the same time."

She rubbed her forehead.

"She's even working while she's here. She has a business meeting scheduled—that's how in demand she is." Trevor shook his head. "I need to get my act together. She puts me to shame!"

Small changes took place. Her body relaxed, detached from the wall. Breathing slowed. Facial expression softened. Her fists opened and closed, rubbed her forehead.

"Mm."

"Rella?"

The movements continued, until her eyes opened. They fell upon Trevor, but looked through him, and Trevor wondered what she was seeing.

"Can I help you up?"

Her open palm went to her neck, again to the forehead. A slight nod.

Trevor extended his hands, supporting her elbows.

"My legs are shaky."

"Rella?"

"Yeah."

"Oh, Rella. It's Trevor. I'm here for you."

They were Rella's eyes looking back.

Morgan called Rella early the next morning.

"Rella, good news—I got you an appointment this afternoon."

Rella paused in her work. "What? What do you mean?"

"Janet called. I know, she can be overbearing, but she's right. You need a checkup, especially if you haven't had one in a long time. When's the last time you had a female appointment?"

"A *female* appointment? Morgan, I don't need to go through that."

"Rella, I insist. My doctor was booked, but this is a medical group, and another was available. Unheard of, to get in with such short notice, I know. Someone canceled, so, you need to take advantage."

Rella was the one who felt being taken advantage of.

Two short beeps sounded outside.

"Hi, Rella!" Morgan waved spiritedly when Rella came out, as if they were headed to a theme park.

Rella trudged to the car. "Morgan, I really don't want to do this."

"It will be over before you know it, and then we'll get you some vegan ice cream."

"I don't like cold things." Rella cringed at the thought of the speculum. "I'm seeing a woman, right?"

"Yes, it's a woman."

The ride much too short, she reluctantly followed Morgan inside.

Rella eyed the other patients in the waiting room. At least none of them had bulging abdomens.

Morgan involved herself in a magazine while Rella unenthusiastically began the paperwork.

Do you have a period approximately once a month?

The only responses provided were "yes" or "no." Rella wrote, *Unfortunately.*

The questions continued—about birth control, partners, pregnancy, and safety in relationships. None of them applied to her.

The last question stalled her pen.

History of abuse or trauma?

Her grasp tensed into a fist.

"Rella Cooper," the medical assistant called out.

"Hello—Rella, is it?" the female doctor said as she entered the room, her eyes on the chart in her hand rather than Rella. "Never heard that name before." She looked up, squinting, as though eyeing a specimen under a microscope. "I'm Dr. Pratt." She glanced in Morgan's direction.

"This is my sister, Morgan."

"I'm a patient of Dr. Leslie's. Rella is here visiting from out of town, and I insisted she have a visit."

Dr. Pratt's head snapped back to Rella. "When was your last pap?"

"A few years ago."

Dr. Pratt tapped her pen critically. She glanced back down at the form Rella had filled out. "You've had cysts in the past."

"Yes."

"And a few abnormal pap smears."

"When I was young, yes."

"You're still young, my dear."

"Not really."

She flipped the chart shut. "Let's take a look."

Morgan nodded reassuringly as Rella uneasily lay back on the freezing table. The paper gown barely reached her thighs, and she was required to be unclothed underneath. Rows of fluorescent lights glowered above.

"I'll perform the breast examination now."

Cold, thin hands prodded her body and Rella tried to pretend she was anywhere else.

"Make sure you are doing this on your own, too."

Rella never had, and never would.

"All is fine there. I'll need you to move to the bottom of the table."

Apprehensive, she did, eyes glued to the ceiling.

Morgan came over by her side and took her hand as the doctor prepared for the pelvic exam.

"Feet in the stirrups, please."

Morgan gave Rella's hand a squeeze before stepping back.

Rella forced herself into the awful position, legs splayed.

"Rella, come down further, please."

Rella grabbed the sides of the table.

"Rella, I need you to relax. You've done this before."

Rella heard the wheels of the stool as the doctor moved closer. She stiffened. The first touch of the cool metal pressed against her skin. She arched her back as the apparatus inserted further, the sensation acute. She wished she could float above it all. It pushed her apart. She dreaded the moment the swab would scrape inside her.

"Ow, ow," she whimpered.

"Come now," the doctor said.

Rella's knees quivered. Her feet drove into the stirrups. She fought the urge to kick the doctor away.

"I just need to collect a few more cells."

Rella's eyes remained shut.

"All right, done."

The doctor removed the speculum and rolled over to a counter in the corner of the room.

"Rella—Rella, it's over," Morgan said, rubbing Rella's right arm.

The watershed of tears Rella had been holding streamed silently down her face.

"You can sit up now and get dressed." The doctor's hand was on the doorknob.

Rella didn't move.

"Give us a few minutes and we'll come out as soon as she's ready," Morgan said.

"We have other patients waiting."

"She's upset."

Rella lay unresponsive.

"This is a routine exam. There's no need to carry on," Dr. Pratt chided.

"And who are you to make a judgment?" Morgan demanded, cheeks flushed.

"Well, it's not normal."

"Maybe it *is*."

"Such theatrics."

"Please leave this room," Morgan ordered firmly.

The doctor snapped the file shut and exited.

"Rella, I'm sorry. I didn't realize."

Rella held her lower abdomen, every artery, vein, and nerve in her pelvic floor weeping.

Forty-One

Prior to leaving on her trip, Garrett had asked Rella if she would be open to meeting with a potential new client in Grand Junction during her time away.

Rella had answered in the affirmative, with enthusiasm, grateful for the reprieve it would provide during the trip. The meeting had gone well, the client accepting the proposal. Now, she had just over a three-hour return drive ahead of her. It was time she planned to devote to Max.

Max had a motorcycle. She turned up the heat, rolled down the windows, and let in the wind. She tuned to an alternative rock station, the kind of music he listened to.

Nearing the halfway point, Rella spotted a sign for a diner and pulled in. Of all the locations where each of the Others spent their time, the two Rella could see the most clearly were Margaret's office, and Max's diner.

A lone structure on a long stretch of road on a castaway route, Max's diner waited. A battered sign, DINER—OPEN 24 HOURS, reached high into the sky, its narcoleptic lights dim. Sounds were scarce in the desolate place. Wisps of paper scuttled across the cracked, uneven pavement and parched dirt.

Rella exited the car, the crisp temperature a biting contrast to the climate she pictured outside of Max's diner, located in a vast desert, low mountains in the distance.

As she entered, she filtered the surroundings to represent where Max resided.

A sense of lost time thickened the air. To the right, in the entrance, a display stacked with brochures for places that may or may not still exist bulged out from the wall.

Just beyond the foyer was the counter where Max sat, his back to the door, a row of red stools along its length. He had a view to the prep area, stocked with pots of coffee, napkin holders, several salt and pepper shakers, and condiments. A clunky cash register cornered a far edge. A rectangular pass-through window provided a partial view of the stainless-steel kitchen, the pincers of a lopsided order wheel on its shelf clipping order slips. The scuffed, grayed linoleum floor, worn in most places, looked up to a yellowed ceiling, a reminder of cigarette smoke from the past. Whiffs of potatoes and oil now hung in the air.

Booths lined a wall of windows to the left, mostly empty, some occupied by staged characters who sat without altering position, a sentence suspended in their mouths, untouched props of food on their plates. A looped program. One where Max could be alone, unbothered. A setting. A place not of moments, but moment. A waiting place.

It's what they were all confined to.

Max's diner. Margaret's office. Katie's tree. Lisa's playroom. Dustin's campsite. Modern Anna's country bedroom. Abigail's floating limbo. Water's ocean. Victorian Anna was the only exception. Rella smiled. She would definitely find the diner distasteful, running a fingered glove over the countertop, displeased as it became soiled from grease.

"Take a seat where you like, honey." The waitress's disruption returned Rella from Max's mute diner back to the noisy present-day one.

Only fitting, she chose a stool at the counter. The seat squeaked as she sat.

"There you go, honey." A plastic menu landed in front of Rella.

Inspecting it for stickiness, Rella skimmed the menu perfunctorily, scant confidence in finding much outside the typical cuisine of iceberg lettuce and battered chicken.

"What can I get ya, honey?" the waitress asked, pen in hand.

"Oh, umm, just a coffee, please." Rella had never ordered a coffee in her life.

"Cream and sugar?"

"Black." That's how Max liked it, and she drew the line at cream and sugar anyway.

The waitress holstered the pencil behind her ear and swiped the menu away.

Rella noticed a faint odor of commercial disinfectant emanating from the countertop and sat back a little further. Her nose twitched. *Sorry, Margaret*, Rella apologized. Her posture straightened.

The coffee arrived unceremoniously with a clang, splashing out onto the white slip of paper under the saucer serving as the check.

Rella regarded the mug skeptically, then curled the handle in her forefinger and took a sip. She scrunched her face.

The man next to her chortled, gut bouncing like a basketball.

"Never had coffee before?" he asked.

"I don't really like it," Rella answered.

"Why order it, then?"

"It's not for me. It's for someone else."

He rubbed his gristly, silver beard, eyeing her strangely, then broke into an amused grin.

"Oh, okay," he said. "I get it—I get it."

He most certainly did not.

Forty-Two

Rella pressed the bell to the apartment building and heard the buzzer as she was let in.

"Leah Cooper," she said to the front-desk person.

"Sign here, please." He pointed to the clipboard. "Room 262."

The carpeted hall rendered her footsteps silent. Heart quickening and pace slowing, she passed 258, 260, until she was face-to-face with 262.

A white-haired lady with a walker exited the apartment across the hall.

"Are you a family member of Leah's?"

"Yes."

To the left of 262 was a small telephone table, a secondhand set of the *Little House on the Prairie* series on the lower shelf, and a small pot of silk flowers on top. A hand-painted WELCOME sign hung in the center of the door.

Rella took a breath, brushed back her bangs, and knocked.

"Coming! Coming!" the voice answered immediately, muffled by the thick door.

She set her shoulders back. She heard the voice again and realized the words were "Come in." She pushed down the handle and stepped inside.

The space was simple, open, not one stray article lying about.

She turned to the hallway and saw her mother, framed by the light of the windows beyond, three feet in front of her.

"Rella," she exhaled, with a sigh of happiness.

At sixty-eight years old, wrinkles had left her mother's olive skin alone. Her hair remained thick and generous, trimmed short around her neck and ears, with only a few specks of gray. Her deep cocoa eyes filled with tears.

"Hi, Mom."

Her thin arms embraced Rella. "I'm so glad you're here." She stepped back and shook her arms with excitement, as though holding two rattles. "A whole day with you! Can I make you some tea? I've got chamomile. Or are you hungry?"

"I thought it would be nice if I took you to a coffee shop or something. I know how much you like that."

"I would love it! Oh, how exciting. Let me get my things. Just give me a minute!"

Rella smiled, pleased with any opportunity to bring happiness to her mother's life. She couldn't go back in time and rescue her from the past. She could only hope to improve her present.

"All ready!" her mother said.

Grateful to be over an hour away from Eastport, everything Rella saw was new, with no reminders.

"Do you have a favorite place?" she asked.

"Well, I usually just go where I can walk to."

"Do you miss being able to drive?"

Her mother had given up her license a few years ago, due to the medication she took.

"Sometimes. But I do get good exercise. It's a little more

difficult in the winter, but I manage."

"It's so nice being able to walk outside year-round in California. You know, whenever you want to come, I'll fly you out there."

"Really? I accept!"

"What about this place?" Rella asked, pointing to a coffee shop. "Looks cute."

"Sure," her mother agreed enthusiastically.

Inside, the dining area was small, but adorably designed in a country cottage theme, with white wainscoting, mint green cabinets, and antique cake plates.

"Ooh, look at these scones!"

As her mother's face lit up at the sight of the chocolate dots atop the treats, Rella wondered what her mother had been like as a young girl.

"Are these vegan?" Rella asked the girl behind the counter.

"Those, yes. The ones on the left, no," she replied.

"Would you like a couple, Mom? For now, and later?"

"I won't say no to that."

After placing their order, they stepped aside to wait. A small terrier hopped around its owner's ankles as the man ordered.

"Is that a Jack Daniel's dog?"

Rella laughed. "It's Jack Russell, Mom."

She giggled. "Glad I didn't ask him!"

The sun shone brightly, warming up the day to an above-average temperature. They chose a table in the sun.

Her mother bit into the scone. "Mmm. Delicious."

"I'm glad we found this place."

"How has your trip been so far?"

"Good."

"Nice to be back?" her mother asked, then shook her head slightly. "I know it's not," she said quietly.

"It's not because of you, Mom." Rella looked at her mother's hand on the table. Slowly, she reached out, and compressed it gently before pulling back.

Rella wished she could open up to her mother, but it wouldn't be the kind thing to do. And she'd risk opening the jaws of the images, whose metal teeth were poised to snap shut, imprisoning her inside.

On the last night of her visit, Rella sat alone on Morgan's living room floor, among boxes of photos her sister had gathered together.

Rella lifted one out, a piece of her past glued on paper. A girl of twelve or fourteen stared back, but she felt only a vague connection. She stood at the edge of the pool, her friends splashing in the background, wearing both a T-shirt and shorts over her bathing suit, as she always had. She'd never thought to question why.

She examined more pictures, studying her eyes, her expressions, wondering if she would—or could—catch a trace of someone else.

CJ had once told her something disconcerting. "Your face changes, when someone else is present."

"I *look* different?"

"It's not something easily noticed," CJ had assured her.

Lisa came by her side.

"Hi, Lisa," she whispered. "You can stay, but quietly, please."

"How's it going in here?" Morgan asked, flopping down on the floor. "Hey!" She snatched a photo from a box Rella had not gotten to yet. "The three of us. We look so young. There's so much captured in pictures; it can bring you right back."

"Put a memory in a box and you'll have to unpack it someday," Rella said.

"Here's Dad and Trevor. The same look, those two. Out to conquer the world with smiles and jokes." Morgan put the photo down and squared off facing Rella. "So, you're leaving tomorrow."

"Yes."

"Talking's hard for you, I know, but always know that I'm here for you. No matter how old either of us gets, you're still my little sister."

"Who are you calling old?"

"You know what I mean. You can tell me anything."

Rella nodded, even though she didn't agree. Morgan meant well, but sometimes there was a price tag attached to wagering trust in her sister.

Rella spotted a bookstore on her way back to the bungalow. She pulled in and parked.

Stepping inside, she inhaled the possibility of adventures through words, invented places, intriguing characters, dually flawed and ingenious, each in their own way. At the same time, danger lurked between the covers. The risk of exposure to reading something upsetting or triggering tucked between the pages.

She entered the children's section. A hardcover caught her eye, a tale about a puppy named Pogo. She flipped through, figuring it would be safe, but still cautious. Seeing nothing bad, she decided to buy it.

It had been a difficult couple of days. Lisa would enjoy a story. She hoped maybe Abigail and Katie would, too, even if only listening from the shadows.

Forty-Three

Wishing she and Ginnie had planned a girls' night in instead of going out, Rella struggled to make her way across the Barnacle Bar through competing conversations and kitchen clamor, to the outdoor patio.

"Crazy night, right?" a guy said, coming up behind her.

"Yeah." Rella moved forward.

"Let me help you." He slinked closer, putting his hand on her back.

"I'm fine." She wriggled and tried to propel away, but hedges of people prevented this.

"Wouldn't want to see you get hurt out there." His hand lowered inappropriately.

Rella felt trapped.

A patron knocked into them, severing his clutch.

She did an about-face. "Thank you for your assistance."

"I'd never let a pretty girl down. How about I get us some drinks? I'll meet you back here."

"Sure."

"Don't go anywhere!" He set out toward the bar.

"Whew, it's as dense as insulation in here!" Ginnie exclaimed, coming up to Rella. "Rella?"

Rella blinked her eyes. "Yes?"

"You okay?"

"Mind if we go somewhere else, Ginnie?"

Returning home from the night out with Ginnie, Rella exited the car, but someone else crossed the threshold. She barged into the house, kicked off her shoes, and left them where they lay. She tossed the purse and went to the fridge.

"There's never anything cold to drink in this stupid place." She slapped the door shut. She rifled cabinets, bottles clanking, until locating something acceptable. She poured whiskey in a glass and added ice.

"Ah," she said after the first swig. "At least she buys this."

"How was your visit to Colorado?" CJ asked at their first appointment upon Rella's return.

"It wasn't as bad as I had anticipated, although I'm very glad to be back."

"Tell me about it."

"Well, I did tell Trevor."

"How did it go?"

"He's amazing. He took it better than I did! It feels very strange, someone else knowing—other than you, of course. It makes it more . . . real. Not sure I like that."

"Your life will be very different from now on. You might find benefits you hadn't expected. Keep your eyes out for that. And your mom?"

"She's good. We had a nice visit. But in trying to recall

details, I have gaps. As usual."

"This trip might have been harder on you than you realized. Perhaps Margaret stepped in more often than you thought."

Rella shifted uneasily. "I have awareness now, or I thought I did, of when I change. Will it sometimes be disguised, as it was before I knew my diagnosis?"

"Yes, it could."

"Hmm. Margaret at it again."

She'd come to call it the Margaret Mechanism. Margaret's sweep, sweep, sweep device.

"Morgan says I've forgotten things from when we were growing up, but thinking back about my mother, there were oddities. She's always paced a lot. I remember from when I was younger. Trancelike. It became more frequent after her time in the hospital."

"I see you, also, shaking your leg, in a perpetual state of unrest."

It's how Rella saw Max: bottling pressure, ready to split.

"She'd be in bed by sundown. It makes me think back to those agonizing nights I had for months after seeing Seth, undulations of harassing thoughts. They were worse after dark. I can't fathom how my mother survived with those memories of the horrors she endured for years. I don't know how she lasted as long as she did before her first breakdown. My mother doesn't have a Margaret, or any Others." Rella looked up at CJ. "Trevor says my condition is an example of resourceful design."

"You *are* an architect," CJ said with a smile.

"Yeah." Rella swallowed. "Changing the subject, I have an unpleasantry to add to the list."

"All right."

"Waiting for Ginnie on Friday night, a guy came up to me. Unfortunately, they often do."

Rella moved as though the fabric on the chair rubbed her the wrong way.

"I have no interest. Sometimes I'm very direct, but usually, I don't speak up. I start to put on an act, what I think they want to hear. I only realize it later. Infuriating. Friday night, after Ginnie arrived on the scene, it took me a minute to be present in the room. I don't want to be like this."

"You are seeing your life as a whole now, for the first time. Have you thought about whether there has been a certain person who comes out in an intimate situation?"

She *had* thought about it, without wanting to.

All of the times in the past when she'd acquiesced to intimacy in a relationship, even when inside she was saying *no*. She'd evaded getting close to anyone for years. It was better that way. A relief. She was happier. She found no enjoyment in intimacy, and it brought pain, from deep within, that lingered for days. Emotionally, it beat her up. And she'd have to resort to toxic drugs to prevent a calamity. She wanted nothing to do with any of it.

To think that perhaps there was one person, an Other she hadn't met yet, who handled only this type of situation—it made her feel sick.

"Maybe there is," she said quietly. "I do get a general consensus among the Others, that none of them want it."

"And how about you? Do you wish to be with someone? What do *you* want?"

"What do *I* want?" she asked sarcastically.

CJ halted. "Who am I talking to?" she asked.

Inside, Rella spun. She shook her head, returned to herself. "How could you tell when even I couldn't?"

"An uncharacteristic tone," said CJ. "Aggravation. Voicing what maybe you can't. Do you remember what she said?"

The expression planed. She sat up further in the chair, hands folded in her lap, back stiffened.

"Hello, Margaret," CJ said.

She gave a curt nod.

"Who came out? Was it a new person?"

She didn't answer.

"Margaret, she might have a statement or opinion on the subject we were discussing."

"I can't let anyone come out whenever they want."

"Of course, in certain situations. But it is helpful in here. And advantageous to Rella to begin to learn how *she* can handle this."

Margaret pursed her lips.

"How do you view relationships, Margaret? The romantic kind?"

Margaret frowned.

"Is there anything wrong with getting to know someone more closely?"

"It's distracting, and a waste of time."

"I understand your caution, and Rella's. Trust is fragile and can be exploited. And relationships require one to be vulnerable."

"Vulnerable comes from the Latin *vulnerare*, 'to wound.' "

"Oh. You are quite a word aficionado."

"That's from Spanish, for amateur."

"I can see I'm digging a hole here. Do you study words, Margaret?"

"No, she does."

"Rella?"

"Yes."

"Rella mentioned she has a hard time standing up for her personal space and voicing if she doesn't want to do something. Have you helped with that?"

"Yes."

"But not always."

"No."

"Does someone else come?"

No response.

"Is there someone else that steps in? Margaret, are you still here with me?"

The hands tightened into fists.

———

She stood in the closet, discarded outfits strewn about at her feet.

She flipped through the hanging clothes. "Dresses, dresses, dresses. Wouldn't be caught dead." She chose a pair of cut-off shorts and a white T-shirt and pulled her hair into a side ponytail.

Bounding down the stairs, skipping the last step, she

raided the kitchen. She bent down to a lower cabinet, her thighs doubling in size, as was normal. "These legs are so *fat*," she grumbled in disgust. "Well, they're not mine."

Pushing past boxes of flaxseed crackers, a bag of dried peaches, and a jar of almond butter, she found a bottle.

"Jackpot."

She straightened her knees and retrieved a glass.

"Alcohol's better than food," she said, taking a shot.

Rella woke up with a headache and her wardrobe in complete disarray. She spent two hours righting the mess. She lined up all the shirts by color. Folded scattered shorts. Neatly rolled socks and tights. The dresses section, intact.

Facing her wall of shoes, all the ballet styles neatly in a row, heels untouched, athletic gear paired, she glanced down to the boots. One pair stood out.

She recalled the day she'd bought them, several weeks ago. Black, mid-calf, studded, thick soles, and long laces. Not her style at all.

Fixing her eyes on the floor where the boots sat, she traveled up, to the ankles, legs, waist, torso, arms, head.

Rella saw her. Thirteen years old. Brown, wiry hair pulled into a ponytail, cut-off shorts. Tension in her muscles and hands, ready to fight. A scowl across her lips. As thin as Rella, she vied to be skinnier. Preferred alcohol over food. Despised dresses.

She spun her cutting tongue from flirty to rude, from polite to demeaning, and enjoyed it.

It took several days before Rella was given her name. Gabby.

"Gabby. The name reminds me of Abigail. Maybe she's a version of Abigail that *can* talk—can let out whatever has been suppressed. Abigail is scared and silent. Gabby is rebellious and defiant." Rella sighed. "My personalities have personalities."

CJ chuckled. "What have you learned about Gabby?"

Rella related what had been revealed so far.

"Do you think maybe she is coming through when you find your hands in fists?"

"Maybe."

"Something to think about."

"She's not at all what I was like as a teenager."

"What were you like?"

"Quiet. Studious. Hated talking on the phone. Read a lot of books."

"I hear you study words."

"I still have my first thesaurus. Thesaurus is Latin for "treasure" or "treasury." Words are gems. Roget was a fascinating man—creator of what we now know as the thesaurus. I've read about his childhood and his love of words and their connections. I would have liked to have met him."

"Maybe Victorian Anna did."

Rella smiled. "Before her time."

"What year was she born?"

"I calculated the late 1870s, as a rough estimate. That

would put her around age twenty-four when she first appeared here, and in her early thirties on the boat. Seems about right, based on what she looks like, and from what I know about events in her life. Roget died in 1869. My mother bought me that thesaurus. I was thrilled. Read it cover to cover several times. I don't imagine Gabby is too keen on it—although I did receive it around the age of nine."

"Any reason for disliking the phone?"

"Distance, I suppose. Inability to see the person's face. Also, it's a waste of time. I prefer learning, doing. Speaking of Victorian Anna, I have more information. I think she had a terminal disease."

"Oh?"

"Well, maybe not as we think of it today, but progressive and degenerative, something doctors would have been unfamiliar with during her time. She found out about it long after her husband and sister had died."

"Quite a bit of detail."

"Not sure what it means. Is my brain making up a story? She doesn't think it's any of your business, by the way," Rella informed CJ, with a sideways smile.

"Is she angry about the diagnosis?"

"I don't feel anger in her."

"Does she make fists?"

"Too unladylike."

"You can still be a lady and punch."

"Nice thought." Rella sat back in the chair. "Sometimes I want to fall into Victorian Anna's life, live in her world, before the melancholy and grief. Wander the paths of her gardens, visit her town, meet the people she knew, see what she saw."

An aperture creaked open in Rella's head. Rella jumped.

"Rella, what is it?"

"A woman. On a cobblestone street."

Damp stones. Streetlamps scattered light. *Someone is after me.*

She took off, the clicking of her shoes loud in Rella's ears, panic rising into her throat.

"There are two men chasing her." Her breath galloped.

"Who? Chasing who? Victorian Anna?"

She clenched her hand around her shirt, over her heart.

"Run," she croaked.

Victorian Anna fled, incommodious skirts and underskirts ensnaring her ankles, a heavy cloak weighting her shoulders, the low heel of her boots narrowly missing the crevices in the stones.

"Ah!" She fell, hurriedly got up, wincing, favoring her left knee.

Turning a corner, she searched for light, activity, but only met narrow, bricked passageways. "They're coming! They're coming!" The burning in her chest intensified.

"Rella, take measured breaths. Reassure her you're here."

Her body finally rested, still.

"Did she get away?" CJ asked.

"We never really get away," Victorian Anna replied softly.

———

The next morning Rella woke at four a.m. to a sharp pain on the right side of her head.

"I'm listening," she said aloud.

I want to hurt you.

The sentence didn't make her afraid. She recalled CJ's words: "Parts get upset if we don't believe and accept what they are telling us."

"Thank you for telling me. Do you have more to say?"

The pain withdrew like a syringe.

"Did you get a sense of who it was?" CJ asked Rella in their next session.

"No. They weren't familiar."

"We haven't visited the Greenhouse in a while. We could see if anyone new is there."

Rather than staying at the beach, Rella entered the Greenhouse.

"None of the lights are on."

"Is there any natural light?"

"Minimal."

An object presented. "I see—a film projector."

"Perhaps it wants to show you something."

She mentally girded herself. "It's starting." The machine softly whirred. A spotlight flickered but remained blank.

"There's only white on the wall."

"Do you sense any kind of apprehension from this part?"

"No. It's just a projector."

"It only holds content?"

"Yes."

The projector went silent, as if the film had been erased.

Forty-Four

CJ tossed her keys on the credenza and looked through the mail, separating out what to keep and what would wind up in recycling. Junk mail annoyed her to no end. She could almost hear the trees crying out.

She went into the kitchen. Twenty-four red roses elegantly stretched from a crystal vase. A bottle of white wine chilled in a stainless-steel pail, two long-stemmed glasses alongside.

CJ's shoulders relaxed. She smiled. One red bud brushed her cheek.

"Happy anniversary."

CJ spun around to see Kyle with a lopsided grin on his face. He pushed his glasses up the bridge of his nose.

"Remind me again how I managed the honor of having a gorgeous Italian woman as my wife?"

CJ kissed him. "The wine and roses say it all. Not to mention you are sweeter than the finest chocolate."

"Speaking of chocolate." He revealed a box behind his back. "Each piece chosen just for you. Hand-crafted. No dairy."

"You pay attention to all the fine details."

"As I should."

"The world is full of earthquakes, with shocks and aftershocks that can prove stronger than the initial quake. I'm so grateful to have a solid foundation with you."

"Sounds like a rough day."

"No more so than others, I suppose. I've just been thinking. Relationships, love—they are complex and precarious for everyone. But for someone after trauma, especially from childhood, it could be like asking them to relive aspects of it all over again, perhaps even with a loving partner."

"Are a lot of your patients single?"

"No. Some are married. Some repeatedly end up with the wrong type of person—and some shun romance altogether." CJ looked down at the top of her right forearm. Visible only with close scrutiny, the thin, white, three-inch scar reminded her of a close call, running through a narrow opening in a chain-link fence while being chased by a wild dog. Eleven at the time, she'd turned around after ensuring her safety, the dog snarling and nipping at the fence, and wondered what had made the dog that way. She'd wanted to console it, pet it, let it feel what affection was like.

Kyle put his arms around her. "Need some time alone before we go to dinner? The reservation isn't for two hours."

"I'm good, but thank you. So, what do we have here?"

Kyle lifted the bottle of white. "A Nascetta. Italian, of course. The wine-seller raved about it, said it's an indigenous varietal that was almost extinct, hard to get in the States, and delicious."

"Let's have a glass, and then I'll shower and change."

As Kyle uncorked and poured the wine, CJ thought about all the attack dogs people placed around their chain-link perimeters, for protection, for warning, for survival.

"You look sad, Abigail," said CJ, at their next session.

I am always sad, she wrote.

"Can you tell me what the date is?"

you will say I am wrong

"Do you know why I will say that?"

Abigail shook her head.

"Maybe we can talk about what it's like where you are."

Abigail dug the pencil into the paper.

I'M STUCK

Her gaze detached.

"Abigail, can you see it's only you and me in the room, and it's safe?"

Abigail dropped the pencil, pulling her hair over her face.

"Perhaps you don't like anyone looking at you."

She continued pulling her hair down.

"I'm sorry if I made you feel uncomfortable."

Abigail searched for the pencil.

eyes

don't like

Her hands lashed out at the air with little force, futilely.

want to go to playroom

"Let's get you to the playroom."

A knock sounded at the door. Both Abigail and CJ jumped. Abigail's arms and hands stiffened into rails by her sides.

"I'm so sorry. Excuse me a moment."

A minute later, CJ reentered the room.

"Won't happen again," she said, shutting the door. "I sense this is no longer Abigail."

"She got scared."

"Anna?"

"Yes."

"Your voice is strained again. Are you in pain?"

"I'm always in pain, even more so when I come out."

"Thank you for coming forward."

"I try not to. The others have more to say."

"I think you all do. How is Abigail?"

"The same."

"Maybe someone could tell her there is no threat."

"There is always a threat."

Laguna Beach—January 2018

Rella sat on the back deck, working on sketches. The faint sound of a bell reached her ears. After hearing it a third time, she stepped into the house.

Someone was rapping on the door.

"Morgan!" she exclaimed in surprise.

"I saw your car in the driveway."

"Morgan, what are you doing here?"

"Oof, let me in!" Morgan pushed past, suitcase in hand. "Rella, this place is gorgeous." She fanned herself with a plane ticket. "And humongous. What do you do with all this space?"

"Morgan, did you send me a message that you were coming, and I didn't get it?"

Morgan paused in her assessment of the house and turned to Rella.

"No, I didn't. And I'm sorry. I won't get in your way. You do what you need to do, and when you have downtime, we can spend it together. I had absolutely no time alone with you when you came to see us. I covered for everyone at the hospital over the holidays, so I told them I'm taking two weeks off."

"You're staying for two weeks?"

"I figured I'd let you decide. Whew, January is hot here, huh? Don't you use the AC?"

"No, I don't like it." Flustered from the ambush, not the weather, Rella said, "Let me help you with your bag." She brought Morgan upstairs.

"This is the nicest guest room I've ever stayed in."

"I'm not quite done with the decorating yet, but all the essentials are here. And you have your own bathroom."

"Wonderful."

"Well, I don't have much work left to do today. Get settled, and we can go for a walk."

"I should walk, but I'd rather go for a drink!"

"Whatever you'd like. I already worked out today."

Once alone downstairs, Rella feverishly texted Trevor.

Did you know she was coming?!

I had no idea.

I'm nervous. I don't want her to know.

Maybe nothing will happen. But if it does, remember she loves you. It might be good for her to know.

Rella ran into her bedroom, to her office, and consulted her calendar. Recently, she'd decreased her sessions with CJ from twice a week to once a week. Her next appointment was Tuesday, five days away.

Tense, vigilantly alert to noises, topics, smells, or sights that could cause a change, Rella still managed to enjoy the Friday evening, and showing Morgan around the beach towns all day Saturday.

Sunday morning, Rella worked on sketches outside on the deck while Morgan sat with her, sipping coffee from a bakery on Pacific Coast Highway.

"California knows how to do pastry. I'm going to put on ten pounds," Morgan said, taking a bite of a banana streusel muffin. "You've barely touched your fruit plate."

"It can take me a while to work up an appetite."

"Wish I had that problem. You devoured everything in your path when you were younger. And never gained an ounce."

The more Morgan talked about food, the less Rella wanted it.

"It wasn't your fault, the eating disorder. Rella, we haven't really talked about what happened to you."

"I don't need to."

"How old were you?"

"Morgan, I remember nothing. Not clearly, anyway."

"How do you know, then?"

Rella saw the Others behind her, shadows stretching back from where she stood. The light that had revealed them continued to shine, but hold back at the same time.

Morgan interrupted her thoughts. "Saying the words out loud could help."

"What words?"

" 'I have been sexually abused.' "

Lisa's playroom came into view. She looked up at Rella, fear in her face. For the first time, Rella noticed her skin was damp, her bangs slightly stuck to her forehead.

"Morgan, can we change the subject, please?"

"I've read that a high percentage of girls who get eating

disorders have been sexually abused. It's a way to gain control over one's body and emotions."

"I know, Morgan," Rella said quietly.

"It's awful—a punishment for having committed no crime, a way to arrest your physical maturity. You lost your period?"

"For three years."

"That's one plus."

Anger bubbled inside Rella at the mention of the red curse. These days Katie surfaced during the first days of bleeding, once the sun went down. Rella always made sure to stay home.

"You ate predictably," said Morgan. "Peanut butter sandwich and an apple every day for lunch. In your playroom. Remember that?"

Rella's vision hazed.

"You wanted to be in that room all the time. You even had an imaginary friend."

"I don't remember an imaginary friend."

"I'd hear you talking to her in there. What was her name? Oh yeah, it was Abigail. Her name was Abigail."

The statement struck Rella, like pelting ice rain, and then she saw it clearly: herself, at the playroom table, drawing, coloring, and chatting with another little girl, one with straw-colored hair and a baggy dress. Only, at the time, Abigail was able to speak back.

Suddenly, the evil face loomed above Abigail, growing into. a man, his body over hers. The playroom fell away.

The terror and constriction in Abigail's throat noosed Rella's own. A door slammed shut, trapping Abigail inside. Rella dropped to the floor.

"Rella!"

Morgan's shout echoed down a distant tunnel.

Someone was coming to get her. She pushed against the ground with her hands but couldn't stand.

"Rella? Rella, what's wrong?"

She opened her hands wide and slammed them on the floor. Then she targeted her legs.

"Rella! Stop this! What are you doing?!"

She used her hands to slide on the floor, going in circles, banging into the cabinets, unable to flee.

"Rella, this is ridiculous! What has gotten into you?"

She hit her head with her hands.

Morgan grabbed them.

She retaliated by whipping her head to the floor.

"Rella—Rella, no!"

A pillow was pushed under her head. She knocked it away.

"I'm calling 911!"

"Hey, Morgan! How's it going? Liking Cali?"

"Trevor? What? Sorry, I hit the 'answer' button by mistake. I'm trying to call 911."

"What? What's wrong?"

"Rella. She's gone crazy!"

"Tell me exactly what is going on."

"She's hurting herself, banging her head on the floor. I need to call the paramedics!"

"What did you say to her?"

"What did *I* say? This is my fault?"

"Where is she?"

"Kitchen."

"Where are you?"

"I ran to get my phone in the living room."

"What is she doing now? Just peek in there—don't say anything."

Morgan huffed. "Well, she's stopped her hysterics, for now. She's rocking back and forth, still on the floor."

"Morgan, can I ask you not to call the paramedics and just observe her first? From a distance."

"Absolutely not."

"Morgan." Trevor rarely took such a firm tone, but on this teeter-totter, he knew which foot he had to put down. "Morgan, take a breath. Rella is safe, not hurting herself, right?"

"Yes," she said impatiently.

"Just take a seat. It's probably over."

"*What* is over? What's going on?"

"It's for Rella to tell you."

———

Hours later, Rella stirred.

The refrigerator hummed Her palms met cold, hard travertine. Her fingers found the low corner of a cabinet. She pulled herself up, her muscles braided like rope.

Tidal disequilibrium almost sent her back down. She rubbed her head, detecting a sore spot, pressed her eyes, the minutes prior to her change slowly coming back.

The realization struck harder than her head hitting the floor.

Rella had the urge to take off to a hotel and hide out until her sister gave up and left.

Rella tiptoed down the stairs the next morning, hoping to leave for the gym before Morgan got up.

"Good morning, Rella," Morgan said, sitting at the counter with a cup of takeout coffee.

"You're up early," Rella said. She turned her back to Morgan and opened the cabinet for a glass, taking a long time at the sink to fill it.

"I had a hard time sleeping last night. Stayed down here for some time, until it looked like you were asleep on the floor. I almost called the paramedics."

Rella whirled, alarmed. "Please, don't ever do that!"

"Well, Trevor talked me down. What he knows that I don't . . . anyway. That wasn't my chief concern. What in the world happened last night?" Morgan asked.

Rella placed the cup in the sink, not trusting her stomach even with water.

"Let's forget about it, okay?"

"Forget about it? You fell to the floor. You pounded at your legs. You were hitting your head!"

Rella turned to face her but kept her eyes down. "I'm sorry."

"Sorry? Something is wrong!"

Rella sighed. She put her hand to her forehead, rediscovering the small bump.

"Was it a seizure? Are you having seizures?"

"No."

"What, then?"

"Morgan, I'd rather not talk about it."

"We need to talk about it. Is this from finding out what happened to you? Is it related to the counselor you saw in Atlanta?"

"He wasn't a counselor. He was a quack. No, that's an insult to ducks."

"What happened? What did he do?"

Rella wanted to deflect the onslaught of questions, but after last night, she knew Morgan wouldn't desist without an explanation. She didn't want to start at the beginning, but it was the only way to get to the end.

"Those sessions —felt like a violation. I never should have gone. I told you I've been seeing another person. It was to undo what he did, help restore my sanity."

"What I saw last night was not sane or normal."

It was to someone, Rella said to herself.

"I finally do have an explanation—for why I don't have many memories from childhood, why the ones I do have are so hazy. The migraines. The pain. And—and for what you saw last night."

"Well?"

Rella hesitated.

"You don't trust me?"

Trust was a net full of holes.

"Rella, you need to tell me what is going on!"

Rella lowered her head. "You're not going to believe me."

"Of course I'm going to believe you."

Rella swallowed. "I have a diagnosis."

Morgan waited.

"It's DID," Rella finally said, aware this explained nothing.

"What's DID?"

"Maybe you can look it up, and then we can talk about it."

"Rella."

"All right. It's dissociative identity disorder."

"What's that mean?"

"It means . . . well, take last night. A . . . a catalyst causes a change in me, and I go away."

"Oh, so it's PTSD then. You see and hear things from the past as if they were happening in the present."

"No, not exactly. I don't remember the past. But—others do."

"Others?"

"Yes."

"You sound like you are talking about someone else, not yourself."

"In a way I am."

Morgan shook her head. "I don't understand."

"I'm still coming to grips with it myself."

Morgan pulled out her phone.

"Dissociative identity disorder," she said aloud, eyes moving rapidly. She put her phone down on the counter. "Rella, you don't have multiple personalities."

"I didn't think so either, at first."

"It doesn't even exist."

"Well, it does."

"Who told you that you have this condition?"

"The person I'm seeing now. And I've had other . . . confirmation."

"Rella, this is absurd. Let's find you someone else to work with. Someone qualified."

"She is perfectly qualified. She has helped me."

"I refuse to believe this."

"It's why I didn't want to tell you."

"So that behavior last night—you're saying you're not at fault."

"It's not a question of fault."

"All that commotion—you don't take responsibility for it?"

"Morgan, do you think this is a party for me? That it's peachy waking up with a headache and bruises, or having something bring on these incessant atrocious images in my head?"

"Bring on? So, it was something *I* said."

Morgan barreled on, recapping their conversation.

Rella quickly put her hands over her ears and ran upstairs to her room, swatting the door shut. She sat on the floor and rocked and thought of fresh air and warm sun and fuzzy animals and every anchor she could to stay Rella.

Forty-Five

Morgan went for a drive, stopped for coffee. More driving.

She was the one who had insisted Rella dig for answers. While Morgan knew there was no way trauma wouldn't have affected Rella at the most profound level, it couldn't be this.

Morgan parked the car along a strip of beachfront in front of a Mexican restaurant. She took a seat on the patio.

"Hola," a waiter in his twenties greeted her cheerfully, setting a menu on the table.

"Margarita, please, rocks, no salt."

"Sure thing."

"Some chips and salsa too, please. Thanks."

Morgan pulled out her phone and repeated her search from earlier.

Dissociative identity disorder (previously known as multiple personality disorder) is thought to be a complex psychological condition that is likely caused by many factors, including severe trauma during early childhood (usually extreme and repetitive), and often before age six.

Morgan reread the passage. *Repetitive trauma.* She needed that drink. She continued reading.

Characterized by the presence of two or more distinct personality identities. Each may have their own name, personal history, and characteristics.

This was too weird.

Lifelong. Treatment can help, but this condition can't be cured.

She dialed Trevor.

"I can't believe you didn't tell me any of this," she said, as she continued scrolling.

"It's up to Rella to disclose this information. How did you take it?"

"She doesn't have this condition, Trevor. It isn't even a real thing."

"It *is*, Morgan. You saw that it is."

"Nonsense. All this time. Years. And suddenly she has this?"

"She's had it all along. It's a condition designed to hide itself. Its whole basis is to guard a secret. It's brilliant—hiding not just the one thing, but breaking it into pieces and scattering them, even across time, and doing it so well, you don't even know to go looking for them. The fragments are entrusted to different individuals who might not be aware of the others' existence, or what they hold. And it's protected Rella, allowed her to live her life, to accomplish so much. That jerk, Seth Jabez, who she went to initially—he really messed her up. But I guess one good thing came out of it. Without him, she might never have learned about her condition."

"She needs treatment, Trevor."

"And she's getting it, from her counselor, CJ. She needs love, support, and acceptance. She's still the same Rella. I may not know everything about it," said Trevor, "but I love Rella, and you do too."

After hanging up with Trevor, Morgan sat in the restaurant

for quite some time, her preconceived ideas popping around her.

Doubts turned to acrimony, targeted at people long dead.

She wondered if she could have done something to prevent it.

Rella's heart quickened when she heard the front door.

Morgan put the keys down on the counter. "Hi, Rella."

"Hi."

"I talked with Trevor."

Rella didn't respond. Maybe the less she said the better.

"I'm sorry for how I acted, Rella. Can we talk about it?"

Rella was exhausted. She just wanted a life where she wouldn't have to talk about it.

"Please."

"You don't believe me."

"I've been reading," Morgan said. "And Trevor explained some things to me, too. I was wrong. I want to know more. You don't have to be afraid. They're all *you*, Rella."

"No," Rella countered, "it doesn't feel that way."

This fact frustrated her, this fundamental facet she didn't think anyone could truly understand.

"They are distinct, outside of me, people I'm still learning about. You ever take a video of yourself? It's weird, right? Watching it? Perhaps you remember it differently than what you see on film? That's how my life is at times. Like a video, often containing partially accessible or lost footage. Physically, it's a roller coaster. Abdominal pain. Throwing up. Stiff neck.

Nightmares. You were right about my ailments. I've suffered my whole life—*they've* suffered—because of what was done to me."

"Tell me about them."

Morgan didn't interrupt as Rella spoke.

Rella descended the next morning. Morgan had left a note on the counter that simply read, *Coffee.*

Morgan had listened to Rella's every word the day before but hadn't said much afterward. They'd gone to bed early.

Rella heard the front door. Pencil poised in the air, Rella waited in expectation.

Morgan entered with a paper grocery bag in one hand and a smaller bag in the other.

"Didn't want to eat you out of house and home." She placed the larger bag on a chair.

"You don't have to worry about that, but thank you."

Morgan sat at the dining table.

"Rella, I'm sorry I was so quiet last night. It—it was a lot to take in. But I believe you. It's hard, *because* I believe you." Morgan sighed. "I should have sensed something."

"Morgan, this is not your fault." Rella didn't want to think about it anymore.

"The brain is a maze."

Rella thought of the Old English word *masian*, "to confuse."

"I didn't protect you enough."

"You were everything a big sister should be. More."

"I would thank them if I could. Margaret—she's done a

better job than I have."

"No. You've both been there for me. Just in different ways."

"Maybe I can meet Margaret one day," Morgan said.

Rella got teary-eyed, both scared and moved by the idea.

"Why don't you let me take you to your appointment?" Morgan asked Rella Tuesday morning.

"I prefer to go by myself. Also, after certain sessions, if they are difficult, I need to do something to, process, I guess is the word. I go by the water or take a walk. So, if I'm not home right away afterwards, don't worry."

"Well, all right."

Plainly, Morgan wasn't pleased, but Rella was proud for making a statement as to what was right for her and sticking to it.

She started her session with CJ by relating what had happened.

"This was disturbing on so many levels," Rella said, "from learning that I talked to Abigail when I was younger, to the horrible images I saw of the evil face and then a man appearing over her, to completely turning into Katie and I'm not sure who else, in front of Morgan. I thought I was doing so well."

"You *are* doing well. That was pretty monumental information."

"Please don't take what I am about to say the wrong way, but I'm digging in quicksand, and it feels bottomless. I may never know exactly what happened to me in the past. There are so many layers of hidden information—this could be an endless quest. I get dizzy just walking up the steps to your office, as though the Others know this is the place they can come out as they wish, and it really keeps me away from most everything else in my life the rest of the day. I'd like to start working on how to live with my diagnosis, how to hopefully keep episodes like the one I had two nights ago to a bare minimum, if possible. I've been trying a few things on my own—writing exercises, talking to them internally—and so far, it's been okay."

"Rella, gaining independence and employing useful tools is a great idea. Thank you for talking to me about this. I must say, I've learned a lot from you. While no two people are the same, especially with this condition, I'm better equipped now."

"That makes me feel good. I'm always looking for what positive things have come out of this. Maybe I can share my ideas with you?"

"I'd love that."

"I am eternally grateful for your help. I'm glad Anna picked you."

"I am too."

Part Four

Sometimes in order to be happy in the present moment you have to be willing to give up all hope for a better past.
—Robert Holden, Ph.D.

Forty-Six

Laguna Beach—June 2018

Trevor heard the faint clang of a utensil through the phone.

"Hey, Trevor!"

Trevor made a point to pay attention to the sound of Rella's voice when she called. For some months after she'd told him about her condition, he'd received random calls from the Others. He wished there were some feature on the phone to let him know who had made the call. He told Rella he would name it the Caller DID app. Rella had laughed. But now, he couldn't recall the last time someone other than Rella had been on the line.

"Hey, Rella! How's it going there?"

"Guess what?"

"What?"

"I ate a whole grapefruit!"

Her favorite breakfast since childhood, Rella had related to him that she'd been unable to stomach its tartness for well over a year. She'd learned to listen to any inner inklings having to do with food, even if they didn't make sense to her. She hypothesized that each of the Others had preferences and intolerances that could manifest within her at any given time.

"Dynamite! You did it. You conquered."

"Well, today, anyway."

"And there are many more victories to come. Speaking of which, you're going to share your diagnosis with Ginnie today, right?"

Rella gulped. "Yes."

"Good for you."

"I don't know. I'm anxious the disclosure could mar our relationship. But it's also not fair of me to assume that outcome."

"You've put a lot of thought into this—and you've asked all of the Others, right?"

"Right."

"Were there more nods or shakes of the head?"

"I'm pretty sure I saw more nods, although not everyone gave an opinion."

"I think you're ready. What happened to you, Rella—it's a killer of relationships. This friendship with Ginnie, it's a triumph."

"Thank you for the confidence."

"You've been okay the past six weeks, right?"

Rella had tapered her visits with CJ over the last few months, attending her last scheduled appointment six weeks ago.

"I do feel stronger in being able to manage on my own." She paused. "You, Morgan, CJ—you're the only three who know of my condition, other than me." She paused again. "Soon, it will be four."

Ginnie arrived with fruit and bread. "Cool outfit. Edgy."

Rella looked down at the gray shorts with frayed ends and her T-shirt splashed with neon orange, fuchsia, and white. A Gabby outfit. She'd sensed her upon waking and wanted her to feel acknowledged.

"Last week you had that beautiful Victorian blouse on," said Ginnie. "I love the way you dress. It's like you're different people depending on the day."

The statement brought a smile to Rella's face rather than tension.

"And you have quite the creation on yourself, as always," Rella replied, admiring the pleated kelly-green skirt and flowy half-sleeve manila-colored top smattered with hand-stitched tulips.

"The bow in your hair is classic," said Ginnie.

Rella touched the accessory. It was for Lisa. She'd wished to meet Ginnie for some time, and Rella wanted her to feel included on this important day.

"So," Rella clasped her hands behind her and rocked on her heels, "I'd said I had something to tell you."

"Yup," Ginnie replied, placing the bag of food on the counter.

Rella's hands shook.

"Hey, it's okay. It's just me."

"I sincerely value our friendship."

Ginnie put her hand on Rella's. "As do I."

"What I have to tell you—it's hard to say. And hard to hear."

"Consider me ready!"

Rella took a deep breath. "Okay."

She began with what she had learned about her mother, leading to what had happened in Atlanta. Ginnie's eyes became moist. Rella dropped her gaze and continued, telling Ginnie about CJ and the discovery of the Others.

Once she'd finished, she looked up. She couldn't quite read Ginnie's face.

"What's that expression Punky used again?" Ginnie finally asked.

Rella scrunched her nose in confusion. "Holy macanoli?"

"Yes, that's it!" Ginnie snapped her fingers. "Holy macanoli!" She launched off the counter stool. "You poor dear. You poor dear!" She took Rella's hands in hers. "Thank you for telling me."

"I wasn't sure if I should, to be honest."

"When we met, it was apparent you were smart, stylish. But this. You've been through such atrocities, and you've prevailed. Your life could have been so different."

Certain thoughts had pecked at Rella for some time. Were her traits of craving order and independence—her fierce drive—a result of what had happened to her, or already part of her? If she hadn't been abused, would she have turned out differently? Where would she be now?

She was proud of her life. To rewind and alter the past could possibly change what she'd achieved. Her most disquieting thought of all: Given the chance to go back and prevent it, would she? Were her successes a result of the trauma, or simply a victory over them?

"Can I give you a hug?" Ginnie asked.

"Umm, okay."

Ginnie put her arms around Rella. "Jagged mountains tipped in snow are majestic and commanding but are no more beautiful and resilient than the small peonies flowering beneath."

"You're a poet, Ginnie. And so sweet to say that. But I'm no peaceful peony. Some days I want to go on a smashing spree. But I don't."

"I'd be shocked if you didn't have outrage inside of you," Ginnie said.

"My life was definitely easier before I received my diagnosis. I still get flashes of information from the Others, randomly. It's difficult."

Ginnie's hand went to her heart.

"I don't know everything they do. I appreciate them, cherish them, for all they've done for me. I'm grateful for each of them—those I've met, and those perhaps I haven't yet."

"I ache for you. All of you."

Rella tucked her lower lip behind her front teeth. "I haven't scared you away?"

"Scared me away? How?"

"This isn't allergies or a thyroid condition. People know what those look like. This . . . when I—when I change. Let's just say, when I'm Lisa, who's seven, I wish I appeared as a seven-year-old, not a grown person. I don't even want to conceptualize how it must look. Crazy, I'm sure."

"It's the crazy people who say they're not crazy!" said Ginnie. "You function with a different blueprint, is all. You found a solution. Exits built into the house of your mind. That's what I call inventive architecture."

"You sound like Trevor. You still want to be my friend, then?"

"Silly girl. Of course."

Watery happiness spilled over.

"Sorry. Seems like I always have some tears left."

"That's because you're meant to use them," Ginnie said.

"Thank you for accepting me." Rella wiped her cheeks with the back of her hand.

"A very wise girl once told me: 'Just like Punky, a girl who broke every fashion rule, stay the authentic you.' Well, you articulated it better."

"Punky Power," Rella said.

"Right," Ginnie affirmed. "There's nothing about you I would change."

Forty-Seven

August 2018

"I've come to hire the best architect in the business!"

"Trevor!" Rella stood from her desk.

"It's so good to see you, Rella," he said, wrapping his arms around her.

"You too. And you've used that line before," she teased.

"And who's this?" Ginnie asked, entering from the kitchen with her newest coffee concoction.

"Ginnie, this is Trevor," Rella introduced proudly, "and Trevor, this is my dear friend Ginnie."

"It's about time we met," Trevor held out his hand.

"Join us tonight at the house, won't you?" Rella asked.

Ginnie put up a hand. "I appreciate the invitation, but the first night of a visit is for family. You two enjoy."

"All right, Friday night then. Eighties flashback?"

"You got yourself a date!" Ginnie agreed, eyes sparkling.

"I can almost see your wheels turning, planning your outfit!"

"What have I gotten myself into?" Trevor asked.

"You'll see," Rella said playfully. "Time now for some grocery shopping."

Trevor rubbed his hands together. "Bring on the healthy."

Despite her happiness at Trevor's arrival, it had been a difficult day for Rella.

After they left her office, the world threw one grenade after another. The bold headline of an article about exposing a child abuse ring hurtled at her from a magazine stand. She'd accidentally overheard a conversation while waiting outside the coffee shop for Trevor, a guy speaking tastelessly to his girlfriend, his hands all over her. Then the graphic images on the poster marquee for a new-release horror movie had assaulted her eyes.

Rella had come to realize that when bothersome things hit her in succession, she had a heightened chance of having a rough night. She exhaled with enormous relief once they were back within the protective walls of her house, the stray bombs fired at her all day shut out.

Trevor's phone rang. "It's Morgan," he told Rella, answering.

"Hi, Morgan!" Rella called out, stirring homemade dressing.

"We're making dinner now. Can we call you later?" Trevor said.

"Hey, wait, let me say hi!" Rella reached for the phone.

"How was your day?" Morgan asked.

"Umm," Rella's spoon paused, the wounds from earlier stinging as though spritzed with lemon.

"I read a story and thought of you. It's about a couple who found this abandoned dog."

"Morgan, I don't think—"

"Poor animal was near death. They weren't even sure it would be able to walk again."

"You can't tell me things like this. Don't you get it?" Rella exclaimed. The phone dropped from her hand onto the counter.

Trevor grabbed the phone. "What did you say to her?"

Rella's hand went to her forehead. She paced. "Mm. Mm," she moaned.

"Morgan, we'll call you back."

Morgan's words had stuck in her head, repeating images mixing with the earlier affronts of the day, intensifying. She hit herself in the temple.

"Rella, please, don't do that," Trevor beseeched.

Another blow.

Rella fought to remain in control. She hurried outside to the back deck, hoping to get in the sun, but it was already setting, its rays vanishing between the trees.

"Mm. Mm." The whirling had begun. She got herself back inside the house. From a distance she could hear Trevor's voice.

She had to be by herself before she was completely gone. She made it upstairs.

"I don't want to remember things. I don't want to remember things. I don't want to remember things. I don't want to remember things. I don't want to remember things. I don't want to remember things. I don't want to remember things."

Trevor heard a childlike voice repeating this sentence from the other side of Rella's bedroom door. "Rella?"

"I don't want to remember things. I don't want to remember things. I don't want to remember things. I don't want to remember things."

Trevor opened the door. "Rella, it's Trevor." He walked to the workspace area and found her standing in the corner, facing the wall, stiff, fists clenched, mouth set, her feet turned in.

"I don't want to remember things. I don't want to remember things. I don't want to remember things. I don't want to remember things."

Strangely, Trevor thought Rella looked smaller. There was a despondency to how she stood.

"I don't want to remember things. I don't want to remember things. I don't want to remember things. I don't want to remember things."

Then: "Don't have to," she said under her breath, as though repeating something told to her internally.

Trevor knew about Margaret, and wondered if she was helping.

Her shoulders eased and her fists uncoiled. Her head dropped forward.

"Rella, come back to me," said Trevor. "It's okay. You won't be hurt here."

"He's making me go away," a voice whispered, and she deflated to the floor.

"He? Who's he?" Trevor wasn't sure if he should approach her.

She curled into a ball, hands returning to fists, arms outstretched into bars crossing in an X over her crotch area.

"Owie." Her legs and arms protected and pushed away at the same time. "Owie, owie, owie," she fired in rapid succession, the voice young.

"Who is this, please?"

"Owie, owie, owie."

Trevor ground his teeth at the thought of what was happening to this girl, her eyes darting, alert for dangers he could not see. Whoever this was, they were not in the same room as he.

Fists pounded her legs. "Mmm, mmm, mmm!" The sound pressed forcefully behind her lips.

"Rella—I mean, please, who is this? Can you hit me instead?"

DID didn't come with a rule book, but Trevor knew restraining Rella wasn't a good idea.

Eventually, her body straightened. She stood. Slowly, her eyes met Trevor's, even, expressionless.

"It is under control now."

"Is this—Margaret?" Trevor asked.

"Yes."

"Thank you for helping, Margaret."

"It's my job. She will be able to sleep."

"That's good. Will she wake up as Rella?"

"She always does."

"It must be hard for you to hold what bothers Rella."

Margaret didn't respond.

"Do you ever feel life is passing you by?"

Her brow slightly furrowed as though she hadn't expected the question.

"What do *you* like to do, Margaret?"

Margaret hesitated. "Read."

"About what?"

"Travel. And books about pottery."

"Hmm. Pottery. I always wanted to take a whirl at the spinning thingy." Trevor chuckled at his pun.

Margaret didn't.

"Margaret, if you could live anywhere, where would it be?"

"On an island."

"An island? In the tropics, nice and warm? That's Rella's dream spot."

"No. A colder one. Like off the coast of Ireland. Open. Isolated."

"Cold, huh? Doesn't sound like Rella at all!"

"I'm not Rella."

"Well, I'm with you. Cold, fresh air gets you moving. Sounds nice. What would you do there?"

"Walk. All day. In the fresh air, hills, by the shore. It's stuffy where I am. The outside doesn't touch my skin."

Rella came downstairs the next morning, head hanging.

"I'm sorry," she said quietly.

Trevor rose from the couch. "Sorry? For what?"

"Last night, of course. I can't remember much, other than Morgan calling, saying something upsetting."

"She'll be more careful next time. And if it's okay, she wanted me to tell you how the story ended."

Rella looked at him cautiously.

"Long story short," Trevor said hastily, "the dog is okay. Better than new. Can walk, talk—I mean, bark—a happy, healthy dog."

Rella wiped away relieved tears and exhaled a trembling sigh.

"Does that make you feel better?"

She nodded.

"She asked me to tell you how sorry she is."

"It's not her fault. If you thought I was sensitive before, it's ten times worse now. If I read or hear or see something bad, it doesn't matter if the ending is good. My mind keeps replaying the beginning over and over again. I live among landmines now."

"We will continue to learn."

"I lost a whole night with you."

"We have many more in front of us."

Rella sat cross-legged on the couch. "When I'm gone for a while, or I've switched several times quickly, a layer settles over my mind, my eyes, my perception. A dissociative hangover."

"Like a beer hangover?"

"Yeah, but without the calories." Rella added a smile to the end of the statement, thankful for Trevor's unfailing ability to put her at ease. "I think they trust you."

Trevor sat a little taller. "Margaret and I had quite a long conversation."

"Really?"

"Yes. Do you want me to tell you what she said?"

"No," Rella replied. "If she shared it with you, it was with you. If she wants me to be informed, she'll tell me."

"Hmm. She's pretty interesting, Margaret. I like her. There's no frills or extras, though, just function! She's there when needed, then gone. No good-byes. Although, I guess none of them do that."

"How many came out?"

"I'm not sure. I just wanted to make sure you were safe. Maybe you could go over with me what to do in situations like this. Did CJ give you any tips?"

"Seems you did the right thing, making sure I didn't hurt myself. With the switching, there's no off switch. The only thing that can help bring me back is calm surroundings, and like what we talked about before, reminding me about my work, and so forth. However, this won't help all the time. There are different levels to it. If I'm very deep, and one of them has completely taken over, it has to run its course. To be honest, I find the best way for me to return is to be alone."

Trevor nodded. "So, talking with them is all right?"

"I trust you. And if they are communicating, building a relationship, I see that as a good thing." Rella squirmed. "This is still weird for me."

"I make mental notes. Each time I learn something. So I can be better for you."

"You are wonderful." Rella stood. "Come on. Let's go enjoy this day. I've been indoors too long."

"Indoors, yes. Rella, there is one facet I think you should know, about Margaret." He related her situation, being stuck in a stuffy place, unable to feel the outside air.

"That's terrible," Rella said.

"She's got your back, that's for sure, but at her cost. When someone fulfills a role so exactly, they are less their own person."

Rella was amazed. Trevor got it. "I appreciate her."

"Maybe there's a way to truly get her *outside*—the kind of outdoor adventure Margaret would really appreciate. Maybe you could take a trip to Ireland or something."

Rella laughed. "That's one solution. I *have* wanted to travel," she added. Rella paused in thought. "She is someone I could be friends with."

"Well, be friends with her then."

"Be friends with her?"

"Yeah, why not? She'll always be with you, stand by you. You've got a friend for life in Margaret."

"A friend for life. I never thought of it like that. I guess they all are." Her allies.

"You have me, you have Morgan, and you have *them*, Rella. That's powerful. And pretty cool."

"Yeah, it's pretty cool."

Trevor and Rella went out for the entire day, meeting Ginnie for her lunch break and then continuing on.

Towards early evening, Trevor pulled out a surprise.

"What's that?" Rella asked, laughing. "A mixtape?"

"It most definitely is a mixtape, and nothing to mock, missy!"

"You made us a mixtape?"

"I did. Straight from the eighties!"

"Trevor, how will we listen? Cars don't have tape decks anymore!"

"Not even my bucket of bolts. This is for show. But I did write all the songs inside, see?" He separated the two halves of the hinged plastic case.

Rella laughed. "You're too much."

"And the playlist is on here." He pulled out his phone and connected it to sound via a stereo aux cable. "Are you ready?" he asked, hand poised over the volume control.

"Play it, homeboy!"

They sang out boisterously to "We Built This City," "Take on Me," "The Power of Love," and "Eye of the Tiger."

As Rella sat with her head against the seat, glimmers of her life came back to her, moments associated with each of the songs.

Wearing Trevor's long-sleeved flannel shirts in January, hiking through the snow at twilight, early November mornings crossing the college campus, the crunch and aroma of autumn leaves at her feet, the warm silkiness of hot chocolate and apple pancakes, dancing in the kitchen with soap and rags as she scrubbed her first apartment the summer's day she was given the keys.

Her thoughts went to the Others. Nineties alternative rock suited Max more than Top 40 eighties music. Margaret selected instrumental and classical. Victorian Anna went to the opera, while soft, melodic voices soothed Modern Anna.

One day, a song by The Bangles had come on, eliciting a response in Gabby that Rella hadn't expected. She wanted to turn up the sound, and Rella had happily complied. She saw Gabby kick her sneaks up on the dash and look out the window, her right thumb, toes, and head slightly moving to the beat.

"Trev, do you have "Walk Like an Egyptian" on here?" she asked.

"Number eight!"

They sat on a bench high in the hills at an overlook that provided a panoramic view of the ocean during the day. Distant stars twinkled against the night sky as the darkened water crashed below.

"I had a wonderful day, Trevor. The sun, your company— makes living in the shadows manageable."

"Shadows are not an absolute black. Just a place of reduced visibility. Peripheral vision is more sensitive than our direct vision. If you look at a dim star straight on, it can disappear. But, if you look at it off to the side, it comes back."

"Wow!"

"It has to do with the rods and cones and stuff. Anyway, maybe living in the shadows isn't so bad. My advice: Don't fight it." Trevor shifted position to face Rella. "I wanted to run something by you. You've said you have to be careful not to change, and around other people, I get that. But what if, when you're alone, you let them . . . out. If they want. Go with the flow. Give them some air, and maybe they won't need to come out at random times. They've been suppressed for so long. No offense."

"None taken. You know, I've wondered about this at times. Who am I to hold them prisoner? I actually asked CJ—in allowing them to come out, am I helping myself? She said yes. There needs to be balance, of course, as to when. I also worry because I don't want the bad images. But I'm no longer living only for myself. I have the Others to consider now. I've asked them to be gentle with me, although I don't think the release of images is something they have control over, either."

Rella paused for a moment, took a breath.

"CJ told me about something called integration, meaning, we would all become one. I shook my head and said no! It didn't sound right. She laughed and said she didn't imagine it would be something I'd want to do. I'd feel like I was killing them and changing myself. Then she told me about cohabitation. We would all live together, like in a dorm. You know how I feel about dorms. This is different, I know. And it could aid me in avoiding unwanted episodes. I'll continue to get a better handle on things; it will be my decision as to who knows, and who doesn't."

Let them be happy. Or angry. Or sad. Let them be all they weren't allowed to be, before, she thought.

Margaret embodied organization and order. Modern Anna was her health advocate. She hadn't figured out Victorian Anna's role yet. Dustin showed early, and didn't like secrets. Rella wondered about him a lot. Katie vented. Max, although a loner, served as a protector. Lisa preserved playfulness and kindness. These were all wonderful qualities, to nurture, not deny. Even Gabby's rebellious, assertive nature had its place.

"It's quite peaceful here," Trevor said, leaning back on the bench.

"Once in a while I come up here to look at the lights."

"I think the longer you look at light, the more it changes."

Forty-Eight

Santa Ana, California—February 2019

Rella waited in John Wayne airport, outside the tightly sealed security gates.

Swoosh. Several people exited. Twenty minutes passed. She had arrived long ahead of schedule.

Swoosh.

Rella felt her mother's presence before she saw her, pushed in a wheelchair by a young girl. Her face shed thirty years upon seeing Rella, her naiveté shining through, a youthful enthusiasm that should never be extinguished, in any person.

"Hi, Mom," Rella said, as the chair was wheeled up before her.

She reached for her daughter's hand, squeezed it. "Now I know it's real. I'm here."

"Your mother has not stopped talking about you," the young girl pushing the chair gushed. "Her excitement alone could have flown her here!"

"Thank you for taking care of her. Why the wheelchair?"

"It was the only way for me to have assistance throughout the flight, to make sure I got to you and didn't end up on another plane somewhere!" her mother said. "Can I walk from here?" she addressed her assistant.

"Yes, of course. Enjoy your visit."

"Thank you!" Her mother waved as the girl walked away.

"I'm glad you got here safely," said Rella.

"Oh yes, no problem. Everyone was very nice."

"Good."

"Let's get out of here and go see this house of yours!"

"Rella, how gorgeous! Such a wonderful, stately place. But the most important question is, do you feel at home here?"

Rella couldn't say if she knew what "home" felt like, but California came the closest so far in her life. She nodded.

"I want the grand tour. But first"—her mother went to her tote on the floor, pulling out a gift bag and presenting it to Rella—"a little something."

"Mom, you didn't have to."

"I can buy my daughter a gift if I want to."

Rella carefully reached inside and found two items from the remake of the Strawberry Shortcake collection: a sheet of stickers and a Raspberry Tart doll.

"Oh, I love them!" She admired the colors. "And look, the stickers are scratch 'n' sniff! Remember my old sticker book?"

"Of course. You spent hours creating it."

"I still have it. You know what else I still have?" She smiled. "Come with me."

Rella led her mother upstairs to a room she had turned into a kind of playroom, even before learning about Lisa or any of the Others, where she displayed toys, books, and figures she'd kept from childhood. On one shelf sat Raspberry Tart's Soda Shoppe.

"Remember this?" Rella asked, pointing up.

It took a minute to register, then her mother's face brightened. "Of course, I do! I'd hid it in the walk-in closet you played in."

"I'll never forget that day. You told me I'd left a mess in the closet, and I was so confused because I knew I hadn't. I opened the doors, and there it was. What a surprise!" It was a memory Rella was so glad she had retained. "How had you even known how much I wanted it?"

"I always paid attention." She brushed the stray hairs away from Rella's face. "I see you. Still the same, beautiful girl. You were born imaginative, always drawing houses with many rooms and hidden staircases and covert passageways."

Escape routes.

"You were about ten when you created that newsletter for the neighborhood kids. *Space*, I think you called it. Yes, that's right. All about architectural design. Your first article was "Dream Up." Such a clever name. Encouraging kids to imagine their perfect fantasy house, and then sample instructions on how they could draw it."

"Huh. I remember the newsletter, but not that part."

"You've always gone after your dreams. No one could tell you otherwise. Negative people and their comments ricochet off you. And here you are, by the water, in the sunshine, with a job you love. Are you happy?"

"Sure, Mom," she said.

There were so many questions Rella wanted to ask her mother—the one person who held pieces of the puzzle no one else did.

Had she ever seen anything strange in her growing up?

How many times had she been left alone with her grandparents?

How old was she the first time they watched her?

How could she have permitted her children to be around them?

Rella would never voice these questions aloud, never write them down, never confront her mother directly. Because she loved her. And she refused to take a knife to her mother's already lacerated kite.

Besides, she knew the answers wouldn't reverse what had fractured her long ago.

Rella descended the stairs in the early hours of the morning and found her mother cleaning the stove.

"Mom, what are you doing?"

"You're a busy gal. I like being useful. And I appreciate you having me here."

"It's not necessary, but thank you. Feels like a deep-cleaning day." The house always felt larger after Saturday-morning cleaning when she was a kid.

"You were so good about it, never fussed. Except when it was your turn to clean the bathtub."

The sparkling morning instantly sullied.

Bathtub.

Tile.

Arms.

Suds.

Water.

Get out.

She couldn't let it spoil the day.

She cleared the images with a windshield wiper.

"I'm looking forward to our whole day together." Rella noticed movement on the doorjamb. She walked over and stooped down.

"What is it?" her mother asked.

"A little grasshopper found its way in here." She cupped her hand and it climbed onto her wrist.

"Rella to the rescue! You always made sure every bug made it safely out of the house."

"I'll be right back."

Rella took the grasshopper outside. Sitting in the grass, she observed the creature, content, resting on her arm. Looking out over the yard, her eyes fell to where the strawberry patch used to be. The plants had never grown back.

"And how are you feeling today?" she asked the grasshopper. Suddenly, she noticed it was missing a leg.

"Oh no!" Tears welled up. Lisa brimmed just below the surface. Her lower lip jutted out, as Lisa's did when upset.

The creature didn't stray from her arm. Its front legs went up to its face and down, to its face and down. Its actions would have captivated her if she wasn't so distraught. Tears continued to stream at the thought that perhaps the grasshopper could no longer take flight.

"Rella? You okay?"

Rella didn't know how long she had been out there. Lisa was still with her.

"What's wrong?" Her mother took a seat on the low wall bordering the garden.

Rella fought to keep her voice her own. "Look," she slowly raised her arm to show the grasshopper more clearly.

"What?" she inspected. "Oh, you mean its leg?"

Rella nodded, crying more.

"These little critters are resilient. I'm sure it will be all right."

"But it can't get around anymore!" She couldn't bear the thought of it not being able to find food or elude attackers. Rella envisioned how to take care of it, while Lisa continued to cry.

"I'm sorry." Rella wiped her face with her free hand.

"There's no need to be sorry! You have always had a tender heart. You are a loving, caring person, and that's a wonderful thing. It's okay to cry, Rella."

It's okay to cry, Lisa.

"Grasshoppers eat leaves. I know a girl with plenty of veggies in her fridge! I'll be right back."

Her mother returned with a small plate of chard. Rella lowered her arm, keeping it steady, to bring the grasshopper to it. Suddenly, it leapt off her arm.

"Wow!" Rella was amazed at how far it had gone, landing right next to the plate.

"See, it's going to be fine. It's lost something, but it can still soar."

Lisa's tears dried as Rella allowed her to extend one of the leaves of chard out to the grasshopper.

"Grasshoppers can do this on purpose, to escape danger," her mother said. "They lose a part of themselves, so they can survive."

Forty-Nine

After her mother's departure, being alone again in the house stirred dark feelings.

Rella called Morgan in an attempt to still them.

"Hey, Morgan. How are things?"

"Fine. I'm finally deciding on paint for the walls. I'm thinking something neutral, but then adding color with art. I saw some great modern pieces at the store the other day. Large, bright shapes."

"Sounds nice."

Rella tried to immerse herself in the conversation, but it wasn't working. She couldn't ignore the sensation of someone at the window. Images of Katie and Abigail being hurt piled up. She couldn't climb out of them.

As though swept up by a cyclone, the world spun. The phone fell to the ground. Pain shot through her abdomen.

She crawled over to the wall and curled into a ball. "Get away from me, get away from me, get away from me," a toddler's voice said. "It hurts, it hurts, it hurts."

She slid across the floor, under the dining table, unable to use her legs.

"Rella! Rella!"

The sound of the name pulled at her, a dangling strand. But she couldn't grab on.

She felt *bad* all around, someone at the window or the door or already in the house.

Katie grunted and hissed and bared her teeth, the only defense mechanisms available to make herself undesirable in a world of predators.

***

"Rella? Rella, it's Ginnie." She knocked gently on the door.

"Ginnie?" a young voice asked.

"Yes, Ginnie. Could you let me in?"

She heard dragging across the floor.

"How do I know you're Ginnie?" the voice challenged, now closer to the door.

"Excellent question. Hmm . . . Rella and I are friends. She's an architect. Do you like to draw?"

"Yes."

"Me, too. Rella and I work together."

"I know."

"So, could I come in?"

"I can't reach the lock. It's high up."

"Oh. Could you try?"

Commotion sounded on the other side, a slight rattle to the door handle. "My legs aren't working today!"

"Don't hurt yourself."

"I won't. And I'm no quitter!"

Click. The lock disengaged.

"I did it!"

Ginnie heard a thump on the floor. "Well done! Can I open the door now?"

"One minute, please." More scuffling. "Okay."

Ginnie slowly opened the door and peeked inside. She saw

Rella on the floor, or, a version of Rella. She didn't quite look the same, which was odd and fascinating at the same time.

"Hello," Ginnie said, shutting the door.

"Hello." She hung her head.

"You don't have to be afraid."

"It's not that," she huffed, pushing her hair away. "I've been waiting so long, and I didn't want to meet you this way."

"Well, I'm glad to finally meet you. Let me guess. Is this Lisa?"

"Yeah."

"Nice to meet you, Lisa. I'm sorry for showing up unannounced. Morgan called and said Rella was upset."

She rocked forward, her hands going to the floor. "Ugh. Ugh. I don't feel well."

Ginnie detected a change in the voice. "Do you need to go to the hospital?"

"There is no hospital on the boat."

"There's no hospital on the boat," Ginnie repeated under her breath. "Well, is there a sick bay?"

"They don't help, they don't help." She rocked. "The spinning."

Benched, unsure what to do, Ginnie kept to the sidelines.

Gradually, her profile relaxed, and the rocking calmed, a storm going out to sea.

She touched the floor. The wall. The wood of the leg on the entry table.

"Who's this, please?" Ginnie asked.

She took a minute to answer.

"Anna," she said, the name wrapped in a breath.

"Anna. Hello. I'm Ginnie."

"I rarely come out. But I know you."

"How old are you, Anna?"

"I'm not quite sure," she answered.

"How old do you think you are?" Ginnie asked.

"Twenty-one," she responded.

"Ah, twenty-one. Now *that's* a good age!" Ginnie said cheerfully. "Although it's not the age when I had my first drink!"

"I don't drink."

"Then I definitely haven't met you before!" Ginnie replied.

"I would like some air, please."

"Of course."

She slowly stood, using the wall for support.

Ginnie followed behind, watching as the girl stepped out onto the stoop and trundled her way toward the yard, keeping her right arm around her abdomen, every movement labored. She seemed to savor a long, unhurried intake of air before gingerly lowering herself. Her hands spread, palms lightly brushing over the blades of grass. She brought her face to the ground and inhaled, as if she hadn't smelled the earth in a long time.

The sun emerged from a cloud, spilling onto the lawn and Anna's skin. She lifted her face to it.

Rella realized she was herself again because of how the world appeared.

When the cloudy cleared from her eyes, she saw that she was sitting on the floor in the living room.

Pieces came back to her. Had she been outside? And . . . Ginnie.

She stood up. "Ginnie?"

"In the kitchen!" Ginnie sang out.

Rella shuffled in. "I'm so ashamed."

"Nonsense! No talking like that!"

Rella sat on a stool. "I'm sorry you got dragged into this." She rubbed her head. "I can't remember much. I assume Morgan called you?"

"She sure did, and if she were to ever call me again to help, you'd better believe I'd come. And that's that. You're not alone in this, Rella."

They looked up at each other simultaneously and laughed.

"Sorry—no quip intended," Ginny said.

"It was a good one."

"Well, as usual, your kitchen is the Sahara."

"It's funny, I'm actually hungry."

"Good. I'll run out, grab and go—that is, if you'll be all right alone."

"I'll be fine. But you don't have to."

Ginnie reached for her keys. "I'll get some wine, too, a bottle for each of us."

"I might qualify for multiple," Rella said, smiling.

Ginnie caught on. "That's better. Clever joke! Although I did learn that Anna doesn't drink."

Rella knew that must be Modern Anna, as Victorian Anna adored wine.

Ginnie returned with dinner, several bottles of wine of different varieties, and a new cutting board with a bright red bow stuck to it.

Three nights later, Rella lay awake. Why can't I sleep? she asked herself.

I won't let you.

Why not?

Because I can't.

Who's this?

Doesn't matter. We all feel the same way.

Rella wondered if any of the Others was part of an alliance, or if each remained separate.

It's not just one of us wearing the mask. It's a memory. Her *memory. Only she and Rella can see it.*

She recalled hearing this whispered during one of her sessions with CJ, but she was no closer now to understanding its significance.

More pain behind the changes . . .

Another stray thought, though not random. None of the messages were. Only cryptic, as if someone wanted it revealed, but only in a way she could handle, drops of awareness rather than a flood of light.

Maybe it was better living in the shadows.

She wondered if there was just one memory that held the key. One that had initiated the loss of a part of herself, enabling the whole to survive.

Had she, Rella, been set adrift? Had *she* lived her life, or had someone else, in her place?

Had she avoided the mirror because she knew she'd see a reflection other than the person presenting as Rella?

Yes whispered inside her.

The mirror we don't see

The mirror unseen

The mirror unclean

She wrote the words down, not knowing what they meant.

Rella awoke two mornings later with thoughts of Abigail, which stayed with her throughout the day. That night, she appeared.

Abigail reached out her hand, the first time she'd initiated such a gesture.

Rella stared at it, white, hovering, an invitation. She raised her own to reciprocate but grew scared at confronting what she didn't want to see, and retracted.

Abigail retreated.

Maybe she would never be ready.

Illusion had meant survival.

But whose?

Margaret built on it. Modern Anna collapsed under it.

The best way to guard a secret: Remember there isn't one.

She wondered if it were the best way to guard herself, too.

Rella thought back to the first day she'd stood in front of building 610, the tall, cold, gray cement block that housed Seth's office.

"Margaret, why didn't you get me out of there?" Rella whispered. "Why didn't you make me flee?"

Her answer came later.

I didn't realize.

Modern Anna had a different reply.

It's better this way.

Fifty

West coast of Ireland—September 2019

Sturdy and resolute, the boat battled its way through the waves, advancing toward its destination. Rain and sea converged on the glass, blearing sense of place, time, and direction, suspending the Atlantic in a void.

Rella hung on to the armrests to steady herself against the abrupt changes in pitch, shutting her eyes at the worst intervals. She had mentally prepared herself for the crossing days prior.

It had been quite a journey thus far, between the long flight to Dublin, a two-and-a-half-hour bus ride to Galway, and another near hour's ride to Rossaveel, the ferry's point of departure.

A staticky message came over the intercom and Rella saw passengers readying for arrival, gathering their personal items and heading for the door.

Bravely, she stepped out onto the deck, near the handrail, gazing over the strip of ocean between her and land. No screaming in her head. No feeling of Victorian Anna.

Once they had docked in Kilronan, the crew worked efficiently, quickly hoisting bags and suitcases out of the storage area, offering a hand for those disembarking.

Rella stepped over the divide from the swaying boat to solid ground. She drew in a deep breath of the fresh atmosphere.

"We're here, Margaret," she said. "We're in Ireland."

Rella pulled her inadequate sweater closer to her neck, searching in her bag for the fingerless gloves she'd packed. She rolled her two suitcases behind her, on the lookout for the meeting spot.

"Are you Miss Cooper?" a middle-aged man asked Rella, wearing a coat fit for the weather, holding a cap in his hand.

"Yes, that's me," Rella answered.

"Right. The van's just there. I'll fetch your bags." He flipped his cap atop his head, lifting her suitcases just as effortlessly.

"Thank you."

"Is this your first time to Inis Mór, Miss Cooper?" he asked as they pulled away.

"Please, call me Rella."

"Rella, interesting name. Mine's Patrick."

"Nice to meet you, Patrick. And yes, my first time here."

"Ah, lovely then. Can't ask for a better place in the world. I've lived here my whole life. It's how Ireland used to be. Almost lost with the Great Famine. Do you know of the Famine, then?"

"Yes," Rella verified sadly.

"Ireland never recovered. Will never be how it was before the Famine. Around twenty-five hundr'd people lived on the Aran Islands, this one and the two others, in 1840. Now, twelve hundr'd, I'd figure. Both worlds cohabit here, life now, and tokens of that time. The land tells the story."

Rella took in the stark beauty of the landscape. The view stretched endlessly, for the depth of the soil didn't seem to support much more than low grasses and brush. "Strange not seeing any trees."

"Yes, they're missed here."

Rella thought of Katie's tree, wondered who'd planted it.

"Different kind of beauty we have, though."

"It's remarkable."

"The first settlers must have thought so, too, I'm sure."

Rella wondered how newcomers had survived on the island under such bleak conditions.

"How did they manage to grow anything?"

"Fair question. The soil here is shallow, at best only about three to four feet deep, but often only a few inches. Underneath is pure rock. We Irish are a gritty lot," he declared, revealing crow's feet. "Stubborn as stone. We find a way. The early settlers mixed seaweed with the sand trapped in the grasses by the wind. They built the soil, so to speak, generations adding to it ever since."

"Incredible."

"Aye. Life favors the resourceful."

"And these stone walls." They mesmerized Rella, roaming the hills, rolling through the fields. "They create a patchwork quilt partitioning the countryside."

"Right you are, miss, for they've been stitched together just so. No mortar, you see. Each stone laid precisely. The land was covered with rock. They had to clear it for pasture, for growing. What better use than for walls? There are over two thousand kilometers of dry stone walls on the Aran Islands.

I build them too, in the winter, once the tourist season is over and the island goes quiet. It passes the time. Hard work, but it's right relaxing."

Rella couldn't imagine it being any quieter. She'd only seen one other car pass, and Patrick had waved to them.

"A few sights, then," said Patrick. "That there, see, is our recycling facility."

Rella tilted her head courteously.

"This, here, is our Blue Flag beach," he pointed proudly. "It's an award, you see. How are you on time?"

"I have no plans," Rella said.

"Let me take you on a proper tour, then. I'll make a call to Dáire. She's the lady meeting you at the house."

"Sounds lovely," Rella accepted, amused by the quirky jaunt thus far.

Patrick's voiced sailed through his phone lyrically, in what she assumed was Gaelic.

"Right. She'll meet us there in an hour," he reported to Rella.

They continued on, a solo tour in a lone, but not lonely, place.

A calf scooted towards two other cows. It made Rella horribly sad that many animals were denied freedom elsewhere, because of their kind.

"I wish all cows could have been born here," she mused wistfully, more to herself than to Patrick.

"Natural lawn mowers, they are. The horses too. Given the freshest air and greenest grass."

"How it should be," Rella declared.

"If you go walking the island, which I expect you will, just up the turn there you'll see a Connemara pony. Gray and white. Gorgeous."

They rounded a corner and Patrick pointed up a hill.

"Many a monk made their home here. Held tight to their practices. Vigils, they'd have. Stay up all night."

"Must be where the word 'vigilant' comes from," Rella remarked.

"You're quite a scholar."

"I admire words."

"Hibernia is the old name of Ireland," he said, "given by the ancient Romans, meaning 'land of winter.' It comes from their word, *hibernus.*"

"Interesting. Like hibernation."

"Never thought of that."

"What does Inis Mór mean?"

"Big island."

"That's not very creative."

Patrick chuckled. "Sounds better *as Gaelige.*"

"Huh?"

"It means, in the Irish language."

"Oh. Neat." Rella retrieved a scarf from her handbag and wrapped it around her neck.

"Summers can be fairly short in Ireland. Last year it was the seventeenth of August."

Rella laughed. "It is rather chilly."

"First day of September can have a winter nip, but we'll have some nice days yet. The sun will shine through to say hello."

The blue sky and fast-moving clouds darkened, followed by a downpour upon the roof.

"The weather changes in seconds here!" Rella said.

"Aye, it does. They say it rains more in Ireland because there's sadness in the clouds. They've seen much heartache. But it grows life, too. The Gaelic name for Ireland is *Éire*, for 'lush land.' It thrives, despite the conditions and the hardships. Have you heard of The Burren?"

"I've heard the name, yes."

"It's a bit similar to the landscape here, but The Burren is over in County Clare, just across the water," Patrick said with a wave of the hand. "The Irish name is *Boireann*, which means 'great rock.' Over seventy percent of the species of flowers of Ireland grow there. Around one hundred and sixty classes of flowers not found anywhere else in the world, from crevices hundreds of feet down." Patrick shook his head in wonder as he turned the steering wheel. "No matter the adversity, one can still reach the sun."

Rella desired for each of the Others the warmth and comfort and healing of the sun.

He drove further, then took a left. "We be stopping here."

Rella exited the van to another spectacular view. Swirled into a painting as land met sky, variations of blue in the still waters and low, white clouds were the only defining separation. Windswept grasses, the same that had gathered sand for the early settlers, tufted in mounds around her ankles as she followed her guide through a graveyard.

Patrick led Rella to a gray block of brick and stone with three plaques affixed. Patrick translated as Rella's eyes roved the surface of the top one, studying the beautiful, curved letters.

"In 1852, fifteen men and boys had their day off, so they had gone fishing. A big wave came, out of nowhere, and swept them all away. The lone survivor, Pat O'Donnell, had his dog with him, who sensed the oncoming danger and pulled him to safety. So, the moral of the story?"

"Leave fish alone," Rella replied.

Patrick laughed. "Always have your best friend by your side and listen to their warnings!"

"What does this say here?" Rella asked, pointing to another area on the monument.

Patrick looked to the sky, as if he'd inscribed the words inside long ago. "These people won't get old, like we get old. Old age won't make them sick and decrepit, and the years won't find fault with them. But when the sun rises in the morning and when we go to bed at night, we will think of them."

"Right then, here we are."

Patrick parked the van in front of a long, one-story house. It was painted bright white and had a low, thatched roof, with four short windows across the front, and a vivid red door in the center. In the middle of the stone wall, a matching red gate led to the entrance path, a picnic table off to the side with a view to the quiet street.

"I'll get your bags. Door's unlocked," Patrick said.

"Thank you," said Rella.

The hinges of the gate rasped as she pushed it back, gravel crunching under her feet. Bushes of fragrant herbs grew beneath the windows on either side of the front door. She was delighted to see it was a half-door, the top unlatched and open. A small black lantern hung to the right, a homemade welcoming sign that read FÁILTE to the left.

Whitewashed mud plaster walls continued inside, exposed beams stretching the length of the ceiling. Cheery red pillows cushioned hand-carved furniture. A red, white, and yellow braided rug lay across the pine floor. A wall made entirely of stacked flat stone housed a wood-burning stove. A reading nook curled itself into one corner.

Patrick entered with the suitcases. "There are two bedrooms. I'll settle these in the smaller one. It can serve as an oversize closet."

Rella walked into the spacious, rustic kitchen, the same beams spanning the ceiling as were in the living room. Skillets hung suspended over the stove. Colorful hand-painted dishes were arranged on open shelves and displayed along the wall.

"I see you made it then." A woman entered from the side door. "Sorry, didn't mean to alarm you, love."

"Oh, no, it's me. I'm jumpy sometimes."

"Come from a city, I gather. You'll be right safe here."

"Hiya, Dáire," Patrick said, joining them in the kitchen.

"Patrick, nice to see you. How are Aoife and Charlotte, then?"

"All's well. Glad to be back in school, in their studies."

"Ah, clever girls. Now, I'm sorry, what was your name again?"

"Rella."

"Rella, right. How ya gettin' on? Enjoy the tour?"

"Greatly."

"Grand. A bit about the house. It can get mighty cold at night, the wind howlin' about. There's plenty 'a wood chopped in the shed outside, to keep the stove going. And some peat briquettes too. You'll love the smell, so fragrant and cozy."

"That's part of our history too, Rella, the fireside," Patrick said, leaning back on his heels. "No records penned in Ireland, not until the fifth or sixth century, thereabouts, everything passed down by way of story, you see. In winter, there's no light, not from about four-thirty in the afternoon until eight in the morning. Many an hour to sit around the fire, talking, handing down traditions, recounting tales. They used to say that peat absorbs those sentiments, holds them, song and soot."

"Ah, Patrick, you missed your calling as a poet," Dáire said.

"These hands are better suited for stone than pen," he replied.

"Aye," Dáire bowed her head. "Now, Rella, here are the keys. The locks are a mite tricky, the doors a touch tight, but give a good tug and you'll manage. I live on the other side of the island, but a skip down the road there is Kilmurvey. The businesses be open till about four. If you're in a fix, or have a bother, they'd be ready to help. Also, in front there is where the men line up for the horse-and-trap rides."

"Horse and trap?"

Dáire smiled. "Carriage might be your word."

"A horse-and-buggy ride," Patrick offered.

"Oh, nice."

"I left my number written down on the notepad in the kitchen. Any questions?"

"No, I don't think so."

Rella had done her research before choosing this spot. There was one small restaurant within walking distance, open for lunch, and no nearby market; thus, she had prepared accordingly before leaving Galway, one entire suitcase stocked with healthy provisions.

"Right. I'll leave you to get sorted then. Enjoy your stay. And be sure not to miss Dún Aonghasa, a prehistoric stone fort on the hill," Dáire said. "A gorgeous hike."

"Thank you for telling me about it. I'll definitely go."

"It's up the road there." Dáire twiddled her fingers vaguely. "Right, Patrick, see you."

"See you, Dáire," he said as she walked out the door. "My number is below Dáire's, if you're needing a ride."

"Wonderful. And thank you so much for the tour. I certainly enjoyed it." Rella held out a gratuity.

"No need for that. Pleasure was mine."

"I insist."

Patrick tipped his cap, accepting. "Much appreciated. Have a nice afternoon, miss."

"You too, Patrick. See you around." Rella already felt like a local.

Rella had arranged absence from the firm, accepting only a handful of smaller projects to bring with her to work on over the next month. She hoped the distance and solitude would allow her time to learn more about the Others.

The next day Rella woke before dawn. Since entering the cottage yesterday evening, she had not heard a single sound. Once light broke, she dressed warmly and went out.

The air was fresher than Rella had ever tasted. She walked in silence, the subtle sounds of the island whispering in her ears. The sky stretched unbounded, welcoming and unsettling at the same time, colors of gray, white, and blue racing each other across the expanse. Golden light shimmered in puddles. While she hadn't seen one car or person thus far, she felt someone's presence strongly, more than she ever had.

She stopped at the small beach located at the bottom of the hill. Carefully stepping along the whitish gray sand to preserve the patterns of ocean etchings, she picked a spot in the center of the curve of the beach and sat facing the water. She was a bit disappointed she could see the mainland in the distance.

She didn't begin writing straightaway, but first inhaled the salty air, letting it linger in her nose and on her tongue, the breeze shimmering around her, and tuned in to the melody of peace that plays when one is alone with nature.

She pulled a notebook from her small backpack and, without much thought, began.

Some buried in the shade. Some at the surface of the sun.

What is the purpose of the shade?

To hide. Underneath. Cold, damp, forgotten.

I could dig some out, into the sun.

No, it would hurt the other grains. Damage them.

Damage?

They are used to it. It is how they have learned to live.

Rella realized she wasn't the only one writing. Margaret had joined, answering her questions.

Rella woke during the night in a sweat, her body heavy from a deep sleep state. Debris from her dream littered her mind.

A girl sleeping.

Light from an opening door snuffed out by an entering figure.

The door closing.

She pushed herself up and turned on the lamp.

She felt a dip in the temperature of the room, her clothes damp and cloying. She changed and added logs to the fireplace. Titian embers flickered. Grabbing a heavy blanket, she sat on the floor in front of the heat.

Did the image of the girl sleeping on the bed come from a specific person? she asked internally.

It was a leak, Margaret answered.

Do the Others dream? she asked. *Dreams I wouldn't have?*

She saw a nod.

Thank you for that information, Margaret.

Rella developed a schedule. She walked in the morning at first light, in the middle of the day to break up her writing exercises, and for an hour in the evening, her back soaking up the last of the sun's warmth before it sank into the clouds over the ocean.

It was the first place Rella ever experienced a complete lack of pollution, of the air, the ears, the eyes. She sensed Margaret more strongly with each stride, until in step with her.

"Go out and explore, Margaret," she said aloud.

Finally, she did. She turned up one of the roads, each footfall purposeful, measured, unsure how many she would have. The cool air didn't bother Margaret, nor the dampness. In her element, Margaret seemed born to live on this island, in solace and with distance from the world; somehow, she'd known it even before arriving.

Margaret continued on. Rella paused along a stone wall, the sun glistening on overgrown vines. "Blackberries!" She tasted one. Perfect. "This is how we were meant to live," she said aloud. "Peace, clean air, fresh food, clear thoughts."

She thought she saw Margaret nod in the distance, her back to her.

A couple of hours later, Rella entered the dry, heated house, cheeks flushed from the vigorous outing, and removed her hiking shoes, placing them at the door. She settled at the table, a cup of tea within reach. Through writing, she'd found a means to be present when Margaret opened her thoughts.

You can escape and never change location. Escape in the same spot. Distance, a stretch of beach in your mind, where only you walk. Reprieve from restraint. Still in the room you've never left, but with the memory of the beach.

Fifty-One

Rella carried in a load of firewood, dropping it into the tin bin with a thud. She rubbed her hands together and tended the existing fire.

Opening her carrying case on the dining table, she removed paper, chalk, pencils, and pens. The items reminded her of grade-school days. She asked herself if she was switching even then.

Yes.

She started the session with left-handed free drawing, accessing the creative part of her brain, and corridors to the subconscious mind. She followed with a free-association word exercise and journal writing, recording whatever came as a result.

Initially, some internal hesitation stalled her progress, and three days passed without much additional insight.

We will cease to exist.

I won't let that happen, Rella said internally. *You are all important.*

You'll forget about us.

No, I won't, said Rella. *I promise.*

She was soon rewarded. She noticed recurring themes in her work—of distance, water, barriers, spinning, sickness, throwing up, and fullness.

At times, she was privy to certain internal conversations.

That's a pretty shade of green. Green is my favorite color, Modern Anna said as Rella drew. *So cozy here, inside.*

Rella could almost see her on the couch, in a sweater and loose pants, long hair around her shoulders, legs folded under her.

This place is lame. Am I supposed to count seconds on this rock? Gabby griped.

Sometimes it's nice having nothing to do, Anna replied.

Hmph, Gabby rebutted.

We used to be friends, you and I, Anna told her.

I don't think so.

You just don't remember. That gets taken away too.

I want to draw a turtle! Lisa piped up. *I love turtles.*

Yeah, so you can be in your shell, Gabby retorted.

I'm not in any shell. Lisa sounded offended.

Abigail looked on silently.

Rella picked up another color of chalk.

Purple is her favorite color, Lisa said.

Whose? Rella asked. *Abigail's?*

No. Katie's.

You know Katie?

She used to like me.

Rella had learned to ask simple questions or respond as neutrally as possible; otherwise, dialogue halted.

I see.

She used to be nice. Then she got all mad.

Then, Rella saw it—the two of them together, at the table in the playroom. But, at some point, Katie had pushed Lisa away—not out of any antagonism directed at Lisa.

Rella wondered if it had been to protect Lisa. Yet another measure to do so.

A thought entered Rella's mind—was *she* Lisa?

She didn't get an internal answer.

Later, Rella went into the kitchen to make a cup of tea.

I'm sick of tea, Gabby complained.

What do you prefer? Rella asked internally.

Shot of whiskey.

You're only fifteen.

While the tea steeped, Rella poured a small amount of whiskey into a glass and took a sip.

Wimp.

"You know I can't drink a whole shot at once," Rella said, then asked herself, did she? "And I can enjoy the taste this way," she added.

Rella returned to the table to write.

Gabby had more to say.

I hate it.

What kind of stupid, no-brained idiot dreams up swim class? Fifteen minutes in the pool, followed by a rushed shower and running down the hall, late, with wet hair. Yeah, bright idea, especially in winter.

Chlorine reeks. It soaks into my bare feet from these scuzzy tiles. My skin itches the rest of the day, and I can smell it exuding from my pores.

There's an out, once a month, if you're a girl. But you still have to show up, sit on a hard bench next to the pool, suffocating in the hot, chemical air, the boys knowing why you aren't going in. A punishment. From a double-wide loser phys ed lump who stuffs his face with cafeteria burgers and "chicken" fingers. Who wants to eat fingers of any kind, anyway? I've never seen him get in the pool. I'm sick of being told what to do. Morons.

As Rella read what Gabby had written, she realized how present she must have been during her early high school years.

The evening sky cleared, unveiling a dazzling canopy of stars.

Rella arranged wood in the outdoor fireplace, using newspaper and a few sticks for kindling. She pulled up a chair and wrapped herself in a blanket, gazing upward.

The cool air tickled her nose. Her eyes followed the scraps of burnt ashen paper as they drifted upward. Her body hummed, tingling with warm blood flow and relaxed nerves. As her eyes fluttered, on the verge of closing, someone inside was ready to communicate.

The end of the day. Sundown. It's over. Quiet.

I clean up in the river. Gather my chair, flute, and pot for over the fire. Baked beans are my favorite. I spend the night outside.

I don't mind being alone, and I'm not quite, anyway. The animals and creatures know me. I won't hurt them, and they don't hurt me. They keep me company. I love foxes. One or two sit at my ankles, long after the sun goes down. Most of the animals only feel safe coming out at night. I don't blame them.

During the day, I wander. I never get lost. The desert is my home. I sit and observe and think. It's how we are supposed to be with nature. Still and observant and thoughtful.

I live in peaceful moments. I wish I could give Rella some of mine. I don't have the bad thoughts she does. I would send them up in the clouds to crystallize into a star and shine down on her as happy light.

The next morning, hair scented by smoke from the night before, Rella reread the notes in her journal.

That afternoon, Dustin added another entry.

Twilight.

Twin light.

I came after Abigail.

I don't mind girls, but I don't like boys.

I wish I wasn't a boy.

Or a girl.

Sometimes I wish I—wasn't.

Sitting in the sand at the small beach, eyes closed, Rella harmonized with the cadence of lapping waves and whiffs of salty air.

Victorian Anna stood on the boat, shrouded in black. The unidentified woman appeared beside her, her back to Rella. The tip of the boat gently swung toward Rella, allowing her a glimpse of the woman's profile. New information was delivered. The woman next to Anna was Margaret.

Rella's eyes sailed open.

In the gray. No one can see me. Protected. Stay small. Stay away. Distance. No bottom. The past not to be caught.

Only receiving trickles of insight into Water's oceanic world had Rella wondering if the aqueous cage held critical keys to herself.

In the middle. Constantly. Up and down. Up and down. Dense fog. No land in sight. Stranded. Never steady. I labor to moor my eyes and fail. Up and down. Up and down. Can't tell if it's day or night. The water muffles me. Hard to keep afloat.

Drowning. Submerged. Swallowing. Murky, horrid, sick, diseased, dirty water. It makes my stomach sick. I'm not just stuck on a boat. I'm stuck in it, in the water, without the boat. Churning, in my stomach. The turmoil in me. I am the water. I am the waves. I can't get out. In the origin.

Rella paused at the last sentence. "The origin," she read aloud, sitting with those words for a few moments as she cast her eyes offshore.

It will drown you.

Rella wished to cross the sea and bring Water back to dry land.

"Hang on. I'm coming," Rella whispered. "I'll figure out how."

The strength. The passage. The raft.

She had to save her. Even if it meant swimming out there herself.

Rella's period came.

Searing hot-poker pain shot up through her. She huddled on the floor, kicking her legs out, willing to push it away. It intensified. She curled into a ball, exhaling in short, laborious gasps. The agony spread to her inner thighs, her lumbar. Her spine arched, head jutting back.

help

drowning

swallowing

spit it up

want to throw up

bloated

liquid

it's dirty water

on face

in mouth

sick

She reached the bathroom just in time, throwing up what little she'd eaten, and the last water ingested.

no air

stuffy

I don't like it

pushed under

pushed down

She ran out of the bathroom, squeezing her head in her hands, the thoughts relentless.

get out of me

dizzy

have to go away

let go

go away

leave the body

She hit her head with the palms of her hands, slamming her inner wrists into her temples. Pain singed her lower parts. "Owie, owie, owie." She pressed her hands over her thighs, moaning. Paralyzed by the burning, she couldn't run, couldn't move.

Being a girl meant being trapped.

"I ain't taking this crap."

The pain rushed out of her as though a valve had been opened. Gabby righted herself against the wall and pushed back her hair.

"Can't *stand* all this in my face." She stood up. "I'm gonna get a gun, that's what I'm gonna do. I'll shoot him. Watch him bleed. Perv."

Gabby turned to Rella, who was still on the floor. "For me, it ends here." She strutted around the room. "'I make my own decisions. Make them better than anyone else. Ugh. I hate this body. I should be the one to say if I bleed!"

She threw herself into the chairs around the table. The forceful act knocked her away.

The person on the floor rocked. "Mmm, mmm, mmm." Black, all around. Pain increasing. A shower curtain. Black tile.

Tile. Tile is hard. Tile can break her head. Then she'll be safe. Hit your head, harder.

That was the answer. The way to end it.

Internally, someone intervened.

Rella remained still for a long time.

Fifty-Two

Rella woke on the floor, cold, sunlight filtering into her eyes.

She stood. The room spun. Surprisingly ravenous, she made her way into the kitchen, using the walls for support.

She scrambled tofu with spinach, thyme, oregano, and fresh tomatoes, and sliced a large chunk of bread made exclusively for her by the kind innkeeper in Kilmurvey, a vegan version of the traditional Irish brown bread, spreading an ample amount of blackcurrent preserves over the top. She ate slowly.

When she'd finished, she picked up the phone to call Patrick, requesting a ride into Kilronan.

"You should take one of the traps back to Kilmurvey," Patrick suggested as Rella exited the van.

Rella looked up, gray varnishing the sky.

"Ah, don't be minding the weather. Give it a lash!" he said heartily. "Tully!" he called out to a man navigating his horse to a stop. "Wait here for Miss Rella and take her back to Kilmurvey when she's finished."

The man inclined his head and touched the tip of his hat, which sat low over his eyes.

"Thank you, Patrick."

"Have a nice time."

Rella perused the handful of shops filled with exceptional

knitwear. She grazed her fingertips over the stitching, appreciating the beautiful variations in the patterns, each sweater as substantial and hearty as the Irish brown bread. She bought two.

Stepping outside, she used the opportunity of having better cell service to make a call.

"Hey, Rella!" Trevor said. "So good to hear your voice!"

"Yours too! I'm in town, where my phone works." She paused. "Lisa says hi." It still felt odd, passing along greetings and words from the Others, but she did it for them. "And Margaret finds it peaceful here."

"How about you?"

"This island is a gift. I've been constructive, drawing and writing daily, working on the exercises I told you about. Information has come out, but so far I'm able to handle it."

"I'm so glad. Maybe this can be a way of processing for you. I wouldn't be surprised if there was less weight on the Others now."

"I hope you're right. Well, I better go. I have a ride waiting."

"Enjoy yourself and call me again when you can. I love you."

Rella walked over to the man Patrick had called Tully, who sat on a low wall encircling outdoor picnic table seating for one of the pubs, as stationary as a statue. "Hello! I'm ready to go back now, if that's all right with you."

"Right, then."

He went around the other side to open the door for her and helped her up the tiny step. The seats were thickly padded and faced sideways rather than forward. "There's a warm blanket there for your legs."

"Thank you. This is quite comfy," she remarked, settling in. "Thank you for being kind enough to wait for me."

He dipped his head. "Ayup."

Taking the reins into his weathered left hand, he flicked them. The horse began a slow trot.

"Name's Mainie Jellett," he said.

"Pardon?" Rella asked, leaning forward.

"Mainie Jellett."

"I thought it was Tully."

He laughed. "Not my name, the *horse*." The way he said it sounded like *hearse*.

"The horse? Oh! Love it. Quite unique."

"She was a painter, born in 1897, from Dublin. I name all my horses after Irish figures in history. It's a way for them to live on. Can't think of a better way than roving these roads."

"What a nice idea. Big fan of her art?"

"Not an iota. Cubism, I think it's called. Right awful. Bunch 'a colors and shapes that don't make sense. But that's life too, right? 'An insoluble puzzle,' her paintings 'ave been called."

"An insoluble puzzle," Rella repeated.

"But, steppin' back, takin' it in, considering all parts on the canvas, we might figg'r somethin' out." He shrugged. "*Cas ar dheis.*"

"What does that mean?"

"Turn right. I talk to her like she comprehends. And I think sometimes she does."

"Animals are more intelligent and perceptive than most give them credit for."

"Aye, right you are. Hold on now, I'll let her open it up." He made a nearly imperceptible motion with the reins and Mainie Jellett's slow trot turned into a canter. Rella bounced in the seat.

Sorry when the ride came to a close, Rella sat patiently as Tully maneuvered his cart to a stop along the stone wall in front of Kilmurvey House.

"Thank you, Tully. And thank you, Mainie Jellett," Rella said. "I much enjoyed the ride. Rella handed over the sum, including a tip.

"Pleasure." He tapped the brim of his hat.

Arriving at the house, Rella spotted a cat in the yard.

"Well, hello there." She placed her bags down and lowered herself, hoping the cat would approach. With a meow, it scampered over, purring as it allowed Rella to pet her. "I think I've seen you at the neighbor's house."

The sun peeked out and Rella sat on the ground to enjoy more time with the cat. She felt Abigail's presence.

"Abigail, want to pet the kitty?" Rella asked her aloud.

Abigail cautiously approached.

"It's a very nice kitty," Rella assured her. Rella noticed a small bowl near the spigot. "Maybe she would like some water," Rella said, standing. As soon as she heard the creak from turning the knob, the sound scraped at Rella's skin, as it never had before. Abigail was gone.

Rella wrote down the name, then any ideas that came.

Abigail didn't like water—not the sound of it running nor the feel of it. Maybe another reason she couldn't ever get clean. Or perhaps no amount of water would ever wash off the dirtiness she felt.

Lost to another dimension, one Rella couldn't access and Abigail couldn't escape from, the little girl was controlled, watched, meant to feel cold, exposed, to wear thin clothing, taken away from herself.

Did Abigail sense that Rella wouldn't be able to handle what she had to say? If Rella looked into her eyes, would they show her unspeakable images held inside?

Rella dreamt of Victorian Anna. In town, head high, her sister trailing behind, giggling.

Rella noticed that the young girl of about eight resembled Abigail, a healthier, lively version, with color in her cheeks and thickness to her blonde hair and happiness in her laugh. Rella enjoyed watching her skip about. She wore an old-fashioned dress, clean, crisp, with sleeves just below her elbows, a low, satin belt attached to it, an oversize half-moon collar, and a big bow in front, with a matching one tying together the two braids in her hair.

The sky darkened. Victorian Anna vanished.

Rella saw the little girl in a basement. Alone. Terrified. Sensing someone coming for her.

Rella reached out. Her arms weren't long enough.

Anna in the distance, flickering between Victorian Anna and Modern Anna. *Help her*, she mouthed to Rella, as if she couldn't get to the small girl either.

Abigail, frozen in time, in that moment. *Help me*, Abigail mouthed to Rella.

Rella engaged her legs to run, but the muscles were jammed. A shadow eclipsed Abigail, and she was gone.

In a room. Can't move. Can't talk. A bad man. Can't say anything. It happens again and again and again. I hang my head. I feel yucky. I hurt. He's always watching. I can't talk. I pretend.

As Rella wrote the words, she came to a possible realization.

CJ had once said "Abigail holds fear." Perhaps Abigail had suffered the longest, terrorized for years, her essence drained. Maybe that's when Gabby entered, at Rella's first period. Gabby was fed up, fought back, stopped it.

Fifty-Three

The pencil in Rella's right hand shook.

She sat staring at the blank piece of paper before her, as white as the dress of the little blonde girl who had first appeared in Seth's office.

The dress that was later covered with blood.

Violence.

No one coming to save her.

No hope of escape.

Up she had floated, released from the body. Perhaps, the very moment she had gone from Rella to Katie.

Rella wrote *Katie* at the top of the paper, followed by everything she knew about her.

Age four

Born of anger

Held down

Can't use her legs

Trapped

Man, forceful

Musty smells

Sunlight taken away

Rella paused, looking at the last two.

Rella's grandfa—his room had been in the basement.

"Margaret, is there anything else?" Rella whispered.

But she wasn't present. Rella honestly hadn't expected

her to be. She didn't think even Max knew anything.

She realized the older ones didn't have any information about Katie or her history. Only Katie did.

Rella never invoked any of the Others to come out, or share what they held. But she knew in doing the exercise, something could appear.

Later that night, in the chasm between the remembered and the forgotten, in the cemetery of memory, lying in bed in the darkness, Katie opened a door.

I'm in the ground. The basement. I look to the small rectangle window high up. Dusty, gray light. The sun's yellow is far away. I want to be outside, where it is warm and dry.

From above, I hear talking. A door shutting. Walking.

Something's not right. My tummy moves inside.

Eek.

A footstep, on the top stair.

On the other side of the wall is where Grandmother does laundry. The smell from the pink bottles gives me a headache.

Eek. Eek.

I could climb on the washer, reach the window. Squeeze out.

Eek.

My heart beats fast. I want to run, but my legs feel like wood nailed to the floor.

"Go downstairs," he had grumbled. I hadn't asked why.

Eek.

How many stairs are there? I wish they would open like a big accordion and shut him inside.

Eek.

Eek.

Eek.

Silence.

I feel heat like the furnace in the corner that hisses steam.

He enters. His eyes burn.

"Get on the bed."

I don't move.

"I said, get on the bed."

I don't want him to touch me and put me on the bed, so I climb up on it. The sheets are stained. I sink low into the old mattress, my feet off the floor.

"Lie down."

No, not on these yucky sheets. He looks angry. I don't want him to push me back. I lie down. The sheets smell funny. The bed moves. My lungs stop.

Rough. Scratchy. His pants. Cold. A button. His hands. Down there. My legs tighten together. He pushes them apart. Then pain. Sharp pain. I scream.

"Shut up."

His hand goes over my face. I want to bite, but it's like all my teeth have fallen out.

My hands become fists and I fight in my mind. Help, I say in my brain. Help!

Then, I see my rescue! Light from the staircase.

My father! He yells and hits the monster away and picks me up. I will be safe now.

Pain shoots up me again. Unlike anything I've ever felt, filling me to my belly button, and I think I will explode like a balloon.

My father is not here. No one is coming.

I have to save me.

I push the pain and smells out.
It isn't happening.
It isn't happening.
It isn't happening.
I float up. And away.

The next morning, beaten up by dreams, lungs waterlogged by tears, Rella went back to the white paper on table. She picked up the pencil. At the bottom of the page, she wrote: *Thank you.*

She raised her eyes to the empty room. "You're no longer alone," she said aloud. "I am here now too."

Her father, mother, sister, brother—no one had come to her rescue. They hadn't been there. But she'd had herself. And that's what had saved her.

Fifty-Four

Rella pulled her new sage green Aran sweater over her head, laced her hiking shoes, and donned a pair of gloves, setting out for a trek.

Having explored the entire island over the last month, she knew her favorite spots, the quieter ones, where the shuttle buses and tourists largely didn't go.

She walked briskly along the path leading to the incline. She confidently ascended uneven rocky steps, enjoying the solidity and stability in her legs after days of debility from the pain of her period.

Cold and hardened and impervious.

"Hello, Margaret," Rella said aloud, receiving her thoughts as she walked alongside.

Rella paused to take in the panorama.

"So restful. You like it here."

Yes.

"I do too."

At the summit, Rella crossed the rocky fields.

Ringforts were constructed with outer, middle, and inner walls, a layout embodying layers of the mind, from easily accessible to impenetrable.

Rella navigated towards the cliffs, careful not to step too close to the edge. Clear of obstacles, the breathtaking coastline stretched limitlessly, this side of the island affording a view of only endless blue waters.

Rella advanced to the boundary where land met sea, variations of hues sparkling in the sun, the pure air sailing up the crag exhilarating.

The might of nature, crashing waves, and the immense power of the wind instilled in her strength, resilience.

She reflected on the past four weeks, all she had learned; on the past year, her entire lifetime. None of it could have been accomplished without them.

"What were your first words, Margaret?"

Margaret looked taken aback.

"You can tell me. It's okay."

Margaret paused. Information was not to give out.

I have to be rigid, so you don't notice me.

"Now that I know about you, it's okay to be noticed."

Rella waited.

Margaret's responses came slowly, each one carried in on a breeze from a distant place and time.

I'm here.

You're not alone.

Let me handle it.

Get out of there.

Rella took it in.

She wanted to turn her head, look at her, but didn't.

They stood side by side, for several quiet moments.

"Thank you for all you've done for me, all these years."

It is what I am here for.

"I think you should live a life too, Margaret. Outside of your office."

Instantly transported, they now both stood in Margaret's workplace.

Rella pressed her feet into the plush carpet. Her nostrils filled with the air of the room enclosed by the cabinets, lockers of the past.

Rella passed through, entered the living quarters, went to the glass wall across from Margaret's couch, and looked out. The view to where they stood now expanded below, over the North Atlantic Ocean, as if the windows represented Margaret's eyes.

Rella's gaze dropped down over the edge. Margaret had kept her away from it, the hazardous knowledge, the precipice, the danger.

"Would it be helpful if I had a set of keys, too?" Rella asked her.

She felt Margaret's response adamantly.

No. The file room was her job. It had always been her job and would always be her job.

"We'll keep it that way, then."

The air gusted.

"How long have you been around, Margaret?"

A long time.

"I wouldn't have survived without you. Without all of you."

Rella knew there were Others she had not yet met.

CJ's words came back to her. *Dissociation does not occur on the first event.* She wondered how many undisclosed shadows still waited in the Greenhouse.

Leaving Inis Mór, Rella felt separated from the strong connection she'd experienced with Margaret. But Margaret was still there, with her, and always would be.

Rella closed her eyes and traveled back to earlier that morning, when she'd taken her final walk down the now-familiar paths through the fields between the stone walls. She'd hiked countless hours over the last month, becoming deeply acquainted with less-traveled curves and inlets, of the island, and of herself. She'd said a last goodbye to the Connemara pony, giving it a kiss on the nose.

A cold and outwardly barren place had received her warmly and given so much. She wished she could fold up the island and put it in her back pocket and cast it off the shore of California, so she could visit whenever she wanted. But she knew it wouldn't be the same. It wouldn't be far enough away.

"It is going to be terribly difficult to leave this place, this island," she had told Dáire upon her departure from the house.

"One always has withdrawal from Kilmurvey," the Irish woman had replied.

Rella had booked a night in Doolin, leaving for Dublin the next day. Her hostess insisted Rella spend her last night in Ireland at a local music house.

To the chords of fiddle and flute, stomping feet on wood floors, encircled by hops, ale, and cheer, Rella thought of all she'd been gifted over the past month. She felt strong, assured, and, finally, herself again. A girl who embraced life and music, animals and insects, kindness and joy.

The chummy group encouraged her to stand and sing along, and she laughed as she fumbled through the words.

432

"Now you must dance!"

"I don't know how!" Rella said.

"We all confront the unknown. Clear your mind. If you're racing in your head, you're racing in the music. Come on, you can do it!"

And she found that she could.

In the stillness at the end of the night, in her room, as all of Ireland fell asleep, Rella sensed she was not alone. They were there. The Others. Standing around her.

She mentally embraced them.

"I love you," she said. "All of you."

She cried, and not all of her tears were sad.

Fifty-Five

Rella crossed the threshold.

Unlived in for what felt like years, the walls and floors of her house had long dissipated warmth and waited in cold.

Rella put down her suitcases and moved further inside, stepping into a memory, a static moment belonging to a former time, of what her life used to be.

Her old reality had changed, her new, not yet fully formed.

"I miss it there too, Margaret."

She turned about the house, realizing she didn't want to stay. She picked up her phone and texted Ginnie.

I'm back. Want to meet up tonight?

Rella arrived an hour before Ginnie finished work, to secure a table. A local musician strummed Spanish guitar melodies. She pulled out her journal, never without it now, using it as a both a discreet way to communicate with the Others, and also to keep a record of any information she received.

Absorbed in her thoughts, she didn't notice the man who had presumptuously seated himself in front of her.

"Mind if I sit here?"

Rella pursed her lips. She did mind.

"I think I've seen you in here before."

"I'm sure you see a lot of people." She did not want to spend her time entertaining this guy. "I'm waiting for someone."

He leaned forward, pushing his chair closer.

Rella tensed.

"Terrible of them to keep you waiting. A friend?"

She crisply nodded confirmation.

"A *guy* friend or a *girl* friend?"

She slapped the journal shut and grabbed his gaze by the throat.

"What does it matter? I'm not waiting for *you*," she snapped.

Surprised at her forcefulness, she realized who she sounded like.

Gabby.

Liberation surged through her, as if she'd been plugged into a power outlet.

She recalled CJ's words. At the time, she'd found them hard to believe.

"Dissociation can be functional. You may find you can depend on the Others in productive and adaptive ways. Remember, you have them as resources, as need be."

Rella stared at him, not backing down. Internally, Gabby sarcastically waved *bye-bye* as he took his drink and withdrew.

Rella opened her notebook and smiled.

The next morning, on the living room floor, Rella went through the mail that had accumulated while she'd been away.

She found a card, in handwriting readily recognized. She carefully opened the envelope.

Dear Rella,

I wasn't sure where to send this in Ireland, so you will get it after you return.

I hope you are enjoying yourself. I know you are. A new adventure. I'm so elated for you.

I can't express how much it meant to me to spend so much time with you in your sunny haven of California. Each moment was precious, and I carry them with me every day.

There is one picture I took of you that I revisit often, when we were on the beach and you saw a dolphin in the distance. You excitedly jumped up and down, pointing it out, eager to share your discovery with me. When I look into the expression captured on your face, I see the little girl I had the joy to raise, and all the memories I have of you.

You've shown me the love that's possible between a mother and a daughter, love and consideration and happiness I never had growing up. Thank you for giving me that. Thank you for you.

I've included a photo of another unforgettable gift, one that exemplifies the generosity and kindness you bestowed on me, and the playful spirit that lives inside you. It's a moment in time I will always cherish.

Keep in touch, okay?

I love you very much,

Mom

The curtain of her tears parted, and the photo her mother had enclosed came into view.

Rella saw a much younger version of herself, a girl still protected from the past, bright, fresh glee on her face as she held up a vivid piece of orange cardboard at an intersection in New Mexico.

Rella lightly traced her finger over the memory.

"Maybe it *was* Las Cruces," she said softly.

We can never know what goes on inside a person simply by looking from the outside. Sometimes, even with ourselves.

To the survivors of horrors and unspeakable atrocities—if it feels all right, wrap your hands around your arms, your waist. Hug yourself, and the little one(s) inside.

To the friends, spouses, counselors, medical professionals, and family members of survivors—your love, encouragement, and support is invaluable.

We all need Others.

Nicole T. Smith, L.Ac. is both an author and acupuncturist, and owner of The Pampered Porcupine Acupuncture, Inc. Writing is a passion of hers that started at the age of five. Other published works include: *Paris Doesn't Fit in My Suitcase*, *Carmine the Porcupine*, and *AcuPass*. She is an avid traveler and explorer, with a love for the whole food plant-based lifestyle. Visit her websites:

www.shadows.group
www.ThePamperedPorcupine.com

Thank you for reading. It was a challenging undertaking, and I hope you found value in following Rella's journey.

I invite you to please leave a review on any or all of the following sites:

www.shadows.group

Goodreads

Bookseller sites

Social media

Any other favorite sites

For a guest appearance at your book club meeting, to request an author interview, or for more information on having Nicole speak at your next event, contact: nicole@shadows.group.

Eager to read more? Join the Shadows Group! Subscribe at www.shadows.group for updates, sneak previews, and secret backstory.

If you suspect you might fall on the dissociative scale, please do not use the information in this book, including the questionnaire, to self-diagnose, but seek out the help of a trained professional.